N

S

E

Brythunia

Hyperborea

Arena

Radolan

Bleak Road

Makkalet

Yvaq

Miras's Farm

Barrens

Hyrkania

RED
SONJA
CONSUMED

RED SONJA
CONSUMED

GAIL
SIMONE

orbitbooks.net

Story by Gail Simone and Luke Lieberman

Orbit
Hachette Book Group
1290 Avenue of the Americas
New York, NY 10104
orbitbooks.net

First Edition: November 2024
Simultaneously published in Great Britain by Orbit

Orbit is an imprint of Hachette Book Group.
The Orbit name and logo are registered trademarks of Little, Brown Book Group Limited.

The publisher is not responsible for websites (or their content) that are not owned by the publisher.

The Hachette Speakers Bureau provides a wide range of authors for speaking events. To find out more, go to hachettespeakersbureau.com or email HachetteSpeakers@hbgusa.com.

Orbit books may be purchased in bulk for business, educational, or promotional use. For information, please contact your local bookseller or the Hachette Book Group Special Markets Department at special.markets@hbgusa.com.

Library of Congress Cataloging-in-Publication Data
Names: Simone, Gail, author.
Title: Red Sonja : consumed / Gail Simone.
Description: First edition. | New York, NY : Orbit, 2024. | Series: Red Sonja ; [book 1]
Identifiers: LCCN 2024008066 | ISBN 9780316475679 (hardcover) |
    ISBN 9780316476027 (ebook)
Subjects: LCSH: Red Sonja (Fictitious character) | LCGFT: Fantasy fiction. | Action and adventure fiction. | Novels.
Classification: LCC PS3619.I56277 R43 2024 | DDC 813/.6—dc23/eng/20240222
LC record available at https://lccn.loc.gov/2024008066

ISBNs: 9780316475679 (hardcover), 9780316476027 (ebook)

Printed in the United States of America

LSC-C

Printing 1, 2024

To my darling husband, who, it turns out, has a bit of a thing for redheads.

Brythunia

Hyperborea

W
S ⊕ N
E

rena

Radolan

Bleak Road

Makkalet

Yvaq

Miras's
Farm

Hyrkania

3arrens

Map by Tim Paul

PART I

1

THEY REMINDED HER OF DRAGON WINGS

So, she went from being the child of a village, loved and nurtured by all, to being a child of nothing and no one, with a swiftness that left scars so deep they might never heal. Every meal was a plan, then a risk, then a danger. Every slumber a sign to the forest's predators . . . an alert in the scent of musk or urine to come and devour the child as she slept in the branches of the tallest tree she could find, an oak that had seen six centuries and offered little in the way of shelter or comfort.

The first nights after everything she had ever known was burned to ash, she sang quietly to herself in the tree's unlovely limbs, bits of a lullaby her mother had sung nightly before bed. She didn't remember all the words and would replace them with a tuneless, dead-eyed hum, more artifact than comfort. A fossil of an age that seemed only the fanciful dream of a drowning heart.

She would think of her mother, bone and burned sinew that she had buried along with everyone she had ever known. At ten summers, she had become her people's last undertaker.

Pilatius III, *The Song of Sonja, the She-Devil*

OUTSIDE THE BORDERS OF TURAN, THE HYBORIAN AGE

Sonja was behind schedule.

To be fair, "schedule" was plainly too fine a word for the heedless, headlong sequence of events she'd set in motion in those cold predawn hours. Even calling it a plan at all was a bit grandiose for what was a messy, unkind affair even by her low standards.

The She-Devil was on the run.

She had not had time to dress properly. Her preference was warmer climes and few encumbrances, her light furs and sparse ring mail making her underdressed for a morning with temperatures just above freezing. Her tan had faded, making her skin paler than she liked, for both practical and aesthetic reasons. A hunter hunted best when difficult to spot.

Further, she had left with an urgency that saw her take only a few items aside from her horse and blankets. A bow (not the double-curved bow of her homeland, sadly), a nearly empty quiver, a sword, and a few scattered items in her kit roll. Not for the first time, she cursed her impetuous nature. She had seen her opportunity and seized it, consequences be damned. No food, no water, and most painfully now, no alcohol.

She had left a warm, generously occupied camp bed covered in silken sheets for three small, scratchy horse blankets and a trail only another hunter could follow. In almost any other scenario, she'd be safe; she'd be on her way.

And she'd be rich.

Unfortunately, she was none of those things. Not yet. Because the Wolf Pack on her trail was led by a hunter whose skills were nearly equal to her own and whose rage would be intractable, even if, as Sonja had to reluctantly admit, it was also clearly justifiable.

She'd stolen from a queen. A queen who missed no trail sign, no matter how insignificant. And to add insult to an already festering injury, that queen had been the owner of that silken camp bed and the warm, lush body within. She allowed herself one regretfully sentimental moment as she brushed her fingers across the gold asp-shaped circlet on her left upper arm. It would fetch a ransom from the right vendor, preferably someone with few ethics and many coins. There was already a generous, if sometimes murderous, potential buyer.

But that was a problem for tomorrow.

Her horse, whom she'd named Sunder after the manner with which he demolished his feed at every meal, snorted in disapproval—whether at the tight grading of the steep hill trail they were ascending or at Sonja's affairs of the heart, only mount and rider could comprehend.

"Look, I never said I was tactful," Sonja said defensively, to no response at all from the horse.

The trail narrowed further as they crested the hill's final grade, surrounded by ominously tall eucalyptus trees, their leaves providing nearly enough cover to block out the coming dawn. In a fortuitous bit of unexpected timing, the greenery gave way at the same moment the sun's light finally hit the clearing at the hill's summit. And for the second time upon seeing what was planted there, Sonja's breath caught in her chest.

"Mitra's fist," she exclaimed. Most of her vulgarities were barroom learned, but in rare moments, only her father's favorite oath seemed to fit, even if the exact meaning of it was beyond her. Sonja dismounted, gesturing the hardy Sunder to stay.

In the center of the glade, hidden to the outside world, was a stone tower, not unlike the turrets and parapets she'd seen on fortresses and castles throughout Hyboria. It was the sails that elevated her heart rate, the four beautiful multicolored sails spiraling in the gentle breeze. She caught her breath just as she had the day it had been first revealed.

"It is called a windmill," Queen Ysidra had said, whispering, as if imparting a secret so delicate that volume could destroy it. The queen was lovely, dark and imposing, but carried her responsibilities like the heavy load they were, and Sonja had never seen her so delighted.

"I...Give me a moment," Sonja had gasped. She'd seen works of art before, primarily of gods and heroes carved in stone, and she had been entirely unmoved. They looked unlike any of the bloody battles she herself had experienced firsthand, with their theatrical posing. The slavering demons of this religion or that had left her thinking only of the madness of artists and zealots, two classes she did her best to avoid.

But this "windmill" was different, elevated somehow, inspired by divinity, perhaps. The sails were dyed in bright splashes of color, some of which she had never seen before. Beautiful but arcane calligraphy walked up the edge of each huge swath of fabric, doubtlessly uttering majestic poetry to whatever blessed soul could read it. She loved it and she feared it instantly, her gut churning with emotions she lacked the vocabulary to express.

They reminded her of dragon wings, and she had never seen anything crafted by the hand of man that was so moving and, to her uneducated eye, unknowable.

"But who...who built this? What is its purpose?" she asked, unaware that Ysidra had been watching her reaction, grinning at her lover's response.

"The people are gone. Plague," Ysidra said flatly, as if discussing the weather. Death was not fetishized in her tribe; Turanian they had once been, and so remained in their hearts. You lived, you died, and nothing of substance was ever gained by mourning. "Come, I'll show you."

They entered the needle's interior through a wooden door, the lock of which had been broken off at some great effort. The clan that had built this wonder had taken pains to keep its secrets unshared, but now its treasure was protected only by the height of the surrounding forest. Meticulous markings on the circular walls seemed to indicate fastidious recordkeeping, but was only gibberish to the Hyrkanian.

Sonja was afraid of no man or beast. But she was superstitious. And she felt ghosts around her as they entered, as if she were herself a violation, trespassing in a tomb.

In the center of the interior, a great flat-chiseled stone disc rotated, at the behest of a vertical wheel and a central rotating wooden pole that Sonja could barely have gotten her arms around, had she braved the vertigo to do so. There were other discs, with carefully aligned teeth. Sonja was no scholar. But she had a keen grasp of cause and effect, and she immediately understood how these gears coalesced from form to function. Ysidra's most learned men were still taking notes and drawing sketches, months after the spire's discovery. Sonja had lapped them in comprehension after just moments. She was frankly smitten.

Ysidra was clearly delighted by Sonja's rapt attention. "You see, they would separate the chaff from the grain. Grist, it is named. Then this is placed on this stone tablet, and the wheel—"

"—crushes the grain. To make meal. I've seen it done with mules as its engine."

"Yes. Yes. Do you understand what this could mean, Sonja, my love?"

For the first time since entering the glade at Ysidra's side, Sonja turned to look at the Queen of Nomads, acutely sensing the urgency in Ysidra's voice. The light through the small windows in the spire's walls glinted off the asp circlet on the queen's arm.

Ysidra smiled, the expression all the more beautiful for its rarity. Her dark eyes and long braided hair were arresting, her face framed by brilliantly colored ribbons cunningly woven into her braids. Red and green, with gold threads at the knots that intersected them. She glowed, in a way Sonja had never witnessed, even during intimacy.

Sonja had felt the queen's hands all over her and knew that the calluses and scars were hard earned, the ransom for a life hard fought for poor reward. The seamstresses of her tribe were famous, not just for the multicolored patterns of their meticulous designs but also for their cleverness and their artistry of deceit. Ysidra's tunic alone pocketed two blades in the soft lining and several jewels in the beadwork, which, true to her tribe's nature, formed the pattern of a gray wolf.

The queen blushed. Despite her position, or perhaps because of it, she had no experience conversing plainly from the heart, and she braced herself to speak as if preparing to leap from an ocean cliff to the water far below.

"It means an end to fruitless toil, Devil. It means bounty and trade. It means no more thievery, no more slavery simply to lift hand to mouth. It means, Green Eyes, that after three hundred years of exile and living in a saddle, my people will have a *home*."

Sonja blinked. She was not one for thoughts of tomorrow, when today could be so nakedly precarious. But she knew how much it meant to the dark-haired woman. Her tribe had been cast from its homeland of Turan for crimes long forgotten, a penance that could never be fully paid.

The queen took Sonja's hand in both of her own. "And you could rule by my side, a wanderer no more. Can you not see the trail, Sonja? To put down our swords? To drink like camels, to bed like rabbits, to eat like pigs? To have roots, Sonja. Roots, beloved."

Sonja merely stared. This was a proposal not without appeal. She turned again to the wonder in front of her, each turn of the sails seeming to bring new emotions.

*   *   *

She awoke from her memory to a familiar roar.

"*Devil.*"

The name was growled with malice by a guttural voice she recognized as Ysidra's. She turned to see the Wolf Pack, the queen's elite guards, flanking their queen, two on each side, bows across their backs, each carrying a black sword. Sonja had once seen Ysidra kill a cherished horse who had broken both forelegs in a ditch hidden by tall grass. Her eyes had gone expressionless and faraway. It was simply an unpleasant task that needed doing.

In stark contrast, the queen's eyes now blazed with a rage that was almost luminescent.

Each Wolf rider wore a short beard braided in two and made no sound, out of respect for Ysidra's position. They had been trained from birth to emulate the wolf, to protect one another, and to hunt with precision. They would not waste their arrows. Sonja thought she recognized two of them; Raganus she knew. Festrel was another, perhaps? The rest she'd never bothered to know.

The queen pointed her sword, kept black by clever use of a forge's flame and scrawled with runes of bloody deeds to its very tip, at Sonja. "You are a thief and a liar. You will give me the Asp and return to our camp for scourging and execution, dog."

Sonja paused, as if considering the merits of this offer. "Am I not granted a hearing?"

Ysidra sneered. "After the execution. That is our custom."

"I must say, that seems a bit unfair to the accused, Ysidra."

The queen's horse reared, its hooves sparking against the rocky path of the clearing. "The accused stole the heart of me and the heart of my tribe. You left on the day of our union!"

Sonja winced...Both the charges were true. But she also saw the riders of the Wolf Pack quickly glance at one another, taking measure not just of their prey but of their mistress. In Ysidra's tribe, leadership came from neither combat nor heredity, but a complicated concept the Devil could barely wrap her head around.

They *voted*. Each person—man, woman, and child alike—put a name on a polished piece of wood, and those marks were tallied and a monarch chosen. At any time, a queen or king could be challenged and overthrown. It was the most unimaginable folly to Sonja, but even she had enough manners not to mention it.

The one stickler in this arrangement was that the new king or queen could, in an effort to prevent future elections, simply declare the previous leader a traitor and execute them. It had a quieting effect upon loyalists to the previous crown. Sonja saw the Wolf Pack riders noting their queen's ire, witnesses to her humiliation.

To bed a comely foreigner was one thing; to propose to a thief—that was something else again. What Sonja felt for Ysidra wasn't love. She wasn't sure she had ever felt such a thing. She was more familiar with sex than sonnets. But Ysidra was walking a razor's edge with her own guardsmen's loyalty and either didn't know or didn't care.

Sonja looked right into the queen's eyes. "Ysidra, look at me. I have never had a home. Do I appear to you to be anyone's bride? I'd ruin the both of us, velvet cage or not."

Ysidra looked down on her, unmoved. "I'll hear no more of your liar's tongue, Hyrkanian. There is still to be a ceremony. It's just that you'll deem it less festive by far."

The riders smiled at this. Here was a queen to follow, who put her people above her loins.

Sonja sighed. "I don't know why so many of my bedmates, high and low, seem to want to kill me immediately after communion. It's very poor manners, if you ask me." She drew her sword. "Come on, then."

The Wolf Pack began to move forward on their horses, each holding their sword aloft, not yet committing to the challenge. From the ground, Sonja felt she might be able to defeat two at best. Four, never. And the queen herself was more dangerous than all of them together.

The queen held up her free hand, palm facing outward. "Hold. First, Devil, order your mount to stay. I know how you fight. Order him, and he lives."

Sonja cursed under her breath and let out an exaggerated sigh. Without turning around, her back to the hulking animal, she held up two fingers and said the word "*Asami*," the Turanian word for "wait." Her eyes never moved from the queen as the Wolf Pack moved closer toward her. They focused on her with the intensity of the wolf they took as their totem. They were fierce, but they were hunters, not fighters.

Ysidra's blade hesitated. "Why do you smile, Devil? You cannot win this fight, and you can't outrun my Wolves. Why do you smile?"

Sonja looked up, a terrifying grin on her pale face, eyes blazing. She lowered the two fingers on her upraised hand, making a fist. The queen's eyes opened wide, too late.

"Because my horse doesn't speak Turanian."

The riders looked up, to no purchase whatsoever, as Sonja's war-horse ran into them headlong, with a lust for fighting none of them had witnessed in a lifetime of horsecraft. Two were dismounted immediately, and the remaining two found their own mounts kicking and bucking in unexpected terror.

Sunder often left that impression when of a surly disposition.

Sonja kicked one of the soldiers brutally in the ribs, cracking three and taking whatever breath he had remaining completely out of his reach. The second fallen man was met with a crashing blow from the hilt of Sonja's sword. The remaining riders were attempting to control their mounts when Sonja's horse began to lay into them with his front hooves.

Sonja smiled. The Turanians were fine riders, and she wouldn't fault them.

But they weren't *Hyrkanian.*

She grabbed the first dismounted rider roughly, his braided beard in her clenched fist. Smiling, she sliced his flesh under the arm, a shallow wound that nevertheless produced a copious stream of hot blood across the frosted grass.

Sonja leapt on the back of her horse, slashing across the leather armor of the closest Pack rider, who was still gaining his balance.

Ysidra swung her sword at Sonja's neck, a killing blow Sonja barely blocked... On a steadier steed, the queen would have killed her, like the horse with the sickly, broken legs. Perhaps with a little joy in the doing this time.

Sonja smashed the flat of her sword against the queen's shoulder, at just the tipping point to knock the dark-haired woman out of her saddle. The woman landed hard on the ground, her foot still tangled in one rope stirrup. The riders, even the wounded, seemed to share an audible gasp. To die in combat was wholly noble in their eyes. To be humiliated was unforgivable.

Sonja looked down at the queen, not without pity, but still altogether irked at the threat of death...

"Hold," Sonja shouted. "You have a badly injured warrior, Queen. If you get him back to camp, he will live. Or you can follow me. You can't do both."

Ysidra stood, holding up her sword. "Death was a mercy, Dévil. I'll find you. I will find you if you bury yourself in the ground like the worm you are."

Sonja smiled; she couldn't help it. Freedom and wealth called, and death had been denied once again, its thirst unquenched. "Ysidra, you worship the wolf and you love a devil. At some point, surely you must begin to question your choices in life?"

Sonja rode away down the hillside, and though it pained her to miss the sun's rays on the spire behind, she did not look back.

2

FROM THE DIRT,
A BOUNTY

It could be truthfully said that Hyrkania was not an important country, in the manner in which scholars and historians measure such things. It produced no poets or artisans of great stature. Apart from practitioners of the arcane, academics of note were almost wholly unknown throughout much of its existence, and it built no great cities. It can fairly be said that there were only a handful of features in the country's story that would make it compelling to any student of its culture, after the end of its age as an aggressive conquering force.

First, that they somehow managed to be successful farmers in the most inhospitable territory in the region was a vexation and bafflement to their neighbors and indeed, even today, remains a subject of some confusion among those who study matters agrarian.

Second, they were extraordinary hunters, swift, silent, and accurate with a variety of weapons.

Third, and not at all coincidentally, they had never suffered a successful invasion for long, no matter how overwhelming the forces. Even grand armies would find themselves dying one by one in the night, either by arrow in the back or by dagger to the throat. It was simply decided their mud huts and livestock were not worth the cost. That is not to say they didn't suffer aggression as their power diminished ... They had been nearly exiled and often harried in matters of trade and policy.

But the achievement they prided themselves on the most, the one thing of theirs that could never be taken away, was their absolute mastery of horsecraft. No bond between horse and man existed like it anywhere else on Earth, and their secrets were never revealed through either bribery or torture, with the most fanciful of minds imagining all sorts of suspicious crossbreeding and spellcraft.

And of course, this arid, unimaginative, unprosperous land had another curse or blessing: It gave birth to the Devil, Sonja the Red.

Sir Failias of Leoni, *The Making and Unmaking of the Steppes*

HALF A CONTINENT AWAY, HYRKANIA

No one, not even his beloved mother, dead these long years at the sad age of twenty-six, believed good fortune would come to Miras, now twice that age himself. He was neither clever nor toothsome to look at. He harbored no thoughts even remotely poetic or imaginative. It might be more accurate, if less kindly, to say that he was unappealing in most respects.

When things went well, he rejoiced. When things went ill, he prayed, scourged himself, and sacrificed in the manner of his people. But what he prayed to, what the god Mitra might look like, never entered his mind. Such business was beyond both his scope and his interest. He had been taught, and thus he behaved. When there was drought, he slit the neck of a goat. When there were floods, he broke the neck of three pheasant hens. As he had been taught.

When he had broken his leg as a young boy, the medicine man of his village had set it, and soon enough, after a span of time he'd completely forgotten, he could walk on it again. It never occurred to him to ask the healer how this was accomplished, what knowledge went into such a thing. Gods and weather were the same to Miras, capricious and inscrutable, but always, always to be respected.

At eleven years old, abandoned by his father willfully and by his mother through dysentery, he found himself the owner of a useless piece of acreage and few other assets of note. There, he set about continuing the crops his family had tended as far back as anyone could recall: cabbages, carrots, and a prickly thistle that was edible only upon stewing the entirety of a day or more, the cardoon. He was to supplement this with the meager meats and milks provided by his small stockyard of a few wing-clipped fowl and a thin, mean herd of goats.

Soon, it was proven he had no talent even for these simple charges, and he came closer and closer to the door of starvation every winter. Loath as he was to kill his only reliable sources of meat, he did as he was taught, and repeated the words of the ritual to the best of his fading memory. Even worse for Miras's lonely heart was killing the animals that were the closest thing he had to friends. They trusted him—he knew that. They would come to his call; they fought for his touch. It had been hard at age eleven and had gotten no easier in the four decades plus that had followed.

He had made the terrible mistake of naming them, against the code of farmers everywhere, and his heart would be heavy for the days before the ritual and agonized in grief for weeks afterward. He'd been to the village many times in his life, once even as far as the capital city, and he had experienced what his mother had called "outside folk," meaning simply anyone not from their own farm. He felt bewildered by simple social interaction, and all in all, with one notable exception, he preferred the goats.

It was the moment of dusk as he bent down to check the sprouts of his crop. He heard his goats, the most spoiled goats this side of the river, and yet they still bleated, asking for his attention, his kind touch. He loved this moment, the end of the working day, because it meant coming home to the warm hearth, his comfortable bed, and Runa.

Runa the lovely, Runa the kind, Runa the notable exception.

He had first seen her when he was but twelve years old, and while there was no question that she was pleasant enough to look at, she had not been enough to overcome his anxiousness at the proximity of so many dozens of villagers in the marketplace, each seemingly vying to take the money from his foolish, inexperienced self.

She was the daughter of a blacksmith, but that vocation seemed hardly to have touched her, so delicate and soft she appeared. He made note, but not more so than he noted the going price for the melons he allowed himself to eat twice a year, once on the day of his birth and once on the day of his mother's death.

In truth, he'd forgotten her entirely until his return to the village two years later. His body had changed; his nights had become colder, and a frustration he could not name was growing within him. He would toss and turn, and more than once, he felt forced to relieve himself the best way he knew how, only to apologize in prayer the entire following week. To whom, he couldn't say. It seemed best not to include his mother in his pleas for redemption for this particular offense.

That year, he returned to the marketplace, with the intention of finding a bride. He had no prospects, so he had no expectations. He knew that he was lonely, and he knew that he would not be able to continue a life of solitude. He brought with him a cart of rough produce, riddled with weevils and holes left by insects. But times were hard, and even these sold for a bit more than he expected. He felt somewhat chuffed with himself, in fact, and allowed himself a rare moment of cautious pride.

It was then that he saw a girl in the blacksmith's stall, and his heart stopped so suddenly he was not entirely certain for a moment if it would ever start back up again. It was Runa.

Not the Runa of two years ago. This was Runa becoming a woman. With fine golden hair, the deep chestnut skin of a clan that worked, partially as advertisement of their commerce, in the sun every day of their lives. Runa who looked up at him and smiled. And his farmer's heart started up again, at an advanced rate, and carrying a new passenger: the blacksmith's daughter.

Runa the exception.

He had nothing to offer her; he knew that. He knew also that she would be the town beauty—it wasn't even in question. There was little wealth in the village and no aristocracy. He wouldn't lose her to a prince or lord. But he was at the bottom of a ladder that went from abject poverty to reliable comfort, and he wouldn't blame her for choosing any higher rung than his.

That night, he returned to his farm. The weather had been reasonable—pleasant, even. The crops were not at risk. So his plan was sinful, never meant to be enacted in times of plenty.

And yet that night, at fourteen years old, he went into the pen, chose his three favorite goats, hating their affection, hating even their trust, and slit their throats one after another, all while reciting the pledge of his family. But this time, he didn't ask for rain or for sun or for the winds to cease.

He asked for Runa. He made the prayer as best he could, and then, to ensure that the gods above heard him, he said it again, louder. Louder and louder until he finally realized that he was screaming as the sacrificial blood seeped into the dirt under his bent knee.

Ashamed, horrified, and exhausted, he collapsed on the heaped corpses of his livestock, grateful for the darkness that followed.

When Miras of the Hyrkanian Steppes awoke the next day, he was aching in his bones and his soul. He was sure what he'd done would offend his ancestors, but he knew he would do it again without hesitation. His gummy eyes opened slowly, and he felt a soreness in the fingers of his dominant hand, so tightly had he clenched his blade.

But the corpses of his goats were gone. This took him a moment to realize, and many more to process. Had he dreamed it? He knew what being drunk was like; his father had exhibited that behavior often enough. But he himself had never touched wine. Had he... had he imagined the entire ritual?

He ran to the pen and counted. There were three missing. The three chosen.

It was then that he noticed the blood on his hands and goatskin tunic. And his shame turned to elation. The gods had accepted his tribute.

Runa would be his.

And so it came to pass. Not that year, nor the year to follow. But something had happened to Miras's fortunes. The hard, thin crops of his meager fields took a turn for the better. Where an acre was barely worth the seeds to plant previously, Miras now found himself in the unusual position of having a routine year-round surplus, such that he was forced to hire one laborer, and then another, and then two more.

Despite his complete lack of education, the village began to treat him with respect, asking his opinion during his now-frequent trips to market. They sought his advice on all matters agricultural, and he learned quickly that if he answered truthfully and said, "I have no idea," the farmers who were his countrymen would walk away bitter and disappointed, certain that he was simply miserly with his successful techniques and unwilling to help others. The resentment was palpable.

And so he learned an affectation. He would sagely nod as one farmer, then another, explained their particular affliction, begging his counsel. Worms, locusts, rot—he would nod at them all, to the point where even the most skeptical and bitter neighbor felt at least listened to properly. Then he would simply make up the first ritual that came to mind, careful to give a different recipe for each of his fellow farmers.

It did not escape him that the very people who excoriated his name for "keeping secrets from his friends" would then hoard the completely invented knowledge he had imparted to each. When asked, they would hold the wisdom of Miras to their breast like the last breath of a favorite child.

It was all nonsense. But it made him popular—beloved, even. And it had to be said that most farms did see an improvement, to the point where tradesmen actively began to adjust their routes to hit his nameless village and its newly prosperous people. It was simply not possible to tell them to mimic his own actions: to go mad in the moonlight, murdering animals and screaming until their throats were bloody. Perhaps the mere belief in his pretend rituals improved his neighbors' lot, but the question was in all ways quite beyond him.

And truthfully, none of it mattered to him, for at age sixteen, it was arranged that he would marry Runa. Nothing else mattered, and in Miras's defense, he worshipped her and was grateful every day of his life. That she loved him in return seemed a better promise than life normally allowed. There had been a gathering, and all the farmers who felt he had saved them paid their due in kind, leading to a need for a larger house to hold the wedding finery.

He was a man who wanted for nothing.

Until that night decades later, that dusk, surrounded by the promise of another bountiful harvest. That very last night of his life.

The goats had stopped calling for him to embrace them, to perhaps share a carrot or cabbage before the night's hard slumber. The tenor of their cries had changed.

To abject terror.

Something was after them.

Miras was no coward. He took a two-pronged trowel that had been propped near the feed barrow and ran toward the pen. His workers had all left for the bunkhouse, too far to be of use. As he ran, he fancied his eyes playing tricks on him in the dark... Small ruts in the dirt, half a meter across, ran parallel to his track toward the pen, as if a great, unseeable wheel on either side of him ran alongside. He would need to investigate when whatever predator that stalked his farm was banished by shout or by injury.

Then the goats were blessedly silent for a moment, and the tracks stopped forming. He ran on, leaving the ruts in the dirt behind him, even as they had knocked through the small lines of sprouts that had lain in their path.

It was not to last; one goat, then another, resumed bleating in terror, the pitch coming brutally higher each time. They weren't merely afraid. It was as if they had felt the devil's teeth already, deep in their guts. They scrambled against the too-solid log walls of the pen, trying to break it in desperation, then trying to climb it, only to fall back to the dirt, more panicked than before. As he was nearing the pen, Miras saw that the ruts in the ground had resumed, still racing toward the pen. But he also noticed similar ruts coming at the pen from many directions, like the rays of the sun returning to their maker.

It was then that he heard the first bones break. The matriarch of his goats issued a sharp scream—it could only be called that—and it was ripped away mid-shriek, followed by a sound he knew well, that every farmer knew well... the sound of bone and meat being pulled from a carcass.

The sound of butchery.

Several other similar sounds occurred as he reached the pen's edge, ready to fight, ready to kill. Instead, he had to resist the urge to void his gorge.

All his goats, his entire stock, had had their legs pulled off while still alive. Some still wriggled pitifully in agony and shock, but their mews were fading. Others were already gone, in the mere seconds it took for him to clear the fields, the smell of sod and cabbage still on his boots.

He let loose a cry of mourning he wasn't even aware of, and the ruts in the ground seemed to turn to face him. Instinctively, he jumped atop the strong fence...Perhaps whatever unseen devils had murdered his stock would be confused. He held tightly to the upper log, one he had cut himself years before, and instinctively hushed his breath. In shaking fear, he watched as the ruts moved toward him, under the fence. They moved slowly this time, without the grim sense of purpose of their initial attack.

He willed himself to be more silent still, and this did seem to slow them even further...He was reminded of the various hounds he'd had over the years, and how they would wander when a scent was lost, unwilling to cease trying to find that scent again.

It was a cold night. He fought not to shiver, not to lose his balance as he hugged the log, its bark cutting into the flesh of his fingers and thighs.

"Miras? Miras, what's happened to the goats?"

In that moment, Miras knew. He had been given many blessings. And this was the night he would lose it all. His beloved Runa was on the hard brown clay in front of their beloved home, wearing only her bedclothes and barefooted. And she was calling to him from across the field.

She sounded a bit like the goats, Miras thought, like a knife in the heart.

"Miras! What *is* it?"

For one moment, his courage failed him, and he did not answer her. He watched the ruts in the ground, and he realized then that they were *in* the ground, not above, turned to point toward the only thing he had ever truly loved. Runa the lovely, Runa the kind.

Runa took several steps away from the house, farther toward the deep sod where their fields began.

"Miras, are you injured, my love? Answer me!"

Then the ruts began to track straight toward her, at a speed almost as fast as a man could run. Miras fancied he could hear the sounds of burrowing, and he imagined again the hideous noise of the breaking bones of the goats just moments before.

He found his courage.

"*Runa!* Stop *yelling*! Don't make a *sound*! Don't make a—"

She turned to face him, clearly confused and anxious. And for one heartrending moment, he remembered when he saw her in the marketplace, years before.

She screamed, an abrupt, horrific thing, as something seized her from below, hard enough to break her bones as she was pulled by the legs through a hole far too small for her. He saw her rib cage crack and collapse and her arms forced together unnaturally in front of her, then above, as she began to disappear into the ground. He loved her, so he prayed she was alive, and then prayed no, prayed that she was dead.

He dropped to one knee, just as he had that night he'd called to the gods of his people, and he let out a loud, screaming lament, just as he had that night. He knew what it meant. He knew what it would call forth.

But he couldn't stop it.

He watched as the ruts arced, then came at him in straight lines from the bloody remains of his wife. He heard the rumble underground and felt the tremor in his knees and hands.

At last, he understood the betrayal the goats must have felt.

3

EVERY HUNTER
KNOWS THEIR PREY

And it is surely unfortunate, but with the passage of time and the growth of her legend, both proper historians and campfire talespinners chose to represent Sonja in whatever manner most appealed to their audience of the moment. Which ultimately led to the schism we have in the narrative regarding Hyrkania's most notable sword-bearer.

One version painted her as a pious follower and tireless advocate of one god or another, and in some cases, she was cast as a disciple of gods she was entirely unlikely to ever have heard of, let alone worshipped. This version tells her ending as one of a martyr, occasionally even lifted from mortality by a grateful deity. Statues and paintings exist of her in white robes, reading from sacred texts, doing various good deeds. One region famously presented her as a learned scholar and healer whose sharp sword was used only in smiting the unholy.

It is perhaps not surprising that this view of her character was most prominently adopted in locations where she had indeed per-formed some selfless function in the distant past and had simply grown into the legend most flattering to her memory out of half-forgotten gratitude.

The other take hews more closely to the truth, even a cursory study reveals.

Sonja the Red, the She-Devil, the Daughter of Destruction, was likely none of these reverent things. Neither a scholar nor a martyr nor a healer. She rather was a reveler, a brawler, and an occasional drunkard.

She was many things, some of the details of which have been lost to the ruin of time. And a case can be made that ambiguities in the historical record have left a great deal to fancy and interpretation, but one thing seems inarguable:

Red Sonja was no one's saint.

Kalifus Hairad, *Heroes and Legends of the East*

It was her second day of riding from the scene of her larceny and betrayal, and she had not slept, trusting her mount to follow the trail even in darkness. She was cold, thirsty, and hungry, and her mood was not improved by the fact that snow had begun to fall, for which she was woefully underdressed. The heavy forest cover and rocky landscape had made traveling at speed a risky choice already, and had she not had absolute certitude that Ysidra's Wolf Pack was following, she might have simply found the nearest tavern and gotten properly drunk at whatever table was nearest the hearth.

Not for the first time, the thought of Ysidra brought a rumbling sensation in her guts. She was aware of what she'd done, but something was bubbling up inside her that she didn't care for at all, something akin to regret. She'd left the bounds of the queen's camp with a sense of a plan done well, a theft of righteous tilt. Half a day later, in the solitude and silence of the forest's edge, that elation had dimmed inexplicably.

Now she was in a state where she questioned her own actions, and she cursed herself for her uncharacteristic weakness. She brought the reins back gently, announcing to the horse that it was at long last time to rest.

A final check for the smoke of a fire or the sound of riders, and sensing nothing, she dismounted. Even for a Hyrkanian, two days in the saddle made her thighs a bit unreliable and tremorous as her boots hit the lightly snow-covered ground.

She'd chosen the bottom of a hill, near a small creek, as her campsite. A bend in the river's path left scraps of wood in its pocket, making it easy to reach pieces that were dry, no hatchet work necessary.

As she gathered up the wood, she caught a glimpse of herself in the water by moonlight. She looked tired, which was understandable. But the pleasant calm she usually felt when at peace under the stars was missing. She searched for a word to describe that look, that missing essence of life that made her Sonja. In a moment as close to poetic as she was capable of at the moment, it came to her.

Bereft. She looked bereft.

She shook her head. This was all too fanciful for her, the woman who thought little of yesterday and even less of tomorrow. Morose or not, in two days' time, she'd be rich. Not just comfortable, but wealthy, for the first time in her life. Cupping her hand, she supped from the icy water, and the chill of it was bracing.

She had markers that needed paying. The Falcon expected her. But she couldn't help entertaining thoughts of competing offers for the Asp. She had no care for her reputation; it was shit, and she lost not a moment's sleep over that fact. But there could be consequences to not keeping your word far beyond disapproving gossip.

She busied herself about making camp for the night. She had three blankets with her, cunningly crafted by Ysidra's seamstresses to resist cold and damp. One would go on the horse. Another would form a tent, and the final thin blanket, which she'd used as a cloak to cover her bare shoulders and thighs, would become a flimsy but welcome bedroll. It would be rough sleeping in the wild, but fatigue weighed on her such that she was certain she'd never waken long enough to feel the frost.

Those tasks finished, she heaped the sticks in a conical fashion and drew her flint from her meager kit, commencing the laborious effort to make fire in the damp night. That accomplished, she removed her moist leather gloves and reached out her hands to warm them against the flame.

And in doing so, she caught the glint of gold and emeralds in the circlet, the fixture of her greed and carrier of her regret.

The Hunter's Asp, it was more properly called. Ysidra had rarely spoken of it, but its value was so clearly outside the realm of the tribe's entire worth that the queen was unable to convincingly hide the way she nursed it, fussed with it, protected it. The thief in Sonja had watched and pretended disinterest, but it had invaded her thoughts nonetheless.

Slowly, Sonja had earned her trust, gotten her to lower her guard. It was a chase, a duel, a race, and one that the queen had lost through a mixture of attraction and trust. Sonja had felt the first often, the second almost never.

The Asp was three coils of gold in the shape of a fanged snake, with two precious gem eyes that glittered even in the lowest light. She stared for a moment, then a moment longer, until she forgot the crackling of the kindling and the cold of snowfall down her back.

It must be said that Sonja was clever, even adroit in her speech. She had wit and a sharp, quick tongue that had both aided and endangered her in roughly equal measure over her young life. But she had little education, and that had been of a kind meant to train her to feed her own tribe, and little else. She lacked the words for this feeling, or she might have said she was transfixed. She might have said she was enthralled. Instead, another word came to mind.

Trapped.

She felt trapped. Exactly like the beasts who eventually entered her family's stewpot. She imagined herself surrounded by coils, waiting for an ungracious and bloody end, to be taken—no, to be consumed—under the gaze of emerald eyes.

"That fire looks most inviting, young lady."

Sonja looked up suddenly, shaken that in her torpor, she'd allowed someone close enough to talk to her, indeed, to reach out and slit her throat if he'd had a mind.

"May I sit a moment, if it would not be an inconvenience?" said the young man in front of her, standing opposite from her place at the fire.

"I don't care," she said, her voice lacking the steel that it nearly always carried.

The young man was not unwelcome, truth be told. He was fair, even comely, with fine brown hair and unworn features. She noted a dagger at his belt, under a thin brown cloak, and she realized that she'd left her sword tied to her thin saddle, inside her makeshift tent.

"Thank you, miss," he said as he knelt, holding his hands near the flames. "In payment, I've a bit of wine, if you're not opposed to sharing...?"

She was not, and perhaps even against snowdrift campfire etiquette, she took the skin from his hands brusquely and drank deeply before allowing him the first swig. He smiled, unoffended.

She ruefully handed the skin back to him. At this point, traditionally, names would be exchanged. But he'd not offered his, and Sonja was in no hurry to proffer her own. Not to a stranger while on the run, even an attractive one.

He looked around as best was possible in the darkness punctured only somewhat by the fire. "And do you travel alone on such a cold night, miss?"

She drank again as the skin was passed back.

"I do, stranger. It is my custom."

"Do you make for Radolan, fair one? P'raps we could ride together come daylight?"

"That is not convenient for me. It's best if you warm your limbs and keep moving, stranger," she said, her eyes steady.

He paused and then grinned, every inch the jovial guest. "Fair enough, I meant no ill. It's simply that these are rough roads, and cutthroats are common. If I were like you—"

She cut him off. "If you were like me...?"

"I simply mean, a woman alone, wearing...well. Wearing what you wear..."

Sonja looked down at herself. She was aware that her clothing, a simple top and loincloth of fur and mail, was considered outright blasphemous in some quarters, but as always, the opinions of others meant little to her. "What about what I wear?"

He hastened to quell any offense. "No, miss, I don't mean that. How could I? I have a man's eyes, after all." He smiled. She was not entirely mollified. "No, it is the ornament you carry...An unfriendly sort might covet it, do you see?"

She looked again at the Asp, this time avoiding the eyes. "An unfriendly sort," she repeated.

He smiled again, but his eyes darkened somewhat. "Yes. Unfriendly. There are terrible people on this road, miss."

"So you have said."

"For example, imagine this unfriendly sort, cad that he is, imagine he decides, rightly or wrongly, that that finery should be his, and only a skinny, unclad heathen trollop bars it from his possession. Imagine further that he therefore offers the helpless girl a choice."

"That is very magnanimous of this stranger."

"Isn't it simply so?" He settled further on his knees, to appear calm. "And that choice is merely this. The girl could *give* him the adornment and go back to her happy life of spreading her legs for the coin of miners and dirt farmers..."

"Do go on—I'm dying to hear the alternative," Sonja said.

The stranger pulled back his cloak, exposing the dagger she'd already spotted but had the courtesy not to mention. She'd spoiled his dramatic reveal, but he was unaware and waited to see fear in her eyes. "Or he could take it off her corpse, miss. Along with her horse and goods and whatever else strikes him."

She stared for a long moment, her face impassive. Then with a seemingly defeated sigh, she began to reach to remove the Asp, and his smile widened.

"Well, it can't be said you weren't equitable in offering a choice, fair one."

"I'm glad we've come to an understanding, miss."

She paused. She looked up at him; he was fit, tall, and no doubt strong. And she was tired and not at all herself. Had it been any other possession . . .

"Oh, but there is one thing, stranger. I feel that if we are to make this trade, my life for this humble trinket, we should at least know each other's names. Is that fair?"

He smiled a smile that doubtless had melted the resistance of a long line of bedmates in its perfect radiance. He fancied himself a charmer and a great wit, she was sure.

"Trogas, I am, miss. And may I know yours, to commemorate this fortuitous meeting?"

She set her gaze to an intensity that she knew evoked terror to many an otherwise brave man. "I am going to say my name, Trogas. You may doubt it, but in your heart, you will know it is true, that I am who I say. My name is Sonja. Sonja the Red."

She waited for a response, but he merely blinked at her, face impassive.

She shook her head. "Red Sonja, foolish brigand. The She-Devil? The Curse of Hyrkania? Terror of the Khitan gladiator pits? *Sonja?*"

He shook his head, and the night went from uncomfortable to humiliating.

"Should I know you? Are you supposed to be renowned or something?"

She spat, her spittle sizzling into the fire. Her previous steel had been mostly artifice, but now she genuinely was spoiling to punch his lovely face in.

"Brave men quake when I unsheathe my blade, ignorant one. My name is known in every barracks and brothel from here to Cimmeria."

"I'm sorry—I'm sure you're very well regarded in some circles, but I don't listen to much tavern chatter."

She turned her head in disgust, muttering in her mother tongue, foul entreaties to gods too dark to be named at night. There was an awkward silence and, if she was being completely honest, a bit of vain pique.

He suddenly brightened. "Wait, now—Sonja, you say? Terror of Khitar? I believe I have heard of you. Yes, most fearsome!"

She turned to face him. "It's Khitai, oh brilliant one, and if it helps at all, it's the country whose borders are only a few days' ride from here."

"Ah. Well, still. Really, it's an honor to steal from such an august name."

She knew he was lying, but she couldn't help it—she did feel a little less disagreeable.

He stood up, all hint of civility discarded. "Now, this business about unsheathing your blade...I can't help but notice that you're not actually in proximity of any blade save my own. So I'm afraid the choice still stands, Sonja. Make it quick, or I'll choose for you."

Sonja sighed again. She reached down with both hands, grabbed two flaming embers, and threw them directly at the stranger's face. He shrieked most unguardedly, and she chose that moment to rise and put her fist into his face with a good deal more force than required, making a loud, flat cracking sound that made Sonja's horse look over with only casual interest.

Trogas, to his credit, found the presence of mind to reach for his dagger, only to find that Sonja had already removed it from its worn leather scabbard and was holding it to his throat, her white teeth clenched and her eyes narrowed.

"I've been weighing your generous offer, Trogas the Fierce."

He swallowed hard and opened his mouth to speak, but she held the blade tighter to his throat.

"You have nothing I want; do you see? I'd take your blade, but it's shit, and that's being kind. Your horse is half-starved. And even your lovely face is starting to swell most ungracefully. So what can you do for me, to pay back this discomfit?"

He gurgled, then got out, "I have some coins. Not much, mistress."

She smiled. Trogas was a man who adapted to new information. "Fetch it. And leave the wine. The horse also goes with me. I'll see it put right, and you will find a new destination on foot, or Tarim help me, I will finish the butchering you've earned this night. Is that clear?"

He could only nod.

She broke her poor camp. There would be no sleep for Sonja unless she killed the stranger, and truth be told, she simply wasn't in the mood. Her temper darkened even as he tried to help her, even as he gave her the few possessions of any value he had. And she was painfully aware that his worst crime had been merely an attempt at a theft she herself had accomplished two days previously.

When all was done and the stranger's mare was tied to Sonja's own mount, she sat in the saddle and prepared to leave. The village he mentioned was less than a few hours' ride, and now she had a few scant coins, enough for proper sleep in a warm inn, perhaps an ale and a hot meal. She could rest and still ride out before the Wolf Pack could catch up; she was almost certain. If not, she'd give them a fight—that much was certain.

Trogas looked up at her, as if a thought had suddenly taken hold.

"Wait. Hyrkania, did you say? That's your home? Where your family is?"

Sonja looked down at him. "I have no home. I have no family."

But it was clear he'd struck something; they both knew it. He smiled a last, mean smile. "Ah. I understand. Then you won't care about the news I've heard. Fair, mistress, fair."

She started to lead her horse away from the already frozen campfire, away from the comely stranger. Then she stopped but did not turn around.

"What news, thief?"

She could not see the dark pleasure in his expression as he spoke.

"The plague, mistress. Hyrkania is riddled with plague."

4

FORSAKEN

Hyrkania and Turan had a complicated, often bloody relationship as neighbor states. Once, they had been two parts of one country, but the topography of that arrangement made governance difficult. During Hyrkania's most aggressive age, Turan was its favorite target for raids and conscription. But as Hyrkania fell in influence, Turan became its unofficial overseer and sometime tormentor.

It is fair to say that if any region of Turan could be said to be excessively philosophical, it would be the colder climes of the North, where the sociological theories of wizards and scholars actually took root and were tested by small clans of hunters and farmers.

No jail had the North. For any born within those borders, there was no dungeon and no gallows. For a people who valued pride and reputation above all, such institutions were almost completely unnecessary, as a far greater punishment loomed for those natives who broke the codes of the people's trust.

Exile.

No punishment accorded the thief or killer brought more pain, more disgrace, than being told they no longer had a place in their own land,

that they would never again call the green valleys and rough, unlovely
mountains home. Worse yet, they were no longer allowed to even call
themselves Turanian.

For a people that attached all virtue to kin and country, it was worse
than torture, worse than death. Those who were so afflicted, who had
seen the backs of their families turned toward them with a cataclys-
mic finality, would often find one another in their nomadic state. They
would form tribes and even, after a bastard fashion, family. They would
survive.

But the cruelty of their punishment never ebbed. And they would find
themselves unwilling to leave the region for long, even as its most unwel-
come guests. To be born Turanian and never allowed to again call it
home tethered the felon to a land that didn't want them and yet wouldn't
let them go.

Of course, if a thief was found who had been born outside the borders
of benighted Turan, the high-minded philosophers of the great thoughtful
land would simply order their heads bashed in with a rock.

Sometimes, what appears merciful is not mercy at all.

Sir Kennon Wrighth, *Lands of Arcanum*

It was the night of Ysidra's return to her tribe's camp, and her people were shaken to see the state of her fury. She had returned with
one able-bodied warrior less than she had left with, and one redheaded, Asp-wearing warrior absent completely.

This was not the Ysidra they loved and feared in equal measure.
This was a raging wolf, tearing at the plush interior of her own tent,
throwing her few gilded possessions at its canvas walls. She acknowl-
edged no voice, not her kin nor her personal guard. She appeared
not to be aware of them at all. The two unwounded members of her

Wolf Pack, the mismatched pair of the stout, beefy Raganus and the younger, thinner Festrel, both stood outside her tent's open door, trying to avoid her gaze. They desperately wished for any other assignment, as protecting the dignity of their queen, their highest duty, was simply impossible at the moment; even the lowliest of the clan stared at the tent's door in open dismay, wonder, and amusement.

"This is unseemly," Raganus said after great length. He was a man who spoke rarely and with little art to his words. But he was also a cautious man, and that had served him well. "Unseemly" was perhaps as vulgar as he was capable of being at the moment.

"One of us should stop her," said Festrel. His voice belied concern that revealed another, thinly hidden emotion. He adored Ysidra. He owed her his position, and more than that, he loved her as a sailor loves a full moon. He felt he was magnificently skilled at hiding his heart. He was mistaken, as his affections were secret to none.

Of the pair, Festrel saw his queen through a fog of devotion and thus did not truly see her at all. Raganus was not given to fancy, but he watched Ysidra's every movement and had done since she took the walking throne. He was loyal. And he was a keen observer. They both looked toward the open tent flap and the screaming, cursing shadow within.

"Perhaps just a few minutes more would be prudent," said Raganus. Festrel nodded, relieved.

Three tribal elders walked toward the tent, and the two guards bowed their heads deeply, placing their hands crossed on their chests in a generations-old show of respect that also provided the benefit of keeping their hands where they could be seen, away from the hilts of their weapons.

The centermost of the robed elders, who had a face lined with age but was sure-footed as a young buck, stepped forward, addressing the men.

"We would speak with the queen, guardsmen. Tell her the elders wish only to console her and express their continued loyalty."

Festrel felt a chill. Turanians did not lie. But there were levels of truth like the different velocities of a whitewater current. And this unasked-for declaration of loyalty seemed far more threatening than if they had stormed the tent with lances.

There was a pause. The two men, proud members of the queen's own armor, were loyal and brave. But Ysidra had slipped on the ice badly, and there would be repercussions.

At last, Raganus opened the tent flap to the full length of its draw and bowed again. "Of course, lords. May we find home again."

"May we find home again," muttered the elders as they stepped inside the queen's quarters.

The three stopped as Ysidra was dissecting a quilted pillow of magnificent beadwork, the hallmark of her tribe's legendary craft. Her teeth were bared, her face pursed.

"Ysidra," said the centermost elder.

There was no response. The tent smelled of oil and floral scents mixed with a hint of musk deer urine, the queen's personal perfume. She continued to tear at the personal luxuries it had taken her crafters years to make.

"Ysidra!" shouted the elder, all patience gone.

The queen turned to look, as if her eyes were adjusting to the sun after an unending night.

Her position relied on what she projected to her people, and her pride was their pride. When she walked through camp, she stood tall. She never stooped. She never stepped outside her tent without her hair immaculately braided. And when she led her people to war, she smiled, as though remembering a private whimsy.

This was not that Ysidra. The wrong word, the wrong twitch of an eyebrow, would be seen as weakness and would lead to the unbearable. Exile, from exile. To be cast out by outcasts.

To be nothing.

She could not find her pride. She had been besotted; she knew it.

She had faced the truth on the long ride back from the windmill she had thought of as their shared future. She had fallen, so deeply smitten that she had given things that were not fully hers to give: her heart, her body, and the sole true treasure of her clan, the Hunter's Asp.

But in that moment, looking to recover her presence and footing, she found something else, something that might do the job, in the moment of need.

Her rage. Her sense of betrayal.

Her desire for revenge.

She turned to face the elders fully and pulled lightly at her breastplate, straightening it slightly. Even in chaos, she knew how to look a proper soldier.

The first elder squinted, then cleared his throat. "Our queen. It brings us no pleasure to have this discussion."

"And what discussion is that, Uncle?"

It was too much for the central elder, this impudence, this lack of humility. He had expected her to be contrite. He had come expecting tears, and instead, her eyes never wavered. It was disgraceful and unwelcome. He stepped forward and raised a gnarled finger at her. "You brought that…that harlot, that…that devil, into your bed and our home."

Ysidra casually brushed back an errant strand of hair from her face. "We have no home. You know that; it was your doing."

The elder continued as if no one had spoken. "She's ruined you, whelp. She's made a fool of you. And she's taken the Asp! You are a god-cursed disgrace! You betrayed us all for the sake of your diseased loins!"

The elder to his left placed a hand on his shoulder and stepped forward, with eyes more sympathetic in small measure. "Our queen. There is nothing to be done for it. Better Turanians than we have fallen for worse bits of dappled arse than the redhead. But for our people…you must step down."

The Ysidra of last night would have bowed and apologized and left quietly in tears, for the good of her tribe, never to be seen again. But this was not that Ysidra. This was a Ysidra humiliated and vengeful. This was Ysidra brought low and reborn in fire.

This was Ysidra scorned.

She reached for the hilt of her sword, felt some satisfaction at the widening eyes of the three robed figures before her, and realized she had always loathed their quiet judgment, the way they were always watching, always daring to grade her performance at every moment.

She pulled the blade slowly from its scabbard.

"You raise fair points, wise ones. Allow me to make a counter-proposal."

Almost exactly a full day later, she and her two most trusted guardsmen, the cream of her Wolf Pack, rode their horses at full tilt by the light of the moon under a fine spray of light rain. She had asked Raganus and Festrel to choose, and they had chosen her. Now the three cut through the hills at a pace only a master of horse lore could fully appreciate.

Above all, Ysidra was a hunter. But she'd never chased prey like the She-Devil. In the rain and the scattered bits of melting snow trampled into mud, eventually even the queen lost the sign.

If there would come a moment when the tenuous loyalty of her men would fail, it would be here, if she couldn't find the body that had come to symbolize the breaking of everything that made their tribe whole.

She knew they would leave her, should she fail. Leave her at best, cut her throat far more likely. And this miserable, wet journey, the debut of Ysidra the Scorned, would be for nothing. She didn't fear death; she didn't fear the pain.

She feared the emptiness of having left nothing behind. No name, no brat, no kin, no home, and eventually, no memory worth keeping.

To be nothing.

In the middle distance, ahead on the path, she saw a lantern. She pulled her horse's reins and headed for the fading light, the flickering glimmer of potential redemption. She didn't order her men to follow; they either would... or they would not.

She came up upon the sole traveler, horseless and muttering to himself. He was attractive enough, if one valued his type (she didn't). The rain dripped off his loose hood, he appeared in all ways miserable, and his face was bruised, as if he'd recently been struck. He did not turn to look up at her, so lost was he in his own malaise.

"Traveler. I seek a woman," she said.

"Join the club," he said, returning to his aimless jaunt.

"No. Not that. This woman, she's... she's very beautiful."

"Those are the most dangerous kind. Please let me be. I have nothing for you. I have nothing for me, as it happens."

Ysidra was losing patience. "Wanderer. If your hand is empty, let me put a proper coin in it. Have you seen the woman they call the She-Devil? A red mane she has, and a shape some find agreeable, besides."

The traveler stopped. For the first moment, he turned to look at the three imposing, impatient riders beside him. Their faces told him his charm would be of no help here.

Ysidra fumbled in her purse for a silver coin. It was far too generous, even if his information was vital. But queens do not haggle with wastrels, not in front of witnesses, in any case. "What is your name, good fellow?"

Trogas had owned knives; he'd even had a favorite dagger, until recent events. But he was inept at all bladework and knew it. He had one true weapon he wielded with any proficiency, and he was intensely aware when it was used against him. The woman was attempting to charm him. He saw there would be no charm for Sonja, should this group find her.

"It is Trogas, my lady. I am at some haste; forgive me if I depart your company. I cannot help you."

He felt no urge to cover for the woman who had humiliated and injured him. He felt no moral compunction of any kind. Indeed, if they caught her and dragged her through the street by her hair, to Trogas that would seem only just.

But he hated the smug looks on their faces, the certainty they had that he would do whatever they commanded. He turned to continue down the path, eager to be rid of the wolfish lot of them.

It was not to be. Ysidra dropped onto the wet path from her mount, eyes ablaze. "I showed you my pleasant hand, footsneak. If I show you my other, none again shall ever call you fair. You've seen her—I know you have. There will be no further warnings."

The guardsmen watched from their mounts, ready. It had to be said, this new Ysidra did have an appealing manner of diplomacy, in their eyes.

Trogas did not turn back. "I'm sorry. I can't help. I have no idea who you are talking about. Good evening, good travels."

Ysidra reached out to grab Trogas's left hand suddenly, too fast for him to even attempt to worm out of her grip. She bent his hand fully up into the air behind his back, forcing him to bend forward painfully and submissively. She pushed his stretched arm down, shoving him to his knees, his face inches from the mud. He grunted in agony and surprise.

He felt her knife's blade against his fingers.

A blinding pain, and two of them dropped into the mud next to his quivering face. He'd had no idea pain like this existed. He screamed, and it took all his will to turn the cry into something resembling speech. All attempts at resistance, even his false bravado, drained out of him like water from a leaky cup.

He was no hero.

"Radolan! She rides for Radolan," he wept, a thin line of drool going unheeded into the mud as his tormentor mounted her horse again and rode away. When he could see clearly, he looked down at his severed fingers.

A silver coin lay between them.

She had never been a leader possessed of unending kindness. But neither had she been cruel or capricious in her punishments or the wielding of her skills.

She felt she had passed a waypoint, somehow. Because of her. Because of that cursed woman.

Because of Sonja.

She would find her. She would have the Asp back. Sonja had no idea of its true value; she had no conception of what its true power was. Ysidra would take it back, and even the She-Devil might be glad to be rid of it, beautiful thing though it was.

And then she would return in triumph to her people. She would rally them. Make them warriors again.

Turan wanted no part of them?

Then they would conquer Turan. Take it and bring it to heel. There would be a reckoning for decades of shame, and once she again had the Asp, all would follow her voice. She would use it for its most terrible purpose, and all behind her would cheer, and all before her would bow or fall forever.

She turned to her men as they rode slowly, resting their mounts.

"May we find home again," she said.

The two guards paused a moment, both thinking of the same image: the three aged men in robes, their tribal elders, all three messily decapitated, their heads stacked in the center of the queen's tent. The guards had faced her, her sword in hand, covered in the elders' blood.

Smiling.

She had given them a choice.

Wisely, they had chosen her.

5

FAR FROM HOME IN FINERY

It is perhaps overlooked precisely what is meant when one calls a Hyrkanian a "hunter." For most peoples, hunting is a survival skill, a method by which a family's belly is filled with enough meat and fat to survive another arid summer's day or cold winter's night.

But for Hyrkanians, it was more. For one, it was the only true source of their martial abilities. Few Hyrkanians of that fallen age (save the most famous, of course) could use or had even owned a sword. But even a child of that land knew the efficacy of a pulled bow or hurled stone.

Their priests and shamans were without exception adorned in the antlers, teeth, and claws of their greatest kills. The art of their common populace reflected the bravery of the hunter and the fierceness of their prey in bold, handmade beads and pigment. And the true currency of commerce was only occasionally the awkward octagonal coins issued by the king. Far more liquid in value was the haunch of the wild boar, the pelt of the mountain wolf.

Nearly every good and service in Hyrkania at that time, from food to shelter to sex, was purchased with something that had been hunted and killed, rather than smelted or drawn.

But more than that, the hunter learned that elevated skill, that knowledge that had made the country so difficult to conquer, regardless of the arms and training and superior numbers of the invader. Never truly a soldier, the Hyrkanian fighter was a hunter first, and to simply survive in that hard land, they learned the elegant use of inelegant tools: the pit, the lair, the spike that had sent untold foreign soldiers to screaming, bloody death.

They learned the art of the trap.

Sage Rowan Aalar, *From Nothing... Plenty*

It was not true that Hyrkania couldn't summon a measure of pomp when events called for it. The kings had long understood the value of appearance, maintained a small supply of banners and horsecloth, primarily for diplomatic missions across the border, to be carried by handpicked men chosen at least partially for their striking looks.

Long-haired and bearded, these were the King's Eye, each group of five, called a hand, kept fed and housed until need arose, then sent out in all their glory, with a captain in the lead and a standard-bearer at the rear. And a fine sight they made to citizen and foreigner alike. They did not smile; they were never drunk in public. For those reasons, a certain mystique grew around them.

But there was an added element, for they had been chosen not from loyalists and barely tethered cousins to the crown, but from men who had grown up hard, men used to discomfort and the hunt. Unlike the ambassadors and diplomats of many neighboring countries, the King's Eye of Hyrkania brooked no insult, and it was known that whatever they lacked in conversation was more than made up for by their skills with bows or blades.

To the king, the Eye served an additional purpose. To see the King's Eye riding by, flags fluttering in the wind, was awe-inspiring to the common people of the land. But to have them knock on your door was a terror beyond imagination. One needed fewer soldiers, fewer guards to police the populace with "ambassadors" such as these, who had burned villages to the ground for showing disloyalty to the Wooden Throne.

Just as, many leagues away, Sonja eagerly approached the unremarkable town of Radolan and Ysidra's truncated Wolf Pack slowly closed the gap between themselves and the Devil, one of the most trusted of the king's captains of the mark led his four men over the barren steppes to the border, with the despised country of Kusan on the far side.

Autius was his name. And he was braver than most, even at this elite rank, and kinder, too. He had no eagerness to spill blood. What he lacked in imagination, he more than made up for in loyalty to crown and country. He would kill if ordered. He would torment if required.

But he took no joy in it, as he knew some others did. All five of the men were armed, more so than usual. Each carried a bow on his back and a spare on the side of his mount. They each carried a dagger and sword and had been encouraged to carry a mace as well, as the very look of them inspired terror among lesser-steeled citizens. To their later regret, they carried no axes.

Above that, no one was truly certain who or what the targets of their mission were, and it was considered well advised to bring different tools for different skulls, just in case. In addition, each man carried an unusual item for such a mission: a simple farmer's spade.

Autius stopped, a barely perceptible tug on the reins halting his horse as if they'd choreographed the moment and practiced for years in the hard clay of the road. His men immediately followed suit. What he saw before him seemed impossible. He raised one hand, shoulder-high, and summoned the newest man in his command. "Tyrus. At my side, please."

The younger man was thinner than the others in this Hand but no less intimidating, with leathery skin covering tightly muscled arms. Without looking, the captain continued as the second man brought his horse up beside him. "You're from near here, is that right? Born back in the valley, am I correct?"

The younger man looked straight ahead down the clay road, unable to avert his gaze. "Yes, Captain."

"And there's a reason why these are called the Barrens, yes? Has it not been at least forty leagues since we've seen vegetation, forty more since we've seen the shade of a single tree?"

"Yes, Captain."

Autius shook his head, as if the soldier's perfect obedience itself somehow caused additional offense. "Well, then, man of the steppes, I wonder if you could tell me what it is we are looking at, as it cannot possibly be what it appears."

Tyrus did not falter, nor did he blink. "It is a forest, Captain."

The captain opened his mouth; he had a myriad of questions. But it was clear that the answers forthcoming would be no more enlightening, and he thought better of it. There had been raids, mostly on farms, but many traders who had serviced a route over a century old had been mysteriously stopped, the wagons and peddlers neither surfacing at their intended destination nor returning to their point of departure. They had simply vanished.

The king could overlook a few dirt farmers gone missing. But nearly all the finer things that kept the Wooden Throne worth inhabiting came from elsewhere—the fruits and shellfish and jewelry and more, they all were imported, and there were rumblings that the roads of the king himself were no longer safe.

That could not be abided. Autius cared nothing for such trade; he loved only his king. And he was prepared to bloody whatever man or beast caused him such discomfort.

Reports had come back from the scenes of the disappearances.

There were no tracks left behind, no droppings from bandit mounts. The marauders had simply vanished. But they had been careless at one farm, where they'd murdered a simple farmer and his wife and all their goats. They had left a hole in the ground that connected to the beginnings of a tunnel that reached into the bare ground, while still allowing the roots of the nearby crops to grow over and sometimes through it. The tunnel expired after ten yards or so, blocked at the end by stone and hard sod.

But there was simply no reason for a tunnel such as that to exist. No animal moved earth like that, and no man had motive. For Autius, the how of it mattered little. If the enemy went down a rabbit hole, then he would take his sword into their warren and kill them, to a man. Indeed, for several days, he had prepared himself for that exact eventuality.

But this, this flock of trees, chilled him. There were no trees of this size in any direction for leagues, and here they were, an oasis in the baked, thirsty dirt. They were hardy and tall, even foreboding with the sun's last light casting fearsome shadows toward the guardsmen. Autius, who was not given to flights of whimsy, fancied that they had been planted to give this exact effect.

No barbed fence or stone wall gave the message more clearly: *Go back. You are not welcome here.*

Autius called for dismount and put his quiver on his back. He pulled his sword from its laced scabbard, and after consideration, he also unhooked his mace for his free hand. "All of you, bows at the ready. Tyrus, bring the torch." And he took his first steps into the darkness of the impossible forest.

His second, an older man from the North named Roja, stood immediately behind him, as he had for nearly five years, in splendor and adversity. "Captain, do you not smell it? Do you not hear it?"

Autius did smell something, and he felt dew on his skin. Here, in this desert region, there was moisture in the air.

"It's running water, Captain. By my soul, I swear it," Roja said.

The captain looked down; there was actual moss under his booted heel. "It's under our feet. An underground river? Is that possible?"

He looked back at Tyrus, but Tyrus merely shrugged, slightly embarrassed. He knew he had been chosen for this mission by the king himself, yet he clearly had no more knowledge here than anyone else.

They moved on. In the veterans of the company, their anxiety manifested as an aggressive confidence. The captain cut at the shrubs and vines in his way with a force that was more than necessary by half. Finally, frustrated, he called out, "*Hear*, untoward and unwanted guests! I am Captain Autius of the King's Eye! Step forward and be counted!"

The men behind him, trained and loyal, nocked their arrows. Everything felt darker than it should, and there somehow seemed less air to breathe.

Autius, who preferred a fight to this... this unknowing, yelled again, clutching the hilts of both weapons so tightly that his palms ached. "I will not ask again. Be counted, villains. Or be cleaved!"

He knew how to put the fear of Mitra's wrath into his words, and strong men had quaked under the sound of his anger. But there was no surrender of bandits, no guilty highwaymen to imprison.

Autius made up his mind. More than anything, he hated being dismissed... and here he was, captain of the king's chosen elite. It was not to be borne.

He gestured with his sword to his youngest man. "Very well, as they like. We'll burn them out. Tyrus, get the rest of the torches. This entire patch will be ashen memory by morning, and the silent ones nothing but seared bones."

Tyrus turned to find his way back, glad to be useful at last.

"Stop," a voice said, from all directions.

The men tensed. Of all things to be expected, being given orders by an enemy in the dark was not at all in their experience, nor to their liking.

Autius yelled, his voice still iron. "Who goes? I say again, we are the King's Eye, and I command you to—

"You command nothing," said the voice, impossible to pinpoint.

Autius raised his voice further, the effect lessened by a small quaver. The men noticed, and he knew they noticed. "As the king's personal guard, I demand that you tell us who you are. At once. Or face the consequences. I will burn you in this foul garden, I swear it!"

There was silence. No man moved. The light flickered slightly as the torch in Tyrus's hand shook. And it began to dawn on Autius where they truly were.

For the men of the King's Eye were not chosen from the pampered and sheltered. They were none of them poets or artisans. They were hunters.

And they knew what a trap looked like. Too late, this time. But they knew.

Autius looked back at his trusted second, Roja, but saw only resignation. They were holding no cards. They were the wild hog in the spiked pit, and both men came upon that realization with a dread that neither could voice. Nor was it necessary.

Autius, the iron cracked, whispered, "Who are you?"

The voice returned. "You know who we are."

Autius shivered. In some dark childhood memory, he did know who they were. The tales of the things that ate disobedient children.

They had returned.

Autius stood up straight. Whatever happened tonight, by the words from his lips or the scars on his corpse, he would give an accounting of himself—that much he owed his king and his clan. "Come on, then. Come take us."

Silence. For two lonely breaths in the dark. Three.

"We will," said the voice from above and below at once.

Roja saw movement and fired into the trees. Another guard gave a panicked shot. There was no blood, no falling body, no outcry. Gray hands with impossibly long fingers and too many joints reached out of the ground to grasp Roja's foot and pull down with impossible force. The tough veteran, famously taciturn, screamed like a baby as his entire body was pulled through the too-small hole, his other leg shot upward by the force of being pulled underground, bones cracking like dry twigs as the man's face was pulled under the dirt and moss, his last scream choked with the sod falling into his mouth, eyes wide and pleading.

Autius, stunned for a moment, threw himself down to grasp his friend, but even a moment's hesitation was too much. His belly on the ground, weapons dropped, hands reaching into the hole in the ground, which was already filling up again, he screamed Roja's name, knowing it was too late, unable to stop. Corpse-like hands reached up out of the dirt from below, grabbing him on each side of his waist, all the way around to his lower back, and suddenly they pulled with awful strength, snapping his spine and yanking him into the ground, bent at the back at a right angle, both his torso and legs pointing grotesquely toward the sky, before he was dragged to whatever hell lay below.

It was too much for the remaining men. They did not fear death they understood, by sword or pox. But this was unholy.

The two remaining bowmen fired but to no better effect. Tyrus panted in fear, and he made a decision, in his terror and shame. He turned to run.

One of the bowmen screamed at him, the words like blades. "You bloody coward, you have the *torch*! You have the t—"

And then he was silent, except for the raucous sound of being eaten by the earth itself.

Tyrus ran as best he could, while everywhere around him he heard nightmares made real, unseen and all the more horrifying for that. But if he could clear the trees…! If he could clear the trees, he could make it to his horse. And no creature of the earth or glade could catch a Hyrkanian on a fast steed.

He could see it, through the edge of the green: the clay road, the desert, and his horse. He could see it. He would live.

And he'd tell the king. Oh yes. He'd be a hero, not a coward. They'd come back with an army of axes and picks and great pots of tar and oil. There would be such a reckoning as to shake the faith of gods and man!

And he'd be captain, he was sure of it. Savior of Hyrkania.

Something cold and hard hit his head, like a stone. He fell forward, dropping both his sword and his torch. His head swam; he could barely get the shapes to stop dancing, when he heard them, all around him.

"He lives yet."

"Easily remedied."

"No."

"But his crime."

"Yes. His crime. There is no forgetting."

"There is no forgetting."

"There is no forgiving."

"There is no forgiving."

Tyrus was unmanned; he was in the dark, helpless; and he'd seen what they had done to his captain. He imagined the searing pain, to be broken like a child's toy, and he could not think of anything else. "Please. Please let me go," he mewled.

"We will let you go."

Hope entered his heart instinctually. He knew he'd be ashamed. But the relief was too great for him to even respond.

"Can you write?"

He was from a good family, with a pious father who valued education, though Tyrus himself had not taken to it well.

"Yes. A little. I can write!"

The voice never raised its volume. "You are to be set free. To tell what you have seen."

He nearly cried. "Yes, yes, I vow, I shall. I'll tell all!"

"But you still must be punished."

Tyrus's face went slack as the fear returned, worse than ever. He sobbed audibly, every memory of being a proud member of the king's guard erased forever.

"Take his tongue," the voice said. And then Tyrus tasted sod as fingers reached into his mouth, wormlike in their invasiveness, and biting down slowed them not at all.

6

THE COMFORTS
OF HOME

And here, the path is murkier yet. Though the written record is madden-ingly sparse, the oral history of the area says she arrived at Radolan with the Asp still in her possession. All known accounts agree, and as stated before, Sonja the Red was no saint.

Perhaps it is because of this that her brief stop in this insignificant region left such tremendous fodder for the storytellers of the area. Her formidable skills in combat, her great beauty, her endless pursuit of fleshly delights, combined with her complete lack of modesty, must have made her a folk hero to delighted patrons of bards and playwrights of the region, some of whom understandably adorned the tale with far more filigreed myth than the truth would allow. Great bawdy pantomimes featuring men in thick greasepaint, donning enormous false cleavage and scarlet wigs, became a virtual subcategory of live performance for many decades to come. Tragedies and romances featuring the She-Devil were also popular, if less likely to fill a room's capacity.

As in many instances, the legend of Sonja blurs the true depiction of events. But it is clear that she changed the course of her trajectory, and in so doing, she made a choice, a change in direction. The why of it remains maddeningly elusive.

But to Sonja, born a Hyrkanian despite all her protestations to the contrary, it must have been like ripping out her own still-beating heart.

Kalifus Hairad, *Heroes and Legends of the East*

Three Days Prior

Sylus Temptree had seen a lifetime of blood, had drawn gallons from his targeted assignments and spilled no small amount of his own in the doing. He was not a timid man; no one living had ever called him "coward."

But he knew he had no power on the lake he was about to cross, the boat he was about to board. There wouldn't be a warrior on Earth who would take him on lightly, but this would not be a fair combat, and he felt a loathsome chill of disgust that he had allowed himself to be called to a table where he held no cards, had no hand whatsoever.

It was the lake of the Falcon. And if the Falcon wanted him dead, dead he would be, though the sickly haggler had never held a sword in his own hand in all his greedy, grasping days.

Sylus summoned his dignity. Even at his worst, he could present himself to the world as fearless and in want of nothing. It was one of his gifts. He pulled his tunic tight at the hem and minded to stand tall, head up. He walked the short, unlovely dock to the small skiff with its driver tied at the end. Neither man said a thing, both uncomfortably aware that they had no choice in their actions. One had been summoned; the other had been told to fetch him. Their wants and will meant less than nothing.

A bitter wind came across the small lake, blowing Sylus's light hair about and stinging his face. He stepped onto the simple plank boat, and the poleman pushed off. His strong arms were tired; there had been many visitors the day before, as the Falcon had called council. He thought, hopefully, that perhaps the fancy gentleman passenger might be killed and dumped in the lake, saving his tired arms the burden on the return trip.

One could hope.

The Falcon's boat was more of a floating house, sat in the middle of the barren lake. All trees on the surrounding hillside had been removed. Over time, as more and more gold and valued objects weighted down the boat, supports were added underneath, making it not actually a boat at all, in realistic evaluation. It was a house, in all but appearance.

And the Falcon, who had many enemies and so much to lose, had decided to live inside nature's moat, surrounded by water filled with sharpened traps. He would die someday, he knew.

But not at the hands of a thief or rival.

Sylus stepped off the boat, and a burly guard, who he first thought was a man but was actually a muscular woman, took his weapons and pointed him in.

The Falcon, coughing and wheezing, skeletally thin, sat on a fanciful cushioned chair, a standing bowl beside him reeking of ejected bile and fluids. *Your time is near its end, despite all your wealth, oh Falcon, lord of coins,* thought Sylus to himself. He bowed in deference. He knew the guards surrounding the Falcon were prepared, perhaps even eager, to kill if needed.

"Sylus. You look fine," said the harrowing figure before him.

"You as well, my lord," the swordsman said.

The scabrous face of the Falcon issued a smile. "Oh, that is kind. Do you know, I feel I have fully recovered from my recent illness. I expect I'll outlive you all."

Sylus's head twitched involuntarily. The pleasantry seemed a threat when contemplated.

"It's the woman, Sylus. The Devil. I've sent her, in my grace and generosity, on a mission to fetch a simple worthless trinket that's caught my imagination. Still, it is a pretty thing, and I want it."

Sylus could not help but breathe a slight sigh of relief. He would not be discarded in the lake's cold waters. Today, at least.

"I do think she's considering backing out of our arrangement. Be a good fellow and convince her—will you do that for me?"

Sylus nodded.

The Falcon started to retch, a guard holding his bowl toward him. The sound was repulsive, the odor unbearable. For a moment, Sylus considered the lake a sound alternative.

When the Falcon had voided his acidic discharge, a guard wiped his mouth. "Oh, and, Sylus, my most favored, if she has truly left the flock, if she's genuinely gone astray..."

Sylus waited. It was best not to interrupt his lord's temper.

"Bring her here and we'll all have a show, won't you?"

THREE DAYS LATER

"Look, I'm not going to stand for any smugly delivered recriminations from *you*—let's get that out of the way immediately," Sonja said, weary from travel yet still smartly mounted as her horse carefully negotiated the downward grade of the mountain trail, watching for stones or loose mud in the path.

The horse, perhaps wisely, did not respond.

"Yes, I know it would be prudent to keep going. And obviously, Ysidra's Pack won't rest until they find us. But we're hungry, we're tired, and we need beer in copious amounts."

Silence.

"All right, all right. *I* need beer. Are you happy? And I'm too polite to mention it, but I could use something between my legs other than your bony spine. Go ahead, throw your judgment upon me, as always."

Sunder snorted.

"Snob," said Sonja disdainfully.

They had let the tired, sagging mount of the would-be thief free in a westerly facing glade, sheltered by rock from wind and cold. Sonja, who loved horses more than people, had hesitated, but for the horse, no master at all was far better than the useless footpad Trogas. She had whispered to the horse in the tongue Hyrkanians knew. "Remember. Remember what you were before the breaking. Eat when you want; rest when you need."

The horse almost capered and did not look back.

It was still night when they arrived at Radolan, and it was not perhaps the thriving, friendly townlet Sonja had been envisioning to make it through the chill and wet of the journey. "Well, this is a complete shithole," she said upon entering.

Even "shithole" may have been generous. Radolan had a single ground well at the center of a thin, shabby circle of wood huts surrounded by a series of mercantile tents and carts. Snarling dogs approached her mount, looking for food or sport, but something in the chestnut horse's stride made them think better of it, after all. Someone had planted perennial flowers around the well, and given that Radolan was the only trade center on this miserable, wet trail, even this poor attempt at hospitality must have been quite welcome to footsore travelers, a splash of color in an image cast through a lens of dull gray and brown.

Another traveler might have been disappointed. But at this exact moment, a shithole suited Sonja just fine.

She heard faint, awkward music and turned her gaze to the largest building in the village. And though it had no sign, she heard the sounds of drunken carousing and argument, and that suited her even more. It was a poor, dilapidated longhouse, like many she'd passed out in previously.

It promised the closest thing to familiar comfort she understood outside of her own recently sour company. Making a click in her throat, she guided Sunder to a hitching post just outside the tavern's weather-scarred door.

"Watch your fine horse for you, lady?" said a rat-faced boy, standing suddenly from his position sitting on a small, presumably empty wine barrel just outside the door.

Sonja dismounted, wrapped one of the three blankets around her against the chill, and flipped him a copper. "See that he's fed and watered. Use the crop, and I'll cut your balls off."

The boy managed a squeak of terrified affirmation before gently, tremulously taking the reins in one hand while protectively cupping his groin with the other.

She gave a last, baleful look, lest he think she was simply being fanciful in her words.

She stepped across the loose wooden planks that led to the door, the smell of charred meat, no doubt spit roasted over a brick furnace, came to her at once, and her gullet and weary limbs responded involuntarily. The warmth of candles and suet lanterns glowed through the cracks in the ill-fitting portal. For a moment, she forgot she was being hunted, forgot even the thoughts in her own head. Her mouth salivated as she swung the door open and entered.

The sound of music and conversation immediately stopped. She was used to this and found the quickest cure was to simply walk in glaring. If she smiled, she invited questions and unwanted company. If she glowered, all but the bravest and most oblivious found other sources of interest.

She walked past the spit roast, where indeed a boar was being burned to a thick, scored crust over an open flame. She found a small table, no cleaner than most others, and sat at the curved wooden bench around it. Normally, she'd not be averse to the more social pleasures an inn like this might provide—gambling, dancing, fighting, and sex, preferably some delightful mix of all of those. But she'd also found in her travels that she could be unpleasant, even downright surly, while hungry and sober. For the sake of everyone, it was best she take care of the visceral needs before scratching any other itches.

The music resumed. Soon a young barmaid approached from behind the bar, wearing a burlap tunic. Her hands and arms were rough and scarred; it was clear she worked for a living, and of all the occupants of the longhouse, only she seemed not to blink at Sonja's presence. Whether she was fearless or jaded beyond caring, it was impossible to guess.

"What is it you're wantin'?" she asked.

"Meat. And beer," said Sonja, already tired of the conversation.

"What kind of beer?"

Sonja was perplexed. "What?"

"We got several beers."

"I should hope you would—this is a tavern, right? I'll be needing several myself."

"No, lady. I mean we got several varieties of beer."

Sonja shook her head. Clearly something was wrong with the girl. "Why would you need several— Never mind. Just bring beer. Until I say 'stop' or can no longer say 'again.' Is that understood?"

"Fine. And what sort of meat would you like? The boar is Cook's special recipe, with rosemary and clove and—"

Sonja slammed her hand on the table. "Mitra's fist! Look. Do you see that fat pig, the one you've set on fire? Cut off a burnt hunk of that and put it in my vicinity. Is that too much to ask?"

The barmaid made a snorting sound, turned, and walked back to the bar, leaving a disgruntled Sonja to rub the bridge of her nose with one leather-gloved hand. When she'd eased the red behind her eyes a measure, she took stock of the tavern, something she should have done upon entering, had her fatigue been less potent. She scanned for potential threats, certainly, but also with a thought to ease the loneliness of the road, and the melancholy of her departure from her last warm bed.

However, despite her wishful boasting to Sunder (who saw right through her, as he always did, to her thinking), she doubted she had the inner steam to function as a proper bedmate at the moment. Two days on the road, in the cold and wet... It did not provide much in the way of kindling for the fire of ardor she preferred. Perhaps it would be best to simply drink, eat, and pass out aggressively in whatever passed for overnight lodging in this compost heap of an inn.

And so perhaps it was apathy that made her pass over his face at first. The smoky air of the common room didn't help, either. But some part of her hunter's instinct made her take a second look, and there he was. Syrus? Tylus? She couldn't recall.

But she knew he was a dangerous, dangerous man.

She adjusted her seat so that no part of her back was to him. In turn, from across the room and over the cacophony, he raised his clay mug to her and nodded. Something in the gesture, which was meant to reassure, only made her restless and guarded. She moved the sheath of her dagger closer to her lap, without even being aware of it. They locked eyes for a moment.

The barmaid returned and none-too-politely slammed a mug of beer and a wooden plate down on the table, breaking the connection with the man across the room. If she'd been cold before, she was downright unfriendly now. "Three coppers. Uncle says if you want shelter, he's got a cot with the dogs behind the latrine, or a room upstairs, cleaned once a month and's got no dogs at all. But he wants you gone in the mornin', that bit's clear."

Sonja drank thankfully from the beer, wiped the foam from her mouth with the back of one forearm. "Did he say why, girl?"

She looked at Sonja properly for the first time. "Says you're a ill tide. Can't say as I disagree."

As the girl left, Sonja turned to look again. There was an empty seat where the man across the room had been sitting. She snuffed; she was too tired to care, really. Let him come take his chances with her blade if he must. She lifted the boned haunch of the boar and tore into it with clean, sharp teeth. *Son of a bitch!* she thought. Even in her black mood, she had to admit that it did have a lovely flavor. She wolfed down several more bites, in case she was to be interrupted by killing or being killed herself. And she raised her mug for the barmaid's attention. No sense in facing death with a clear head was her philosophy.

"'Ill tide,' is it? That seems most unkind, even for a devil." She turned to the sound of the man who had somehow managed to approach her unawares. It was not the simplest of tasks; few could accomplish it on her worst day. Suddenly his name came to the front of her skull.

"Sylus, is it not? Sylus Temptree?" she said, grease from the boar's flesh running a bit down her chin.

"I am as you name me, Hyrkanian. May I sit for a moment?"

She shrugged.

He cocked his head and stared as if examining her right through to the bone. She fancied his eyes glowed yellow gold, but it was just the lantern light reflected. His soft light hair was quite pleasant to Sonja's eyes, and if she'd been a tad less grim in temper, she'd have been quite willing to tumble him until he broke.

"I wouldn't take it personally. The news from Hyrkania is... not excellent, and people fear carriers from there," he said.

She looked at him, less pleasantly this time, and shrugged not at all.

"I know who follows you, Devil. And I know why." His eyes showed a hint of compassion, but not enough to shame her with sentiment.

He was handsome and strong in his features, with that shock of silver hair, only beginning to gray at the temples, and a taut form that suggested a life of some wealth, but not accustomed to opulence or indolence. He carried two sheathed swords, one belted on either side. His manner was polite but not sickly sweet, and she admired that in a killer. Which he most certainly was.

He took a stool from an adjoining table, even less hygienic than the one Sonja had chosen. "You know my name, Sonja. So you must know who I am and why I'm here."

Sonja continued to eat but kept one hand in her lap, near her dagger. "You work for the Falcon, yes? You're his Blood Man."

"I would not say it as such aloud, but as you wish. Mostly, I am his scout. Occasionally, his bill collector. I spill red only when absolutely necessary."

"And which function do you serve tonight, Sylus? I ask because I am new to these parts and am uncertain which cutlery is appropriate for our supper."

He scooted in closer. "No cutlery necessary, Sonja. I'll simply take the Asp and go, and the Falcon will arrange payment. He never overpays, not by a single copper. But he never underpays, either."

Sonja looked at the man; he gave her the same regard he had previously from across the room. No overt threat, no posturing at all. He had no need of posture. Then she looked at the Asp, and in a gesture quite unlike her, she put her opposite hand gently on the circlet on her arm, her fingers cradling its coils, warming them slightly.

She turned to face him. "And if I don't?"

He shook his head sadly, unconsciously twitching the fingers of his left hand against his belt. "I had hoped you wouldn't ask that, Devil. But you know the answer. I tell the Falcon, he bounties your shapely head, and soon every cutthroat from here to Cimmeria wants your pelt. You'll never sleep a night in peace again. And while I have no doubt that these brigands can't outwit you or outfight you ... they are legion, and you are but one. Eventually, they'll drag you to nothing and extinguish you like a campfire gone cold. They'll take your hair as trophy and your organs as sport. You know...you know all this; you've no doubt seen it done."

She unsheathed her dagger openly, placing it flat on the wooden table in front of her. "That is a bleak telling of my fortune, sellsword. I have another. It's shorter but vastly more compelling."

The Blood Man stared at the dagger, clearly weighing his options, by the light of the flickering lanterns and the fire of the cooking pit. Now that Sonja's appetite was diminished, she found herself almost eager for another challenge. Sonja watched the fingers on his left hand twitch, almost as a drumbeat, as they lay on the table. He seemed unaware of it entirely.

His eyes closed in silent contemplation, to de-escalate the threat, until that moment when the threat was irrelevant. "Sonja, why? What possible reason do you have to keep this...this gaudy worm trinket? A fortune like this, it can never stay in the grasp of our kind. We will live and die paupers, until our usefulness is at end."

Sonja drank deeply from her second beer, but she did not sheathe the knife. "Have you ever felt regret, Sylus? Have you ever felt...I mean, in your guts, in your bones, have you ever felt remorse?"

He sat up straighter, and his face went blank, as if he was carefully weighing his answer and Sonja's ability to understand it. "I...I have not. I am not like other men in many ways. Are you suggesting I will regret our conversation? Because I must say, I find it pleasant to speak to another like myself. Regardless of what happens next, it is amenable."

Sonja pushed her mug forward. Something in his response raised the fine hairs on her flesh. "I had thought of returning it. I am not certain why, entirely. But I have not yet decided what to do with it, to be honest, Falcon's bounty or not."

"You owe your loyalty to him, Sonja. He hired you, after all."

Sonja shook her head. "I owe him a chamber pot of nothing, Sylus. I do not give my allegiance as carelessly as some I might mention."

Sylus stood, sighing. "I see. Well, we are who we are, I suppose."

Sonja quickly reached for her dagger.

He held out his hands, palms empty. "You misunderstand, Sonja. I will not hinder you. I didn't see you, and we never met this evening. Do as you will."

She recoiled almost as if slapped. Of all possible reactions, she had not expected mercy. "You... you'd do that for me? Allow me my freedom?"

"It's not for you, Hyrkanian. It's a matter of self-preservation. If we fight now, I believe I will win."

She allowed herself a small grin. "But you're not—"

"But I'm not sure. And I will almost certainly have scars on my bark afterward, which affects my ability to survive and produce income." His fingers twitched at his left side. Again, he seemed oblivious. "I give you the courtesy of the night to rethink this. But no more."

Sonja reached for her cloak to wrap back around her. "Then our business is done, scout. Thank you for your company." She turned to leave, carefully, turning her back to him fully, out of respect.

"Sonja." She paused at the quiet, mournful tone in his voice.

She did not turn back.

He continued, "If you leave for good, if you truly run, I will be forced to chase you. And I will do my best to kill you. I'll stalk you, hunt you, and when you are convinced you are safe, I will cut you open. I need you to believe that."

She turned back slightly, not quite facing him, addressing him for a final time that evening over one cloaked shoulder...

"Do you know, I think I preferred being hunted in the open," she said. "And I suggest you get a healer to look at those fingers... They'll betray you, someday."

And she walked out into the night.

7

FOR LOVE OF COUNTRY

It is often said that all roads lead to one place or another, but historically speaking, roads are often less important in that regard than rivers, and all rivers eventually lead to a bureaucrat's pocket. Not every country has a brilliant general as its monarch; not every land is ruled by an indomitable warrior.

And yet which countries somehow manage to survive, and even thrive, without an army of any significance? Those that learned that the art of war carried over well into the art of economics, and economics in those times meant trade.

But those countries that had made enemies of all their neighbors, that had routinely burned villages and sacked temples, found themselves on the losing side of history, as countries with vast trade networks flourished and often had less want. The intelligent warrior-king might see his power diminish, without ever really understanding why.

As many a game young man, measuring his potential fortune and life span, would put down his sword and pick up an oar.

Thedren Sysfan, *Economics in the East*

There was a moment when, sitting by the campfire, her sparse and leaner Wolf Pack keeping guard, the exiled queen wanted nothing in her life more than to turn around and be back among her people.

To forget the Devil, forget the Asp. To forget being queen, if such a thing were possible. Her heart ached with the burden of continuing to pump ungrateful blood to her limbs. In every direction she looked were pain and disgrace.

But she'd left too much blood at her camp. Coming back without two treasures, Sonja's severed mane and the Hunter's Asp, intact and in full power, would mean banishment from the banished, and she could not abide such a thought. It felt like a never-ending frost-cold rain, and no solution seemed imaginable. Not even to her, the Fool Queen, the mockery she had made herself out to be.

She'd even, gods help her, wondered, daydreamed, what would happen if the Hyrkanian came back and begged forgiveness. She had briefly pictured them reunited, abandoning the past and all they knew. She imagined burying her hurt and shame, laughing like a madwoman.

She had never loved. Never truly been loved.

All the deeper the sting.

She felt like there were rats in her skull where her brains should be. She knew her cunning, her tremendous skill for outthinking her opponents—she knew it was deteriorating. She would laugh that it was heartbreak that was making her weak, but even she was forced to admit that the sadness, the weight of it all, was crushing her ability to see the path clearly.

And alone, here in the dark with the flickering light of the fire, normally her most beloved and serene state . . . the rats were winning.

She knew what Sonja would do. She'd head east through Turan, heading for her homeland of Hyrkania. Cutting through Turan was impossible, inconceivable for any of Ysidra's tribe. They'd been banished. Being caught in Turan was shame unimaginable, and the only felony that earned a death penalty and worse. But beyond that, it meant the end of hope. The end of any possibility that someday, some kind king or prophet would open their arms to her tribe and say, *Come back—all is forgiven. Welcome. Welcome.*

Welcome.

Sonja knew all this. Knew that Ysidra who loved her, Ysidra who sometimes laughed, sometimes even made ribald jokes at dinner, could never see herself being so disloyal, so faithless, to her home. Which made her strategy all the more painful. That Ysidra would choose anything over further ignominy.

But this was not that Ysidra.

She felt Festrel's eyes upon her in the dark. She knew he wanted her, knew he ached for her touch. How simple it would be to pass him a gentle word, a tilted gaze, and ensure his loyalty forever. But she knew he deserved better than to be her fool, and tomorrow, she would have to tell her loyal guards her plan. That they would follow the Devil and run her to ground, border or not, banishment or not, death awaiting like a child for its mother or not.

She did not expect them to follow. She hoped they would, or at least one. She would be glad of the company, and the arrow to kill the Devil if Ysidra failed to do so herself.

There was a time when she would have put aside her throne for Sonja's embrace, her fiery touch and kiss. When she could never have harmed a hair on her head.

But this was not that Ysidra.

They didn't know it, on the dirt path made muddy by the pouring rain, but to everyone they passed in the dark, at the alehouses and tumbledown sheds housing far beyond their capacity, they resembled nothing so much as mice. They had similar dark hair and the deep chestnut skin of most of the population of their home. But they had survived only by the leavings of a careless world, and when the rainy season had begun, they'd bought the cheapest, ugliest fur coats available. Neither of them, the young man Dalen or Aria, two years his junior, were vain, despite being clean of limb and eye, and altogether pleasant to see and touch. But there was still something unpleasant about wearing stinking fur of undetermined origin, made even more rodent-like in appearance by the matting of its poorly tanned and patched fur.

The tanner had been too drunk or lazy even to cut the tail off properly, and thus, drunkards found the pair deeply amusing in the dark, which both Dalen and Aria pretended to ignore. They themselves didn't drink, because they had a shared purpose and could not waste the meager wages they made cutting and carrying wood.

So they looked like mice, nothing ferocious about them. And being completely truthful, they smelled more than a little like rodents, as well. It was the aesthetics of poverty, where a minor beauty looked like a princess when bedecked with gems, and a stunning specimen looked downright untouchable when the dirt and wounds of a life hard lived caked every inch of them.

But scrimp and save they had. It had been Aria's plan; she was always the planner of the two, while Dalen was more thoughtful and reserved. "You're twice dear to me, Dalen, but you'd watch the stars while walking right off a cliff."

And because he loved her, he could take no offense, but only grin. And no flimsy garment, no positively hellish rainstorm could make her any less lovely to him. They were far from home, and both knew a great and terrible truth; neither of them would have survived this far without the other.

They were bound together, and as in all such cases, sometimes it felt like silk, and other times like chains.

They would not trade each other. They were certain. They'd never said it aloud, even on the day of their wedding. But they yearned for each other after the briefest time apart. Theirs was a genuine love, but circumstances had forced it to be a quiet one.

They were too far from home, their existence too fragile... When they had a warm fire and a roof from wood they'd cut, perhaps then. It was there between them, they were both assured, but they'd never truly been tested.

Dalen dreamed of a day when Aria would wear fine clothes. He had no aspirations to greatness, no hope of renown or wealth. But he wanted to see her live in safety and comfort. He knew such a day was not to be, and it stuck in his stomach a little.

They walked along the ramshackle buildings of the forgotten port village, along the bayfront, past boats and skiffs not strong enough to brave this weather, the water on one side, the populace trying to stay warm by whatever means their destitution left them. In the places where the rain was too much to see through, they each extended one arm and grazed the buildings with their fingers to stay true to their reckoning.

Until they came to the man relieving his bladder in the mud, the only living soul besides themselves foolish enough to stand outside sober on this worst of nights.

"Sir," said Aria, impatient and somehow oblivious to the circumstances of their meeting. The man was old, perhaps in his fifties, and where most of his advanced years were a wrinkled, boiled lot, he instead appeared to have his skin pulled far too tightly over his skeletal frame. Ridiculously, he didn't wear a hat or coat and yet seemed completely unbothered by the torrential downpour.

"Just a momen', lass. It's slower goin' out than goin' in, if you catch my meanin'," he said, wisps of vapor coming from his mouth with each breath.

His business concluded, he reached out a hand, which the young couple hesitated to take. "Ah, yer right, where's me manners? Best not, best not." He turned as if to walk away.

"Sir!" exhorted Aria, more forcefully this time. That tone had made many a potential suitor stop in their own footsteps, puzzling at the mouse of a girl who made a noise like that.

The man turned back. "You have somethin' you want me to hear, tha's plain, and it's only right I should listen."

Dalen stepped forward, pulling the hood of his shabby cloak back from his face. He couldn't be certain, but they'd both found that when conducting business with men of a certain age, they had better results when presenting a male face to their partnership. "We seek passage," said the young man, his voice friendly but firm.

"No, no. I don't take steerage such as you like, always more trouble than it pays. No. The answer is no, not if you two were the teats of the goddess, raining milk down upon me."

Aria couldn't help herself; she stepped forward. "We can work; we can earn our keep."

The man cackled. "Earn yer keep? Doin' what, lass? There's nothin' in the hold, won't be for days. An' if you think you can spread those legs for it, yer right out of luck—it's been a dead fish in my breeches for years. No, no. I'm sorry. No."

Dalen gently guided Aria back before she planted her feet, which he was certain would lose them the entire catch. "We can pay," he said simply. He was used to negotiations and knew well when to lay the trap.

The older man looked thoughtful. It made little sense; two penniless indigents wearing rat jackets in the rain could likely not afford the piss he'd just taken in the street, let alone passage in his hold. But there was something there... It wasn't nobility; it wasn't some sense of value that the young man had. It was simply certainty. He'd seen it on the faces of dozens of sailors, convinced this was the sailing that would bring them wealth. He hadn't lied to those men, not precisely, when he'd promised them blessed returns. But nonetheless, their certainty had come up to be yet another crashing disappointment, more debt in their ledgers.

This young man had a look about him; he was convinced of something, convinced it was important. The old man was certain he would know that same feeling the sailors felt when they came back poorer than when they left, wondering how they would explain this to their families and their debtors.

The young man thought he had a destiny. The old man didn't believe in any such thing. But if the young man had a purse, if he honestly had the coins, the old man with his leaking, creaking flatboat had no right nor reason to deny him his delusion.

"It's not a pleasure craft, my boat. She's a workin' ship," he said. He'd already decided to take the money, but appearances were important.

"What my sister said was right—we'll work. We'll work hard."

The old man made one last attempt; it was better to be sure that these young ones knew who it was who watched the helm, as it were. "You'll be responsible for your own care an' safety, that's flat. My men gets lonely, don't let her go toyin' with them, or I'll have you both over the side, are we clear?"

Aria considered showing her knife; they each had one of a matching set. And they were skilled with them, as all their kinfolk were. Dalen raised his voice, knowing her thoughts. "You keep them away from us, then, for their protection and yours. Or it might be you swimming home."

The old man smiled; he couldn't help it. He liked the boy. "Fair, lad. We've only to work out the details...Where am I takin' you to, 'xactly?"

Dalen looked back, as if for confirmation. But Aria only stared straight at the man.

"Hyrkania. We go upriver to Hyrkania," she said, ice in her voice.

8

ONE ROAD
TOO MANY

Where do you ride, my love, my love?
I ride to war, my wife, my wife.
Why do you ride, my love, my love?
For my land and my king, to give my life.
But can you not stay, my love, my love?
I could not stay, I'm now naught but bone.
But you are not gone, my love, my love!
I've been dead an age now, and you are alone.
I've been dead an age now, and you are alone.

Traditional Stygian song of the soldier

Sonja sat on her horse for a long time, simply staring at nothing.
It couldn't be called a fork, because neither path was truly a

road. They were more like simple trails, kept viable by the shoes and hooves that had the misfortune or poor planning to end up on a path with nothing of value on either end. But it was a choice, nonetheless. One path led east, the other west.

But that was merely the topography of it. More cuttingly, one path went to the making of her, her homeland of Hyrkania. And the other, as far away as it was possible to be and still be on the same continent. Even fully fed, her stomach ached. She felt the Asp's coldness on her arm. But she did not take it off.

To the east, to Hyrkania, was freedom, at least for a good while. She would cut through Turan, and her followers, Ysidra and the remains of her Wolf Pack, were banished from that land upon punishment of death and, worse to their pride, eternal shaming. To follow her to Hyrkania, they would have to go around the borders, putting them days behind her trail, perhaps weeks.

And what Sonja could do with that much lead time…She might as well be a phantom to her hunters. She would never be caught. All she had to do was turn right, to the east. She did not fear the plague, because she did not see tomorrow. But she did, this once, think of her yesterday.

To the east was the land of her birth. To the west, only Mitra could know. But she'd be hunted and quite likely caught.

She was tired. She wanted away from the shithole village and away from the Blood Man and, for the hell of it, away from memory entirely.

She pulled the reins. She would not return home.

West it was.

Sylus had a single mug of the inn's fine beer. He did not carouse; he did not take the pleasures of the flesh.

He was the Falcon's Blood Man.

He took pride in it. As a child, he'd gone with his mother to market in the nameless hardscrabble town of his birth, and he'd seen the pantomime there. Children laughed and squealed at the bright colors and merry pratfalls as their weary parents threw what copper bits could be spared in gratitude for their children's distraction.

He had been transformed. It was a lesson, a revelation of the true nature of adulthood that he somehow understood, even as a child. He knew it marked him, the absurd caperings of the two actors, playing all roles in dyed wheat wigs. He knew now, to his very bones... adults could have secret lives.

Who they pretended to be didn't matter. There was an underbelly that must be Hidden—it had to be kept painted. They would smile when there was nothing mirthful in sight; they would laugh when furious; they would fuck while rife with loathing. He was just a child, but he felt filled with this sudden thrilling, terrible knowledge.

He saw it all. And he knew that the slumbering dolts who made up his fellow children were blind to it, had no notion of the thing, the Hidden thing, that each adult had long since learned to conceal. Their true soul, covered by the fleshy paint and hide we call our skin.

He looked at his mother, who was holding his hand. She looked down at him and smiled. She didn't love him; she didn't love anyone. She kissed him suddenly on the crown of his head.

And with his heart breaking, he knew it was another pantomime.

He drank from his mug, wiped his face. When the surly waitress came by, he pretended to be drunker than he was. He thanked her, left her twice the cost of his single drink, and grabbed her ass firmly enough for her to feel it, but not so much that she'd remember. It was expected of men like he was, like he pretended to be.

She took the coins and smiled, as close to flirtation as her misery allowed her to present. He saw it, her Hidden. Like all men, but all women in particular. With women, he could see that they might have more reason to pretend, to simply survive in a world where a man's passing attention could lead to death or worse. But even for that, he hated the women more, as the only one who he'd ever thought truly cared for him, his mother, had been the most cruelly false of all. To her deathbed, she had maintained that facade. But he had seen the greasepaint and colored wigs, and he knew no woman ever told the truth about anything.

With men, he knew that most thought they lived with their secrets in solitude. That their Hidden was something shameful, something contemptible, something cracked in their personal pottery. But he had seen the truth, in a mud field, with his mother smiling down at him.

And he'd never believed another human being's words, not fully, ever again.

He walked at a deliberate pace, staggering the tiniest bit, then almost comically straightening his back, as if recovering a dignity that was precious to him. He knew what they thought... *There goes a gentleman— couldn't keep his cups, but a gentleman nonetheless.* His fingers tapped a Hidden code he did not understand on his flank, and becoming aware of it, he made a conscious effort to still them, lest his inner turmoil be detected by the hideous creatures all around him, pretending to be human.

He left the tavern and closed the door. He didn't notice the cold once outside; he never did. His Hidden was always preoccupied, always planning, always thinking. He shivered, from habit, for appearances. But he was a Blood Man, and it didn't do to show too much weakness.

He walked to the stables, where his mare was housed. The same little rat-faced boy who'd taken her in to brush her and remove her rig came up grinning, grotesquely subservient.

"Come for your fine horse, sir? She's a beauty—hate to see 'er go."

Sylus smiled at him. He remembered his mother's smile and displayed the same practiced rictus. "She is, lad. And I appreciate your fine care of her. Saddle her, please. There's five copper bits in it for you if you finish before I'm done making water."

The boy beamed at the fine man's compliment. Such a gift was rare in his orphaned, abandoned life. "Yes, sir, with haste!"

He hadn't lied to Sonja; he prided himself on never fully lying, never completely surrendering to the obscene lack of character that other "people" exhibited, hiding their lust and greed in a false sheen of kindness and goodwill. He bent the truth, yes—it was necessary to stay Hidden among the things that walked upright like men. And it truly had been pleasant to sit with someone who, if not the same as himself, with his wide-open eyes, was at least similarly aware of how near the precipice all actual humans remained. He'd met a handful of beings in his life who he thought might have a fraction of his vision, and the redhead seemed to see the world he did, or at least a glimpse of it.

It had been pleasant. But then…she had rejected his company, broken his trust. His fingers twitched at the thought of it.

She had seen his Hidden—he was sure of it.

And that could not be allowed.

Sylus opened his leather britches just outside the large double door of the stable. He dropped his belt, its two swords still sheathed. His true soul stirred but remained quiet. He pissed on the faded wooden side of the dilapidated building, enough to indicate a healthy stream, and not a drop more. He stopped with his bladder still not completely voided, for appearance's sake.

"Oh. Do you know, I did have a question, boy. It's nothing serious, just a curiosity."

"Sir?"

"The female. The flame-haired one. You must have seen her."

The boy grinned, suddenly conspiratorial, as if sharing a secret. "Too right I did! I think she fancied me, if I'm being honest, sir."

"Very good," said Sylus. "But you see, I need to find her. There are people following her, and they mean to do her harm. I need to warn her. And I need your help, son." Sylus sadly saw the boy's Hidden was being born right in front of him, lecherous and jealous. A shame, really. But all children grow up, and innocence always dies.

The boy finished pulling the understrap on the gray mare's saddle taut, buckling it. "Oh, ayeah?"

"I need to know which path she took. East or west. It's worth a silver to me, and you'd be saving a defenseless, virginal maiden from despoilment and death."

The boy snorted derisively. Innocence dies, all of it. "Begging your pardon, sir, if she's something to you. I meant no insult to you nor the lady—it's just...Never mind. West, sir. She went west, sure as rain."

"Excellent, lad, many thanks, and you've earned your reward," said Sylus, reaching for a coin in his purse. He realized, looking down, that he had forgotten to close and lace his breeches. That wasn't like him; he never allowed a glimpse of his true self, his Hidden, like that.

And yet, *Be fair*, he thought...it wasn't the first time he'd slipped lately. When a pretty streetwalker had forced her exposed bosom directly into his face in the last town previous, he'd responded with instinctive disgust and revulsion that even the drunkards had noticed, shoving her hard into the street. It hadn't helped that the slut had started screeching, as if she'd had virtue to actually defend. No one had cared that a gentleman had abused such a woman, but they had noted the look on his face. That sour, disgusted look that revealed his true self.

There had been other instances.

Was his time at hand?

He pulled out the shiny silver coin, more money than the boy would otherwise see in a year. The boy looked at it with that way of the habitually wounded...a mix of hope and doubt that struggled to manifest on the same face at once.

Sylus snatched it away. "Ah, but there is one thing I just thought of, lad. And it troubles me, I must be honest."

The boy, skeptical of being humiliated and worse, said nothing. He was certain there would be no silver from the man and hated himself for daring to believe.

"It's this: What if you are not the stout, loyal, decent young man I fancy you are? What if her pursuers come here and ask you where she went?"

The boy blanched. "I'd never!"

Sylus shook his head. He could clearly see the boy's Hidden, his true soul, showing through. He'd only get worse from here on out. "I'm afraid I don't believe you, lad."

The boy never even saw the dagger that ended his life. The Blood Man moved with such swiftness and cruelty that all the boy knew was pain, blinding pain. Five punctures in the boy's guts and chest, at a speed so quick the blood from the first wound had barely begun to spurt by the time the fifth cracked a rib bone upon being retracted.

The boy dropped. Sylus stared for a moment, careful of the blood spray. He then wiped his blade in the boy's hair and pulled the corpse into the piled straw and hay.

His true soul grinned. His pantomime remained unmoved.

The woman. The Devil.

He didn't like her. He wanted her to like him, and he was certain he'd managed that simple feat at first. Bedding women had long since lost its sheen as a challenge for him; the mix of manners and danger in his shadow laid them out like gutted fish, with an accompanying warmth he found distasteful, like from a dying campfire.

But even out of practice, he knew he'd charmed her. It was what he did. He knew he could have her with little effort; she'd as much as said so. And while death often did arouse something in his true soul, something resembling passion, this time he felt only rage. He showed none of it, so it burned internally, using his guts for fuel.

He knew the cause of it. It was her. Sonja.

He'd felt it almost immediately. He'd been wrong—it wasn't that she saw his true self; it wasn't that she could see inside him.

She didn't have a Hidden. She didn't have a pantomime. How did he miss the signs so badly?

She did not have a secret being. She said what she meant. She smiled when she felt like it. She ate and drank what she liked and cared not a dog's testicles what anyone thought of it.

She was free, free as no adult he'd ever met had been.

But that also meant she had no true soul.

The very concepts he'd lived his life by. The secret only he was perceptive enough, cunning enough, to have comprehended fully. As a *child*.

She somehow found a way out of it all, out of pretense, out of the constant maskery of simple existence. Of knowing you had a monster inside you and yet never letting anyone glimpse its rough, stained hands.

She was free of it all.

He pulled his breeches down fully, standing with them around his ankles, and screamed. He picked up the crude, rusted pitchfork and stabbed it heedlessly into the pile of straw where the boy's body lay, over and over. He hated it. He hated, inside and out. He felt like the cage had cracked and the pantomime player that he was every single day shrank back in fear.

And Mitra help *anyone* who dared come into this barn while the beast was loose. Mitra help them, because Sylus the Blood Man would rend them and prod them and rip them inside out.

He lay down in the hay where he fell, exhausted as he had never been in his life, from his manic episode and the swiftness of his murderous actions. He had no concept of time. His eyes focused in and out on the roof. *There are so many holes, it must be like the gods pissing when it rains*, he thought.

He sat up. He made himself presentable, as best he could. As a last measure, he dipped his jade comb in the small satchel of hog's fat he carried, and steadied his hair artfully. His true soul was silent—whether sated or enraged, he had no notion.

There were two options, as he saw it. The simple one was to follow Sonja. Her skills as a tracker were legendary—perhaps it was time to see what her talents were as prey.

And yet there was another thought. Amid the confusing bright light of newfound hatred that he had for her, was death really enough? Was torture really enough?

In some primordial response, he knew that it was not.

But there was a way.

What if he could bind her, rip her somehow so that she could not escape...and whisper into her ear, just before she died, that he had killed her lover? Forced her to an awful, dehumanizing end?

What expression would the Devil show? What would her eyes say?

Would her anguish last forever? What would happen if he attacked the soul of a being who was—how else could he put it?—completely *bereft* of that godly asset?

He would find out, by all the gods. He had learned many artful torments as the Falcon's Blood Man, and he would try them all out on the woman who had scorned him this evening.

But first, on her love, the one she'd already betrayed.

He mounted his horse, noting the skill with which the boy had saddled her, and nodded in acknowledgment. He corrected his posture, tall in his saddle, as befitted a man of his responsibilities. Decorum was important.

And then the Blood Man headed south.

In the tavern of the humble pub in Radolan, the waitress was scooting out the last reluctant local sot, as she had every previous working night. The same faces, the same fanciful tales. It wasn't the work that weighed her down; it was the tedium.

Tonight had been a bit livelier...There was that rude woman, the redhead, of course. She'd been glad to see her depart.

And then there was that lovely gentleman, who'd left such a generous tip in his wake. If only she could be blessed with more customers like him.

9

VOICES IN THE DARK

It is important to note that in this age, nomadic tribes represented only a tiny fraction of the land's population, contrary to common understanding. In fact, the nomadic tribes had centuries before made up the bulk of human endeavor and were dwindling at a rate that, culturally speaking, must have felt like a way of life fading into the mists.

A tribe would find a forest and remake its entire civilization. Another might land on the rocky shoals of the West Coast and make generational mounds of the shells of local seafoods, many stories tall and a source of great pride. The old ways were dying. Tools, craftsmanship, and above all, trade routes meant entire peoples and cultures were subsumed and conjoined, to the point where the historical record very quickly erased all clues of where these tribes began, or even hints of their centuries of wandering. For the Hyrkanians, it was horses, great open fields of wild horses.

A way of life was dying or, more precisely, had already died, its corpse forgotten. But salvation came with four legs, it would seem.

Dr. Severen Lyban, *Hyrkania: Origin of Destiny*

In slumber, she found herself freezing.

Had she been awake, she'd have cursed her threadbare blankets and the earliness of the hour, with dark still reluctant to give up its share of the world. She shivered and tossed from one fit of discomfort to another. It was not her way; she was known as a deep sleeper, "dead to the world and all who walk upon it," a brief and pleasantly muscular and willing bedmate had said of her.

The same companion, raven-haired and firmly attracted, had said of the one night that she'd been uncharacteristically fitful that she had "danced with the ghosts," which he felt was why she'd woken up tired.

He'd been a soldier, educated for his trade and merely repeating phrases he'd heard a thousand times as a child. But Sonja had been less discerning in those days and far more willing to believe the pillow gibberish of a vigorous partner, and she had taken it to heart. Had she danced with ghosts in her sleep? Even now, she couldn't say with certainty either way.

She missed her soldier. She missed her errant queen. She wanted no family, but a cold morning under a damp misty sky made the thought of other bodies cheerful and compelling.

Tonight, her soldier had been prophetic. She saw faces in the fog; she recognized them. Her tribe. Her brothers. Her family.

She had been their last undertaker. She'd thought of herself as the lost sheep of the herd that no longer existed. And yet here were their faces, floating above legless bodies in the directionless night.

Their mouths moved, and she realized that she could understand what they were saying, if she listened. So she consciously chose not to listen, which seemed to alarm the phantasms wearing her family's faces. Their words were not for mortal ears, she was certain.

She had forgotten what they looked like entirely. She was only ten when they died and she hid in the tall grasses, far enough not to be seen but close enough to hear the screams. But there was no question. These were her family. She spent no time wondering how this could be; the soldier's fanciful talk explained it...There were ghosts in the world, and they broke your slumber in their loneliness.

She began to turn away. She found no comfort in the past. But she saw her mother reach out her deathless arms to her, and her will nearly broke. After a few moments, her mother brought her arms back across her breasts, and her face fell, her heartbreak evident even to a daughter who did not want to see.

Her father put his pale arms, the same arms that had lifted Sonja into the air to riotous laughter as a toddler, on her mother's shoulders, in whatever passed for comfort among the dead. Her brothers stared at her with a disapproval she did not understand. What did they expect of her? What did they want of her?

She scarcely remembered them. Months went by without her thinking their names. Did they want to see her break down in tears at their feet?

She would not. She would never.

They had abandoned *her*. *They* had left her alone to face horrors both human and otherwise. Her mother had stopped making her delicious meals, leaving her to eat the worms and insects of the deep woods. Her brothers had stopped mocking her, stopped protecting her from bullies and would-be suitors, leaving her to negotiate the lusts of men as a child.

Worse yet was her father, who had been the tree she had clung to in every way possible. He had gone without teaching her a trade, life skills, even their family's history. She had a clever tongue but could barely write and could read only slightly better. She had little ability to live among strangers and made a poor friend in all ways.

Bereft. They had left her bereft.

She didn't need them, and they would never see her cry.

To the underworld with them all, each one.

*   *   *

Sonja awoke briefly to find herself bleeding.

She'd taken the extra precaution of setting up camp in tall grass with no fire. The weather in the North was unexpectedly a bit warmer, a surprise benefit for both horse and rider. She had considered a tree; she'd slept in enough since first losing her home as a child, but the idea felt melancholy and fully of unwanted memory. She'd examined a cave…but if the Wolf Pack found her, she'd be trapped.

So the grass it was, cold and damp though it had become as night had fallen. She thought of Ysidra. It was never her habit to be remorseful. But there was something, a feeling in her heart, mind, and loins, that was unpleasant and insistent. A yearning. She'd heard many a bard or poet say the word, and it always seemed a bit grand for the simple emotion it was meant to convey. But she caught a glimpse of it somehow, in the same manner the artists intended.

Minstrels may take an age to say it, but Sonja knew it simply as a physical desire, no need to put honey on it.

Still, in this case, she yearned. She yearned for Ysidra's company, for Ysidra's hands on her body, her lips on Sonja's own. And this baffled her somewhat, as hands and lips were plentiful and willing, from sea to sea, mountain to valley.

But she also yearned for something else, something slippery in the dawn light. Forgiveness? Redemption? She chided herself. It was foolishness. What was done was done. Any more of this and she'd become a useless singer of songs herself, to her eternal disgrace. Being a thief and killer was one thing; being a *minstrel* was simply not done.

It was exhausting, having a conscience, she decided, so she chose to be rid of it and made up her bedroll and meager campsite.

Eventually, she slept, if fitfully. She knew she'd dreamed—she woke up angry, but no recollection of *what* she'd dreamed came to her. She wasn't afraid, exactly; if her own senses didn't warn her, her mount's would. But she was anxious—"jumpy," her mother had called it. Fatigue, hunger, and that third thing...the *yearning*...and finally, they led her to a deep slumber quite beyond her normal time of rest. She pulled her rough, thin blanket tighter and was blissfully empty of thought for a time.

She awoke abruptly in the dark, the taste of blood in her mouth.

She sat up, reaching for her sword without conscious thought, her speed blinding. She heard something. Something in the air.

Sonja raised to a squat—it wouldn't do to lift her head above the cover of the tall grass for any Wolf Pack archer to put a few shafts through it. She looked at her mount, Sunder, who had not stirred, but neither was he sleeping. And again she heard the wind.

She considered. Bow or blade? If the enemy was near, she had one (slender, unpalatable) chance at surprise: that they might still think she slept. In that case, a bow was the weapon of choice, but to scan the area, locate and puncture an enemy in the dark, at no known distance...

So it was the blade. She'd heard some noted swordsmen had named their swords, and in drunken revelry, she'd been asked to name her own. "Sorrow," she had said without thought or hesitation. "It is named Sorrow."

The tavern had gone quiet, in contemplation of the blood that blade had drawn, but Sonja herself had been unable to keep up the pretense and burst out laughing loudly. She paid for no drinks that night; a good jest was enjoyed by even the drunkest of men.

The sounds.

There were many. One whisper became two. Two became ten.

Mitra's name, had they brought a battalion?

They whispered words she could not quite hear, and worse...they were circling around her.

And coming closer.

She held her sword, checked her knife, and laid the bow and quiver at her feet, facing her, so they could be grasped as needed. She'd known her death wasn't going to be that of an aristocrat, pampered and surrounded by well-wishers. But she hadn't thought it would be so damn *soon*. Her well-worn soft leather boots slipped perceptibly in the damp grass.

Only then did she reach up to touch her face, drawing back red fingers on the glove of her free hand.

She was bleeding from her nose. And she was cold, colder than she ought to be. She flexed the fingers of her free hand, open and closed, open and closed.

"Slit my throat," said a gruff, emotionless voice.

She didn't respond but merely curled her toes tightly, in case she had to spring and needed purchase.

"Slit my throat," the voice said again. She saw a shape, manlike and shambling, but no detail to add context to the encounter.

Another voice responded, "Cut my belly open. Cut it right open, warm guts on my boots."

Were they *asking* her to kill them? Was she still asleep and dancing with the dead?

A woman's voice said, "I hate her. I will hate her until there is nothing left."

She shivered. She was certain she'd heard that voice.

Shrieking. Wailing. And then becoming silent.

The first voice said, "Devil. We *see* you."

The woman's voice said, "Look at you, proud as a cocksman's wedding. You make me sick, Devil. For what you did to me, what you did to my husband."

A shambling figure in the mist came forward, his mouth somehow paralyzed, drooling. "Ah ill eee. Ebil ill eeee. Uht eye aaaay."

The woman's voice returned, rageful beyond understanding. "Do you see? Do you see? I had a virile, handsome husband, in the thief's fine trade, and now I spend eternity with *this*. Because of *you*."

The voices spoke over one another, listing their grievances. "She put an axe to my head," "She speared my gut and threw me overboard," "She set a burning arrow to my ship." Many of the shapes shambled, as if carrying the weight of their wounds into whatever misshapen land they were bound to.

Sonja tried to speak but found her voice unaccountably dry.

Then a closer voice came to her, and she knew this came from someone still among the living.

"*Hey*. You're routed! You're *pissed*. Put your sword *down*, harlot."

She turned and saw clearly three urchin youths, perhaps twelve or thirteen, all holding rough tree limbs they'd clumsily sharpened, the points away from Sonja, the blunt ends aimed at her. All girls, with close-cut hair, perhaps to resemble boys at a distance. She'd done that trick herself as a child.

Living. Thieves and footpads, maybe even roadway killers, but they drew breath. And she saw they had the angry smirking faces of the youth who had known hunger and saw all those who were fed as the enemy.

Sonja started to relax. "Children. I am not your enemy. Just let me go on my way and..."

The second of the girls whacked a fair blow with the side of her makeshift spear against Sonja's head... It was her own fault; she'd been paying attention to the one who'd spoken and was sure they were not a threat.

She rubbed her head with her free hand. "Ow! You little swineworn *shit*!"

The girls grinned. Sonja reached for the spear of the child who'd hit her, instinctively. The lead thief took the opportunity to even the bruises on Sonja's face, laughing all the while. They reminded her of her brothers' taunting, which put her in a fouler mood still.

"God-cursed little dogs! I'll swat the life from you!"

They stepped forward as one and spun their spears around so that the sharp points now faced Sonja. "Just give us what you've got. You've got enough and should be happy to share."

Sonja sneered and for her bad manners was poked lightly in one thigh, which helped her mood not at all.

"All right, gods damn you. Come get supper, bratlings."

The girls stepped forward, smiling. This was good sport *and* a fat prize.

But Sonja was ready this time.

She knocked their spears to one side easily with the weight of her weapon. They were fast, but she was mean, and in this case, mean was better. Still holding the pommel of her blade, she punched the lead girl in the face, bloodying her nose far less delicately than fear had done for Sonja herself only minutes before. The lead girl was tough, but a child, and went down hard.

Her friends were loyal and tried to repull their spears into killing position … but none of them had ever truly killed, and they hesitated. Sonja grabbed the little brute who had first hit her and flipped the girl ass over stewpot, knocking her out completely.

Sonja slapped the third backhand-style, as her brothers had taught her, and she felt the girl's jaw rattle.

Somehow, the fight left them, and they sat still, expecting dire retribution.

Whether because of the fitful night or the morning cold she felt, Sonja simply didn't have the will at the moment. In fact, she felt she owed them her thanks for the distraction from a morning she didn't want to recall.

She took out the few meager coins she'd taken from the handsome bounder she'd met on the road and tossed them to the girls.

"Look. No hard feelings. You're only doing what you need to do," Sonja offered.

The lead girl only glared.

"In exchange for the coins, is this the road to—"

The girl spat, eyes full of rage.

"Something you want to say to me, girl?"

The girl sat up straight, defiant. "Your hair is stupid."

Sonja's left eyebrow arched upward.

The girl helpfully continued, "You look like a loose girl with a dead red rooster on your head."

Sonja found this less amusing. It was, again, too close to the taunts she'd received as a child. She tried to remain calm.

"And your armor looks like the wire on a hogpen."

Sonja pulled back her fist, then held back at the last possible moment. "You're rude little brats, I'll give you that." The girl's eyes burned, but she was silent as she rubbed her reddened face.

Sonja bridled her horse and packed up her belongings.

As she rode away, she was certain she heard them laughing. One of them screamed out, "Goodbye, stable sweep!"

"Should've cut their nasty tongues out," she said to Sunder. "That's my problem—I'm too nice."

Leagues behind her, the Falcon's Blood Man was nearing the camp of Ysidra, the exiled queen. And he was smiling.

10

BONES ON
THE ROAD

*It was not the sharing of thought from land to land that shaped the rules
of castle building, for in those days, great architects were coveted, not lent
out or sold easily. Often, they were slaves, regardless of the affections of
their ruler. So the learned experience of one citadel artist tended to stay
within a single land's borders, and a traveler felt the change from one
country to another almost immediately. One king preferred elegant spires,
another fierce turrets. Materials and the recipes to make them varied
from border to border.*

But some elements remained consistent even if unspoken and unguilded.

*For example, no castle, regardless of land, would be built in a val-
ley when a mound was available. This meant a lifetime of extra labor
to bring water and trade uphill, but that choice was made again and
again and again, without the sharing of knowledge from one builder to
another. It is certain that there were military benefits, such as the ability
to see oncoming pests at a greater distance, but even those high castles still
tended to retain guard outposts for an even greater allowance of alarm.*

*No, it was simpler than that. No king wanted to have peasants pass-
ing by looking down on them. Ideas were formed that way.
Terrible, traitorous ideas.*

Tophen Lamar, *The Philosophy of the Fortress*

She continued her journey away from the safety of her homeland
and toward Zamora, always with an eye on the trail behind her,
for sign of the Pack hunting her. For a time, she followed the river
along the Bleak Road.

If it could be called a river. On the other side of the great water
(a lake, she always called it, thinking the name "great water" a bit
grand for its purpose) of Vilayet Sea was Hyrkania, which she kept to
her back and avoided looking at entirely. But the desert was around
her in every direction but one, the sparse vegetation along the nameless creek she walked beside.

She had only a vague destination in mind, and no fixed point on
the map beyond. Sonja's mind, lethal and cunning as it was, tended
to wander in her solitude. She was aware that she was being hunted
by both former friend and former employer, the Wolf Queen and the
Falcon's Blood Man. But she had barely seen anyone on the road
since sunup, had not spoken with anyone since the trio of brats she'd
been forced to educate. And so she could not help it. She felt the danger less intensely, the need to move less keenly. She took the creek
path to avoid encounters, for her sake and theirs, as she was in no fine
mood at all after the events of the last few days.

She wanted an inn, something a bit merrier than the shithole in
Radolan, perhaps, but not too much finer. A fire, a drink, a meal.
Her needs were simple, even if her appetites were unending.

She'd chosen the Bleak Road, which had existed in some form

since antiquity. It'd been grand once, fit for the conveyance of noble carriages, with signposts elegantly painted and a series of heavy stones carved to tell stories in sequence, of great battles and triumphs by forgotten rulers.

Those days were long gone, the signs used for fires and the stones worn smooth by the harsh desert wind.

Her mount voiced no objection to the route. To him, access to water and palatable greenery made the trip almost pleasant. Until the stones.

At first, random pebbles on the river's edge, small enough to be noticed, but not a hindrance. But they grew larger and more numerous, and eventually, she dismounted entirely, walking alongside her horse with no lead or reins. They weren't necessary. She was, despite her recent choices, Hyrkanian to the bone.

As the rocks became larger, it was too treacherous to continue the simple path, which had clearly not been intended for mounted riders. More likely, it was made for fishermen and tradesmen, a shortcut to the border, perhaps useful to avoid the presence of guards. A broken leg for her mount here meant no outcome but death for even the most loyal of horseflesh, and that was a thought she could not bear. So she faced a choice: leave the road, crossing the desert to find a larger, smoother trade route over the sand, or actually walk in the river itself, for as long as she could, where the stones had been diminished and polished by the mountain water's endless care.

She removed her boots, whistled, and stepped into the water, which was briskly cold, she knew, but somehow, she didn't object, while her horse sighed audibly, relieved by the cool, placid current.

It was the horse who smelled the smoke first. Sonja's mind had simply wandered away from the tedium of the march. But when she looked up, she saw it, the wisps of smoke from a small campfire.

And it was indeed small. Too small for a garrison, or even a hunting party of any significance. She did the unconscious weapons check that had long ago become habit, and they moved toward the fire, quietly but not so quietly as to startle. After all, she was the newcomer, and it wouldn't do to be shot for a simple lack of roadside etiquette.

There were bodies in the road.

Three, maybe four corpses, freshly removed from all earthly concerns. Flesh melted and faces pulled open in violent crimson rictus, bone joints and tissue exposed. They'd been set on fire, which chilled Sonja a bit, because of the effort expended... There was no wood nearby to speak of, and what vegetation did break through the desert surface was too damp and too hardy to burn well.

Someone had prepared this tableau. Someone had hauled the fuel to set these souls burning. There was a sign, with an ornate scrawl she could not read and an image of a white spider, red-eyed and fanged. Although the writing was meaningless, the message was clear: This road was restricted. The spider, she knew, meant it was under Zamoran order.

And there was an old man, toothlessly grinning at her as she stepped from the water. Whether out of malice or lechery, she couldn't say and didn't care.

He was bald but for wispy tendrils of hair, and his posture indicated a life of hard, repetitive labor. He sat next to a small, empty pullcart that had been fitted with harnesses. Harnesses for men, not beasts. She suspected it was these unfortunate burning remnants who had pulled their own funeral pyre to this remote location.

"Well. Now, this is a fine sight for my tired eyes. Welcome, your lady, welcome," the old man said.

"My thanks, old one," said Sonja. The scene made her wary. She'd seen enough corpses and little understood the use of them as trophies. Upon standing closer, she noticed the sizes of two of the burned bodies... Children, without doubt. A family, then. They'd made a family burn together. She wondered if they'd had the courtesy to kill them first.

"Begging your leave, pretty. But your voice and rigging say that you're Hyrkanian—have I about placed your birthland?"

"You have, elder."

"And you can't read the sign, then."

She blushed. This was not a topic she enjoyed discussing with strangers.

"Be not ashamed. Few can, as it's in the high court script of the king. I myself had to have it read to me several times by a man wearing scent like a fancy whorehouse. Again and again, until I got it just right. Any errors meant the lash, you see."

"I am sure none of this is my business, and I'll be taking my leave, sir."

He grinned widely again, and she could see the remains of unchewed breakfast on his gums. "It *says*, 'Travel from Hyrkania is *forbidden* under penalty of *death by fire*.' And it's signed by the administrator of the high court hisself, pretty pretty and all. Do you ken?"

Sonja merely stared, emotionless. "The plague."

"Aye, the plague. *This* little family of rats and beggars ignored the sign, which is quite against the king's policy, you see. I struck the flame myself, as his loyal subject, keeping the horse-screwing savages away." His smile disappeared, and it occurred to Sonja that he fancied himself some kind of hero for this miserable duty.

"How very valiant of you," Sonja said, unable to mask her contempt fully.

"I hear your tone, pretty. I may not be able to fight. But I am able to serve. And serve I shall."

"Perhaps. But I suspect you needn't *enjoy* it so much."

"A tart tongue you have, pretty—I hear it, I hear it. And there's naught I can do, old and diminished as I am. Except to say, red one...that there are them at the border who are not old and not diminished. And they'll make you eat your tongue if you answer them with acid. You'll bow and scrape if you want to live unmolested.

Frankly, even that may not be enough." His grin returned but was quite devoid of goodwill.

Sonja started to turn away. The entire scene nauseated her, and her temper was already short. More discussion with this worthless functionary would lead only to more revulsion. "I'll keep it in mind. Good morn."

Suddenly he moved toward her, quickly enough that she put her hand on the pommel of her dagger, the fastest-retrieved weapon she had. And while she felt no danger of being overwhelmed by the rickety and grotesque figure, she couldn't help but shudder at his touch on her bare shoulder.

"You don't understand, pretty pretty. Go back. It's plague your people carry. You could be fresh as a spring foal and someone'll claim you have a peculiar odor or that you sneezed too loudly, and that'll be it. They'll tear you to pieces, burn the corpse, and piss in the ashes. Go back."

She shrugged her shoulder from his loathsome touch. "I'm going to Zamora, elder. You can burn all the luckless travelers you want, but that's the direction I'm headed. Touch me again, and I'll show you what else Hyrkanians export—are we understood?"

But the old man wasn't listening. He was eyeing her arm, his eyes moist and his entire figure trembling. He was staring at it, gazing at the Hunter's Asp as if he were starving and it was the last food on the face of the land. He gasped, transfixed.

And then he took Sonja's gloved hand.

And knelt before her, head bowed.

"My lady. My lady of the Asp. Forgive me. Forgive my useless, thoughtless words."

Sonja looked down at him, head cocked in bafflement. She looked momentarily for counsel from her horse, who provided only indifference.

"I only did as my king requested, lady. Forgive a stupid old fool."

Sonja disliked genuflecting to anyone or anything and found that she liked it not a bit more when she was the subject of the unctuous toadying.

"Tarim's balls, get up. How far to Zamora, old one?"

He stood, but it clearly made him uncomfortable. He kept his eyes averted, as if from the sun when all the sands around him were blinding. "Lady, I beg of you. Go back. They will not... The guards are not kind. Fearful of sickness, they are. They will not treat you proper."

"How *far*?"

He raised his arm, clearly defeated, and pointed wearily to the west. "Two days. Two days, lady. May the gods light your way in the dark."

Sonja looked at the still-burning remains and turned her gaze back to the old man. "Bury them. Dig a proper hole; place a marker. Let someone else be the bloody scarecrow for the court. Do you understand? Do it now. *Now*."

He contorted physically, as if struck. "My lady, the *king*—"

Sonja snorted, her eyes narrowing. "The king can eat my arse after three days' ride. Do as I say."

He contemplated, then nodded slowly, resigned.

Sonja was moving back to her horse when a sudden thought hit her.

"Also. Your lady has a final order. Slap yourself in the face. Hard as you can."

He didn't understand. "My lady...?"

She put steel in her voice. "Quick as a whip now, hard as you can. *Now*."

He dutifully did it, knocking the strength out of his own legs and drawing blood from his toothless mouth. He fell to hands and knees, disoriented.

He said something unintelligible, a mere mumble.

She mounted her horse. Every instinct she had told her to go.

"What did you say, peasant?"

He stood up but still would not look at her. "I said, 'May the frost never reach your heart, lady.'"

She stared at him and looked again at the burnt bones of her countrymen, and for a moment, she realized that the safest and most satisfying thing would be to simply cut his head off and watch it tumble, gathering sand in the wounds of neck and body.

Instead, she turned away. And guided her horse in the direction he'd pointed. Toward Zamora. Toward food and flesh and beer overflowing. Away from this staged carnage, this meaningless cruelty.

She had things to say to the man, unkind things. But she wanted away from the smell of him and the corpses he tended. She rode away—the road to Zamora was mostly uphill from here, at higher elevation, and she didn't want to run that span in the dark. She suspected everything the old man, that bloody marker, had said was true and more. Best to see what was ahead, if the road was to be full of vipers.

And the road behind full of wolves.

She felt chilled, despite the warming proximity of the blazing desert sun.

On the road to Makkalet, city-state of Hyrkania and its capital, a soldier marched on, dead-eyed and silent. His slack lips drooped, and if the road dust and sand carried by the breeze entered his mouth, he didn't notice or react.

His shoes and fine uniform were torn, as if to manifest his descent, his fall from gracious station and duty. Only days before, when he passed by, men paused and women admired him. He'd grown used to it. Even liked it, to a degree.

Respect. He craved it. And no small measure of fear. After all, he was of the King's Eye, was he not? Chosen envoy of the Wooden Throne?

He was. And he fancied he still was that person, although the few reactions he'd received on his long trek home had been more of the horrified stripe. But his fragile mind had not allowed a full reckoning of his situation. It was merely marching steps—one two one two one two three four *three four*—as he'd been endlessly taught, enough so that he could do it in his sleep.

Or in his torment, it turned out.

If he'd had the clarity of mind to know what he really looked like, if he'd stopped to drink in a cool, reflective stream... he might have lost what little sense remained in him. Clothes torn, most of his hair pulled out in huge clumps, leaving raw bloody scalp and even some exposed skull. One eye gouged entirely. Claw marks down his face, and a long trail of dried blood from his mouth, down his chin and neck, all down his formerly fine uniform.

Even if bystanders had had the grace and kindness to ask if he needed help, he wouldn't have been able to answer them. He had a message he'd memorized at some great cost... but it would have to be written, if he could summon the wits to move his hand.

His name was Tyrus. And he had no tongue.

11

EVERY HEART
A PRISON
GUARD

"How deep shall I mourn?" I once asked the Earth.
"As deep as a mountain, determine your worth."
"How long shall I mourn?" I once asked the Sun.
"Till I've become frozen, that's only begun."

"How far do I mourn?" I once asked the Sea.
"Until you can walk 'pon the surface of me."
"How much do I mourn?" I once asked the Sand.
"Until molten rivers devour the land."

"Buy why must I mourn?" I asked the New Day.
"Because what you love has all blown away."

Traditional Hyrkanian grief chant

Despite her impatience, despite the tartness of her tongue, Sonja did not dwell on the hardships of her life. She'd made a point of it. If her blankets were threadbare, she thought of the desert and warmed herself in its memory. If her food was rotten, she'd fill her belly with thoughts of the hunt for breakfast the following day.

There were many things she had no use for, fools chief among them. And she'd seen too much cruelty and death to be shaken like this, like a child without its—well, like a child.

But even the Devil, who laughed often at nothing and never failed to carouse when given the opportunity, was beside herself after the encounter with the old man and the tragic pile of burned bones.

So what if they did have the plague? Send them off, lock them up, let them...let them die with something like dignity. She pictured the mother holding the children, the father holding them all in his strong but tender arms. She imagined the parents pleading for the lives of the children, and she suddenly felt very tired.

Tired in the soul, as if her strength was sinking from her head to her leaden feet. She almost had a memory she'd long buried, but it remained prey she could not track.

It was too much. She'd hoped to make it closer to Zamora before nightfall, but she'd been through a great deal, and she had nothing remaining to push herself on with, having left whatever inner fuel was in her at the warning post with the cackling old man rife with delusion.

The nearest outcropping of sizable rock was on the other side of the creek, which had now opened up enough to be called a river, if a shallow, murky one. She made her decision impulsively, as she always did. Guiding Sunder's head with just a gentle nudge, she led him into the stream. It was warm and pleasant, actually, and both were grateful for the soothing water.

But it was muddy in the middle, and she almost lost a boot more than once. Sunder grunted at pulling the great weight of his legs through the deep muck. Then stopped for a drink and seemed unwilling to go farther.

She could have forced him. Cajoled him, even punished him. He would have obeyed, but he would have seen her differently, no longer as friend, as family, but more as attempted master. Instead, she leaned on him with both hands, gently breathing him in, as she waited for him to move on.

When they made it to the other side, she found a spot of shade, where a bit of raspy cowslip grew, enough to keep her mount busy and contented, if not precisely overjoyed. She knew the day was warm; the sun was reddening her skin. But she still felt a chill, and so she started to make a fire, a chore she normally enjoyed.

As the flames started to grow, she imagined she heard the screams of children, and she kicked at the scrap wood she'd positioned carefully, scattering it to uselessness.

She checked one last time on the trail behind her, on the other side of the water. It came to her that she'd been lying to herself, as stubborn as the giant horse in the running creek. She'd been running from the Wolf Pack; that much was true. But she wasn't truly afraid of death. She valued her life dearly but knew her end was likely to be violent and possibly the work of someone she'd genuinely wronged.

What she was afraid of was Ysidra cornering her, leaving her no choice but to kill to escape. And that seemed a tragedy more for gods than for her kind, homeless rider that she was.

She laid her back against the rocks, adjusted her back for comfort, and lowered her head, as if laying down a burden as well.

As she often did, she tried to think of the memories that made her happy. But they seemed so distant and circuitous, she gave up on trying to cheer herself and went to the one comfort that had never completely failed her.

She quietly hummed her mother's lullaby.

*   *   *

She slept. And despite her discomfort, it was a deep sleep.

But it could never be called restful.

In dreaming, she caught her prey.

She was ten years old. By then, all the boys in her village, and many girls, had declared what their vocations would be. The villagers did not use money among themselves; the idea of keeping a stack of coins buried somewhere would have been roundly ridiculed by her people. Even with others, they traded primarily for pelts, crafts, or things grown in their fields. And truthfully, rarely even that, because they had need of so few things.

In times of plenty or of want, if a traveler needed a meal and a bed, they fed them without payment. But they also gave a gracious but firm invitation for them to leave in the morning. The lack of need for imports extended quite completely to outsiders of all stripes.

On occasion, a young man or woman would fancy someone from a bordering village, or even a traveler, and while it was never strictly forbidden, it was felt as a loss in the economy of the village's assets. A strong young boy or a stout young woman was a loss, certainly, after the years the village had spent feeding and caring for them. But if they wanted to go, it was better they go than remain and be diminished with grief.

And to be fair, the village council was not above a dowry, regardless of size.

Sonja wanted to be a hunter. Her mother kept the family and was a fine craftswoman; her loaves and jewelry were prized, even outside the village. And her father, with arms like tree trunks, was the blacksmith. But the truth was, most of the villagers were farmers first and did their specialties and passions when the goats were fed and the crops tilled. The care for their most precious commodity, the horses, was shared by all, and none called it a chore.

She either could not or would not remember the names of those villagers, but then, they had been her tribe, and her world.

Sonja, it was decided, embraced a wide variety of things she simply wasn't good at. She was clumsy with the forge, having nearly set the village on fire twice. She lacked the patience for growing things and became bored even at harvest. She had no sense of pattern or agility with the polished stones of her mother's bracers and necklaces. "You are chaos, child," her mother often said.

Her father put it more forcefully. "No. She's the Devil."

Even in slumber, her arm ached under the Asp, perhaps in memory of her mother's craft.

The name should have been hurtful, but she found it amusing, after a time. It had rather stuck in her community. From her point of view, it was vastly preferential to her previous nickname, the one her older brothers called her incessantly.

She was ten when she finally declared her vocation, essentially choosing the pattern of the rest of her life. "I'll be a hunter, Father," she told him one evening after supper as they slopped the pigs, and with all due gravitas.

Her father, strong as he was and respected by all, was in most ways a gentle man. From her point of view, looking up, he seemed surrounded by the stars. He looked in her eyes, and there was something there ... some hesitation. Then he smiled, tussled the hair that had become the bane of her existence, and said, "I think that's the road chosen for you, Sonjita."

It was true—she was born to hunt. Whatever rare gift had allowed Hyrkanians to survive their darkest times, times of raiding and famine and disease, it ran strong in her. She was slovenly; she was often thoughtless. Her mother's attempts to teach her letters had been an agony for both teacher and student.

But she was relentless.

She could run a short distance faster than any man, woman, or child in the region and could continue long after others' legs gave out. She had eyes that spotted still fowl in the trees and huddled game in their burrows. And she could scuttle through endless brambles without making a sound. And she saw pride in her father's face, though he tried to hide it with scowls and tsks of disapproval.

Above all, her skill with a bow seemed a near miracle. She aimed well, instinctively, upon first picking it up and practiced every available moment for months. When she stopped, her father asked why.

"I don't think I can get any better, Father," she said. And he didn't understand at first, thinking she'd become bored or frustrated. Rather, it was a simple statement of fact. It was unlikely that she could get better, because she had mastered the thing entirely.

At ten. Ten years old. He was equally astonished and proud.

But he hesitated. He knew a truth that he was not strong enough, for all the thickness in his arms, to say aloud.

The daughter of his heart would never be a hunter.

He had three sons, two older than Sonja. Arrick and Ozkar, who both watched over their sister with protective eyes and attempted always to make her as miserable as possible, their way of showing love. And the gods had blessed the family with an unexpected son, Shia, still a toddler, more fair-haired than any in the clan, under his mother's constant adoring gaze.

They would likely become hunters, all of them. The elder pair were competent. More than competent, certainly. They lacked Sonja's gifts, but they never failed to return with meat for the pot, whether it was a squirrel, a pheasant, or the one time they'd excitedly brought down a stag and called for the village to help with the haul. It'd made them a bit heroic that week, and other village girls already looked at them admiringly.

But the truth was, it was Sonja who had spotted the stag they'd dragged home. Sonja who had said nothing as the boys were soundly praised. Sonja who'd dropped her bow when she'd had the beast directly in her sights, utterly unaware.

His little Sonjita, family clown, father's pride...could not kill. Had no taste for it at all.

He'd wanted to be kind. He'd wanted to explain to her that her heart was tender and that that was to be respected. But he couldn't. That kindness would mean hunger. It could mean illness, even death, eventually. Her mother defended her, said she'd grow out of it. But he wasn't at all certain.

Sonja saw the moment's hesitation and was saddened by it; she knew what darkened her father's bright eyes. She decided she'd go on the hunt the following day—she would not be talked out of it.

And *she* would make the kill.

It was Ozkar who said it first, on the hunting trail the next day. Ozkar who, she knew, loved her best of the brothers but also loved tormenting her most. "Mitra's hairy bunghole, *keep up*, Tomato Head!"

She took the core of the pear she'd been eating and hurled it at the back of his head, with a good deal more force than necessary, and was rewarded with a string of the best curses a fourteen-year-old boy who'd never really been anywhere could muster. But the sad truth was, Ozkar was plain, neither hideous nor pretty, and possessed of no particularly distinguishing features. She'd attempted many insults toward him, hoping one might sting. But there was no wilting response to "Tomato Head," and they all knew it. In childhood parlance, that was the killing blow.

She was certain she'd be called that for the rest of her life, curse her ridiculous mane. If only she could have the blond locks of her younger brother. She looked balefully at her elder siblings in annoyed silence.

Arrick was a year older than Ozkar but always seemed a bit behind in all regards, somehow, despite being adept in the limited academics available to him in the village. He couldn't resist joining in. "Have a care, Brother. I heard her condition is contagious. One wrong word, you might catch her horrendous symptoms."

This was too much for Sonja. "I hope you *do* catch it, down *there*, assuming either of you ever *grows* a man's patch!"

Her father laughed, which only made her angrier. But behind the smile on his face was worry, and she knew his thoughts were always of the coming of winter. It was the time when the crops failed and game fowl moved south. He had six mouths to feed, and there were those in the village who would need help, who were long past their hunting days. She listened to the elders at meetings. She knew their worry.

"Also on your skinny asses," she said, to the boys' confusion. "Red hair by the bushel!"

Ozkar simply laughed as they walked. "Men don't grow hair on their asses, Tomato Head."

She looked up at her father with her guileless green eyes for confirmation. "Do they not, Father?"

"None to speak of, Sonjita."

So she crossed her arms, one more red mark on her side of the win/loss tablet, and she pouted for a good half mile. Until she saw something, something the boys had overlooked. She knew immediately what it meant, and she couldn't wait to tell her mother and the baby back home that this time, it was *she* who found the stag. This time, *she* would feed the village.

She should have told her father, she knew. But she'd been raw ever since last season, seeing the boys get credit for a kill that should at least partially have been credited to her. And she had something to prove to her father, and to herself.

She took off. She sprinted ahead on the trail, bursting between her two brothers, almost knocking them over as she passed.

"Out of my way, bareback boys," she shouted in passing, quite pleased with herself. It sounded dirty, but not so dirty she'd get a whipping. Just right.

Her father yelled at her to stop, but she was already reaching for her bow and was in full run...and when Sonja chose, Sonja could fly.

And fly she did. She ran up the trail, never slipping on that edge of the hillside that was all loose shale, her feet barely making contact with each step. She leapt the big elm that had fallen and not yet been chopped and bundled.

She ran, smug and delighted. She knew this...this was the day. Wouldn't her brothers be heartbroken when the village applauded her harvest? Wouldn't they just want to die?

She didn't know, couldn't imagine, that both her brothers were secretly rooting for her. Perhaps a bit was guilt—they had taken the accolades, it was true. But more than that, and though they would never say it, they loved their sister and had since being brought into the midwife's tent to see her tiny, perfect form.

She came to the first glade, the last great grassland of this hill, and she saw it.

A white stag. The biggest stag she'd ever seen, pure like the clouds that watched over them and brought the water for their crops.

It didn't see her. Its brown eyes were still as it grazed. She found that she hadn't been breathing and had to gasp once quietly just to catch up. She carefully pulled her bow from her back and the single arrow from her quiver, beaded with love by her mother in a swirl of reds and greens.

Sonja's colors.

She nocked the arrow. He was too close to miss.

She pulled back. The fear was there, and the inexplicable mix of feelings that came with killing anything at her age. Her hand shook a little. She could miss the target if she—

But no. She stood straight, took her breath... and fired.

The stag fell.

Elation quickly gave way to sadness, and if she could have, she would have reached through time and clipped the arrow out of the air.

She didn't move. She simply stood there. The feelings were too big for her small shoulders.

Then she came to reason, hearing her father and brothers crashing through the tall grass and brambles. Her father's face was panicked, distraught like Sonja had never witnessed. He grabbed her by the arms and yelled at her, yelled as he had never done in her entire rebellious life. She quivered under the force of it. *"Sonja.* You stay *here.* Do you hear me? Stay *here.* Swear to me. *Swear* to me!"

She had nothing in her experience that taught her to comprehend this moment. She blinked, wide-eyed. Had she done something wrong? Tears threatened to fill her eyes.

He shook her again, as if trying to wake someone from a dark fever. "Say you understand!"

Silently, she nodded. Her father let her go and turned around while reaching for his bow, never looking back as he ran back into the brush.

Then she saw it. Smoke, from the direction of her village. Too much smoke by far.

Ozkar looked back at her and said a single word, like her single arrow through the stag's brain.

"Raiders," he said before running off to follow his father, followed further by Arrick, both swallowed completely by the tall green grass.

It was the last day she would ever see any of her family alive.

*   *   *

Hours later, cold and abandoned, newly orphaned, utterly alone, she knew what her first real use in the village would be: that of the undertaker of everything and everyone she had ever known.

Crying unheard tears down her dirty, smoke-stained face, she pulled a spade from the remains of the garden shed and began to dig.

12

WRITTEN IN BLOOD AND FANG

I fought for king
I fought for land
I fought for beer
And maiden's hand

I fought for life
But now I sleep
Where I will stand
And guard the keep.

I learned my trade
By fire and sky
I cursed my blade
Yet held it high

My flesh is red
My wound is deep

And yet I stand
To guard the keep.

Traditional soldier's ballad

Once past the last high steppe, Sonja knew the road, and by late afternoon, she knew she faced a choice. The Zamorans were not to be trifled with. Their militia was trained and motivated, and they detested outsiders even during times of peace. Tradesmen were cautiously welcomed, tourists contemptuously tolerated... Bannerless wild women from a plague state would be executed on the spot.

In particular, they remembered Hyrkania from its violent heyday, when its people had been plains raiders and had made endless raids touching thousands of the Zamoran population. Direct hostilities had long since ceased, and trade routes had been established.

But Zamora had not forgotten.

And it had turned to darker arts. No one was certain who had first named it "the Spider Kingdom," but whether it was a domestic title the Zamorans had originated or a curse from neighbors that they took a fondness toward, the name stuck.

Sonja had chosen her fate, to go from her homeland and not toward it. And if Sonja had a defining trait, it would be that she was stubborn. Her father had observed that she must be part mule, until her mother had asked, "Which part?"—which seemed to end the conversation entirely.

Her choice was simple, but the results could be lethal. Did she continue on in broad sunlight toward Zamora and attempt to bribe her way past the guards, or did she wait until cover of night and enter as a sneak? A misstep in either approach meant death. But she was tired and hungry and more.

She decided to continue on. The most outlying guard patrol would still be a day's ride away. She could decide then.

Or so did she reason.

Until she saw the spiked helmets of the Zamoran outreach patrol.

Sylus found them sooner than expected, just half a day's ride from the stable of Radolan and the site of his latest indiscretion. This was not the outcome he'd expected, based on the advice of his informants... They'd been quite effusive in their praise of the skills of his targets, both the two guards and the errant royal they served.

Their reputation apparently was an overfilled bladder, because he saw two of them at the edge of a small pond, delinquent in their duties entirely. They had fair cover, surrounded by trees and shrubs. But he was the Falcon's Blood Man, and he'd killed in much less hospitable scenarios many times. The fabled hunters boasted and laughed as if in a crowded tavern, one short and thickly built, the other a younger man, slender and lithe. He was almost disappointed in them. He'd expected a challenge. He considered the strategy... Were his swords in order?

They wouldn't be the first overrated local heroes he'd gutted. He could likely take both out with his bow before they could even react, so poor was their position. Certainly one of them, and the other would be knifework, as easy to do as it was to say.

But that wasn't what pleased him. He would never see their Hidden that way, never know their true souls. And while he doubted either of these simple hired men had anything new or compelling in their inner selves to reveal, he nonetheless received no pleasure without knowing. He did not ambush, but it had little to do with honor and more with a bone-deep need to see what death displayed on the faces of his targets.

"We're tossed fools, Festrel, you know that, don't you?" said the heavier man, warming his hands by the campfire. Both hands, Sylus noted with contempt. Leaving no hand anywhere near his weapons.

"And why are we such, Raganus? Enlighten a poor guardsman," said Festrel.

Sylus would never admit it, but the private conversations of normal men fascinated and inspired him. He would overhear the most mundane of chatter and try it out later, to aid in passing as one of them. The word "enlighten" in this case thrilled him, in the peasant soldier's casual use. Sylus knew it was sarcasm; he vaguely understood the concept. But he tended to misinterpret it as contemptuous hostility, little understanding that it was also common as a bonding ritual quite beyond his capacity to discern.

"Because we follow a queen who is likely to be hung upon our return to camp, regardless of the success or failure of our mission," said Raganus, a sour look on his face.

"Oh, I don't think that she—"

"She killed the elders and stacked their heads like melons, my friend. And do you know what? They'll make a trio of nooses, I'll wager. Curse be on us for following her, they'll say. And we *chose* to follow her."

"She is our queen. I did as duty demands."

Sylus made a note in his mind. *I did as duty demands*—that phrase could come in handy someday, as the other guard seemed to change tactics immediately.

"You fool none, my friend. Your queen, is it? And you follow her, this virtuous monarch, for no other reason?"

Festrel shifted, suddenly finding urgency in stoking the campfire with a stick. "I don't know what you mean. And that's enough chatter—we'll be heard."

"We've seen no track of anything all day except rodents and lizards, friend."

"Nevertheless."

Raganus grinned broadly. "And if your dear queen were to disrobe in the firelight and show you her wounds…what then, Wolf soldier?"

The younger guard's hand reached for his sword, his eyes blazing. He opened his mouth to speak but seemed unable to form the words.

Raganus laughed. "Stand down, my friend. Every man is allowed his wants. But I fear we'll come to a bad end long before you taste her peach. Stand down—I was merely jesting."

"You jest too much, Raganus. That's all I'll say. Too much and more. It's likely to get you killed one day."

Raganus sat on the heavy stones outside the fire. "If I'm to be killed, better you do the deed than many a less loving hand. Back to my homeland, I'd be."

Festrel sat across from him, stoking the embers. "How you older ones pine for a land you've never set foot in is quite beyond me. But every man is allowed his wants, I suppose."

Sylus had reached his limit of patience. The bittersweet tone of the conversation annoyed him. It was like listening to foreigners speak a language and catching only every fifth word.

He knew he could walk toward the fire and charm them; he had no doubt of his abilities in that regard. Get them calm, get them drunk, slit their throats. It would be all too easy. And he could look in their eyes and see what no one else could.

But then he remembered Sonja. She who had seen him, the real him, not the polite creature he pretended to be, even if only for a moment. It had disconcerted him, made him feel exposed in a way that lingered uncomfortably. And she would not care a whit if these men died in tears—he was certain of it.

It was the girl. The forest "queen" in exile. That was who Sonja had betrayed; that was who she felt guilty and responsible for ruining. If the She-Devil knew that her insight had led to the miserable torment of Ysidra—Mitra's *name*, that would be glorious to witness.

It was decided. These two were meaningless. He'd shoot them from ambush, silent and swift. Let the empty sky witness their last breath; he had better game.

Sylus knew there would be hell to pay from his ostensible employer, the Falcon. He had a mission, to take the Asp and kill the thief he'd hired to steal it, who had broken her word and kept the damn thing. The Falcon would not like him killing merely for the sake of it, for the *enlightenment* of it.

He smiled as he realized the guard had given him the perfect defense. When the Falcon called him to reckoning, he'd stand tall, head up, and say, *I did as duty demands.*

It would work. He'd tell the Falcon that no physical torture would make Sonja's last moments destroy her as this would: knowing she'd caused her love to die. In agony.

"I did as duty demands," he whispered to himself.

It was perfection. And the dead man gave it to him as a parting gift.

It was all too delicious.

He raised his bow, nocked an arrow, and pulled the string back slowly, soundlessly.

The tall one would go first; he looked quicker witted and therefore more dangerous.

Sylus took aim.

And felt a sharp sting on the back of his neck. Just enough to break the skin.

A woman's voice came quietly from behind him, and he keenly felt his complete vulnerability.

"Who are you, and why do you target my guards? Quickly. You will get no second answer," said the voice.

His mind was a miasma. He knew, simply *knew*, that she wasn't bluffing and that in all the fights he'd been in, all the duels, he'd never been so close to death.

"I am simply a hunter, lady. I'm camped nearby and heard voices; I saw their swords. You can't murder a man for being cautious, can you?" He knew this wasn't a perfect approach—something about it didn't sound fully human. But he was scrabbling up a rock face and had yet to find purchase.

"No. You are not a hunter. A tracker you may be, since you clearly found *us*. But a tracker doesn't expect the prey to fight back, and a hunter understands the value of a blind. And so we find ourselves," Ysidra said.

He had no answer for this. He felt like a snake with impotent venom.

The queen pressed the knife tighter against his already bleeding skin. "Put down the bow, tracker."

The man slouched for a moment, then visibly straightened. He knew this woman would not be intimidated, and he had no faith that his honeyed tongue would save him here.

Very well. He would behave like the demon he knew himself to be. "No, lady. I won't."

"Make no mistake, tracker. I will kill you and not feel a moment's regret. Do you believe me?"

"I do, lady," Sylus said. "Only, I wonder…"

"What is it you wonder, odious one?"

He had a genuine look of confusion on his face, not that she could see it in the dark and shadow.

"It's only that I am certain I can kill one of your guards before you kill me. Even *while* you kill me, if needed. See my arm, lady. It does not quiver; it does not tremble. So that's one of your guards with an arrow in his eye—that is not in question. And so I wonder…" He paused.

"Which one of these two over-loyal idiots is your favorite, lady?"

13

THE WOODEN THRONE

I fought an age
I killed a throng
Low was my wage
Men sang no song

Then at the gates
Was stabbed and fell
And so the keep
Can go to hell

I bowed and knelt
Before my king
It didn't mean
A goddamned thing

My guts now lie
Upon the grass

And so the keep
Can kiss my ass

Traditional soldier's dirge (revised)

Hyrkania had been a brutal neighbor for a span of years. What it lacked in technology, it made up for in ferocity and more than a little cruelty. Great populations of elephants had been trained to move weapons and crude siege machinery that no armies could stand against. And when the Hyrkanian cavalry arrived, few defenders could stand against them.

But those days had gone. Disease had taken the massive war beasts, leaving only scattered tribes, ill fit for combat. The same disease hit the population centers, with only the most isolated communities unaffected. When Hyrkania reached out for help, it was found that few countries were feeling particularly charitable to their former raiders.

The Aesir and Cimmerians, working independently, revisited Hyrkania's previous bloodthirst many times over, leaving behind the desiccated bones of the once-feared nation, deeming what little was left to be of too little value to conquer. And the former slaves from Zamora and Zingara took their recompense in blood and fire. Only Turan maintained an uneasy truce in those early days, perhaps due to their shared family tree.

Hyrkanians set store by burying their dead, which they did by the tens of thousands. And a culture that exported only pain soon realized that what they had previously taken from others, they would have to grow or hunt or make themselves. Their craftsmen had been killed or enslaved, and the land was left without.

So soldiers learned to fish. Weapons makers learned to farm. And generals continued to raid, as some simply had no other skills. But it was done in secret, and often, they did not wait for the politeness of leaving Hyrkania's borders before their attacks.

Such a raid had been the making of Sonja, and the last time she heard her mother's voice. Those who knew her story were not surprised she felt no warmth for her homeland.

At some point, it became clear that there was precious little left in the land to take, and even their most covetous neighbors lost interest, thinking of Hyrkania as a defeated land, a lost cause, a sour well no longer worth plumbing.

It was then, when armies lost interest, that Hyrkanians learned to once again fight back against raiders with the remaining tools at their disposal: their cunning, their horses...and having lost everything, their absolute willingness to dispense as much miserable, furious *pain* on any invader as humanly possible.

People again began to fear the name of the land.

Hyrkania.

They had had a proper throne once.

It was telling that a country with no gold mines and no precious gems had a grand throne festooned with jewels and drunk with gold filigree. Slave artisans had built it, making it entirely an endeavor of stolen materials and labor, certainly. But in the eternal nature of man, "grand" it was considered, when spectacle was part of a nation's pride.

The first man to sit upon it was considered the father of the country, not coincidentally because he'd had the previous keepers of lore boiled to death publicly. Danska was his name, and he was father of something else, too: a great passel of vicious bastards, enough children to alter the temper of culture in diminishing concentric circles around his proximity. Those women who birthed them...They had also been stolen, many of them.

Nevertheless, he was a king to be feared by friend and foe, and his justice was swift and arbitrary. When he died by a stolen woman's hand, she suffered greatly for her deed, but secretly, even her torturers thought her more hero than assassin.

The current king, Gahresh, and his son, the prince Arahka, could trace their line directly, centuries back, to Danska himself. The first king had never married, not even in the clerical sense of many a court. His future lineage in doubt, it was decided that the closest available of his bastard sons would be suddenly "discovered," and the story was quickly concocted that Danska the Fierce had kept the child in secret, to save him from potential assassination. It was a flimsy story, but belief was enforced at sword's edge, and few were motivated to question it. Even the bastard himself came to believe the legend, despite having lived the reality.

His mother, it was said, lived handsomely but quietly in the Far North, a pampered ward of the court, forgotten by all but the clerk who refilled her stipend every two years, and she stayed alone, mother of the king, until the end of her long-ago days.

Danska had at first sat on the golden throne humbly. He felt inadequate, unsure of himself. But a golden throne and a complete lack of consequences change a man, and he himself became greedy and spiteful. It was then that Hyrkania again became a raider state. If it had want, it took, until it wanted no more.

It was a country with few allies and fewer friends.

The throne had in golden relief scenes of Danska's greatness, his courage, his strength. There were multicolored gems in the arms and crown. It had to be said, the finery actually made the chair quite uncomfortable to sit in, and among the court, the legend was that that was a deliberate sabotage, the only revenge available to the slaves who were tormented into making it.

Nevertheless, it was a symbol of pride for Hyrkania and of intimidation to outsiders. It was the last grand thing disloyal members of the aristocracy, such as it was, saw before hanging. It meant something to all who surveyed it, and it represented the land and the man who led it.

It was the first thing taken when the capital was sacked.

The Zingarans and Zamorans ran through the city, burning everything they couldn't murder, plunder, or consume, and could have, with a bit of time and planning, taken the entire throne by force, back to their own homelands, as a trophy and torment. *Look at what we've done to Danska's memory—we've pissed on it every day since.*

Instead, they chose to destroy it, break it with axes and hammers, take the gold and the jewels, scrape the relief sculpting to scrap, and defile the worthless remains with their scat.

It took centuries before Hyrkania began to defend itself at all. But once it did, something was recovered, a spark of worth that had been all but forgotten. A new throne was needed.

And it would not be run through with gold, stolen or otherwise. It would not be a target for enemies. The king of the day, Korath the Wise, deemed it good that the new throne should be made of wood and be utterly without value to anyone outside the borders of the land.

So it was made by the finest remaining carpenters, cast in beautiful, rare woods from all corners of the country, depicting landscapes and vistas of Hyrkania, and in every facet, the horse was celebrated.

It had an effect no one had expected: It was beloved by every true Hyrkanian soul who saw it. *This is who we are,* it said. *We are of the earth. It cannot be changed; it cannot be stolen.* Even the worth of the king went up considerably. They saw themselves in its lacquered surface.

It meant nothing to an outsider, and everything to those who had survived the sieges, the purges, and the sackings.

And the man currently sitting on it, King Gahresh, seemed meant for it, for he, too, was polished and smooth seamed. But underneath, he was intractable.

The throne sat on a dais, a humble platform not meant to impress. Nothing in the king's courtroom would ever be allowed to outshine the Wooden Throne. He drank ale, perhaps too much ale, while sitting in judgment, but these were troubled times.

His son, Arahka, stood beside him. No prince was more loyal to his king and father, but as is the way of princes, he could not help but imagine a time when he himself would sit on the throne and, after a suitable period of grief, offer his own philosophy and judgment upon the land. He'd proven himself a brave man in battle many times and had prevailed on each occasion. His father felt that the proud young peacock could use a good dose of the humility that comes with failure but had never spoken this thought aloud.

On the other side of the throne was the king's lord high general, Dahmarhk, growing old in the way of soldiers who have been without war for too long. He had made a habit of never telling his opinion fully, in a manner so artful that everyone he spoke with came away feeling a great soldier agreed with them fully, even if he agreed not at all. It had been a decade since he put a blade into anyone, but he still wore the dueling totem of his youth, the crimson scarf of a forgotten fine lady, every day to court. Perhaps it was a reminder that even old stallions could kick and bite, as needed.

The three of them waited together, without speaking.

A soldier had been found on the road to the capital, and he claimed to bear witness to information they'd been waiting for. He would speak to no one but the king, it was said.

The truth was crueler still. He would speak to no one, not even the king. Ever again.

A sentry—Gahresh could not recall his name—entered and bowed before the Wooden Throne. He appeared shaken, despite his attempt at protocol. "My lord, we have the soldier of the road. He… I don't know how he's alive. Tyrus of the King's Eye, my lord."

They had offered to aid the soldier, to carry him in, to provide him with a seat, or a guard on each side to prop him up at least. But Tyrus refused to meet his king for the first time on any but his own two feet. And so the shambling, half-dead creature who walked into the king's court did stand on his own. After a fashion.

The blood from his mouth, where his tongue had been ripped out, had long been covered in dust and dirt. His clothes were torn, his breeches wide open at the knee, bloody underneath. His face was bruised from having fallen forward many times, too fatigued or too injured to prevent the collision of skull and road. His hair was filthy and wild; his eyes were dim and full of memory. All three of the men on the dais had seen death and near death many times, but this man seemed in both states at once.

The king paid him the respect of showing no pity. That dim flame of pride might be the only thing keeping the soldier from giving in to death's cold caress. "King's Eye Tyrus. Welcome. I am told you have news."

Tyrus looked up at his king's voice. He had only a vague awareness of his appearance. But something in his Hyrkanian heart swelled and pumped enough blood to do his duty, even if for the final time. He tried to speak, having forgotten. He'd done it often the last few leagues, even tried to sing a soldier's song once or twice. He was past shame for the inarticulate grunts that came out, and soon, he would be past any emotion at all.

He scribbled in the air with his right hand, and papyrus was brought to him, and a wooden brush with dark green ink made from sap and juice. He found the strength to write, somehow. He'd always been proud of his letters; they provided the grace his voice never would again. THEY COME.

The general squinted. He always assumed the worst, but in this case, that might be underestimating the coming calamity. Dahmarhk leaned forward, taking the natural command of the superior officer. "*Who* comes, soldier? Do you have no more for us than that, after all your trials?"

Tyrus scribbled again, and another papyrus tablet was brought. The letters were large and certain, despite the pain it took to create them. FROM UNDER. FROM THE DIRT. THEY CRAWL IN THE DARK.

Dahmarhk and King Gahresh did not look to each other for acknowledgment. They had been at each other's side in peace and war for too long to need such trivial communication. But the prince noticed that they were silent just a moment too long.

Whatever strength had brought Tyrus here over leagues of dirt road was nearing its end. He began to write again. THEY CRAWL IN THE DARK. THEY CRAWL IN THE DARK. THEY CRAWL IN THE DARK.

The prince raised his hand to the sentry. "Get this man out of here—get him to the healers at once. Go."

But it was too late for such efforts, and Tyrus fell forward and did not rise.

Later, it was decided. The prince had been adamant. He would lead the hunting party, the last great run of Hyrkanian soldiery. They would do what they did best—track and hunt—and preferably trap the enemy, whether they walked by land or crawled like worms.

Gahresh had tried to talk him out of it. It was purely a shame that his son had chosen this moment to become a man and not a subject of the king. But if this didn't work, the kingdom was doomed anyway, and his son would not be spared in the massacres to come.

In his chambers, Gahresh had Dahmarhk sent for, and they spoke in secret, without even the king's most trusted guards or servants. The old general had arrived looking tired, certainly, but also with a glow in his eyes that had not been seen by the king in many years.

Gahresh himself poured wine for both of them. Something he'd never done for his friend and most loyal protector. Dahmarhk took the goblet reluctantly at first, then simply nodded before drinking deeply.

"Are we in agreement, General?" asked the king.

"We are, my king," said Dahmarhk.

"How do you find our prospects, then, I wonder?"

The general drank deeply again. He lowered his gaze. "Bleak. Will you let me escort you to the mountains? Will you allow me that honor?"

"Hide me, Lord High General? That is your military advice?" A bit of steel came to the king's voice, and his military counselor realized there would be no saving his king, no preserving him from torture and death and worse.

"What would you have me do?" Dahmarhk asked.

"Dust off your armor, my friend. At dawn, you leave with my son. Protect him. Keep him from death. He knows not what horrors he faces," the king said, his face betraying the bitter grin of the convicted man, doomed to die and fully aware.

"I so swear, my lord." Dahmarhk knew his king; his time of counsel was over. He left the goblet on the king's desk and turned to leave.

"How do we fight them, Dahmarhk? Is there a way?" the king asked.

There was a long pause as the general considered his answer. There was false hope, illegitimate bravado, and the saddening truth. In the end, he chose the last.

"I don't know, my king. I am sorry. I have failed you."

The king turned to the window, as if to check for an army just over the horizon. "We won't even see them coming—that's what is so maddening."

Dahmarhk nodded sadly. "They crawl in the dark, sire. And we'll be in the ground with them soon enough, cold and blind, alone until the end of days."

The king did not turn around. "As we deserve."

The general opened the door to leave. "Aye. As we deserve."

14

THE CHOICE OF BLOOD AND BONE

Despite the borders and cultural differences that manifested later, few countries in her age were as closely bonded by history as Turan and Hyrkania. Indeed, many scholars have claimed that Sonja the Red was in fact from Turan by birth and became known as Hyrkanian only after her clan's migration, which may have occurred when she was a mere babe or toddler.

While in all available records, Sonja made it very clear she considered herself a Hyrkanian, born and bred, many villages in neighboring Turan acquired a small amount of notoriety by claiming that she'd actually been born in proximity. The most common story was that jealous travelers stole the child to raise as their own, perhaps sensing some nascent greatness within her.

While it is impossible to confirm or discredit such talk, neither is it outside of her possible origins. Records for the birth and death of peasant stock were virtually unheard of throughout the region, and Sonja herself may not have known the full truth.

However, if true, it makes certain events that would occur in her adult life all the more heartbreaking.

Sir Fenir Al Sabanot, *The Melancholy Queen of Turan*

Ysidra found herself wondering if she'd heard the man correctly. She hadn't intended to kill him, but merely to frighten him away, perhaps with a dueling scar for his trouble.

But his voice.

It wasn't fear she detected, not even a drop of it. Nor was it mirth or whimsy. It took a moment, but she placed it.

It was eagerness. She saw his fingers twitch.

"Say that again, sneak," the queen said quietly.

"It's very simple," Sylus said. "These are your guardsmen, yes? And I have my bowstring already taut. One will die tonight; it is as certain as the moon."

"Then you'll die, just as certainly."

"That is not in question, Your Highness," he said. "But one of your guards will be dead, and I do not see how you can avoid responsibility. It will have been your choice, and when you think of his lifeless skull with an arrow through his eye socket, will you feel no remorse?"

She was silent in response. The firelight reflected off the ribbons in her long, dark braid.

"I would," Sylus said. "A loyal soldier, doubtless stout in heart and willing to place his head on the block for you without question. Killed from ambush, in such inglorious fashion? I would be overfull of regret."

She spoke carefully after a moment's pause. "If I but move my wrist, assassin—"

"You'd slit me open. Yes. But I swear to you, it won't be before I loose my arrow."

Ysidra stood a little taller. "I'm a queen. Do you think I've never had a soldier die under my gaze?"

"Doubtless you have—it is the way of monarchs. But you rather gave the game away, my lady, by pausing when I placed my bet on the table."

Sylus's body hadn't moved, not a hair's worth. "No, I'm afraid this is the poor bargain we must make. You kill me, but one of your loyalists never sees his home again. To me, it is merely scratching with the claw I have remaining."

Ysidra considered. If these men had died during battle, she'd have mourned them, missed them, and felt pangs of guilt, certainly. But to die this ignobly, for nothing—it caused her steel to soften, somehow.

"As I say, I'm a good sport, lady. Do I shoot the heavier one, the life-long soldier, whose life is centered around keeping you from harm?"

He let a small bit of malice creep into his voice for the first time.

"Or do I puncture the dreamer foolish enough to believe you will love him in return, some faraway day? I leave the choice to you."

"I'll scream. Sound the alarm."

"Yes, very good. Do that. Or...shall I? Here, give me leave. I'll yell at them myself, see if they can outrun an arrow I fletched by hand."

"I should have killed you the moment I saw you draw your bow," she hissed, all the rage and frustration of having been made a fool, and worse, simmering out of her for the first time since leaving camp.

"Oh, on that we concur. That would have been the prudent thing—more's the pity," Sylus said agreeably.

Every instinct told her to kill him, there, from behind, in the dark. Instead, for one of the few crucial times in her life...she wavered.

"Think, sneak. Is it truly worth your life, simply to kill a guardsman I can replace with the raising of my hand?"

"It is a fair point, lady. It is a life without a moment of consequence, but I've grown dearly fond of it over the years," Sylus said. "Would you suggest an alternative path?"

"I step back five steps. I will count them. You may take your leave. We will not follow you. It is the best offer you will receive in this lifetime."

"And what of our weapons, lady?"

"We keep them. If you break our treaty, it will cost you."

Sylus's gift was pretending to be what he was not, and right now, he knew that the calm facade he presented baffled and confused the queen. In truth, he was seething, furious at himself for having been so careless. To be caught with his dick out like this—it was disgraceful. Worse, it was sloppy.

She would be counting on him keeping his word, or she would be counting on the limited use of a bow in close combat.

He cursed his selfishness. He should have killed both guards, but he'd been too cocksure, and now his life, *his* life, was in mortal peril, from this dirt-covered, self-appointed "Queen of Nomads."

It was more than he could bear. He knew his tendency for self-recrimination; his true self would punish his foolishness, possibly until the day he died. But the alternative was simpering for mercy. To this runted whore, thinking herself a *queen*.

And he was not capable of that.

But *she* didn't know that.

"But then, I'll have a bow . . . Could I not simply kill you from the forest's edge?"

"Keep your bow. By the time you turn to run, we'll have ours. And that puts us both in the same bear pit. I give my vow. You keep your word, you keep your skin."

For a moment, he was the silent one.

"It's done, then. You take your count of five. I'll keep my bow trained on your good men, there. And then—"

"And then you leave, and we never see you again, night thief," she said, straining to keep the ice from her voice.

She thinks me a thief, Sylus thought to himself. To have a specimen like himself right in front of her, so close he could feel her breath on the back of his neck... and she thought him a thief.

"It is agreed," he said. Sylus lacked many of the normal emotions others, from commoner to king, told of. It had been his life's work to mimic and present a convincing imitation of such. But for a moment, he felt time crawl, and without moving his eyes, he had a strange feeling of being present in the moment, in a way he'd never felt without someone near him dying. He smelled the smoke of the fire; he noticed the shifting colors in the flames. He even had a moment of reminiscence triggered by the trees all around him, that of chopping wood with his father, one of the last memories he maintained before his revelation at the puppet theater.

He felt his true self rise. He'd been suppressing it, he realized.

It wasn't fair. Not to him, not to the woman.

And not to the guardsmen. He owed them this.

Carefully, quietly, Ysidra took her first step back. "One," she said.

He didn't move. She'd been prepared if he had. But he kept his word.

"Two," she said. She was far enough back now that it would not be impossible for him to turn, perhaps drop his bow and make a play for her knife. It was only going to get more dangerous with the coming steps.

He stood like a statue... the only movement a fatigue twitch in his forearms.

"Three." She stepped back again, confident that at this distance, she could throw the blade before he could spin, aim, *and* fire. But this was the last step she could take where that would be so.

"Four." Now was the risk. And she knew, if he even began to turn toward her, she'd have to throw her knife, her only weapon at hand.

"I'm sorry, lady," said Sylus. And he loosed the arrow toward the campfire.

She heard the thud of the arrow into flesh, followed by a wet gurgling cry, and her eyes widened. She moved toward him, unthinkingly shifting the grip on her blade to overhand so she could plunge it into him. She had the advantage; she was too close, too nimble, for him to nock another arrow and kill her. She was sure of it.

But he didn't reach for a second arrow. He dropped his bow entirely, making a quick, odd gesture of one hand to the sleeve on his opposite side. She heard a savage scream of shock and grief from the campfire beyond the bushes but couldn't yet see who it was who was spared. Then she saw it, in the firelight's flicker...a silver-handled knife. They were evenly armed, and he was twice her size.

Sylus couldn't help but smile. This was going to be a high moment of his time traipsing the skin of this world. An epiphany, he was sure of it. He'd killed many a nobleman and more than a few fine ladies...but even a degraded queen who slept in the dirt was still a queen, after a fashion. And he'd see her last moments and know what she kept Hidden.

The technique he'd perfected, and last used on the simpleton stall boy, five quick stabs, deep and fast as a witch's curse. He'd trained on it, meditated on it, thousands of times. She would never see it coming; no one ever did.

But curse his greed.

He'd forgotten the other guardsman.

The stout, muscular form of Raganus tore through the bushes behind Sylus, screaming in a foaming rage, like the crash of a broken ship on the rocks. He rushed at the Blood Man with a speed quite belying his frame. He came at Sylus, fists raised, either too rageful to have drawn a proper weapon or too vengeful to miss the opportunity to pummel the assassin to death.

Once again, Sylus was furious at himself. And he knew he was going to pay for his carelessness once again. He'd misjudged the guard, thinking him stupidly loyal to his queen.

But he apparently was equally loyal to the man with the arrow in his brain. The first fist hit Sylus across the face with enough force to dislodge two teeth. The second cracked a bone in his cheek.

Raganus raged, fully prepared to tear the man to pieces. "You killed my friend, offal. My friend!"

Sylus steeled himself against the pain and focused on keeping his grip on the blade. He had no other chance of survival.

But in concentrating, he received a third blow from the guardsman. And this time, Raganus put some muscle into it.

The fist was enough to briefly lift the Falcon's Blood Man entirely off the sod under his boots. And when he went down, he did not immediately get back up. He'd never experienced pain like this before. His true self screamed at him to get up, to fight back, to run. Anything but face those fists again.

Ysidra, recovering her wits, placed a hand on her guardsman's shoulder. "Raganus," she said, "don't kill him. We need to know why he came for us."

The guardsman turned his face toward her over his shoulder. His scowl so dark, so bleak, she stepped back involuntarily and grasped her knife even more firmly than when she'd planned to attack the intruder.

Raganus, without words, without slowing, reached down with both hands to lift the assassin fully off the ground with a grunt. He'd been a quiet man, really, for most of his life. He'd happily taken the position of man of the queen's Wolf Pack. He never made any attempt at promotion. He was happiest when left alone. No one ever called him ill tempered. But grief had stripped him of his kindness.

"I'm going to bite his eyes out," said the guardsman.

There was a flash in the moonlight.

Sylus had kept his blade in hand.

Bloody in multiple locations, vision blurred, and two teeth missing, he slashed out. He couldn't quite manage his signature death move, but nonetheless, he hit flesh and was rewarded with a splash of blood on his hands and face.

Not his blood. Not this time.

Then the guardsman dropped the Blood Man, who somehow maintained his feet, if a bit unsteadily. He looked at the butcher's bill of the encounter so far: one dead, one injured, one staring at him with frightening eyes, whore or queen.

He turned and ran. A knife stuck in his shoulder with a solid sound and did not fall out as he continued toward the forest's edge. Not a good sign.

He called to his Hidden, his true self, to ask for counsel.

But there was no answer as he stumbled in the darkness.

He ran until fatigue and blood loss took him.

If he'd had the makeup of a normal man, he might have realized he didn't need to run so far. No one was following him.

Ysidra was checking the wound across her stout guardsman's chest. He looked down, the fury subsiding into grief. His breath was labored, and she worried about the depth of the ugly slash through his shirt and flesh.

"Leave it, Queen. See to Festrel," he said.

"We have to make sure that—"

"Leave it."

She sighed. In the part of her that remained queen, she knew every dark thing, every torment her people had faced since she had fallen in love with an outsider, a devil, was her fault entirely.

"Come to the fire, at least, Raganus of the Wolf Pack, bravest of all."

"All respect, Queen. Save it. By your leave, I'd rather not hear such sodding rubbish at this moment."

She nodded. She parted the large bushes where Raganus had come through, seeing the only thing she could imagine worse than seeing poor, kind, lovestruck Festrel lying dead.

Which was Festrel lying there still alive.

The assassin had been true to his word, and he'd placed an arrow right through Festrel's left eye and into his brain. But curse every goat-humping god and goddess, it hadn't killed him.

He lay on his back, the fire throwing his agony into sharp relief, arrow pointed toward the heavens. His elbows were bent, hands spasming into claws helplessly in the air. Blood gurgled as he breathed.

She felt it was the worst sound she'd ever witnessed, helpless and agonized.

She sat beside where he lay. She placed a hand on his chest, and for a moment, his arms stopped their chaotic jousting with nothing. And he calmed his breathing.

"Qua—qua . . . ," he managed.

"It is your qu—it is Ysidra, Festrel. I'm here."

"D-d-dark."

She wiped away a tear with the back of her sleeve. No Wolf Pack soldier had ever seen her cry.

She suppressed a sob as his good eye moved painfully to gaze at her, but he was already beginning to see another world in the mist. His face succumbed to a misery beyond the pain.

"F . . . f . . . failed. Failed you."

She took his hands, clasping them to her breast.

"Never. Never."

She sat up for a moment so her tears would not fall into his face, and she said to him the thing everyone in her tribe most desired, perhaps now true for one poor guardsman.

"May you find home again, Festrel the Fearless."

She reached her face over his, kissing his lips, lingering. Waiting.

He breathed his last breath into her mouth.

15

A CIRCULAR MOTION

It is not wise, nor indeed entirely possible, to attempt to compare what the so-called "rights" of women were in the long-ago age to the freedoms (and responsibilities) enjoyed by the modern woman of today.

While today's woman is best satisfied with a life of service to church and family, she is also allowed (within reason) to pursue an education, even a vocation entirely separated from her parents, husband, or other responsible party. It might be said by reasonable observers that she is granted access to the fruits of civilization in a fashion unequaled in human history, for good or ill.

These same observers might be aghast at the tales told in scrolls of flimsy parchment, and the cuneiforms on stronghold walls.

Certainly, a female's "rights" varied from country to country, even from village to village. It is perhaps not surprising that those lands ruled with an eye toward religion were more moderate in the allowance of such "freedom," but even in such cases, some factions allowed women workers, craftspeople, and even clerics, though time has seen much of this now regarded as the well-meaning folly of a softhearted paternal presence.

It is of particular note that many countries allowed, even fostered, a sort of independent, "emancipated" warrior class of female fighter. There were even some armies that relied on these women, mostly unschooled tribal wives, to attend the soldiery in all manner of need and comfort.

Fewer, though, were the women who were truly independent and yet lived by sword and bow. They were tolerated and even, in precious few cases, respected.

An even smaller number yet were feared.

Professor Archibald Mecurtin, *A Brief Treatise on Sex*

Sonja was still in a foul mood, brooding on the bones of the family that had been burned and displayed like the prize hog at a town fair.

Her anger was interrupted by the five men on horseback bearing down on her on the final stretch of the Bleak Road. She weighed her options and considered them all unfavorable.

She cursed her choice to walk beside Sunder, rather than ride. The Zamoran outreach patrol would have bows, but had she been riding, her Hyrkanian blood would have given her a chance at escape.

On foot, it was hopeless.

She could fight. The guards wore only the traditional spiked helmets and leather, and bore swords on their belts, but in typical Zamoran fashion, each held a short spear as a combination weapon / walking stick / adornment, each painted with a web pattern and a single red-eyed white spider. She was certain she could take two. Possibly three. She had been focusing on the road behind and not the road ahead, in open terrain, visible at a great distance in every direction. That was her error, and she already regretted it.

She could bluff them. In this part of the world, the name Red Sonja carried a ledger of some note. But five men, five proudly uniformed men in light armor, would have a difficult time backing down from a single unarmored woman, even if they wanted to.

Or she could simply be surly and unhelpful, a Sonja staple. Often, she found, they simply decided she was mad or too much trouble to bother.

She walked not around them, but directly toward them. She saw five sets of eyes under deeply tanned brows look at her body. One gave a lecherous sneer, and she realized . . . she'd miscalculated again. And it was quite likely to cost her.

They had the look of soldiers who had been told the enemy was fair game.

She raised one hand higher on her horse, closer to the hasp holding her sword. But not so close as to raise alarm. And though it pained her, she lowered her eyes and moved slightly to the side.

She was almost past the front line when the patrol's captain shouted, "*Hold.*"

She wasn't afraid of death. She wasn't afraid to fight. But she had no stomach for it this day and couldn't shake the feeling she'd lose.

A chill ran down her spine.

She stopped but said nothing. The captain turned to face her.

"Where do you hail from, woman?" he asked, and she couldn't help but feel relieved, reassured, somehow, by his dull tone. To this one, the captain, she was merely a task to perform. He was profoundly disinterested in some waif with a potentially unrideable horse. Or perhaps he had orders elsewhere. And blessedly, he was the man in charge.

She did not look up but kept her eyes fixed on the graveled path. "Turan, sir."

The captain, white bearded and face lined with age, walked toward her but instead looked at her horse, examining the few slight possessions she carried. The men all wore the stylized badge of Zamora, the white spider.

"And where is your destination?"

Anywhere but Hyrkania, oaf, she felt like saying, but wisely told a partial truth instead. It was well she had the gift of many tongues.

"My father sells Zamoran mead to the western realms. He's ill. I go to bargain in the market for stock for the season."

Without warning, the soldier who had leered at her slapped her across the face, rocking her head to one side painfully. Her head was forced down; she could taste a trickle of blood from her now-split lip. But when she raised her head back, she looked him in the eye. She had narrowed her options down to one, in a matter of moments. And this pig was going to fall first.

"Liar. I hear the Hyrkanian swine in your lineage when you speak, harlot."

She squinted but said nothing.

"Like all the slatterns of your land, you reek. But this time, you smell worse than the sty, somehow," he said.

She knew what these insults meant. She was not to be a bit of sport to torment and then forget. She was to be punished, humiliated, for reasons known only to the guard, if a reason was indeed needed at all.

Sonja said nothing. Words were no longer useful.

A second guard's gaze hardened as he dismounted his horse. "Your possessions are forfeit. You'll accompany us to the garrison. Where if Mitra is just, they'll quarter you and burn the pieces. And may every one of your pox-laden mud people follow, man, woman, and child," he said. "Resist, and I'll cut your feet to the bone and drag you."

Again, she'd misjudged. These men were not fully under the

captain's sway. They would do as they wished, with the captain's disapproval or not.

She inhaled. She could plead; she could beg. She could act when called upon.

One look in his eyes said it would mean nothing to these men.

Instead, she spoke two words. "Sunder. *Hadash.*"

The horse immediately spun to cave in the guard's head with his back hooves, right through the guard's iron helm. The denting made a single loud clanging noise, then blood flowed down his face, and the light from his eyes dimmed.

Sonja grabbed the dead man's spear as his body realized it was no longer viable and fell to the ground. The four remaining guards rushed toward her, and she swung the spear's bladed end in a high arc, positioning the other end against her body for leverage. The guard who'd sneered had a new mouth to match the previous, only this new one went right through his windpipe in an altogether expected yet formidable spray of blood.

She could win this; two were down already. But Sunder was in the way and too close around the length of the guards' spears. With her free hand, she slapped her mount's haunch, hard. "Sunder. *Sarat,*" she shouted, turning to regain her balance once the horse bolted from her.

The third guard approached head-on, no subtlety at all, and she plunged the spear tip toward his throat and let his momentum tell his story to the gods.

It was then that the fourth guard, the farthest back moments ago, slammed the carved wooden butt of his spear across the side of her head with a force she had not prepared for. Her ears ringing, she took a stumbling step back, only to be hit again even harder.

Cheeky little bastard, she thought.

And then all thought left her mind entirely. She fell to the ground, the spear rolling sadly from her open hand.

*   *   *

The two guards, captain and private, stood over the woman, looking down. The lower-ranked man—Tias was his name—who'd only just missed being gored by his comrade's own weapon, kicked her in the stomach in spite. And then again, for even less reason. He thought he felt a rib go under his boot.

His captain forgotten, he reached down to touch her hair and to make sure she was still breathing. "She's pretty, in a peasant way." He touched her skin roughly. He dismissed the Asp as trash finery, the pretend airs of a scullery widow. It would never have occurred to him that a woman walking alone and covered in road dust would be carrying something worth the value of an entire village.

Removing his helmet, he reached a gloved hand to pull her hair roughly away from her face. He bent to kiss her lips. It was his right, wasn't it? He'd taken the witch down, hadn't he?

He was solidly slapped on the side of his head by the hand of his superior, Captain Grapas, who was always a joyless, bossy sort, the younger man felt, too old to serve over men like himself. He reached for his sword instinctively.

"The *plague*, you fool," said Grapas. "Did you forget the *plague*? You want the pox, that's your concern—find a tavern and have at it. You want your tackle to rot, keep wagering on her flesh, boy."

The guard stood, removing his hand from the hilt of his blade. "I suppose you're right. Still. Almost worth it, eh?"

"You were always a dim lad, and now you're a dimmer young man, Tias. Might as well take your own knife to it as get stuck in *that* bit of rump."

"Well, then," Tias said, smiling a smile he didn't feel at all. "What do we do with her?"

The older man stroked his full beard thoughtfully. "The garrison will be wanting answers, lad. We have three dead and nothing to show for it, not even horseflesh. And yet—"

Tias's face lit up a bit. "She'd be good sport, wouldn't she? A Hyrkanian savage, as she is?"

"Yes. We carry her to the outpost—it's not far—and take her by horse from there. Gods, what a mess she's made."

"And you'll tell them that I took her down? You'll tell them, won't you, Grapas?"

The older man grinned generously and slapped the young guardsman on the back. It was the captain's turn to show false camaraderie.

"Of course, son. Of course. And then, tomorrow or the day next…"

Tias brightened again, certain that this would be the making of his career. "She dies in the arena."

"Yes, lad. She dies in the arena."

Sylus awoke no calmer. Despite the depth of the wound caused by the knife still stuck in his shoulder, his actual scream came first due to the pain of his bruised and damaged face. He had a moment of confusion while his fingers on his left hand twitched and trembled.

Then he remembered how he acquired those wounds. And he received, for the second time in his life, a revelation from the gods themselves. He should have known; he should have put it together long before it cost him so utterly. But he hadn't.

Two people had come out ahead of him, the redhead and the pretend queen.

How had he not realized?

Women, both of them. They were women. And he'd treated them as men, creatures of purpose and lacking in guile. He'd been a fool for that, certainly. But all the rest? He saw, with the clarity of the dawn horizon, none of that was his fault.

It was the women.

They couldn't beguile him, couldn't appeal to his groin, and both had somehow seen that, seen that much of his true self. So they had both resorted to the natural armament that every woman possesses in surplus: wicked, hateful deception. He saw it all.

No woman cared about the stain on their soul from betraying a man; no woman had a depth to which they wouldn't stoop to achieve whatever selfish goal their capricious and endless wants envisioned. Even his mother, even his *mother*. All the harlots and virgins he'd met, he could see it now—they saw him in his perfection, his purity, and it savaged their hearts. They couldn't allow him to exist unmuddied.

He'd been blind, and worse. He'd thought himself free of the madness of the flesh. But perhaps even *his* great intuition had been sorely tricked. He still raged at himself. But perhaps this pain, this ignominy, was worth it to understand the evil, the true soul, of the entire world.

He screamed. But he was not aware that he had.

He heard a trickle of water…a creek. He stood up, forcing his remaining blood to his legs and heart, and walked drunkenly toward it. He sat in the soft-flowing creek, warm to his flesh through his bloodied clothes, no more than a few inches at its greatest depth.

He took a deep, ragged breath and saw his purpose. He'd had the targets right; he just hadn't understood the *urgency*.

He reached back and pulled the blade from his shoulder in one motion, biting hard on the teeth whose number and formation had recently been rearranged. This scream, he did hear entirely well.

Like a child in a puddle, he slapped his hands onto the surface of the creek's water, over and over again, loudly and without thought. When his tantrum ceased, he saw the blade of the queen's knife sparkling in the water.

It was decided.

This was the weapon he'd use to kill them both.

16

ALL THE SOLDIERS MEET THEIR END

Of course, regardless of position or piety, all in that age had a vice, or more likely, a full deck of such. A healer might partake of his own potions; a brewer might drink his profit; a gambler might find himself having spent all on events of no import at all. In the matters of the flesh, a king might, indeed likely did, establish and maintain a harem of elite courtesans, while the peasants and merchants living under him might trade what little they had to local women and men to drop whatever shabby garments collected their modesty.

Some countries would maintain a fitful and uncomforting mix of abstinence and tolerance, under the somewhat vague threat that one god or another was looking down on them and could see the full depth of their depravity. Laws and punishments were indeed enacted wrathfully upon those hapless practitioners who met in secret to lie with or drink the forbidden fruit. Many a man had his balls clipped; many a lady adulterer would be given tonsure, scourged, and banished to a nunnery, and often those were the lighter of punishments.

But there was a truth in even the most pious land, and though it was unspoken, it was also ubiquitous: People are mortal and well prone to show their finger to their gods.

Pilatius III, *The Song of Sonja, the She-Devil*

In her dreams, she saw the windmills.

And for a moment, despite the frost she felt, she was happy, remembering a time when she felt she was seeing something...worthy in the workings of man. Something that had no blood attached, that required no slave to fashion. Something that awoke a spirit in her heart.

A possibility.

But then in her dream, she saw the small curved door of the mill's turret open in the mist, and the colors of the fan's sails seemed to drain to gray, and the surrounding forest to darken as if abandoned by the sun.

Two gray men came through the doorway from inside, and she heard their mournful drone. One stood on each side of the door. She could not see their faces, but she knew who they were...and her vision began to fill with a red that came from no other source but blood, until the entire landscape was that color, making detail difficult to see, particularly of the two figures in front of that now-crimson curved doorway, staring back at her, making a sound like a wolf with its leg caught in a trap, waiting to die.

She couldn't see them, but she knew who they were.

By the spikes on their iron helmets.

She awoke to the miserable stench of breakfast, a swill that, rather than served in a fine bowl with a proper spoon, was instead thrown upon her through the bars of her tiny cell. At first thought, she felt the liquid and mean small bits of meat were boiling hot, and flinched in her awakening. But she realized quickly that it was nearly ice cold, and her body had lied to her in shock.

She was not manacled and had the freedom, as it were, to move about the straw-strewn, rough stone blocks of her cell's floor. Her head was still leaden, but she'd had things thrown at her for her entire life and had grown a sizable dislike for it.

"Breakfast time, harlot." And as her eyes adjusted, she recognized the smug face of the young patrolman who'd nearly caved her head in.

From her position on the floor, she smirked. "Hello, jailer. How's your garrison?"

The young soldier's face soured. "As you like, miss, as you like. You killed three good men, and there's some lovely justice coming for you, in that."

She wiped some of the gruel off her skin. Hungry she was, but she'd not give this dog the satisfaction of seeing her eat his scraps.

Well, maybe later.

"And how's that, love?" she said.

He leaned in closer to the bars. "It is simply this, dead girl. When you walk into the arena this afternoon, you will face two men, both unbeaten in this venue. One bites, I'm told. The other...Mitra only knows what goes on in his mind. He claws, you see. After the dispatch, he claws out bits...organs and such. Bone, sometimes. It's not to my taste, I'll grant it. But in this case..." He shrugged.

"I'm honored, brave one. And am I to fight these two empty handed? I'm not sure I can guarantee proper sport, if this is so," Sonja said, with perhaps a bit too much sincerity.

Tias of the Zamoran outreach patrol paused, as if the thought had just struck him. "My, yes, they'll both be armed, but you—oh no, how tragic! You set your horse to run with your sword still attached! Well, that *was* poor planning!"

Sonja raised an eyebrow. Even while he mocked her upcoming death and dismemberment, she found the man tedious company.

"But wait! Brave Tias again comes to your rescue, dead girl! It seems I foresaw this predicament and brought something to even the odds—made it myself, I did! I know you'll love it."

From his belt, he unhooked it. A dingy mess of a sword, so covered in rust that it looked like the side of a Khitan cliffside exposed endlessly to the sun. It was the size of a small cutlass and perhaps had been useful for its intended purpose. But that was long ago, and now the "blade" was a featureless thing, the point deliberately dulled into flat, thick impotence. It was useless and would likely break the moment it struck a harder surface. The hilt had rusted to the point where holes ran through in spots... Even holding it might wound the wielder, not the target.

Sonja, mistress of the sword, was going to die holding a cracked relic that could no longer even in jest be called a blade.

He tossed it to the far side of her cell, where it clattered noisily. She did not reach for it.

"What, no gratitude? I may have saved your life, saddle whore. Alas, I have to leave. I have to get good seats, you understand."

Sonja was no longer amused. "And what happens if I choose not to fight at all, guardsman?"

He smiled. "Oh, that's the best part. Do you know what Zamorans do to gladiators who choose not to participate? We have an old lady, a basket weaver in town—quite cunning she is yet, and she sews the fighter's mouth shut. Do you see? Even if they change their mind and fight, even if they *win*, they either starve to death or go mad trying to pull the stitches out. It's quite comical. Do you have any further questions, Hyrkanian trash?"

"I do, brave one. I wonder if I might ask a favor...Regarding the crier, would you convey a message for me? As a last request?"

He grinned; he clearly enjoyed her having to beg favors on the last day of her life. "Of course. What shall I tell them, dead girl?"

It was rash, she knew it. If she missed by an inch, she'd crack her hand open or, worse, rip her fingers loose. But such was life, she decided, as she threw her fist directly through the bars of the cell and into the man's crotch.

The man crumpled and fell backward in an instant, eyes wide and throat gurgling inarticulately. He grabbed at his own midsection and howled like a toddler deprived of teat.

She gritted her teeth. She reached to see if she could damage him further or take anything he had of use, but she perhaps had put a bit too much enthusiasm into the blow for that. He gasped, incapable of finding air.

"Tell them this, soldier. Tell them *Red Sonja* graces their stinking city—do you think you can remember that?"

He did not respond, his face now several vivid colors not in his original configuration.

"And one more thing, brave one. A special message, just for you." She put her face against the bars.

"You are very fortunate that you are not more generously endowed."

She opened her mouth and snapped her teeth down twice, lips pulled back, sharp white incisors flashing, *clack, clack.*

And then, as the soldier loudly vomited, she did it again.

Clack.

It was Captain Grapas who came to take her to the arena, the pride of the city of Shadizar. Sonja noted that there were eight soldiers total as her escort. Whether this was merely showmanship or genuine concern for what the Devil was capable of, she didn't know.

"You've quite unmanned my patrolman, lady," Grapas said as he unlocked the cell doors.

"Not a great loss, I assure you, Captain."

She stood up, dusted herself off, and walked forward pridefully, without looking at the cautious guards around her. They'd all heard of what she'd done while likely concussed, and of the shape of poor Tias's manhood. It was said he would fully recover, but there were doubters, and no one wanted to share his fate.

Grapas pointed for a soldier to grab Sonja's "sword." He disliked this; it felt ignoble to humiliate a brave woman. The game was already fixed—everyone knew it. But the sight and scent of blood were a powerful attraction to a crowd that had few real pleasures of note.

They walked uphill on the red stone road, the dyed path to the arena. There were hawkers and bettors, brewers and prostitutes. Death had a whimsical cast on a day like this, and Sonja found herself hating the lot of them.

She was manacled to a post in the gladiatorial pits, a bunker on one side of the round theater, the farthest side from the pavilion reserved for nobility. She again felt a curious frost inside her.

She waited. She was to be the main attraction, it appeared. Near her, a thin, terrified young man with calloused hands, clearly not a warrior, shivered, eyes wide, in utter terror. He was dark skinned with beautiful eyes, the corneas seeming shrunken in the pools of white displayed around them, as if, unable to make his situation disappear, he was forced to witness all, everything, in what were likely his last moments. He looked a farmer to her, and she wondered how this terrified man had ended up as blood sport for an audience of ghouls.

A pattern emerged. Two seemingly random prisoners would be uncuffed and led at spearpoint to the arena. A short time later, only one would come back. On two occasions, no one came back at all.

Her companion sighed in despair. She had little energy for empathy now; she needed what strength she had, but finally spoke to him softly.

"Hey. Keep moving. Let them tire of chasing you. Act fully the coward—do you hear me?"

The young man looked up at her, as if in a reverie so deep, he had to be pulled back to reality.

She continued, "Then, this will take some steel. Find your strength, do you hear? Draw them in. Let them think it's over, you're too frightened to go on. They'll raise their blade; they'll make a show of it."

He squinted, as if trying to understand.

"Then gut them. Swordpoint, not blade, right in their stomach, and twist, twist again, pull out, and stab again and repeat, three times total. Say you hear me."

He shook his head.

"Say you *hear* me."

He nodded. "I hear you."

It was his turn next, and a tall, muscular man of golden skin was chosen to go with him, which he did, grinning, as if he'd been impatient for this.

A few minutes later, only the golden man returned.

When all other bouts were done, the sawdust and sand of the arena pit floor smelled of blood and spewed intestine. For the pride of the city, she found the arena a shabby, dirty spectacle, and she allowed disgust to come to her face. She was taken to the arena entrance, and the barn doors were closed behind her by Grapas himself.

"Good fortune, Hyrkanian. I wish you honorable victory," he said.

"Hump off, Zamoran. I wish you to choke on a goat's pizzle," she replied.

Sonja had no heart for slave killing, and they were all slaves here. Slaves to whatever upright sacks of scat paid for this mockery. Win or lose, this was a poor way to spend an otherwise perfectly acceptable day.

The other two fighters today were special, beloved by the locals, and thus entered the arena from a private entrance under their own power. There were no spears pointed at their heads, and they smiled and waved to the crowd.

They loved this.

One, she assumed the biter, had shaved his head and darkened his eyes. He made eye contact with her and bared his sharpened teeth. The other was all muscle, glistening with oil to thrill those in the audience who were hardened or moistened by bloody death. He was their avatar, and they loved him. He'd painted his hands red, as if they were already stained with blood.

Sonja felt ridiculous, with this useless block of dingy iron and its rust-whittled handle. But such was life, and the arena was no place for dignity.

The crier shouted under the black-and-white banner of Zamora, but few turned to look at him in his silken finery; their eyes were fixed on the two local favorites and their preening display.

"*Good people.* For our last blessed contest, we have a woman who *claims* to be the great Red Sonja! I know you scoff, but *twelve soldiers* did she kill just this morning, with only her teeth and pretty fingers! It is said she ate the *heart of a lion* and now his spirit guides her! *See* her ferocity!"

Sonja rolled her eyes. She'd never been in an arena yet where they didn't tend to run on a good deal.

The crier shouted again. "And our two heroes, showing their grace and fealty to grand Zamora, *Sharptooth* and *Filus*! And as added reward for their fine service, our lord mayor has stated that after this combat, the two fighters will be *set free* to live with *honor* in our fair city!"

The crowd, who had apparently been bored during the previous combat, found this almost too rousing and stomped their feet with abandon and approval.

"Last call for *wagers*, good people! Bet well, bet generously…for you'll certainly tell all you were *here* the day *this* honest duel came to be!"

And then it was a hush as Sharptooth pointed at her, grinning his hideous smile. The two opponents took their swords from plush pillows the arena's runners brought out.

Sonja looked at them, cocked her head, and with her good hand, gave them the finger, grinning hugely.

The audience gasped…It was such a tasteless display during such a dignified murder game. This wasn't done; it wasn't done at all.

Enraged, the two ran toward her, swords raised. She calmly watched them run. In truth, this was her element.

The She-Devil was home.

When the two creatures were halfway toward her, both screaming, she calmly walked back toward the barred door she'd entered the arena through. A guard on the other side held his spear up to warn her, assuming she was going to beg to be allowed back inside, to the safety of the pit bench.

Instead, she turned to the stone wall of the arena and, with all her strength, swung her useless "sword" at it. The weapon splintered mightily and loudly, the blade now no more than half its previous length.

But much more interestingly…the remaining section of the blade was now shards of brittle, razor-sharp metal, the interior where the rust had not penetrated. It looked to her like the razored crags of the Zingaran shoreline. She held in her hand now not a toy, not a joke at her expense, but a splintered, multifanged, short-but-lethal weapon of convenience.

The two men coming at her were big. They had thought she'd destroyed her weapon, to surrender. They had no interest in her surrendering. Not when there was sport to be had.

She was to be overwhelmed and torn bloody.

By the time they saw what she held in her hand, they were almost upon her.

Unable to stop in time, Sharptooth swung his sword level to the ground, where her head had been just a split second previous, his own strength twisting his midsection beyond his ability to recover quickly. She stabbed into his side, twisting each time before stabbing again.

Three times total.

Filus was not an intelligent nor educated man, but he quickly realized that he'd made a terrible mistake, and turned to back away. Sonja stabbed him in his lower spine, the backside of his rib cage on his left side, and then deeply and finally between his shoulders. Filus dropped his sword, throwing his hands open in agony, eyes wide.

It turns out they were indeed both set free that day. After a fashion.

The crier, whose job it was to declare a victor at this exact moment, found his throat incapable and simply stood agape.

Sonja picked Filus's lifeless head out of the dirt, raising part of his still body, and she plunged her makeshift blade into his throat. Maybe she did have a bit of showmanship after all.

Crouched over, still, standing between the two bodies, she grabbed the two swords of her fallen opponents, waiting for the guards to come, ready to show what the Devil found entertaining. She breathed deeply, over and over, almost ferally, her face spattered with the blood of the fighters. She might have growled; many swore they'd heard her do so. She waited for her arrest and execution.

Instead, the audience cheered.

It was good sport, indeed.

17

THE MANY REWARDS OF DISHONOR

Astonishingly, there were those who faced the arenas by choice. Some found the applause agreeable, or perhaps they simply were plying the only trade they were good at.

These were often former soldiers, road thieves, or freebooters, who for whatever reason accepted the challenge and risk of the gladiator's life or, more insidiously, were addicted to it.

It was possible for a particular city-state's fighters to gain a pleasant notoriety, even fame. For these gifted few, it was common to be lent out or traded entirely to other arena masters to keep the proceedings fresh.

Unfortunately, records do not exist on how many of these lived long enough to retire, as there were significant hazards to the occupation, fame notwithstanding.

Renee Albergi, *When Life Was Precious*

But of course, they were prepared. If not for Sonja herself, certainly for a fighter who chose to turn their weapons on the arena guards. As she turned to face the door she'd been forced to take to enter the coliseum, the blades of her now-deceased foes in her hands, her reward was not freedom, nor even confrontation.

It was simply archers in the stands. Six in all. Each had an arrow pointed directly at her. Still, she did not drop her weapons. She knew the mathematics of what she'd done today... They wouldn't be so careless next time. She'd heard of disobedient pit fighters given a dozen opponents to face, even exotic and dangerously mistreated animals, often with no weapons at all.

And circling the arena, banners of a red-eyed white spider, an image she was losing all fondness for, if she was being frank.

Sonja was nothing if not practical. It might simply be better to take her chances now, as loaded as the game dice were.

Until she heard the voice of Grapas.

"Red Sonja of Hyrkania, known as the Devil," he stated clearly, but not without some tone of empathy, or perhaps respect, in his voice. "Drop your blades. There is no exit for you save the arrow, otherwise."

There was a long pause. She heard the bowstrings pulled taut.

"Sonja, will you acquiesce?" he asked. "Or will you die and be forgotten?"

Sonja spat, partially for show but also because her split lip had started bleeding again. "I'm *thinking*."

Grapas scratched absently at his beard. There was something sorrowful in the gesture. "They won't wait, girl. Your life is water pouring out of a cup with holes in the bottom. This is your last chance."

Sonja grunted, wiped the arterial spray from her opponent from her eyes with the back of one gloved hand. She dropped the swords into the dirt.

The gate immediately opened, and two guards with spears rushed in, screaming at her as if they had heroically disarmed her, rather than stood cowering behind the barred door. In the days to come, their part in the story would grow considerably under their telling of it.

"On your *knees*, woman!"

Reluctantly, she did as she was told.

But it was worth noting that the guards kept as distant as possible for the task they found themselves doing.

Grapas was respected, considering his position, that of an old workhorse soldier. That is, when he was noticed at all. But there were whispers that he was soft, ill fit for the job. He was even accused of the suspect quality of mercy, seen entirely as weakness by the younger soldiery.

As Sonja was dragged through the holding pit, he did not speak to her. And when she was not as obliging in her pace as the guards required, he did not stop one from backhanding her across the face. If there was an opportunity for kindness to prevail, he did not rise to it.

Sonja harbored contempt for men like him, even more than the openly brutal, common guards. Eyes of sympathy, heart of cowardice.

She was prepared to be returned to her wretched cell. But she made a vow to herself: The old soldier would remember her name for the rest of his days, for good or ill. Preferably the latter.

When they returned to the red road leading downhill toward her cell, she was surprised to find they had taken a sharp turn to the right, to an outer door of the arena. There were two more guards in front of the door. They didn't look at the filthy, blood-spattered woman being escorted inside, but merely held their post as Grapas held the door.

Sonja had been an unlikely guest in many great estates and even a palace or two in her violent life. This wasn't that. But to her tired, sore, deprived body and soul, it was close to paradise.

The room was beautifully appointed; there were two large, soft beds with down pillows and warm blankets. There was a table of food, more than she could eat on her hungriest day, warm venison and hot crusty bread with cold butter and preserves on the side. Sliced cheese, fruit and sausage, and fig tarts as beautiful as any pastry she'd ever seen.

Much more importantly, there was a keg of beer and a small cask of wine.

The room was lit not by crude lanterns but by beautiful scented candles, reminding her of herbs and flowers, some that didn't grow anywhere near Zamora. There were drapes and a great tapestry of a hunter cornering a wolf. She recognized them as the illusions they were; they had the effect of concealing the bars on the windows and the cold stone doorless walls. But their bold colors reminded her briefly of windmills.

And Ysidra.

Grapas spoke after she'd taken it all in. "These are the quarters…" He corrected himself. "The *former* quarters of the men you dispatched today. Understand the following rules: There will be no cutlery, any attempt to exit without leave will get you back in your previous lodgings, and it's expected to rain tonight. Are we understood, lady?"

Her mouth was watering; she couldn't stop herself. She nodded.

"Additionally, there is a bath with attendants provided. A woman, or a man if you prefer. It is your choice."

She thought quickly; she was prepared for more hardship and was momentarily not fully herself. "Woman. No. *Man.* Wait. Can I have both?"

Grapas smiled indulgently. "Certainly. Would you prefer bath first, or do you wish to eat while the food is hot?"

She thought again; such urgent matters were to be weighed carefully. "Both. Both first." She paused, then added, as if pained to say it, "Please."

Grapas tipped his helmeted head toward her. "As you request, lady."

Unwilling to be entirely compliant, she pointed at the cask of wine on the sideboard. "I suppose you'll want me to use a glass."

Grapas opened the door to leave. "If it's not too great an inconvenience, my lady."

The crier, a tall, theatrical man who functioned as the lord mayor's overseer of the arena, waited anxiously outside the star fighter's quarters as Grapas walked through the door into the open square.

"She hasn't got it," the old soldier said.

The crier shook his head. "You're no healer, guard. How do you know? Do you realize the danger here at all?"

"No. But I know a sick one when they pass right in front of me. Did you see her cunning on the killing sand? If that's the plague, may Mitra strike us all down with it. I'd have seconds, personally."

Sonja indulged.

She wolfed her share, and more, of the food on wooden trays. She filled her glass and tankard equally often.

And she bathed.

In her lonely, often solitary life, she rarely made hygiene a priority beyond scraping the crust off in a frigid stream once in a while. She'd showered, after a fashion, even sunk her form into warm spring pools on occasion. But she'd felt no particular romance for it, and when stepping out of immersion, she tended to put on the same road-befouled clothes she'd had on before washing up.

But she'd never really *bathed* before. Grapas had been as good as his word and sent both a male and female attendant, equally comely, to bring her hot water and keep her plate and glass full. They were both well paid, she'd discovered, and perhaps it was the wine, but she soon had thoughts of herself bathing both, instead of the arranged proceedings.

They poured dried scent from a clay jar into the tub and insisted on helping her disrobe. She had little compunction about others seeing her body, and she knew in the right light, there was something arresting about it to a great many onlookers. She was pleased to hear a suppressed gasp from each.

So she ate, she drank, and she felt her days of riding fade from memory. The chill that had somehow followed her across the steppes and the desert seemed to dissipate nicely. When she was finished, her attendants helped her from the bath and dried her with care, in no haste whatsoever.

And then Sonja indulged again.

Her first indulging was thirsty and needful, and the three hadn't even made it to the bed.

She indulged again with a warm pleasant feeling, a pact of wellness in the world, and in that instance, she climaxed with utter contentment, and a howl that was both inarticulate and voluminous and left a jittery grin on her face after.

And in her final indulgence, she was a bit surly and athletic, and if she was being completely honest, that might have been her favorite carnal mood of the entire evening.

For the first time in many days, she did not need to sing her mother's lullaby, as she sank into a smiling slumber, like that of an emperor's spoiled cat, the black and red of Zamora's colors wrapped around her in something close to silk. She heard no voices, felt no touch of sadness, for the first time in a long, long while.

She didn't know, or perhaps didn't care, that she was being watched.

18

A TENUOUS GRIP

It isn't exactly clear when the ideological shift regarding death ritual passed from appeasing the gods to remembrance of loved ones, but a gradual evolution in matters of ceremony is clear: At some point, a conversation with the deities took on an additional tone of tribe/family solidarity. People all over the world added an institutionalized component of personal loss and the understanding of grief as more than a visceral reaction, as something that quite possibly never completely faded.

To this day, each people, indeed each individual, processes the death of someone vital to them with different ratios of the personal and the social, and each has an expression formed by custom and social viability.

But it is also clear that to many, these rituals aid in the journey not just from life to death for the subject, but from unbearable grief to a tolerable amount of the same for those left behind.

Professor R. A. L. Bazzer, *How to Live After Death*

Ysidra and her sole remaining Wolf Pack protector stood at a quiet, flat outcropping of rock near the creek bed. They couldn't know it, or their day would have been violently different, but they'd been less than a hundred yards from the man who'd murdered poor Festrel.

To leave Festrel lying alone as his body cooled in the forest was inconceivable. Her people were not capable of abandoning their own to the elements and scavengers. It wasn't done, not even with enemies at their heels.

It was a delay. The queen in exile was aware it meant Sonja was putting distance between them, but it was simply not possible to move on without the proper rites. She was certain, though he hadn't said as much and, in fact, had stopped speaking almost entirely, that Raganus would have abandoned his vows, tribe, and queen entirely had she pressed him to leave Festrel unattended.

Festrel's body lay on a long bed of twigs and logs, hands at his chest. It had been her duty to remove the arrow from his skull, and the sound it had made coming out still haunted her, even hours later.

Raganus, rather, took the chore of putting his friend's spear in the corpse's hands, in case the road after the fire was a dangerous one.

Ysidra stood at the head of the rock. There was no performance in her heavy heart, only regret and grief and guilt. Raganus looked up at her balefully.

"Our brother, Festrel," she began. "He wished harm on no one, save to protect his family and his . . . his queen. I pray to the gods that someday, I will be worthy of his devotion."

She looked toward Raganus, whose expression only darkened. She realized she was falling short, somehow. But the truth was, she didn't really know her Wolf Pack. They'd somehow all made an unspoken agreement that familiarity wasn't allowed. There was the Pack, and there was the queen. Nothing good would come from blurring those lines.

She knew she was faltering, but she continued, "Festrel, I remember he laughed often, making the watch less dour. Stouthearted protector and trusted friend…"

Raganus spoke. "He had a son. Wife died. Son died last year."

She kept her voice calm. "Yes. Loving husband and father. Is there anything else we should say, Raganus?"

The burly man shook his head, then averted his eyes from her entirely, his voice catching as he started on the fire. "Just that he loved a queen and thus died a complete fool."

Festrel's shirt caught first, and soon enough, he was consumed.

They silently packed their horses and made their way, at last, toward Radolan.

Sylus kept turning at the sound of a mournful voice over his shoulder, which he was certain was death.

It would only make sense that, as the only human in all the lands who understood what humanity truly meant and what his mission was, he would be personally watched over by the guardian between worlds.

But his mission was not accomplished, it was clear. He'd tied a bit of his cloak around the wound in his shoulder, which was painful and awkward, and he simply assumed this pain was sent from the gods to their favored son as punishment for his weakness, first with the redhead, then the cursed Turanians. Instead of simply being a professional, being expedient, he'd wanted to toy with his prey; he'd wanted to drink in the look in their eyes as they died. He told himself he was a scholar, collecting truth, but lying to himself was shameful, like being caught masturbating, and he admitted balefully that he'd simply wanted the experience. Two devoted warriors and a queen were a meal he'd not been able to turn down.

It had cost him.

After he regained consciousness and set his wound to rough justice, he whistled for his horse...the call long ago developed and taught to his mount, like the song of a small bird, to keep enemies unaware.

He climbed up awkwardly. There was tremendous temptation to simply rest a bit, but favored by the gods or not, he knew that was self-treachery and that he would never awaken from such a slumber.

He knew a sanctuary; the Falcon had men of use scattered all around the region. He'd go see Radhi, the healer. Sylus couldn't let him live, of course—he'd tell the Falcon of the Blood Man's weakness.

That was fine, he decided. He couldn't remember the last person he'd killed, the last true soul he'd witnessed.

Either in blood loss or simple cruelty, he'd simply forgotten there had ever been a queen's devoted guard or a stable boy in Radolan at all.

Ysidra and her "Pack," if one grief-stricken guard could be called such, made it to the village just before nightfall. Sonja's trail was of course demolished; they'd wasted nearly a full day preparing for poor Festrel's last watch, and it was a trade route, though admittedly a backhanded, unofficial one. Her tracks were no longer distinguishable.

The queen had the same thought she had every time she wandered into such a place. *These people, even these people, have a home.* There were those who had grown to love the nomad's life, but she wasn't of that mind. She wanted her people to rest and to plant. She'd searched for a way her entire adult life and thought she'd found it, with colorful sails circling in the wind on the top of a forested hill.

Instead, she'd found disgrace and death.

They dismounted and walked their horses to the stable, but

though there were still torches burning, no one came to offer assistance. After a time, they simply stalled their horses and gave them hay and water from the big clay trough. The other horses in the stable appeared skittish and timid, despite being solid work beasts.

They'd taken to barely speaking. It hadn't felt necessary, and both knew it would bring no comfort. She wondered if her sole remaining Wolf stayed with her out of loyalty or a desire to see Sonja gutted.

Across the square, they took stock of the town, such as it was. It had few buildings; most were in disrepair. No one seemed to be out on the streets, though it wasn't fully dark yet. She was amused to find that someone had planted flowers around the town well in the center of the square, and she found this somehow heartwarming.

She knew Sonja would call this a "shithole," and she wouldn't be factually wrong. But to Ysidra, always moving, never welcome, it seemed inviting.

The few sounds she heard came from the tavern, some rough planks helpfully bridging the mud in front of the entrance. She walked toward it, knowing her shadow followed.

When the door opened, the scent of roast meat was immediate and irresistible. All the patrons, mostly simple townsfolk, turned their eyes toward the visitors. She was a queen, well used to eyes on her. She looked for an empty table, and there were several. There was no music; few people were even talking. Slow night, perhaps.

It seemed to her that this tavern felt like horses, timid and shaking. "Spooked," she'd heard Sonja call a person of nervous disposition once, and it fit. The tavern was spooked.

They sat at a rough table. Her tribe took their meals outside, or under a tent in wind or rain. The thought was upsetting.

A barmaid in a threadbare burlap tunic came to their table, with a sour aspect to her face. *Perhaps outsiders aren't welcome*, thought Ysidra. "Welcome. What do you want, strangers?" she asked, without warmth.

"Do you have wine? A glass of wine and whatever my...friend wants, please."

"We have a variety of wines from all over the— Never mind. Yes, and you, sir?"

"Ale. Two. One for our Festrel, his last in this realm," said Raganus. The queen ordered two plates of the intoxicating goat roasting on the spit. The barmaid expressed little interest in their order or their grief and turned to leave. Ysidra gave her guard a look. *Don't share our business*, it said with authority.

"Wait," said Ysidra, placing a hand on the barmaid's rough-skinned arm. "Forgive me, but this party seems...a bit grim, somehow. Has there been an illness?"

Even the meager chatter at the tables nearby ceased. The young woman pulled her arm away as if Ysidra's hand carried poison. "There was a killing. Young stable boy named Atus. Murdered and mutilated. Poor child of little brain, never harmed a god-cursed thing. Cut open and left to die."

Ysidra was taken aback, but the barmaid only sneered at her shock. "Apologies if we ain't exactly in a festive mood, Your Grace."

The woman started to turn away, thinking the matter settled. Ysidra stood, and there was fire in her voice, fire of the war field. "You leave when I say you leave, woman. Who killed the boy? Who did this?"

The barmaid saw something in the queen's eyes, something like a lightning spark, and her ill manner changed abruptly. The patrons around squirmed uncomfortably; some thought to get up and defend the local girl from this madwoman, but then Raganus stood and none felt inclined to anger the professional soldier with the dark, angry eyes.

"Some awful woman. Sat at this same table. She was seen heading for the stables. She was a bit like you," said the barmaid, recovering a bit of her cheek. "Rude. Arrogant. Ten minutes later, Atus lies drained of blood in the same hay he slept in. He didn't deserve that. No one does."

"What did she... Tell me, what did she look like?" Ysidra knew the answer but hoped she was mistaken.

"She had a great long shock of red hair, like a cooking fire, if you must know. Red like the blood she got out of Atus... five stab wounds from guts to glory, and if you know her or know of her, I venture to say you are not welcome here."

Her voice raised a bit of courage in the townspeople, and many stood, including the cook, with his gleaming butcher knife.

Ysidra saw the odds. "We know her. The truth is, we seek her for other crimes. If you are sure... if you are certain, then this boy's torment will be paid and repaid, I vow it."

Raganus did not remove his hand from his spear, but he did lower it.

"Did anyone... Good woman, I grieve for your loss. But we need to find her before she commits more evil on this land. Did anyone see where she went?"

A man with a hard-bitten face, an outdoorsman's face, stepped forward. "She went past my spread, riding like the devil. On the run, I mean. I'm east of town, off the Bleak Road."

Ysidra noted wryly how he described her ride, but said nothing.

"She heads toward Zamora. The road leads to Shadizar. She knew we'd think she made for Hyrkania, the cursed minx."

The barmaid's face dropped, showing her genuine grief. This time, it was she who grabbed Ysidra's arms, squeezing more tightly than perhaps was needed. "Please. We aren't fighters," she said. "If you're going to chase her, find her. Hunt her down."

Ysidra nodded, meeting the woman's tearful eyes.

"And cut her heart out slowly," said the woman.

"That'll have to do, son," said the old healer. He'd used sewing needles and thread to shut Sylus's wound, which, being infected and pus-ridden, proved to be extremely painful for the Blood Man. But, calling upon his god-given exceptional gifts, he was able to avoid screaming, giving out a few manly grunts and curses at best. He'd seen so many men die in pain, it was easy to mimic their terse pangs of agony.

In truth, he rather enjoyed the theatricality of it.

Radhi, the healer, was a small man, pale of skin and with eyes so light that they often appeared to have no pigment at all. He lived, as most of the Falcon's men did, simply, away from people. It wouldn't do to be easy to find, not in their profession, not with the Falcon as their master. A small, isolated hut was easy to equip and abandon at need. There were dozens of such huts scattered across three countries, all for those in the employ of the Falcon. Their residents left no mark upon departure.

"Heh, some host I am. I forgot to bring you some wine to numb the pain. Forgive me, my friend," said the small man, bringing a half-empty bottle of cheap wine. Sylus's insight was working, at least. He saw immediately that the smaller man had not forgotten anything, had simply chosen to withhold the very thing that might ease his friend's suffering. He made note of it.

Radhi smiled, smugly certain that he was in no danger. "Sorry this happened, Sylus. Missions get away from us sometimes, don't they?"

He hid his true self; it was not to be wasted on men such as these. He attempted a bit of the hearty, soldierly chatter of the men he'd ambushed... He'd already forgotten their names, and he said simply, shrugging and grinning, "I did as duty demands."

Radhi raised his own glass. "To duty, indeed, my friend."

The healer's eyes never left the bottle, and he reached for a second glass greedily. *A drunkard, then*, thought Sylus. *I read your story like a puppet show, old man.*

It was disappointing. A coward and a sot. There'd be no revelation tonight. Something in Sylus's demeanor—perhaps it was the fatigue and blood loss; perhaps it was a bit of contempt for the poor quality of his benefactors—caused Radhi to see something in the way Sylus stood. The small man's eyes opened wide, and he dropped the wine to reach for a dagger clumsily, and fatally, hidden in his pocket.

"Sylus, *no*," he said, but Sylus was on the third of his five deep punctures in the man's body, and the small man was already past the point of further alarm.

The five cuts finished, Radhi started to drop, and the possibly senile old tosspot looked up with his poor, uncomprehending vision and said, "What's this, what's this?"

Sylus saw nothing but fear in Radhi's last moments, no further step on his journey toward understanding.

"Disappointing," he said, this time out loud, as he set the small hut on fire.

19

FALLING INTO FIRE

Quiet child, so fair and deep
Mother will watch you as you sleep
Restless eyes and dreaming heart
Father has loved you from the start

Quiet child, and be at peace
Brother will make your nightmare cease
Tribe accepts you as their own
Sweetest infant ever known

Quiet child, hear my song
You won't be a child for long
And if you leave us all someday
We'll be here to light your way

Quiet child, wrapped in fur
Sleep in silence, do not stir

Daughter, sister, mother, wife
We'll walk beside you all your life

Traditional tribal lullaby, Hyrkanian region

Sonja awoke in the arms of a dead man.

She was ten years old, and while she slept, her village had become a crematorium.

She shrieked in horror at the cold embrace of the corpse that seemed to completely encompass her. She pushed at his heavy arms, arms that had threatened to crush her into submission. When his fingers opened from their interlacing, she burst forward to her feet, shuddering and shaking off the feeling of chill, the feeling of death that seemed all over her, crawling on her like insects on a scrap of meat.

She looked at what remained of her village. She cried, or rather, she sobbed, and tears fell from her eyes. But her denial was such that it felt as if those tears came from some other child, some other redheaded village girl. She found herself walking about in the cooling ashes, collecting horrible images, one after another, many that would plague her dreams for years to come. To Sonja, this was her world, and her world had just ended.

She had *tried* to keep her promise to her father. She had sat in the tall grass, anxious and confused. But then she saw the eye of the white stag she'd killed, its body still steaming even in death. And she knew she couldn't stay. Later, as people told the story of her life, they'd speak of her remarkable courage, at ten years old, running headlong to join the battle against the raiders of her village.

The truth was nearly the opposite. She was afraid to stay with her kill.

And so she stood and gathered up the blood of her family in her veins and did something that would have been unthinkable even an hour ago: She stepped to the stag, and with a grimace on her face, she removed her arrow. It wasn't broken and it had held true. She would have that, at least.

She had a blade, as well. A skinning knife, not the big ones her father and brothers used, that was for rodents and small-catch fowl. She thought briefly of her father's hesitation, and she knew what he was worried about—that she could not bring herself to kill. And she shared that worry.

But she had killed the white stag.

Maybe she was Hyrkanian after all.

She prayed so. And she ran through the tall grass, in the footsteps of her father. As fast as she was, it seemed to take forever.

She smelled the village before she could see it. Black clouds of smoke, unlike anything she'd seen before. She had just enough presence of mind to squat in the grasses outside her village.

What she saw broke something innocent and precious inside her. Her people screaming as the raiders cut down everyone they could reach—man, woman, child. They poured a dark fluid on the huts and storage sheds. She tried to understand it and failed. Why destroy what they couldn't use? Why leave her people with nothing?

And in their laughter, in their blood-flecked smiles, she knew the answer.

Because it amused them. It fed something dark and hideous in them, and worse...it made them laugh.

She heard their chatter, their boasting. She heard her people begging, raging, wailing in grief. But she could not process it. Something in her heart or head kept most of the words on the funereal wind from her comprehension. Blessedly.

She heard the raider's chief calling the tribeswomen cows, unworthy of their attention, worthy only of the axe. He called the men weak, the children infected. They were doing them all a favor, he said.

There were men sacking the huts. She could have told them it was a complete waste; there were likely less than twenty coins in the entire village. But they pulled out children who had been hiding under their beds, and for a moment, she felt she would never be able to breathe again without smelling the burning flesh, not if she lived to be an elder's elder.

They were Kothians—she recognized the symbols—or at least most of them were. Koth had suffered several years of famine and could no longer pay for an army's upkeep. Word had been given that they were free to take what they needed—*outside* the Kothian borders, in exchange for continued service when called upon. She'd heard it enough times, but it had meant nothing to her child's mind. She shook her head clear, trying to see where she could use her single child's arrow in a way that might do the most good.

It was impossible; she knew that on some level.

Then she saw her mother holding a wrapped bundle protectively. Her baby brother, Shia, she hoped, and Sonja really *did* forget to breathe. Somehow, even in the tall grass, her mother had seen her, locked eyes with her. Sonja started to stand, but her mother shook her head and mouthed the word *Run*.

But she couldn't, as from behind her mother, one of the raiders, laughing, lifted his sword, aiming to stab downward through her back, and possibly her unexpected son.

Sonja screamed, "*Mother.*"

But it was her father who blocked the blow, with the largest hammer from his forge. The raider was big, no doubt strong. But her father was a blacksmith and pushed the man's sword away with such force that he fell backward, his head, helmet and all, completely caved in and, indeed, fully impacted into the sod below.

He pushed Sonja's mother behind him and swung his hammer with arms that lifted anvils unaided. Two more raiders approached him, and one learned the folly of trying to block a smith's hammer with a wooden spear. Her father's hammer crashed through his breastbone, heart, and spine like an axe through kindling.

The other stepped back. Whatever else this raider was, "brave" did not seem to be among his qualities. It was then that an arrow pierced her father's side, just above his great hide belt. He didn't slow; he took his hammer and threw it at the mounted bowman with all the force in his great arms, breaking the man's arm, ring mail, rib cage, and internal organs as he fell, foot still in the stirrup of his terrified horse, who dragged him well past the point of death a few moments later.

The raider chief saw this last loss, and a grimace came over his face. Whether annoyed by the failure of his men or the stubborn refusal of the sheep people to simply die, Sonja had no idea.

The bandit chief, mounted on a black horse caked with white paint and terrible symbols of red, trotted up behind her father, who was looking for a weapon to replace the one he'd thrown. He settled on his first opponent's sword and reached for it, unaware of the chief, his spiked ball and chain dangling in his free hand, thirsty for blood.

This was the moment. This was what she'd been given her talent for—she knew it. She could save her family, possibly the entire village. The chief raised the heft of his weapon, the spiked ball at the end of the loose chain already flecked with flesh and cloth.

Sonja drew her aim on him.

And Sonja never missed.

In that moment, she understood. She could kill. She *would* kill.

She just needed a *reason*.

She nocked her arrow silently, aimed for the chief's eye...

But she was grabbed from behind by arms almost as large and as strong as her father's. "Ah, see what I find? This is why Kreval gets the choicest vittles, the softest bed. Because Kreval is a thinker, girl."

His foul breath was in her ear. She felt his long beard on the back of her neck, his sharp armor against her simple tunic. "I'm afraid you're in for a bit of a rough time, girl, being veal such as you are. Your people gone, your home burned. But Kreval has an answer— would you like to hear?"

Sonja's eyes widened as the chief's weapon demolished her father's head. Oblivious, Kreval continued speaking, lizard-like, into her ear. "Come away with Kreval, poor Kreval, always alone. Come with me and live. You'll forget all this . . . this unpleasantness."

She struggled, but he held her firmly, crushing her a little, to weaken her, take a bit of breath and fight from her. She watched her brother Ozkar fall, pierced with arrows.

Kreval squeezed her again, harder this time. "Now, I'm losing patience, my fine toy. Kreval is kind, but he has a bit of a dark side when pushed. And you are beginning to *push* me!"

Sonja struggled, freeing one arm, more through jostling than cleverness or strength. Kreval smiled. "Aw, what you going to do, dolly? Are you going to shoot me with your toy bow? Can't have *that*, poor kind Kreval says."

He stepped on her arrow, her single arrow, which she had thought, as a child thinks, she would use to save her people. She heard it snap and break.

Kreval grinned as raiders dragged Sonja's mother from her hiding place by her hair, her beautiful red hair. "Well, child? What say you?"

Then his eyes opened wide as she showed him what she held in her free hand. Her skinning knife, a gift from her father.

"Wait," he said.

It was the last thing he said. Still in his arms, she held it underhand

and jabbed it into his leg, ripping upward with all her strength. Blood poured out of the wound, gushed out onto both their legs.

She could kill, it turned out. *Would* kill.

She just needed a reason.

Kreval squealed, then issued a guttural yell, squeezing her so tightly she felt her ribs begin to bend. She was going to be crushed, and the man who would do it was already dying. There would be no mercy.

He fell forward, his full weight slamming her against the ground. On the way down, she thought, *I hope I don't burn to death.*

Then there was pain, then nothing for a good while.

The Kothians had been thorough, but it seemed as if at some point after the initial frenzy, that distorted, perverse party of blood, they had simply burned their tracks and left. Sonja could not imagine them regretting their behavior, but nonetheless, they did not linger. Perhaps the amusement of slaughtering unarmed farmers and horse breeders felt beneath them, somehow.

Some animals were missing; the raiders would likely be eating them or selling them this very night. All the horses were gone, which made Sonja think that perhaps those horses, Hyrkanian raised and trained, might have been the real purpose of the raid. The rest was just... ash and bones. Bodies scattered and crushed by the raiders' horses' hooves. The food stores were gone, taken or burned. There were no artifacts, no real commodities to recover or preserve. Everything that made their tribe have any meaning at all was in their hearts and hands, and those were as cold as the stone, and equally still.

No one came. No neighboring villages.

It started to rain. She'd found one good spade, scorched but sturdy. And in the rain, in the cold, she began to bury her people. She did the best she could, sorting bones and laying graves near where she remembered their huts had been. It was hopeless. But it was what needed to be done. So it fell to Sonja.

For two days, she worked without food, hands blistering to the point of constant ooze. She wouldn't use the word "trauma" even if she were familiar with it, but when a passing small caravan came through, simple craftsmen taking their wares from town to town, she was suddenly skittish and mistrustful. She had no one to tell her otherwise. They could be raiders; they could be Kothian.

So she once again hid in the tall grass. Not far from the corpse of Kreval. There would be no grave for him, and she spat at him as she squatted down, waiting for the train of small carts to stop, wonder at the tragedy before them, and move on, realizing there was no money to be made in a cemetery.

When they passed, Sonja looked at the corpse of the man who'd meant to destroy her but somehow accidentally saved her life. She hated that she knew his name, hated that she'd remember his face.

She looked around at the valley of her home. The shale hillside, the tall grass, and the ashes in the wind and rain.

She reached down and pulled the cloak off the dead man's body, rolling his stiff form over to gain access. She took his fine sword and belt, tied it twice around her tiny waist.

She took a look at the road. Each way led to a village, to people, within a few days' walk. People. Campfires. Families.

Sonja turned her eyes from the road to the nearly impenetrable forest to the south and walked into it, swallowed by the lush green trees.

20

UNEXPECTED VISITORS

Whether or not it was Sonja's example is difficult to say. But as her name grew from amusing anecdote, as in "I saw a woman fight two men and win," to the creature of campfire legend that she became, it is clear that a small, but fearsome, fighter class of young women emerged in areas she'd visited, however briefly.

Young women previously given the choice of acolyte nun or stolid wife began to pick up arms, most particularly hunting bows and lightweight swords, again, whether intentionally or unintentionally following Sonja's lead. They found heavy armor difficult to navigate, but more importantly, it negated what speed advantage might save their lives in combat.[*]

So they stuck to leather armor or what light scale or chain they could afford that would not restrict their movements. They often wore war paint; sometimes they wore dried bits of their defeated opponents in their hair. This gave the benefit of frankly terrifying their detractors, while

---

[*] Referenced in Tophen Lamar's *She Wore a Helm*, pp. 216–218

also providing a sense of belonging to a confederacy of isolated fighters.
The fashion leaked past borders and across religions to become a sym-
bol, a message to say, "This woman is a fighter—approach at risk."

The final thread could well be completely coincidental. But wherever
these women appeared, on the trail or the battlefield, they were called
"wild women."

Or, more simply, "Devil Women."

Reverend Albert Commecci, *God and Gods*

They were a day beyond Radolan. Ysidra had been heartsick, almost willing to abandon her hunt entirely, until visiting the tiny village.

But she'd insisted upon seeing the stables. There was blood everywhere still, on the floor, the walls, the hay. She'd known Sonja could be merciless; she'd even admired her ferocity at times. She'd felt she'd chosen a life partner who would never cower, never retreat, and it had warmed her insides. She'd felt a bit of that ferocity when they touched, even in the tenderest moments.

Before seeing the stables.

The townspeople were certain it was the rude flame-haired woman who'd slaughtered a boy, just barely more than a child, apparently, and left without a word. Had he offended her somehow? Had he made a transgression?

But no, nothing could have deserved that. An unarmed youth, a tender of horses, without a coin to his name. She was no longer sick at heart; that would have been selfish. She was sick in the pit of her stomach, as if a rat were crawling in her intestines. Sonja had to be stopped. She had to be taken off this earth entirely. It was the only just choice for the She-Devil; perhaps it was even her only true destiny.

They stopped at the creek along the trail to water their horses. Raganus looked at her as if to say that time was passing and the trail only getting colder. She said nothing, instead crouching and leaning over the water's edge to wipe the dirt from her eyes. She looked at her face in the water. The light in her eyes was gone. She tried to smile for reasons she didn't understand, and found she couldn't; the muscles that pulled her flesh simply failed to respond.

Sonja.

She howled like the Wolf Queen she was, in grief. Festrel, the elders, the stable boy—all their deaths were on her back and in her guts, and she howled it to the heavens. Raganus joined in; it was what the Pack did when words failed them.

She turned to him after their throats were raw. "Give me your knife."

Raganus, as if startled from a stupor, said, "What? Why—"

"Mine is stuck in that murderer, guardsman. Do as I *say*."

Nothing good would come from this—he knew it. But she was queen.

She took the knife, and looking in the water, gritting her teeth sharply, she brutally, painfully sawed her way through the two long braids of dark, thick, beautiful hair, braids that had been entwined with gorgeous ribbons beaded by the best of her people's craftsmen. Two colors they were.

Red and green.

Sonja's pleasant dreams were interrupted. She heard voices in the dark, and she sat up, realizing her bedmates were gone and her only company was the soft sheets and pillows she'd used so ingeniously for leverage a few short hours ago.

Then she saw the corpses at the foot of her bed, staring at her in the darkness. She heard a dripping sound and realized it was the sound of blood trickling from their wounds as their empty eye sockets looked at her with accusation.

She felt that she must be the subject of some sort of hazing or ritual. That perhaps the guard Tias had recovered from his bruised, possibly ruptured groin and intended some sort of revenge. If so, he'd quite miscalculated. Sonja avoided sorcery; she disliked it, even feared it.

But she was entirely used to the dead.

"Well. You might as well come out—I won't shriek for you," she called out.

Then the bigger of the two raised his hand to point at her, and she shrieked a little, causing her to grit her teeth in embarrassment.

She squinted as her eyes adjusted. She recognized them. They were... What were their names? Sharptooth and... Filus, was it? Yes, Filus. The gladiators she'd defeated yesterday.

Dead as dogshit and standing in front of her.

Sharptooth looked at her with dry, dusty eyes. *"You. You are in my bed. Why are you in my bed?"*

Sorcery, then. She shivered and shrank back toward the headboard.

Filus looked around. "These... these were our quarters."

Sonja simply nodded.

He looked sad, dirt falling from his face and mouth, dirt of the shallow grave. "We're dead, aren't we? You killed us."

She nodded again. She had no weapon at hand but simple cutlery, if they came for her, which given the circumstances seemed entirely justifiable.

He sank, as if resigned. "Where do we... where do we go?"

Sonja spoke again, her voice an unlovely croak. "I don't know, gladiator. I'm sorry."

He looked at her mournfully, as if about to weep. But instead he simply shrugged. "You're cursed, you know. Not our doing. But you're cursed. I can smell it."

Sharptooth seemed to lose interest in the conversation and appeared to fade, like fog on water after the sun bursts through.

Sonja sat up, hoping she was still dreaming. "Follow your friend, Filus. He seems to know the way."

Filus reached around to the gash she'd put in his spine and pulled back a handful of blackish-red blood.

"Yes, Sonja. See you soon."

And then he faded into nothingness.

She did not return to sleep that night, neither the restful postcoital bliss she remembered nor the haunted, hunted type she'd experienced of late.

"Cursed," she muttered to herself. And she felt a chill.

She'd felt cold quite a lot recently. Too cold.

She looked at the Asp on her arm. It was beautiful, but she cared little for adornment. Was it possible—

There was a crash against the door, a fumbling of keys in the lock. She leapt out of bed, fully naked, and grabbed the only weapon available, a small cheese knife.

"Mitra's bloody stool," she cried.

As if corpses weren't enough, two giant rats entered the room.

Sonja squinted, assuming the entire night's proceedings had to be attributed to the copious amounts of alcohol she'd drunk when she hadn't been servicing or getting serviced.

But no, she saw the rodents were in fact people inexplicably wearing coats that made them look like giant rats. As before, Sonja cared little for fashion or adornment, but this seemed a form of self-cruelty.

The taller one, male, she thought, under his hooded, inexplicably tailed fur cloak, looked toward her with something approaching euphoria, and she briefly saw the bodies of the cell's two guards as he closed the door behind them. "Sonja? Lady of the Steppes? You must be her. Red Sonja?" he asked, unable to contain his joy.

The girl seemed more cautious, perhaps wiser, Sonja noted.

"I don't remember having any giant rats in my social circle," she said.

He frowned and shook his head. "What? Oh. No, no. We..." He stumbled on. "We're not rats. We've been in hiding." He took back his hood, and she couldn't help but notice that he was handsome indeed, almost pretty, with dark hair and blazing eyes.

"That's one mystery solved, then. Perhaps your sister would like to remove her rat cap, as well?"

"I'm not his sister," said the young woman, sheathing her knife. *That took some confidence*, thought Sonja, even as she stood before her naked, with only a knife still stinking of cheese as her weapon.

The man came forward as if to touch Sonja, and she stood her ground, holding up the knife ridiculously. "Your lover, then. If you've something you wish to say to me, best say it. Also, I might be a very little bit drunk. A little."

Surprisingly, he knelt in front of her, reminding her painfully of the old man with the burned bones on the Bleak Road. "My lady. We are not vagrants or vagabonds. We are loyal Hyrkanians."

Sonja cocked her head. They did indeed look like most of the people in her tribe. She'd been an awkward, often painful, flame-haired exception. The girl was fiercely lovely but clearly more cautious in her words and manner, letting the man speak in his breathless way.

He stood. "I am Dalen; this is Aria. We were on a mission we thought was hopeless. Until we heard of your battle in the arena. You are a gift from the gods."

Sonja dropped her knife back on the cheese tray, causing a clatter. "I often think that about myself. Lovely to meet you, please fuck off—I'm getting all the telltale signs of a hangover." She turned away, walking toward the welcoming bed.

Dalen was alarmed. "You don't understand. It is the greatest need. Hyrkania will *fall*."

Aria sniffed contemptuously. "She doesn't care, Dalen. She's no use to us, just another drunken, hopeless trollop."

Sonja pointed a single finger at the girl. "Well observed, fair one. Now, if you'd simply quietly take your rat friend somewhere far away enough that your chatter can't be heard?"

But Dalen refused to be swayed. "Lady. Please. Your homeland needs you."

This raised Sonja's ire; she felt she was being trapped, and would have none of it. "My homeland? You utter jackass, my 'homeland' is under the cloud of plague."

Aria stepped forward, taking the sole remaining bit of sausage on the room's hospitality table. "No, it isn't."

Sonja shook her head, for clarity's sake. "What's that? Speak up, rodent. What are you saying?"

Aria stepped forward, eyes facing the She-Devil's directly. "I'm saying there's no plague."

Sonja struggled to understand. Dalen spoke up. "It's true, lady. The king, King Gahresh of the Wooden Throne, he and his advisors spread that story, even falsified evidence. Now it is accepted truth. Though no one has witnessed a true plague victim in or outside of its borders."

Sonja shook her head; it was beyond comprehension. Why would the king— But no. It made no difference. Plague or no, she wanted no part of Hyrkania.

"Even if that's true, which I doubt, it makes no difference to me. Hyrkania let my people die and left me to rot. I owe them nothing, not love, not loyalty, not the crack of my ass. Do you understand? Go away—you've come to the wrong devil."

Aria smirked and said, "I told you, Dalen. You tried. But she's not worth your adulation."

"Sonja of the Steppes. I beg of you. What ails our land is not an illness. It's an army. An army of rageful creatures unlike any other on or under the land. And they are headed for our capital city of Makkalet. There, they will conquer us and all our people."

Sonja, dizzy with the events of the night, sat hard on the soft mattress. "And why, if this is the case, are you two bold defenders not there, fighting this phantom army?"

Aria stepped forward. She drew herself up to her full height, as best she could muster, but her face betrayed her shame. "Because we are deserters, Dalen and me. There you have it, Flame Hair. We left our posts. We are traitors—do you understand? Going back means death the moment we are revealed."

Sonja looked up, directly in the young woman's eyes. "And yet you're going back."

Dalen nodded. "We are. We were of the King's Eye. We abandoned honor and have been living as peasants. It is no more than we deserve."

Sonja reached for a mug, hoping against hope, but alas, she'd already drained it. "Have at it, then. Sonja wishes you well. May you slay a few invaders before you get hung—that's my wish for you both." She looked at the moon outside the barred window and said, "If you're going to be heroic martyrs, may I suggest you get to it, as the guards outside will be spotted soon enough."

Aria grabbed Dalen's arm. "Come, Dalen. She won't be moved, and we can't wait for her."

But he did not move. He simply stared at her, as if she were hope.

Sonja felt oddly exposed by his stare and wrapped the sheets around herself. "Look. Maybe Hyrkania was my homeland. Once. But that time was long ago and fraught with pain. I have nothing, I have no one, to go back there to fight for—do you understand? You're asking me to leave all this, all this food, the roar of the crowd, all the naked bashing I can conjure..."

Dalen said, at last, "I understand. You prefer your cage."

Sonja laughed. "For a day. For a few days. If Sonja wants to leave, then leave she shall. Do not wager the house on this one, pretty fellow."

Aria was already at the door. "She's right, Dalen. They'll see the guards. We have to go."

Aria's contempt meant nothing to Sonja; she had lived as a scandal most of her life. But Dalen's quiet, broken stare made her feel a bit guilty, somehow. "Truthfully. Good luck. May you redeem yourselves and your honor and slay many enemies."

"Thanks ever so much," Aria said with a snort.

Dalen started to turn. "It's not true, you know."

"What's not true?" Sonja asked.

"What you said earlier, about having no one," he said, reaching for the iron door latch. "Your brother is alive."

21

AS ABOVE, SO BELOW

May death mistake you for your worst enemy.

Traditional Cimmerian curse

That night, within Hyrkania's borders and just beyond the great bay, the outsiders attacked their first full city.

PART II

22

THE DEEP FOREST

We know that Sonja's whereabouts during this time were not recorded by historians or storytellers.

Using the best artifactual cartography available, we know that there were small villages within a relatively leisurely horseback ride, but even afoot, it would have been a matter of only days for her to find refuge in the closest townlets. They surely would have taken in a young girl of her age, particularly one with her skills as a rider and hunter. She quite likely would have apprenticed to one craftsman or another, or even been adopted whole into a clan who, perhaps, had lost a child (or children) in those turbulent times.

They may have even been happy times for young Sonja.

It is pleasant to imagine that—the girl having a warm bed, a loving family, and food enough to survive.

It appears that for whatever reason, such was not the case.

Enid Cascardin, *Young Sonja of the Steppes*

The ten-year-old girl who walked into the forest covered in the ash of her entire clan, blisters on her hands, was not recognizable when she stepped back out two years later.

Whereas Sonjita, beloved by her family and tolerated affectionately by others, had stepped past the tree line, it was Sonja who stepped out.

And she had forgotten much.

The first night was cold, with only Kreval's stinking, tattered cloak to wrap around her. She heard sounds in the woods, and though she was a hunter's daughter and a hunter herself, she was still a ten-year-old girl, suddenly brotherless, motherless, and fatherless.

Her hands bled with the effort of two days of grave-digging, and her eyes were red with ash and momentous sobbing. She knew some woodcraft. She'd been on field hunts. But this section of the forest, no one went to alone.

The sounds of wolves howling gave her pause, and there was something else, something bigger. She looked back at the tree line behind her one final time and moved on, holding the dead man's sword in front of her.

She heard the second sound again and made a decision, possibly a poor one, to climb the nearest heavy-branched tree. It was the same sanctuary she used when her brothers' heckling got to be too much.

It began to rain again. She hugged the tree's trunk, under the dubious cover of its stout limbs, and sat, unable to move, overwhelmed with loss and hunger. She thought longingly of the stag she'd downed, doubtless torn to bits by scavengers, and her stomach growled almost as loudly as the wolves.

Ten years old, lost, abandoned, alone, she cried in the rain, in the treetop, first clutching at her breath, then letting out body-shaking, punishing sobs.

At some point, she wailed.

*   *   *

In the morning, her stomach woke her. Her arms ached from the previous two days of labor and holding unnaturally tightly to the treetop. Through the pain, grief, and guilt, her hunger brought a truth that she'd never had to face: Tears meant hunger. More tears would mean starvation.

She imagined her father seeing her now, his daughter the hunter, unable to feed herself or slake her own thirst, unable even to properly clean herself. She knew he'd be kind but disappointed, and that made her less tearful and more determined.

It was just dawn. She had a cloak, a bow (no arrows), a sword (no sheath), and a knife with a terrible man's blood dried fast to its blade. She had no shelter from rain, cold, or claw.

The first duty was to find water. Then she had to make something resembling an arrow. The sword was useless for food gathering, and it already felt heavy enough to weigh her down if she needed to flee. She knew how to make basic spring traps, so she left the sword in the lower branches of the tree and was grateful for the knife.

The first day, her arrows were useless, lacking the weight in the point to puncture a target, as well as proper fletching on the butt of the shaft. She built crude traps in a concentric circle around what she was calling the "home tree," but they remained empty and unsprung when she awoke after a second night of hunger and fear.

She found some red berries that she knew to be safe, but something had cleared the majority long since. She had stopped crying, but starvation was still a very real possibility.

She worked feverishly, from morning till night, that second day, for the results to be no better, and when she woke the fourth morning, after three nights clinging like a baby at her mother's teat to a tree completely indifferent to her survival, she found her head woozy and her steps uncertain.

She stopped. She'd been working entirely on instinct and the little bit of forest wisdom she'd gathered almost by accident in her village. But she hadn't really been thinking. It wasn't her favorite activity, to be fair.

The arrows needed shale, pounded to a point. She'd done it often enough to amuse herself and please the village elders. She would also need feathers or something else that would stabilize the shafts in flight.

Additionally, the traps had her scent on them, and no bait, she realized. They were useless, worse than useless, as they had taken up much of her day when she could have been foraging.

She walked to the creek and drank, using her cupped hand to lift the cool water to her lips. She was contemplating what the forest would do with her emaciated corpse, when she saw a flash of silver in the stream.

Her tribe were not fishermen. It would require too much effort to feed the village, with the tiny creek running through the high grass next to them, and the water was needed for crops and their horses. She slapped her forehead... Fish. She'd forgotten fish.

She smiled for the first time in many days and ran downstream along the small creek. As she got farther from her home tree, she became more brazen, less careful, as she leapt and ran along the gurgling stream.

To a pond. A clear pond, surrounded by vegetation. She saw the flash again. And another. And another.

Her "arrows" were useless for their intended purpose. But for this, for this they were perfection. She crashed into the water, knee-deep, holding one of her thin shafts, with its roughly pointed tip, like a fragile javelin as the fish, oblivious to her presence, swam around her. She stabbed downward too hard the first chance she had, and broke her arrow, reminding her painfully of Kreval's stepping on the arrow she'd hoped to save her village with.

So she adjusted. Two more fruitless jabs, and then, on her fourth attempt, she felt the thin resistance of the fish being punctured, and carefully lifted it out of the water…It was just a bit more than the size of her hand, still wriggling and precarious. She took it by its tail fin and smashed it unceremoniously on a rock at the pond's shore. She shoved the gauzy white flesh into her mouth, scales and all, not even tasting as her belly filled a bit, greedily, miraculously.

She laughed and hopped foolishly in the water. Catch the fish; for every three, eat one; use the rest for bait. Supplement with roots, leaves, and berries. While strategizing, she caught another. Her mind raced at the thought of a roaring fire, fresh fish and meat each night. Joyfully, unbelievingly, she caught two more. She stuck each one on a separate stick and placed that stick in the ground as she went back to work.

She'd have to ration, she thought. Everything relied on this pond, and if she was careless—

She heard a roar behind her, and she was shaken out of her dreaming, standing stock-still. She turned slowly. There was a massive black bear on the shore, mere feet behind her, beside the stick holding her day's catch.

Too late she understood. The bear had claimed this water, and this catch, as its own. She was standing in its supper bowl. It roared again, its hot breath enough to blow back the stray strands of hair over her face. Her knife was on the shore, her arrows completely meaningless as weapons. Spittle flew from the beast's angry maw. Worse still, to her child's ears, was the roar, which sounded like thunder flying past the beast's teeth.

It swung at her, claws out and the strength of the forest in its reach. It missed her more because she fell in terror than because of any savvy on her part. She scooted farther into the water, splashing all the way.

The bear hesitated a moment and then started to walk on all four legs into the pond after her.

23

ALL MANNER OF THINGS

"Matron, matron, where are you bound?"
I say that I heard the most awful of sounds.
"Matron, matron, what did you hear?"
It sounded quite like a babe, I fear.
"Matron, matron, where does it lie?"
I know not—can you not heed its mournful cry?
"Matron, matron, is it near?"
Hush your voice now, child; I'm trying to hear.
"Matron, matron, where is the sound?"
I vow it comes from deep in the ground.
"Matron, matron, where is the babe?"
It's living still, I fear, inside its grave.

Traditional Zingaran song of mourning

You are a *liar*, rodent," Sonja said, eyes narrowing. Her brother, alive?

The two in their shabby fur coats had pulled the bodies of the Zamoran guards inside the room, lending an eerie pall to a space meant for celebration and reward. Two hours ago, she'd been cavorting and was fully fed, enjoying the pleasures she'd denied herself the past week. Now she shared her quarters with two deranged killers and their victims.

Aria stood as tall as her small frame allowed. "It's not a lie. It's the truth."

"Do you know how I know you lie, rat girl? It's because I *watched* my family being murdered. And when I came to consciousness, I *buried* them all."

Aria was unmoved. "And yet *you* survived. Somehow you survived. Is it so beyond your imagination that, as a mere child, you were mistaken in this instance?"

Dalen, as always, tried to be kinder. "My lady, I assure you, we of the King's Eye do not lie well. Can you not see we are telling the truth?"

The memories were buried deeper than she had buried the villagers who were the only family she'd ever known. When she'd awoken, the fire had been burning all night. She'd had to guess at so many remains, and the gods had surely laughed at the awkward, mixed-bone skeletons arriving at their thrones in the afterlife.

"I don't believe you. And I'm not wandering into a plague swamp on your wild delusions." And it was done, she was certain. She'd made her choice. They were liars; she was alone—the alternative was too much to contemplate.

And quiet reason was never her greatest skill.

Aria nearly shouted, "There *is* no plague, lady. It's something the king's court dreamed up to keep invaders away from Hyrkania while it lies in weakness, undefended. But death is coming to Hyrkania; it spreads like the sickness they have used as cover." She stepped closer. "Will you let your brother be slaughtered, now that you know he yet exists? Will he call for his sister with their claws in his belly, do you think?"

Sonja's eyes went cold. "I think, girl, that you are very fortunate I don't have a blade."

Aria refused to flinch and squared her small shoulders. "The guards have swords, lady. If you won't fight for your people, perhaps fight for the blessed relief of having some sense knocked into that empty skull of yours."

Sonja smiled. "Gladly, girl. But I think it fair to warn you, I can be downright surly when hungover. I'm actually known for it."

Aria reached for the two swords of the deceased guards, her pride not allowing a retreat. Dalen shook his head in disbelief. "Aria, dearest one, we do not have time."

Aria seemed to shrink at his comment, perhaps for the lack of faith in her it expressed. But she stood to her full height and handed over a sword to Sonja, hilt first. "If I cut you and you live, you come with us, agreed?"

"No wager, chipmunk. And if I cut you, you won't live at all."

They raised swords, and Sonja thought, as always, only of the moment of approaching death, hers or the girl's. It was her gift to make the world disappear when called for. And it was called for with a regularity that would have made her sad, if she were the type who carried past regrets in her bedroll.

The door opened, and a Zamoran guard stood in the frame, sword raised.

Sylus was a tracker, it was true. A tracker of men, the occasional woman. Once or twice, a child. And he was good at it, renowned in the manner of his trade, even famed, if it was indeed possible to be famous among only a tiny selection of assassins and bounty hunters.

But the truth of it was, he was not skilled in the way of the Hyrkanians or Turanians. If forced to hunt for food on his own, he'd go hungry as often as not. If obliged to hunt a man through the woods with nothing but his wits and senses, like as not that man would escape his fate and never receive the five punctures the Blood Man of the Falcon specialized in.

No, his tracking was at least partially an aspect of his true self, the ability to ask the right questions, to discern the truth of them. He thought of himself as an evolved hunter, capable of feats the dirty, unlearned tribalists chasing rabbits and worse could never even conceive.

On some level, he knew he was unraveling.

He told himself he was chosen by the gods, granted insight and agency beyond normal men. Certainly beyond his prey, who all fell to his blade eventually.

But another part of him realized that he had departed from reality, and it was getting worse. Last night, he'd had a miserable headache that kept him from sleep, and he counted the heads of those he'd killed. Usually, this was a pleasant pastime, but last night, he felt their ghosts had taken up clubs and pounded his skull from the inside.

He was proud of his vocation, proud of what he could accomplish with nothing but a knife jabbed five times into various targets, while he watched their spirits fade. It was his opera. It was his puppet show.

And the victims even danced like marionettes, at the end.

But since meeting the woman, the Devil, he had begun to go off the mountain trail, even fully aware of the razor-like rocks below.

He was certain he could reattain his grace and gifts with her death. And in the meantime, he knew his skills as a gentlemanly deceiver were still ample enough to flummox the peasants of the area until he found her. And then he would kill her, and his *true self* would exalt and become arisen, and this momentary lull in his greatness would become memory.

He came upon three young girls on the Bleak Road. Dirty, useless orphans, most likely, trying to look fierce enough to not be simply stolen and used by people less civilized than he. They might have seen Sonja go by; she was certainly memorable, as such things were measured.

He would practice his charm on them. He would smile at them, compliment them. Speak to them as if they meant something in this world. He would make them feel, if not worthy, at least *significant*. Likely for the first time in their destitute, unremarkable lives.

And if they were uncooperative, well, there was always Queen Ysidra's knife.

The guard captain Grapas was no coward. He was a veteran of many skirmishes and had been wounded more than once, nearly mortally so on two occasions.

But neither was he a braggart or fool, and when Sonja in all her terror rushed at him with one of his own guards' swords nearly singing in the air toward him, he knew he lacked the heart and youth to even attempt bravado.

"*You,*" Sonja hissed. As her blade impossibly stopped at the very skin of his throat, he did something he'd never considered in all his storied career. He dropped his sword with a loud clatter on the stone floor.

"I yield, Red Lady."

Dalen pulled the old guardsman in and slammed the door shut hurriedly.

"Kill me if you must, but may I remind you that I was the one who saved you from death or dishonor on the Bleak Road."

Aria made a loud snorting sound at the word "dishonor."

Sonja replaced the blade at his throat. "I believe you, guardsman. And do you in turn believe me that I still dislike you a considerable amount?" He nodded, vigorously but carefully.

"I have questions for you, Grapas the Bold," she said through clenched teeth. "Have you ever actually seen a living victim of this Hyrkanian 'plague'?"

He considered. "No, lady. I have not. Only a few corpses, all burned before examination."

She paused before speaking again. "My...compatriots here allege that there is no plague, that the Wooden Throne sent warnings to nearby Zamora to keep people from crossing the steppes into my country. Is that conceivable to you, Master of the Outreach?"

He pondered. He didn't know the answer that she wanted to hear, so as a last resort, and remembering his pride, he told the truth. "It... is conceivable, Red Lady. Though why, that is less easy to imagine."

Dalen stepped forward, his voice calming. "He did you a service, Sonja. We could bind him. He needn't die."

"He's not going to die. He's coming with us," she said. "And one more question, Grapas. The most important question of your miserable life."

He looked up. He wanted to live.

"Where the bloody hell is my goddamn horse?"

The plan was simple, even a bit thoughtless, really, but Sonja would not abandon Sunder, no matter the risk.

Grapas was in front of the pack, as was dictated by military custom in his country, but also so that Dalen could walk behind him with a knife hidden under his cloak. Sonja walked behind Dalen, as a respected but not fully trusted gladiator, and behind her was Aria, a final "guard." She and Dalen wore the uniforms of the guards they'd killed only half an hour previously. Aria seemed particularly vulnerable, as even the smaller guard's armor was overlarge on her petite frame.

Grapas spoke to the man at the stalls, who was agreeably intimidated by the guardsman's rank. "We'll need four horses, good stable master. Oh, and make one of them the horse we liberated from the prisoner two days back, a chestnut roan, I believe?"

The man in charge of horses had been assigned the post as punishment by his superior officer, who quite felt that endless days of cleaning shit out of the wooden stalls would be "character fortifying" for his imbecilic brother-in-law. His expertise in the field of horses lay mostly in avoiding being kicked or thrown, but he was only partially successful in this regard.

"Oh, I wouldn't, sir—he's a mean 'un. Bites. Kicks too. Loves his feeder, hates his rider, I say of him. Can I get you a nice overlander? Calm as kittens."

"The chestnut, good sir. And my commendation for your excellent advice. I will be certain to mention it to the deputy mayor."

The man brightened visibly. He only hoped that the white-bearded guardsman might pass on his regards *before* the horse threw and trampled him. "Faldo is the name. Thank you, thank you, sir!"

When he returned, with four horses on two leads, a strange thing occurred. The vicious, untrainable horse, the horse that had sent two of his assistants to the healer with broken bones, pulled the lead right out of his hands to run to the redheaded woman, who stepped toward the largest of the horses and threw her arms around his neck. He was not a poetic man, but even the awkward Faldo was moved to compare the two, both beautiful and dangerous as a night viper.

Grapas knew enough not to caution the Devil. Dalen and Aria stared with understanding and jealousy. A Hyrkanian could love many horses.

But they were lucky if even one in their life truly understood them.

They were half a day's hard ride from the Zamoran border along the Bleak Road, back the way they had come, now heading toward Hyrkania, instead of away from it, when Sonja called the quartet to a halt. She had not spoken the entire time, whether processing what she'd been told and weighing the truth of it on the only scales available or being reluctant to share the information in the presence of a loyal Zamoran, the rest of the group did not know.

They did not stop for water or feed. It was as if Sonja recovered her full self only while on Sunder, and stopping even for a moment was not to be borne.

But she finally put her closed fist up, and all stopped. Grapas sighed, certain that his compliance had done nothing but delay the inevitable. He seemed to sink into his saddle.

Aria stared at Sonja, gauging what was to come next. Sonja pulled her borrowed sword from its sheath and faced the Zamoran.

Dalen spoke, calmly but with conviction. "We do not need to do this; there's no benefit to us, lady. He's done nothing to us."

Grapas grimaced. "She's already chosen, lad. But thank you."

Sonja rode to where Grapas's mount stood, and she laid her sword casually on the guardsman's shoulder. If she simply withdrew her blade quickly, she would slice his throat, quite likely to the bone.

"I have, Grapas. And you did save me from the inconvenience of death or worse. On the other hand, you jailed me, stole my horse, and threw me in a gravel pit to fight two of the ugliest bastards I've ever seen. Hard to forget, you understand."

Grapas said nothing. He'd recovered his pride.

Sonja leaned in but didn't remove the sword. "If what these two former rodents say is true, guardsman, there are going to be refugees from my country by the hundreds. Thousands, perhaps. And having few options, many of them will attempt to cross your border. Do you understand?"

Grapas nodded. Carefully.

"So you will tell your mayor this message from the Devil. From Sonja the Red," she said, steel in her voice. "He will make room for those seeking safety in their time of want. Every single one who shows at the door. They will earn their keep; they are used to working for their supper."

Grapas showed no emotion at all.

Sonja smiled. "I understand. You are envisioning his response to this message. No doubt his court will laugh."

"It is quite likely, lady. They care not for the troubles of your kind."

"Yes. So add this to the end. Tell his lordship that if he fails to heed my request, I will place the Curse of the Hyrkanians upon him. Not his people, not his soldiers, but him."

Grapas blanched.

"Every wound, every injustice visited upon the refugees will be thrice paid for. It will be an end so excruciating that his own family will run from the mention of his name. I will see it done. If not myself, another Hyrkanian will fulfill the curse. And if no Hyrkanians are left... then our bloodless ghosts will come at night, and that will be the worst result of all. Do you understand?"

Grapas only looked ahead.

Sonja nicked his throat to bring his attention back to the road and blade. "Last time. Do you understand?"

He nodded, unable to speak.

She slapped his mount's flank and sent him on his way.

"Goodbye. And thank you," she added, under Dalen's judgmental glare.

When they turned back to face Hyrkania, the three remaining in the company realized there were two more riders on the road, facing them, riders who had taken advantage of their distraction.

The lead rider was Ysidra, Queen of Nomads.

24

PUT THE SUN UPON ITS TRUTH

History is written by a ship shrouded in fog. We may see the calm sea in front of us and completely miss the mountainous coastline beside.

Kia Aberahti, *Wisdom of the Prophets*

Yvaq was a trading city in Hyrkania with a small population for its economic importance. Though solidly loyal to the Wooden Throne, the population was in constant flux as craftsmen and merchants came from four countries to trade their wares in the giant marketplace.

Only Hyrkanians were allowed to buy land officially, but anyone with enough wealth could easily find a proxy or bribe a landowner. During the warmest seasons, it was one of the few thriving sources of revenue in the kingdom. Purchasers came for crafts and horses; sellers came bringing virtually everything else.

Because the entire region benefited from Yvaq's prosperity, it had lost all pretense of having any standing soldiery to speak of. The small armory and barracks currently stored grain and were watched by a rotating shift of two guards sharing one cot and cooking fire. The walls that were to have been built to protect the city's banks were abandoned and left unfinished. It was common to see plants growing in rows upon the remaining skeletal turrets.

There were thieves. And the local khan, Asran Kiat, knew how to catch and deal with them so swiftly and silently that custom was rarely interrupted. Thus, though he had never held a proper sword, not even at celebrations or council functions, he was well liked by the only real power that mattered in the area, the movers of money, and King Gahresh found his rule useful.

He had been kind. No one, not even thieves, had been executed under his two decades of oversight. He allowed his wives lovers, having little interest in amorous pursuits himself, and not wishing them to want for physical affection. And he presented a figure of prosperity himself, being a generously proportioned man of immaculate dress.

Seeing him dragged through the dirt of the market square to the town dais, clothes torn and body bleeding, was a brutal shock to the populace and, under any other circumstances, might have led to an uprising. But the crowd, the city's citizens, surrounded by blazing fires and nightmare invaders, had lost all stomach for revolt.

Even the stoutest-hearted of the gathered populace kept their eyes down, avoiding looking directly at the creatures who had come to them as destroyers, and most would have traded their homes and possessions to be virtually anywhere else in the known world at this moment.

They could see the hideous, filthy bare feet of the outsiders, who were branded with elaborate, ornate snakelike scars up and down their legs, in designs that crawled up in raised, hard red flesh to their thighs and beyond. They'd been ordered to keep their heads down, but in all truth, none had needed that command.

The khan was dragged to the wooden dais, where each day, trading and town news was announced by the town crier.

His hands were tied behind his back. Asran Kiat was not a brave man, even as bureaucrats go, and he had offered little in the way of resistance against the treelike limbs of the outsiders, whose rough skin tore the flesh of his arms with each touch, and who smelled unmistakably of the grave.

He was shoved down to his knees painfully. Each contact seemed to come with enough malice to bring pain, even needless pain. He had already given the outsiders control of the market and city in his mind; he was in fact barely keeping control of his bladder.

He knew there were degrees of death. He knew there were worlds between dying in your bed, surrounded by loving faces, and the slow, never-ending death of careful torture. He knew in his heart that if he died today, it would be a very poor death indeed.

The outsider who had dragged him to the dais hit him hard with a club or baton, he couldn't see which, the tip of it right between his shoulder blades. This was not something done in haste or without forethought. It was specifically designed to agonize him, to emasculate him, in the most painful manner possible with the least effort given. He bit his cheek enough to start blood flowing down his lip, the acrid taste surely a hint of things to come.

"Eyes *down*, maggot," said a voice, and dutifully, Asran obeyed.

Two feet came before him. Grotesquely elongated and prehensile toes coated dark with dirt and the intentional branding that had appeared on the others, with thick yellow toenails, sharp and irregular. He knew looking up would bring another sharp rebuke from his captors, but there was no danger of him raising his head, perhaps ever again.

His bladder let go entirely. He was not a brave man, but he was surprised to realize he still felt capable of shame. His pale skin was covered in sweat, and he trembled visibly.

"You are the khan," the outsider in front of him said, and all Asran could think of was the voice of his father, the older man dying of infection, when this position had passed to him. He had been terrifying, in Asran's memory, even to his end.

His father had been strong. Stronger than Asran. But the khan wanted to believe even his father would have had to quiver in the face of such creatures.

His father had choked up black blood as thick yellow and red fluid was drained from his wound. And his voice had still had some thundering hooves to it, but there had been a sound in the tone, in the occasional quaver of the big man's throat, that sound of death calling.

Asran remembered. And he heard it again in the voice of the thing looking down at him.

The baton hit him again, in the same exact spot, with a ruthless accuracy that dropped him forward, face unprotected, right into the wooden platform where he had spent so many days imagining himself and his deeds to be important. He tasted more blood and found himself unable to raise his head at all.

The captor reached down, grabbing him by the hair with hands tapered into those same clawlike nails, pulling him up effortlessly.

"Cower before Emperor Tol, maggot!" He felt his flesh tear on his scalp, perhaps on purpose, perhaps from a simple inability to measure the ferocity of each contact. Blood began to drip down from his crown to his face.

"I am, Majesty." The idea of this . . . this thing being an emperor, outranking him, seemed utterly sacrilegious, and his sense of class, of lineage, ingrained in him at birth and reinforced every day by his father's hand, was lost in the dust, every scrap of it.

There was a silence; even the babies in the crowd had ceased crying.

"Do you know who I am, 'Khan'?" The voice thundered through him, to his bones.

"I do not, Majesty. Forgive me."

"It is just as well," said the voice. Tol, Asran supposed he was. "Tell me, 'Khan,' do you believe in sorcery?"

"I...I am not sure what you mean, Majesty. Forgive me, but—"

"You ask for forgiveness a great deal, man of coins. I ask you, do you believe in dark gods? Do you believe in a world beyond and below? Do you believe there are great plains where no light has shone for a thousand years?"

Asran was lost completely. "I...do not know, lord. I've seen conjurers and entertainers, but I don't know that I have ever seen anything like what you...what you are speaking of."

Eyes still lowered, he sensed the "emperor" squat before him, voice somehow more sepulchral. "What if I told you I could cut off your head and sew it to a cow's body? What if I told you I could cut you open, fill you with rats, and stitch you back up, chained in madness as they consumed you from inside? And you, 'Khan,' would live, be aware, through it all?"

Asran's skin, already pale, became almost ghostly, even where he'd hit the wooden floor. "Can...can you do that, Majesty?"

A pause. A breath. Asran waited—for what, he was uncertain.

Tol stood.

"No. We are just men, as you are. Say it. Say we are men."

"I...You...you are men, Majesty." Asran's voice quailed.

"Just as you are," the emperor said.

"Just as...just as I am."

"Yes. Yes. Thank you, Khan Asran Kiat of Yvaq. You are a most gracious host, and we accept your hospitality."

"Of course, Majesty! Anything, anything you want, anything you need!" Asran could not help but brighten at this seeming change in hostility.

"Yes. Most gracious. My followers, they do not remember the politenesses and pretty speech of your kind, Khan. But I do. And I believe there is but one last matter to attend to before we can discuss the future of this city."

Asran wept in relief... A trader! The creature in front of him was a trader—he *wanted* something.

And Asran was *lord* of traders!

"Bow your head at my feet, khan of Yvaq. Genuflect, and then discussions can begin."

Asran, in his haste, nearly fell, but he managed to bow his head all the way to the wooden platform's rough surface. He knew... he knew that he would have these drooling creatures begging for his favor once he found out what they wanted. He would own them; he would... he would conquer other cities, entire trade routes... Who could stand before him?

Tol's face gently came down toward his, close enough for Asran to see just a bit of him out of the corner of his eye. And his hope fell like an unwanted child thrown from a cliff top.

Tol spoke in Asran's ear but seemed incapable of whispering. "About the future of your city, Asran Kiat."

Asran wept, a level of terror he didn't know existed.

"There *is* no future for this city."

Tol stood and placed his rough, leathery foot on the back of the khan's head, holding him steady with the yellowed, clawlike toes, then stomped his foot completely through the man's skull and face, clear through bone and flesh, all the way to the wooden surface of the dais. The last legacy of Asran Kiat, khan of Yvaq of the Bleak Road, descendant of warriors, was a wet, popping sound like a ripe melon hit by an axe handle.

The crowd began screaming. Men and women shrieked; people bleated like the animals they had forgotten they were. A few tried to run, only to be ripped apart by the outsiders.

Their captor spoke, oblivious to the terrified screams. "What do we do with them, lord?"

Tol scraped the last memory of Asran Kiat off his foot with the rough edge of the wooden stage. He looked out at the crowd. He didn't smile; he'd forgotten how to smile many ages of man ago.

"Show them our hospitality, Garek."

He raised his arms up to the sky, and his small army followed suit, howling a sound that carried on the wind but was still somehow subterranean.

On his right arm, close to his shoulder, was a golden Asp.

25

BETWEEN LOVE AND HATE

Three bandits robbed the travelers who passed along their way;
Red Lady cut their heads off and threw them in the bay.

A dragon from Zamora burned all the castles down;
Red Lady put a saddle on and rode it into town.

A giant in the mountains crushed the locals good and dead;
Red Lady cut its legs off to crush its ugly head.

Then the king sent off his army just to bring her full to heel.
She brought mountains down upon them and told them all to kneel.

Great Tarim stood tall before her, and he warned her of her doom.
"The graveyards are piled with death, and there is no more room!"

"Red Lady, stop your murdering, for I won't warn you twice."
She smiled, drew her sword, and said, "You did not ask me nice."

Song excerpt from the northern lands
burlesque *The Red Lady*

S onja knew there was no good end to this.

The Queen of Nomads said nothing, merely looked at her with eyes that made her heart sink. The hope, the brightness that she had seen grow in their time together were gone. Ysidra's heart was shattered, Sonja knew it.

And Sonja herself was the cause.

She knew Ysidra. She knew herself. Her stomach flipped. But the instincts that had kept her alive when she should have died years ago, those refused to be silent.

Raganus, the queen's faithful guard, was on his mount beside her, his bow already drawn and an arrow nocked. Sonja had seen him shoot. At this distance, and with them caught foolishly unawares, he could kill two of Sonja's party, possibly all three. But certainly, by the look on his scowling face, the first shot would drop Sonja herself before she could clear her sword, let alone her bow and quiver.

Dalen and Aria must have known the peril they were in but lacked context for the hot rage and regret that seemed to weigh down the air between Sonja and the riders.

Sonja spoke, with some difficulty. "Ysidra. Dear one. I..."

Ysidra replied in a tone Sonja had never heard from her even in her hardest mood. "Don't call me that, monster."

Sonja hated regret; she loathed facing the darker mistakes of her life. But above all, she hated the look of betrayal in the queen's eyes.

She struggled to find something to say. "Your Wolf Pack, why only one rider?"

Ysidra's lip trembled once, and no more. "You sent two to the healer's tent. Festrel was killed two nights ago. By someone looking for you, as it turns out."

Sonja had known and liked Festrel, fully aware of his devotion to the woman whom Sonja had been sharing a bed with. He looked at her so plainly in love, all the while certain he'd been so clever in his subterfuge as a soldier simply loyal to his queen.

"I'm sorry, Ysidra. I genuinely am."

Ysidra's eyes grew hard. "Just another stone in the path of blood you trail everywhere you go, monster. Thief. Betrayer. And now murderer of children."

Sonja's puzzlement showed in her expression. "What? My love, what are you talking about?"

Ysidra pulled her sword from the scabbard at her side. "I'm talking about giving the Devil her due, her long-overdue punishment for the pain she has left behind her like the droppings of a diseased animal."

She pointed her sword at Sonja, her jaw hard.

"For my men. For Festrel. For the innocent boy. Take your sword, Sonja."

"Queen of Nomads, you are a great fighter. But you are not good enough to beat me. You know this."

The queen was unmoved. "Today I am. Today, this day, I am, Sonja."

Sonja looked in her eyes and knew at once that it was true.

She pulled and twisted at the golden Asp on her arm, trying to take it off, though it seemed reluctant, somehow. "Ysidra. For you. For the us that used to be. For your people. Take it. Take the Asp and go home. Forget me. I erred, but I never truly deserved you in the first place, and that gnawed on me every time you embraced me, every time we were alone together."

"Stop, creature of lies."

"Ysidra, I—"

"I said stop. Everything you ever told me was a lie. Every kiss, every touch, you were only thinking about the *Asp*."

Sonja shook her head. "That's not true. Take it. I'm sorry—I don't even *want* the thing anymore. Just take it and go home."

Ysidra smiled, a rare event even in happier times, completely grotesque in this moment. "I can never go home, Sonja. You robbed me of that, as well."

Raganus's face fell, and he spared his queen a glance, still holding the bow. "What? What are you—"

Ysidra did not look his way, merely said calmly, "I'm sorry, Raganus. But you have been following a campfire tale. You know I killed three elders. We will never be allowed back in our tribe. Not if we live a thousand years."

Sonja watched as the guard's face cracked. *This is the moment. This is the moment I could tell Sunder to rout them,* she thought. Instead, she fought back tears for the first time in many years. Her childhood had taught her the uselessness of tears. *Tears mean starvation; tears mean death,* she had chanted to herself.

A suddenly weary Sonja tried one last time to break the wall between them, one last time to save as many lives as she could. "Please, dear o—Ysidra. Please. Take the Asp. Go back. Try to make peace. Go build your windmills... You are their queen. Take it—take the cursed thing." Sonja's eyes pleaded. "And forget you ever knew the traitor to your heart."

The dark-haired woman laughed a deep-bellied laugh with an edge of hate enveloping it, somehow. "'Cursed thing'? At last, you say something true, Devil. You actually think I came for that... that unholy serpent?"

Sonja was stunned. "What?"

"You fool, you lying, murdering *fool.* I came for revenge, it's true. But I loathe that thing. I hated being its carrier with every bit of my flesh and bone. I was glad when you took it!"

Ysidra urged her horse to move two steps closer. "You once said I had 'haunted eyes,' Devil. That, too, was true. And soon, if you defeat me, so will you, and I will make certain that you are pushed to madness. You will beg to be free of it; amputation will seem a blessed relief, and yet it won't be enough. You have no idea of the true price of your thievery, and this alone, in all the world of swift rivers and icy mountains, brings me joy. No, it brings me unfettered delight to imagine."

She smiled without warmth as she faced Sonja. "And that 'cursed thing' will be the means of it."

Ysidra dismounted; Raganus hadn't moved. Dalen spoke to Sonja in the quiet manner of the King's Eye. "Sonja, you don't have to do this. We have bigger worries to face. We can rush them."

Sonja put her hand on Dalen's arm and smiled a hopeless smile at him. "When this is over, go back to your land, Dalen. Hyrkania calls its straying son home." She looked over to see that Aria, sensitive, insightful Aria, was on the verge of tears, holding them back only for her companion's sake, as he didn't fully understand.

Sonja pulled her sword and dismounted. Sunder stamped anxiously. She placed one hand on his muzzle. "Stand down, Sunder the Faithful. *Hralat, surit hralat.*"

The two women then faced each other, swords held away from their bodies, as was custom in duels in both their lands. Once they pulled their swords in, there would be no ending the fight until at least one sword could no longer be held at all.

Ysidra drew first blood.

26

THE WOUND
BEFORE THE CUT

"Sonja, will you confess?" said the jailer to the She-Devil.
"Mitra knows my crimes already. Let's get this execution started."

Sonja's alleged last words (unconfirmed)

Ironically, the queen's sword cut Sonja along the arm, a graze, mostly, but it would have been far worse, potentially ending the combat, had Ysidra's steel not nicked the golden Asp and diverted its course.

Sonja pulled back instinctively; she couldn't remember the last time she'd been tagged first in combat. But she knew a strength she had that Ysidra did not, could not.

Sonja was not afraid of blades. Not wounding, not the pain, not the blood, not dying. She had long since accepted that it was the likely method of her death, inured herself to the fear that even great warriors feel. When she looked down to check the butcher's bill on her arm, she felt nothing but anger that she'd let herself be touched at all.

And something else: a desire to live. Regret could come later, but only if she won.

She'd been called the Devil since she was a child, since she was Sonjita. If forced, she would unleash the truth of that name.

Ysidra came at her again in a low arc meant to build enough momentum to be unstoppable so close to Sonja's torso. These were not the dueling foils of the bored elites in Zamora; these were heavy swords—savages' swords, they were called sometimes.

Well. How fitting, Sonja thought.

Rather than attempt to block the flash of steel coming for her middle organs, Sonja spun away, fractions of an inch from the swinging blade, matching its arc to avoid the connection that would surely end the fight.

She used her pirouette motion for velocity, but she'd mischosen in the moment; her sword was in the hand away from Ysidra. So instead, she balled up her leather-clad fist and used her spin to smash her hand into Ysidra's face.

Blood splattered under the queen's shattered lip, and Sonja expected a moment of strategy and reevaluation from her. Instead, she grinned and came at Sonja, sword on high, bringing it down as a huntsman would an axe.

For the first time, Sonja realized, Ysidra had been right. This day, this one befouled day, on a duty path of nothing, the queen *was* good enough to beat her. With no room to spare, Sonja thrust her blade up past her shoulders, past her head. She held it flat, parallel to the ground, her gloved hand holding the tip of the blade, her other hand on the hilt. Ysidra's sword clanged loudly, and a shudder went through Sonja's arms, but there had been no other block that would have saved her skull from being cracked noisily in half.

Her arms felt the ache of the impact, and she knew she couldn't work up enough force in them to swing the blade while Ysidra was so close. She took one booted foot up to Ysidra's belly and *heaved* it forward with every bit of strength she had. Ysidra was thrown backward, hard, arms pinwheeling seemingly in slow motion.

Sonja caught sight of a flash in the morning sun.

Ysidra's blade had fallen from her hand as she landed hard on the stony path, hard enough to lose her breath.

Raganus, enraged, pulled back his arrow. But he'd lost his focus, and Aria and Dalen, Hyrkania's finest deserters, both crashed into his mount with their horses, hundreds of pounds of muscle and bone colliding. He howled in rage as one leg, his left, was caught in the crush of the horses. As his bow lowered, Dalen had his knife to the Wolf's throat. "I wouldn't" was all Dalen said.

Ysidra, on her back, realized that her sword was out of reach, and she began to reach for her belt. Too late, as Sonja leapt on top of her, driving her shoulder into the queen's soft belly flesh with her full weight. The queen gasped for breath, failing to take the air into her lungs. Sonja punched her face again, rocking her head sideways.

"So today was not the day, dear one," Sonja said to a dazed queen. She raised up her sword with both hands, blade tipped down, pointed at her former lover's heart, as she squatted over her, one knee on each side.

There was no choice, she told herself. This was survival, she told herself.

She hesitated one moment. And looked down between her legs.

Ysidra's fist held a dagger, the blade tip right against Sonja's stomach. Her eyes narrowed.

"You...you could've easily..."

Ysidra struggled to breathe and did not meet Sonja's eyes.

Sonja stood up in surprise and horror. "You wanted me...you wanted me to kill you?"

She had the presence of mind to kick the queen's sword away and lower her own, in case the knife, borrowed from Ysidra's guardsman, suddenly found its way to Sonja's heart.

"Ysidra, in the name of Tarim and every god living or dead, *why*?"

The queen simply turned over on her side, away from Sonja's gaze. She had rarely cried before another soul since childhood and wouldn't today. But Sonja heard her muffled sobs.

Aria came from behind, now dismounted, and placed a hand on Sonja's shoulder, a kindness Sonja deeply felt she did not deserve. "Red Lady, we can't let them follow us. You know this. I'll do it; you do not have to be here."

Sonja stood silent, wondering how one moment of weakness had destroyed so many lives.

Ysidra mumbled, not turning to look at her. "She's right. I will follow you, Sonjita. I will become your eternal shadow."

Aria waited for the word, hand on her sword.

Sonja picked up Ysidra's dagger and flung it a small distance away; it shimmered in the sun like a lake in a desert.

"No. Take their horses. Leave their gear. If you disagree, King's Eye, then you can go save Hyrkania without me. Is that understood?"

Aria looked at Sonja, then down at the queen, who was still sobbing for the loss of everything she loved. "Yes," she agreed, "but it might have been more merciful my way, Red Lady."

Sonja started walking toward Sunder, who was bored now that the fighting was clearly over. Ysidra's voice called her to stop.

"Sonja. What do you mean, 'go save Hyrkania'?"

Sonja did not stop. "If these two wild dreamers are telling the truth, which I have no certainty that they are, there is no plague. We are being invaded by monsters, or pirates, or monster pirates or some such thing."

Ysidra was silent, her sobbing replaced by an eerie quiet. As Sonja mounted Sunder, the queen finally spoke.

"May you do your people less harm than you have done me, Sonjita."

Sonja and her two companions turned and trotted away, down the Bleak Road, as if to outrun the queen's last words.

27

NO LOSS OF WORDS BETWEEN THEM

She wasn't the only legendary fighter of her age, of course. There had been brave generals and heroes of war; gladiators of great renown beloved by their audiences; even those of lower character and repute—thieves, reavers, and slayers from lands both near and far.

Many of these shared some similar origins with the She-Devil. More than one had survived a massacre; many were lowborn and rose in stature by the strength of their sword arms or the courage of their leadership.

Regardless, there was only one Red Sonja.

Sonja, who spent most of her life trying to avoid the trappings of the so-called civilized, and who would never read any of the multitude of books written about her.

There was only one Red Sonja.

And she seemed to carry carnage and chaos with her wherever she went.

Author unknown, *Artifice and Legend*

Neither party was aware of it on that day, but they were both on opposite ends of the Bleak Road between Turan and Zamora. And they were headed toward collision: Sonja's morose party and the Falcon's increasingly unhinged Blood Man.

Sylus was of two minds, more than he'd been since the stable boy, whose murder he'd already fully forgotten, when he saw the three urchins at the edge of the Bleak Road, laughing at some horrid jest (of low character, no doubt).

It was a question of approach. There was no doubt that the young peasants—girls all, he came to realize—would die. Five punctures each, no more, just enough to ensure the light would fade from their eyes for him to witness. This was not under debate.

The question was whether to simply kill them outright or to revert to his skills, his remarkable charm, before the deed. He was certain he could use the practice, after being admittedly unnerved by two separate women in two separate humiliations.

They were hardly fair sport, but he was not a sportsman. He cared not for "fairness" and, in fact, thought it quite cruel at times, to give the lesser of two creatures the belief that they had a chance, whether at the reward of a wager or freedom from the noose. Gladiators were never evenly matched, making the concept of rules governing "fairness" absurd, even malignant, in his mind. The lesser gladiator would die, and the fancy folk in the royal boxes could pretend that he'd had a chance, that they had been wise, even kind, in their "fairness."

He had no use for it.

He rode up to the girls for a better look than he'd given them previously. Close-cropped hair, perhaps thirteen years of age. They draped scraps of Turanian silk over their torn, filthy clothes, an adornment more sad than fetching. But they laughed together, a mean, judgmental sound, as he approached, and he, an evolved being, a singular creation of the gods, blushed and felt hot shame, for no reason he could understand, except that they were young and laughing. Laughing at him.

Still, he had his steadfast weapon, his blade of charm.

"Hello, ladies. May I say what a pleasure it is to see you three young women on this dry, dusty day? Becoming, all quite fetching, you are." He smiled and bowed his head, the very picture of traveling grace.

They looked at him silently for a moment, and he feared he'd overplayed his hand, that they might believe he meant something lascivious rather than perfunctory civility. Did they believe he meant to—

They all burst out in laughter. Derisive, and somehow painful. How could these three unscrubbed trash children mock him, laugh at *him*, the Falcon's chosen one, the premier Blood Man of the entire region?

"Keep riding, scrote," the obvious leader of the trio helpfully suggested. "We haven't time for the likes of you."

His surface facade slipped; he knew it. He could feel his smile crack like an egg over a fry pan. His right hand moved down toward his knife. He noticed not as his fingers flexed repeatedly. But he would stay in control; it was his gift...or he was nothing, a fraud, and that was a possibility not worth examining closely.

"And yet I have a trade to offer you, perhaps. A significant reward for no effort, and then I shall bid you good day, but you'll walk away richer. What say you?"

They hadn't stopped walking, and he was obliged to slow his mount beside them to keep up. "We have nothing we're giving, and you have nothing we want. Ride on, ride on, swaggerer."

His smile became a weight to be carried. "You misunderstand, girl. I'm looking for a woman."

This caused the trio to burst out laughing again. "I'm *so* surprised, sir," their leader said.

He shook his head. Were they really this obtuse? "No, no. A specific woman. A redheaded woman, green eyes, barely dressed, riding alone on this road? Tell which direction she went, and it's a gold coin for the lot of you."

The leader stopped, and the two other girls came to a halt immediately behind her. The laughter died as they turned their heads toward him, their expressions dour. "What would you want with this woman of yours, bluebird?"

It was almost more than he could bear, the insults, the scorn in their eyes. He longed to knife them, one at a time, watching their eyes for any sign that they had a true self, youthful though they might be. He realized that the last of them would have watched her two compatriots die unaware of the nature of their deaths, but the last one would know. She'd have seen them die. Would it alter the spasms of her own passing, that awareness?

He licked his lips.

He said, "I want to help her; she needs my aid. She's chosen an impossible task, and I want to help."

The girls didn't believe him. But neither had they eaten properly in days. The lead girl hesitated, weighing her options, then pointed east, toward Hyrkania. "That way," she said. "She'll be at the Winding Stair by now."

He smiled again, a bit of a recovery, really. Seeing there was nothing but a peasant's greed gave him his confidence back. He still intended to kill them, but suddenly, he felt like continuing the game, giving them hope before taking it away.

Three dead girls in the road. It delighted him to contemplate it, somehow.

"Thank you, ladies. I am in your debt, and as promised..." He chose a coin from his purse and gently flipped it, glittering, toward the girls. They ceased mocking him to scrabble for the coin in the sand of the Bleak Road, he noted. Even peasants could be brought to reason if they missed enough meals.

As they stared at the coin, oohing and aahing, he gently took out his knife. He'd done this many times. Many times, indeed.

But not with children of this age.

He was excited. It was almost carnal, which was a realm he'd not entered into willingly in many years.

The lead girl, sensing something amiss, pulled her crude spear in front of her, and the other two followed a split second later. They pointed their spears—sharpened sticks, really—at him in defiance.

He grinned, fully allowing them to see inside. They would not forget.

It was then that they all heard the clatter of a small caravan, nomad merchants most likely, their wares on hooks tied to the exterior of their cart. Three mules pulling, four adults visible, taking the turn onto the Bleak Road and coming toward them.

He sheathed his knife, the queen's own blade. He wasn't sure if the girls were lying or not—it seemed entirely likely that they were. But then again, they were peasants, and peasants weren't cunning enough to fool Sylus the Blood Man.

"I bid you thanks, ladies. May our paths cross again someday," he said, adding quietly, smiling, "the sooner, the better."

And he turned his mount toward Hyrkania.

Sonja had been uncharacteristically silent all day since leaving the queen sobbing in the sand next to the Bleak Road.

She had questions that needed answers, but she had lost all interest in asking them. When they stopped, Dalen caught a rabbit for a fine lunch, dressing and cooking it himself. Aria watched as the redheaded woman, of whom she'd heard so many impossible tales, seemed to shrink and shiver, though the day was perfectly warm.

Was it possible Sonja was not the great warrior of legend? she wondered.

Sonja didn't eat, despite kind Dalen's prodding. She took water from the creek, not even looking at it before drinking half-heartedly.

As lunch wound down and Dalen and Aria were sucking the marrow from the cleaned and gnawed bones of the rabbit, Sonja stood suddenly and uttered something inconceivable to both the guards, still wearing their stolen Zamoran uniforms.

"I have to go back," she declared simply.

Aria's face showed her shock. "What?"

Sonja walked past the campfire toward Sunder, who was cheerfully grazing what small amount of hardy grass had pushed through the sand and rock.

Dalen stood, alarmed. He was situated at the other end of the fire and thus found himself uncomfortably in her way. "Lady, you cannot. It's impossible."

Sonja said nothing, merely shoved him forcefully out of the way. As if she couldn't hear him.

Dalen recovered his footing. "Lady, your people need you. Your *brother.*"

Sonja reached for her horse's blankets, tossing them on without thought. "I'm going back. You two do as you feel need requires. But I'm going back."

It was Aria who said what needed to be said. "Sonja. Heed my words."

Sonja was already in the position to mount. In moments, she would be gone. But she turned her head slightly, not quite looking at the smaller woman.

"She'll kill you. Or you'll kill her."

Sonja hesitated, then swung her leg over, fully mounted.

Aria ran to stand in front of Sunder, fully aware that the horse could crush her without effort.

She said, her eyes set, "Sonja." Aria breathed in heavily. She knew this was cruel, impossibly cruel, in the face of the loss and guilt Sonja was already experiencing.

But it was necessary.

"Sonja. She doesn't want you. Can you not see that? Every moment you spend with her brings her unspeakable pain."

Sonja sagged on her mount. Dalen's face melted in sympathy. Aria wasn't finished.

"You've destroyed her. Do her the last kindness left to her, and face your horse away and never turn back."

Sonja sat in silence for several minutes.

Dalen asked his love, his voice thick and labored, "What do we do, Aria?"

Aria gathered up their few campfire possessions. "We ride for Hyrkania, Dalen. What choice do we have?"

Sonja was unspeaking, and it was entirely possible to forget she was even there as they continued down the road to their homeland.

They came by midday to a grotesque display just on the side of the road...Dalen audibly gasped. It was intended as a plague warning, clearly. But it spoke of a cruelty and spite for life that was quite beyond him.

Sonja did not look up but merely stopped Sunder in front of it and waited. She'd seen it before.

It was the small pyre, long since cold, where a family of ostensible Hyrkanians had been burned to death while in one another's arms. If her two compatriots were being truthful, they'd been killed and set alight for nothing, and no plague truly existed.

She'd ordered the old man, the minder of this hideous display, to bury the bodies, but she could see why he hadn't done that, as he was lying dead on the roadside in front of his shabby cart. Some sort of carrion eater had been at him, and she found she couldn't remember if he'd told her his name.

The burned bones hit her again. And the smell caused her to gag.

It was familiar, too familiar, even years later.

It was the smell of her village after the Kothians arrived.

She was racked with sobs suddenly. Dalen and Aria were respectfully silent.

Sonja dismounted Sunder, who was used to the smell of corpses and remained unaffected entirely. Sonja began to tear through the meager holdings of the old man's cart, until she found what she needed . . . a loose-handled and ancient spade.

Aria cleared her throat. "Sonja, lady, we don't have the time for—"

Sonja looked back at her, eyes flashing deep green. "We're Hyrkanians. We bury our dead."

In the end, they all took turns digging a hole big enough to allow the nameless family a place for the rest of all days. Beside the Bleak Road itself, the ground was heavy with sand, and each shovelful excavated let another half shovelful back in the hole. It was sweaty, arduous business, and no one spoke, not even cheerful Dalen.

In the end, they'd made it as right as they could for the souls who had perished for this hideous display, and Sonja's hands blistered, as they had when she was ten years old and the last of her tribe.

But they'd made it as right as they could.

The old man, they left for the vultures.

28

FALLING ENDLESSLY

After the great fall of Hyrkanian military might, and the slow but steady picking at the remains of the once-feared nation by the former targets of their raids and expansions, the Wooden Throne saw a decline to match.

King after queen after king promised to restore Hyrkania's "glory," though the hazy retelling of its history tended to seem both brighter and more valorous than perhaps reality would dictate.

They had been great warriors, once, sought after as allies and respected as enemies. A Hyrkanian king once held sway over every land at his nation's borders and many beyond, with few brave enough or strong enough to stand in his way. There was something in the Hyrkanian heart that ached for a return to that feeling, and many were willing to overlook the bloodshed that paid for that respect.

But there were just as many who were tired, exhausted of the conscription, the war dead, and the taxation, both economic and familial, that paid for their monarch's vanity.

These Hyrkanians adapted, many eagerly. To trade, craft, crops, and the hunt. And of course, the keeping of horses.

Always, always the keeping of horses.

The days of Hyrkania's "greatness" might well be past, likely forever.
If one counted greatness solely in the coin of the conqueror.

Evan Smythe-Wilder, *The End of the Soldier King*

As night fell on the Bleak Road, Aria watched as Sonja began to shiver, almost to the point of convulsion.

As Hyrkanians, they could sleep in the saddle, "ghost riding," as soldiers called it, the act of maintaining enough awareness, even fully asleep, to keep their mounts on the necessary path. It would not work with even the finest horse from Zingara or Cimmeria.

It required a horse of Hyrkanian blood raised by Hyrkanian hand.

But her shaking alarmed Dalen so much that he insisted they stop and build a fire. He had already wrapped his stolen Zamoran cloak around her. Aria did not argue overmuch. Seeing the state of Sonja, she began to feel that the Devil's value to the cause might be more inspirational than martial. If she lived to make it to the front at all, which seemed increasingly in doubt.

As happened often on the steppes, the sands went from burning during the day to bitter cold at night, and all were glad there wasn't enough moisture to form rain to further torment them. They found a likely spot, with enough rock to shelter them from the chill wind, and sat down to a spare but welcome fire, which seemed to rouse Sonja considerably. She even deigned to eat some of the stew Aria cooked using the last of their saved provisions.

For a time, they were almost merry. After dinner, Sonja scooted closer to the fire, for their first real conversation in many leagues.

"Why did you leave the King's Eye?" she asked, staring across the fire at the pair somewhat brusquely.

Dalen and Aria looked at each other before dropping their eyes back to the fire. Sonja knew that look; it was the look of a soldier who had failed in their duty. "We were in the same company," said Dalen softly. "And we grew feelings for each other while on guard, in the mountains. Makkalet seemed so far away."

Sonja shook her head. "I've been a soldier in many armies. Soldiers stick themselves into each other routinely—it's encouraged in some regions. They'd not punish you for that. It's allowed."

Aria spat a bit of bone into the fire. "But marriage is not. Our commander said it quite clearly: 'Bed, do not wed.'"

"Ah. You're married. Yes. And you disobeyed a direct order from your commander. You'd be hanged, certainly."

Dalen's face darkened. "We are wed. We sought to run as far as we could, become different people entirely. We are not cowards. We just..." His voice trailed off; he'd run out of words for what was in his heart.

"If you expect scorn from me, pretty ones, I'll simply remind you that you saw the results of my recent romantic choices yourselves," said Sonja.

Aria bristled noticeably. "We aren't asking for your approval, Devil. Your ardor is legend and well noted. This isn't about rutting by the side of the road. It was about a love you could not understand."

Sonja sipped the last water from her flagon. "Love. Never saw the need for it, myself. It's like swallowing a poisonberry; it sickens you more the longer it takes you to shit it out."

Dalen snorted, but a deep scowl was Aria's only response.

Sonja displayed a rare moment of tact and chose to move on. "And this invasion you mention. What is it, and why the charade with the false plague?"

Dalen responded, noting his wife's sour expression. "We don't know, Devil, not for certain. But there were defectors from Hyrkania's army, running leaderless in every direction. Brave men and women they were, but they bent to whisper when speaking of what made them flee. Something horrid, coming up from the ground, they said. Like demons, more creature than man."

Aria grew impatient and cut him off. "Gahresh, king of the Wooden Throne, and his council, they feared that if our enemies knew we were under attack, we'd have many enemies marching on the capital, not one burrowing up from underneath. As our sources say, the plague is a fraud in its entirety."

Sonja shook her head again. The fire seemed to take away the chill, even while her thoughts were cold, indeed.

Aria took note. "Is there anything else on your mind, Devil?"

Sonja took a deep breath, as if to enter a frigid pond. "You said something about my brother."

Dalen stirred the embers. "Aria was in the court's guard, my lady. A favorite of many, noted for her loyalty and quick-wittedness."

Sonja raised an eyebrow. "And yet she ends up posted to a mountain covered in snow in the middle of nothing?"

Aria raised her head, her pride rising. She couldn't help it. "There were…advances made by a nobleman. I won't say his name. He was insistent and took my lack of willingness as an insult to his manhood."

Dalen added, "You said you wouldn't ride his diseased pommel upon pain of death, also."

"That failed to further endear me, yes."

Sonja smirked. She liked this girl. She knew it wasn't wholly mutual, but she liked this girl.

Aria continued, "But I was liked and trusted. Well, it is perhaps fairer to say that like all useful servants, I became invisible to them, unseen even in proximity. 'Aria the Reliant' quickly became a fixture, like a wall sconce or a favored tapestry. I was unseen, and in being unseen, I saw much."

She stood to stretch. She wasn't used to speaking; guards and soldiers were not valued for their oration. "There was a festival. I saw two noblemen of unapproachable reputation discussing the matter.

That a nobleman's wife was barren, and they needed a child. A babe young enough to be unable to remember being stolen and sold."

Aria turned to look directly at Sonja, her eyes softening a little bit. "They said there were two survivors of the raid. And one of those survivors grew up to be Red Sonja.

"*You*, Devil," Aria said, not unkindly.

Sonja dug into her memory, to the days she'd spent a lifetime forgetting. She knew she'd seen two brothers fall.

Two brothers.

But she'd had three.

"Shia," she said. "His name was Shia."

When they cleared a small patch of sand of all rocks and twigs, Dalen and Aria wordlessly laid their bedrolls together, worn but still comfortable, made for the outreach guards of the Zamoran border. Sonja shivered, and there was a brief moment of uncertainty, her waiting to be invited, the fire still glowing softly in the dark.

Dalen said to Aria, "She's shivering. She'll need to huddle next to one of us for warmth."

Aria paused, then grunted a noncommittal sound.

"Hell with it, I'm freezing." Sonja laid her blanket next to Aria and got under, scooting closely to the guardswoman—for warmth or comfort, it was not immediately clear.

Aria sat up suddenly. "I don't want you lying next to me, Devil. Your hungers are, as stated previously, of legendary stature, and all I want at the moment is sleep."

Sonja sighed elaborately, throwing off her scratchy, inadequate blanket. "Fine. I'll move to the other side."

She stood up, and Aria couldn't help but gasp at the vision of her in the firelight. It was more than simple beauty. Something that took the air from the lungs.

Sonja started to lay her blanket by Dalen's side, and he moved to welcome her. Aria shouted out an instinctive "*No.* No. Not that side. He's only— No. He needs his sleep as well."

Dalen stated simply, "I'm not that tired."

"Yes, you're exhausted—just look at the state of you," Aria added helpfully.

Sonja stood once more, snorting in frustration. "That leaves precious few alternatives, girl."

Aria looked up again, her view encompassing all, from leather boots to hair of flames and every bit of fascinating topography in between. Perhaps she'd been unkind. Sonja had been through so much, and she was so utterly alone.

"The middle, lady. Take your rest between us."

Dalen scooted over to make room, and Sonja lay between them. Both turned toward her, putting their arms around her, to keep her warm.

But also to touch each other across the breach of flesh between them.

Sonja slept, as comfortably ensconced as she could remember. It was pleasant, and the tumult of her heart two days previous had quieted in the warmth of warm bodies and the diminishing dance of the campfire.

She was fed, she was coddled, and she had a new hope, a new reason to ride.

A brother.

If it was true. If it was true, she had a brother.

In her dreams she fancied meeting him, and in those dreams, he was still a baby, carried by their mother.

In her dreams, she could remember things she'd made every effort to forget... the placing of her bed in their house, the smell of iron from her father's forge. It was her most peaceful evening in longer than she would want to admit.

She imagined Shia playing, crawling because he could not yet walk, on the edge of the forest, making giggling, happy, nonsensical noises as Mother and Father attended their chores. Only Sonja, ten years old again somehow, could see him. As his big sister, it was a job she took begrudgingly but also adoringly, a pair of watchful green eyes on him always.

She heard a noise in the trees. Whatever it was, it was large. And her baby brother was completely unaware.

"Shia. Shia...look out. Alarm! Alarm!"

But the villagers, including her parents, paid no heed at all.

She began to run. She had no weapon; she had no help.

"Shia, I'm coming. I'm coming for you," she shouted. She picked up a stout bit of tree limb from the central firepit's supply and ran... flew, really. And when Sonja flew, she was very fast indeed, hadn't everyone always said?

"Shia!" she screamed.

A massive bear, drooling and roaring, burst through the trees, snapping limb and branch, and snatched up her brother. She heard the horrid sound of it crunching through his skull, its jaws and teeth snapping together.

Her dream went all red.

Tears meant death, she thought to herself, never fully awakening.

She had been asleep, thinking she was awake. Now she was awake, thinking she was yet in a dream.

She was alone in the dark, her comrades gone, somehow. She lay on her bedroll, under her sparse blanket. They'd left without her—of course they had, and who could blame them? She'd been abandoned so many times before, she almost came to expect it.

She looked up, and where the stars should be, she saw that a demon stood astride her. Tall and ragged, naked against the cold. She did not recognize him from the many temples she'd hurriedly passed in her travels. But she knew the source of his voice. It came from the Asp.

He was at least eight feet tall. Dirty, covered with lines of what looked like scar tissue, but placed deliberately, crudely artful, as if made by a burning rod over a period of years. The shape of spiders appeared all over his flesh.

He had long, untamed hair, full of twigs and leaves over vestigial pointed horns. His mouth protruded a bit more than was comfortable to look at, and he grinned down at her with too many teeth by half, all too pointed and white.

His fingers and toes were extended and crowned with hideous broken nails. She could see his monstrous manhood dangling down, lines of burnt tissue swirling in its circumference.

Worst of all, he had slightly bulbous eyes. The eyes of a goat, not of a man.

He wore an Asp, like hers, on his taut, scarred arm.

And he smelled of the grave.

"I found you. In the dark, I found you, female."

Sonja gasped and reached for her sword, but she could not find it in the dark.

She didn't fear death. But the mere sight of this monstrous thing and the funereal sound of its spidery voice took her speech from her.

"You don't even know what it is that you have," he said. "But it doesn't belong to you."

Sonja at last found the strength in her legs to kick away, pushing herself backward, from under his splayed legs.

She still had her knife with her, and she pulled it and held it out. Beast or man, she would not die quietly. "Who are you? What do you *want?*"

The creature smiled, revealing an entire additional row of teeth, saying nothing. Sonja was certain she would know soon enough.

She stood up. She was a traitor. She was sick and tired and unloved by anyone. At that precise moment, she was willing to spend her life slaying this abomination, if indeed it was possible to do so.

He faded into dust, his grin the final remnant of his presence.

She woke up in the throes of panic and fury, her legs and arms striking out chaotically. She felt his arms around her and struck out, trying to find purchase. She hated to admit it, but she struggled not to fight...but to escape.

"*Sonja.* You're *dreaming,*" came a voice, so different from the beast's that it seemed to her to be made of honey.

It was Dalen. He repeated himself, taking her unaimed blows. "Sonja. Calm yourself. You're walking with the ghosts."

She looked up and saw that she was still in her bed, though her thrashing had kicked the blanket and bedroll away. The two guards had their arms around her, though she'd been hitting outward at close to full strength.

They hadn't abandoned her. Dalen looked at her with concern and empathy. And when she turned her wide-eyed gaze to Aria, she was surprised to see his care mirrored in the young girl's features.

They hadn't left her. They had stayed beside her all night, and she wasn't alone. She felt a lump in her throat that made words impossible.

She reached her hands out, calmly now, and wrapped them around the backs of the heads of the pair, one hand for each, and drew them in.

"You didn't leave me," she managed to croak out, painfully.

Dalen responded, surprised, as if the idea had never occurred to him. "Of course we didn't."

Sonja closed her eyes and shuddered, thinking of the beast. "You may yet wish you had."

She kissed each on the cheek, not too gently. Dalen first, then Aria. Both seemed surprised as she fell back to the sandy ground.

"Thank you," she said, through her hoarse throat. "Thank you, guards of the King's Eye."

Aria's eyes warmed. She'd been lying next to a legend and awakened next to a lonely, hopeless woman.

"Go back to sleep, Sonjita," she said. "We'll keep watch. Rest."

Aria made to leave the bedroll.

Sonja's hand, laid flat on her belly, caused her to stay.

Sunder had watched the entire event, first with alarm, then with relief. He snorted in impatience. He'd smelled something bad, very bad, and had forgotten it almost completely a few minutes later. Now he was witness to his people talking, always with the endless, meaningless talking.

Why all this chatter? There was breakfast to be considered.

29

RISE OF THE PASSIONATE SUN

When you're hungry to your bones
A rat's as good as pheasant
But when hungry in your nether parts
There's no time like the present

Hyrkanian drinking song

Sonja's last visit to heaven had been the servants at the gladiators' suite outside the arena, and before that, she'd been athletically trysting with the queen whose heart she had broken. Neither filled her with warm memories at the moment. Indeed, she only felt her loneliness more keenly when thinking of those nights.

This was not that.

This was healing.

Aria put her hand over Sonja's on her own belly and gave a minor squeeze, wordless and somehow thrilling. She looked to Dalen, who smiled, kindly and without jealousy or even possessiveness. He reached across Sonja between them and put his hand over his beloved wife's. Their eyes made full contact.

I love you, his eyes said, and hers returned the sentiment.

They'd all be exiled. The spouses had hidden their true nationality; Sonja had been on the run from the pain her own memories refused to diminish. They'd each done everything possible to avoid speaking to others from their land.

And here they shared a bedroll. They had ridden together as Hyrkanians. They had a shared purpose.

Aria and Dalen felt Sonja's loneliness and were sorrowful for her. Even in their penniless, exhausting run from their home in the East, they had a wealth she couldn't fathom even with the golden band on her arm. They had each other.

Their brief look in each other's eyes said, *Can we share, my love?*

Yes, we can share, my love.

Dalen leaned over, kissed his wife full on her mouth, while Sonja held her breath, unsure if she was to be a witness or a participant.

Three exiles found a piece of their homeland in one another.

He then kissed Sonja, and after a moment, she opened her mouth to him.

Aria took Sonja's head in her hands, lying beside her, and kissed her with even more ardor. Their breathing became louder, and each touch more arousing.

Sonja sighed as she felt hands on her breasts, unsure and uncaring of whose hands they were, exactly. She reached down to feel the hardness of one and the softness of the other. She felt their hands touching her in unspoken unison, surrounded by heat and pleasure.

And Mitra look away, she felt the sweet softness of their lips on hers. She came.

And then she came to life.

30

ALONE AGAINST
THE BEAR

It is important to note that when serious-minded historical researchers first attempted to retrace the steps of Sonja's journey, they did indeed find a cave and pond that matched the description she'd passed on, allegedly during drunken revelry while attached as a freebooter to a ship along the western coast. The retelling of this remarkable series of events has survived only due to forensic study of one of the few remaining scrolls of the era, and that itself was told as part of a theater performance, rather than a scholarly study.

Whether confirmation bias or outright academic fraud was a factor, it is not known. Creeks and ponds dry up, land is developed, landmarks are forgotten or moved by way of nature or commerce.

But even so, the final land survey of the area does lend some small credence to the tale. There was indeed a cave near the suggested location by the retelling of Sonja's time alone in the forest. There is now a quaint village over the whole of it, and it is unlikely that in our lifetimes we will ever find credible evidence of her time there, if in fact she didn't make the entire thing up or wasn't misunderstood or misreported.

However.

It still must be remembered that as fanciful and thrilling as her tale may be, Sonja would still have been a child, only ten years old, at the time of this event. She would have been on her own and traumatized at the very least. And it is inarguable that even the hardiest and most remarkable child is still a child.

It is thus quite probable, in this author's estimation, that the young girl we call Sonja (there isn't even evidence that she used this name at this point in her history) simply could not have lived through these trials on her own and that the story is a deliberate padding of the details either by herself or by the scribe telling her tale.

And yet who is to say for certain?

Maybe in this case, legend reflects historical truth.

Pierre Roux III, *Reconstructing in Red*

Ten-year-old Sonja stumbled back, directly into the pond, her feet slipping out from under her, not in muck, but in loose shards of rock brittle enough to break under her step. And every step backward put her legs and lower body deeper into the water, slowing her escape even further.

She knew with terrifying certainty that she was about to be slaughtered. She would die of what her brother Ozkar jokingly called "claw-and-fang disease." She'd shivered at the campfire jest then, imagining appalling ferocity and speed, only to find reality far worse than her imaginings.

She'd once seen a sickly foal that'd been dispatched in the same manner. Its guts had been strewn over an area larger than her home's entire footage, and though the village had been roused in moments, the entire rear haunch was ripped off and taken before her father could put his shoes on.

The tracks had led into the forest, and her child's mind imagined, even as she fell under the surface of the pond, that this bear, the one about to rip her apart while she drowned, was the same bear that had killed the young, squealing foal her father had failed to protect.

The bear leapt farther into the pond, all four legs furiously churning the water, mouth agape and roaring, tongue horrifyingly trembling beneath its teeth of razors.

She lost her footing completely under the water and felt the brittle rock shoot out from under her sandals. She realized it was shale, undisturbed here perhaps for centuries, slippery and sliding out from under her feet.

She felt claws at her leg, swiping down effortlessly, grazing her skin. *I was the salmon*, she thought, *the fish on the headless arrow.*

She would not be so lucky again; it'd be teeth next time.

She was now completely on her back, choking and wide-eyed. She kicked her feet for purchase and found none. She kicked at the bear in panic, to no effect at all.

Failing to get her feet under her, she reached backward toward the pond's bottom and came up with a handful of shale in each hand. Her eyes were already filling red, her lungs burning.

The bear was enough of a force in the small pond that each of its steps seemed to have its own gravity, pulling Sonja off-balance.

But Sonja was fast. The fastest in her village.

She pushed herself up and back, more animal instinct than strategy, and sprang out of the water with such ferocity that the bear, who feared nothing, paused.

When her feet hit the solid foundation again, she hurled the shale shards at the bear as hard as she could. But she was ten. Had she her father's blacksmithing arms, she might even have caused the bear to consider another meal entirely.

But such was not the case.

The bear shook its head, annoyed and outraged, and roared again.

There was no possibility of fight. Her sword, her knife, and even her ridiculous arrows were on the other side of the pond, behind the bear. She turned to clamber up the side of the rocky hillock above. At first, her feet found purchase, and as the bear emerged from the pond below her on the slope upward and away from the water, she was able to move just fast enough to stay ahead.

She spat and choked out as much of the pond's green water as she could as she scrambled up the slope, her breath screaming in resistance. She would make it to the top before the bear; she was sure of it. But to what advantage? She knew the bear could climb the trees, outrace her in the shrubs. She was simply delaying the supper of her living flesh.

But then her hands slipped, and her feet again shot out away from her. The hillside was covered in loose shale. She began to slide, with a small section of the hillside's rock cover, down the hill to the bear below.

She yelled out in fear but also in frustration. It wasn't bloody *fair*. Every attempt to scramble upward only dragged her farther down.

In desperation, she threw herself painfully onto her back, arms spread wide, to slow the descent back down to the water. She summoned every bit of strength into her legs and began kicking the shale below her as hard as she could, each kick lowering her down by inches.

But the shards flew from her feet as well, and this shower of sharp rock was not to the bear's liking at all. He roared; he pounded his massive paws against the solid rock around the pond's edge. He raged like the lord of the forest he was.

But he did not face up to her, the bizarre, unknown, and terribly tenacious little creature he'd mistaken for an easy meal. After many rocks flying at his sensitive eyes and snout, he turned and headed back into the pond. It wasn't retreat; he was still hungry.

At the far side of the pond, he was distracted by the skewer of fish Sonja had helpfully stuck into the ground. He ate them in moments, gathering strength to finish the wriggling hairless thing on the hill to his cave.

But when he turned back around to renew the attack, Sonja was gone.

She had escaped, in a fashion. But she knew she wasn't safe. She and the bear could not coexist, could not share this patch of trees, nor the little honey basket of fresh water and fish below.

As she raced up the hillside, she saw a cave in the rock, concealed from most vantage points by an overhang of solid stone, topped by dirt and grasses. She'd been right under it and not seen it. For one wild moment, she headed inside, thinking, *It won't see me in there.*

Then it hit her: The cave belonged to the bear, and every day when it awoke, it had just a short jaunt down the hillside to water and food. To enter would be to become trapped, for however long it took the bear to sniff her out.

Something stubborn arose in her. Had she not lost her family? Had she not found the pond and the fish inside? Below her, she heard the bear climbing and snorting angry breath from its muzzle.

It was coming for her.

She looked about for something, anything, big enough and sharp enough to defend herself with. But the shale up this far on the hillside was smaller and thinner. It wouldn't last. There were larger, volcanic rocks, and this surprised her...She'd seen it before—obsidian, it was called—and the child in her was lost for a moment in her reflection in the black glass of it.

She found a large stone, big enough that she could barely lift it.

But from her uncertain place on the hillside, she couldn't guarantee she could throw it, let alone with accuracy.

She picked up the stone and walked up past the cave, each foot shaking with effort, each step sinking into the soft dirt and loose vegetation. Her goal was the overhang of the cave entrance. And her knees began to wobble halfway up.

She prayed, in her family's name, silently.

She climbed, pushing the stone the last few feet, with great effort, to the end of the cave entrance's overhang. For a moment, she felt it would collapse, sending her right into the bear's mouth.

She took the large stone to the edge of the overhang, as far as she dared without being seen. The bear, sniffing and snorting, now completely confident in its surroundings, padded across the stones to the entrance of its cave.

And Sonja pushed the heavy stone with an effort that nearly made her fall right along with it.

The stone made a sickening crunch as it collided with the bear's skull directly below. The bear rose up, blood running down its fur, one eye completely destroyed and bits of white skull showing. It wasn't dead.

"Hello, bear," she said. "That was for stealing my *supper.*"

And taking the two shards of obsidian she'd stuck in her belt, she leapt down onto the bear's back, teeth first.

The forest had a new lord.

She giggled as she skinned and segmented the beast, as she had once helped her mother do with the kills from the family's hunts. She laughed and capered over her campfire at the edge of the cave. *Her* cave now.

Over the next days, she sharpened the bear's massive ribs and planted them in the hard rock of the cave's entrance, points outward. A warning to all creatures, two-legged or four... Sonja lived here now, and it would be best to leave her unmolested.

She tanned the hide and used Kreval's ratty cloak to make a quite comfortable bedroll, stuffed with grasses she'd washed in the pond and dried in the sun. She even used the bear's blood to draw pictograms of her victory on the cave wall. They made her feel less alone, somehow, and she was certain that Tarim would be pleased.

And soon, very soon, she'd start on those damn wolves.

But she was ten years old, orphaned and abandoned. Remembering was painful, so she stopped remembering. Thinking of the future was painful, so she stopped dreaming entirely. Thinking of the people in the world, going on without her, without everyone she'd ever known—that was most painful of all.

So she stopped thinking of other people.

After six months, she stopped talking aloud completely, except for the brief singing of her mother's lullaby, the words of which she began to forget after a time. It left just a sad melody that made her hurt without quite knowing why.

She made her system. Harvest berries, plant seeds, catch fish, cook one, use two for bait, maintain traps, check traps, cook anything they catch, make use of the remains, sleep.

But every second she wasn't doing her chores, she was holding the sword. Kreval's sword. She'd clean it, sharpen it, look at her own reflection in its bright surface.

And she would spar with it, until the weight of it meant nothing. It was her poetry; it was her dancing. She was fine with a knife; she used it many times against predators. But the sword . . . the sword was her instrument.

On her eleventh birthday, which she left unremarked and unobserved, she would have appeared more animal than girl to most passing eyes.

And a year later, she packed up her small collection of possessions and headed for the tree line, from the only home she remembered fully.

She headed back to people.

31

THE TWISTED STAIR

ACT TWO: SCENE ONE

Sonja faces two soldiers in armor on the drawbridge of a grand castle.

> *SONJA: I seek entrance, soldiers.*
> *SOLDIER ONE: To what purpose, lady?*
> *SONJA: To speak to your king.*
> The guards laugh scornfully.
> *SOLDIER ONE: I'm afraid our king is long since past having*
> *any use for you, fair one.*
> *SONJA: Very amusing, and perhaps it is so, man-at-arms. But I*
> *wonder if you might tell him of my arrival, in any case. I*
> *would hate for him not to receive the gift I will bring to him.*
> *SOLDIER TWO: Are you mad, woman? You will not see the*
> *king today, nor ever.*
> *SONJA: Oh, that is a shame, then.*
> *SOLDIER ONE: And what gift was it that you wished to give*
> *the lord of our land?*

SONJA: *It's two things, really.*

Sonja unsheathes her sword.

SONJA: *I was going to bring him both your heads for your lack of manners.*

The two guards quickly stage-whisper to themselves.

SOLDIER ONE: *It appears that our king is indeed receiving visitors today, gracious lady. Please go right in.*

Sonja walks past them, clicks her tongue.

SONJA: ...

SONJA: *Pity.*

> Author unknown, excerpt from the Khitan spoken tradition play *Sonja the Red* (note that the translation is speculative in parts where artifactual support is not complete)

They were nearing the end of the Bleak Road from Zamora to Hyrkania, far closer to her homeland than she had been in years. They were nearly at the momentous Winding Stair, the natural rock bordering Hyrkania from the west, below the great lake.

To the immense relief of Dalen and Aria, Sonja appeared to be in better spirits, though her increasing chills and shivering made both anxious. Even while she was riding Sunder, they worried she would fall from her mount, perhaps crack her head open, and returning to their homeland with a legendary hero might be dimmed somewhat if she were no longer of the living persuasion.

But she did speak to them both, and even more to her horse, which they both found amusing and disconcerting in equal measure. She even smiled.

They both decided that satiety suited her, tremors be damned.

Aria went ahead to scout for game, a chore she seemed to relish, leaving Dalen and Sonja alone for a moment. Sonja watched her race ahead to do the hunting she normally would do for herself.

Dalen smiled. "She idolizes you, you know. Has since I've known her. You are the Red Lady. You were all she ever talked about in the frost mountains."

Sonja's look was disbelief, so he continued, "It's true. When we were hungry for the voices of strangers, she would ask about your legends and tales. You are the reason she joined the King's Eye."

"Huh," said Sonja. "She must be bitterly disappointed that I don't fit in the boots of my legend."

"You do, lady. To Aria, you are the woman of choice, the woman who made her own destiny. Kings and wizards fear you, and every morning, you decide which direction you will face, and follow that path."

Sonja snorted derisively. "I am also the woman without family, without child, without friends, without a country. And you saw how my previous romance ended. Better the girl follows in someone else's shadow, I'd say."

Dalen rode quietly for a moment. "You underserve your worth, lady. And I echo Aria's heart in this."

Sonja fell to silence.

It felt rude to continue to protest. And she did feel for them both. Good hearted, caring, and generous, the pair of them. And their love for each other seemed unshakable.

But she could not deny that at that moment in her life, with the choices she had made, she did not feel deserving of their adoration at all.

As they crested a brief hill in the road, they saw that Aria had not gone far ahead and was stopped in the road, speaking with three urchins. Sonja's eyes widened, then the civil conversation was forgotten.

"Those . . . those little *brats*. They *walked* here from Radolan? I owe them each a swat across the crown!" She leaned forward, and Sunder raced ahead, leaving Dalen in the dust.

Aria turned on her mount, momentarily baffled. The three young girls raised their hopeless spears, ready to do whatever violence had kept them alive without shelter or family.

"*Bratlings*," said Sonja, raising her sheathed sword. She wasn't going to *kill* them; of this she was certain.

Reasonably certain.

The girls raised their spears, cleverly enough, but they aimed at her, not at her mount, and this gave her pause.

"Lose your nerve, Flame Hair?" chided their leader. "Come at us, oh great warrior of the cesspit!"

Sonja stopped but did not let go of her sword. "Why are you on this road? Why are you headed east, when you know there is plague?"

But she had already guessed the answer.

The leader said, "There ain't naught plague, and you must ken that, too, unless you're more lost than you seem."

Sonja put her sword away. "You're Hyrkanian."

The girls did not lower their eyes. Penniless and homeless, they had pride and hung on to what bits of belonging were available to them.

"Yes. We're Hyrkanian, even if we aren't fancy-born like yourself."

Sonja felt a wave of emotion that was difficult to interpret, like walking through a swamp toward a light that keeps moving. "You're right. But there's evil and darkness. Go home, girls. Be safe."

The unspoken lay between them, that they had no home to go to. "That's very nice, giving us commands when we sent that loathsome gent off your trail."

Aria looked curious, but Sonja held up her hand. There would be time to explain later. "What loathsome gent, girl?"

"The man who looked like he wanted to skin us and eat the

remains, that gent. We sent him eastward, knowing you'd gone west. Now, like a fool, you've only come back this way, and he'll be waiting!" She shook her head, once again amazed at the lack of common sense that adults seemed to have.

The second of the girls spoke up. "We're goin' to fight the giant worms. You can't stop us, lady."

She guessed their ages to be twelve to thirteen, around the age when she'd still been fighting bears and living in isolation.

"No. No, I can't. Stay well. Strike from a distance; strike from shadow. Remember, above all, you are hunters, not gladiators," she said, reaching into her purse for the few remaining coins she'd stolen from Trogas the thief so many days before.

The girls took the coins but did not thank her, nor did they bow.

"*Hunters*, ladies," Sonja said, and rode on ahead, fighting the urge to look back.

"Also, you're still utter brats," she said to herself.

The incline of the journey kept going up gradually; one hill would rise, then subside a bit, just as another hill would appear. The road became rockier, less sandy, and for a good distance, there was no vegetation at all. It was the border that nature and the gods had created; man had no say in the matter.

At the apex was the Winding Stair, which was not truly either of those things, but was a series of narrow switchbacks, uneven and without rail. Even the best riders preferred to walk their horses, as the vertigo from the far, far distance to the bottom could be overwhelming to the strongest stomachs.

Sonja dismounted and made for the first of many diagonal legs of the cliff face. But Dalen bade her stay for a moment.

"It's our first time back. We never thought we'd see home again," he said. He appeared near tears, and Aria held his arm tightly, taking in the majesty of the Hyrkanian Steppes from a viewpoint made by Mitra himself.

She couldn't bring herself to point out that once they set foot on that path, they would be traitors in the land of their treason, eligible for immediate execution. Besides, if she was to be honest, she had a lump in her chest as well.

The view to the desert far below was breathtaking. Plains and rock formations that made her stare like an infant does at their mother's countenance. Bits of green fields, streams of blue from the higher elevations. It was overwhelming.

Why did I stray so far? she thought to herself. Even Sunder seemed anxious to brave the stairs, to return to the land of his birth.

Aria squinted and pointed outward, to the farthest reaches of their view. "Hold. What is that?"

She followed the arc of the girl's finger and saw it, saw the massive, still-burning circle that had been the city of Yvaq. It was quiet. She heard no moan or cry; she saw no movement save the glowing spots where a massive fire still found fuel.

The smoke was acrid and bitter. It smelled of death and irritated the eyes and nose equally.

Sonja shook her head. This wasn't war; this was...this was something even more hideous. Had they taken the citizens, all the tradespeople?

Aria put her hand on Sonja's shoulder. "Sonja..."

Sonja simply looked ahead, the lingering soot in the air making her eyes water.

"Why does everything have to end in fire?" she said, knowing no answer would ever be good enough.

The second day after meeting the urchins, Sylus knew he'd been tricked. Lied to. Betrayed.

By women, or soon-to-be women, of course, of course. He was furious, and yet he giggled in his rage. He was angry, but he couldn't stop laughing, loud barking laughter.

He finally had to stuff his head into the small outpost's rain barrel and hold it under until his survival instinct overcame his uncharacteristic mirth.

He'd find them. He'd ask for the Falcon's assistance, his network of informants. Sylus would surely have to give up something grand in return; the Falcon was not in the business of favors.

But those three children were certainly on his list, along with Ysidra and her soldier, and the redhead. Always the redhead.

He was gathering quite the little list of pleasant chores.

He'd been sent directly on the wrong path, but it didn't matter. However one denies their homeland, knowing it is in flames makes a loyalist out of most. She'd catch up.

And he'd be waiting.

Five swift punctures with her lover's own knife.

32

FULL OF FIRE
AND FURY

On the matter the other books choose not to discuss, I give you the contentious subject of sorcery.

Many will read this and scoff. This author takes no position on the existence or lack thereof of anything supernatural in Sonja's story. Certainly she believed it. It is in the record many times that she spoke of her gods, particularly Tarim and Mitra.

But religion is different, you say, and I quite agree. Few faiths even to this enlightened day are completely without some element of, shall we say, magic. Whether it be healing, miracles, arcane beasts, or even the resurrection of the dead. Are we prepared to dismiss all such parables?

And even disregarding matters of faith, there are multiple assignations of the impossible in the records we do have, from widespread countries and innumerable unrelated sources.

Perhaps they are simply tall tales. The mixing of real people who lived and died real lives and the routine mythification of their deeds is a common practice.

Or perhaps something has long since passed out of this world, for reasons unknown to all.

And perhaps one day, a fossil will appear of a giant worm with wings, or a horse's carriage connected to a man's torso.

And that day, we will have to reconsider everything we believe we know.

Samuel Brydon, *Great Monsters of Myth*

It took three hours to make it to the floor of the cliffs. Even Sunder was showing signs of fatigue, so carefully did each step have to be placed. The two horses they'd stolen for Dalen and Aria were simple Zamoran horses, almost completely hoof-blind in comparison. All involved were sweaty and footsore, and it was turning to nightfall as they reached the lower surface of the Winding Stair.

There were other routes, easier routes. But they would have caused much delay, and the simple truth none of them admitted was that they had wanted to see Hyrkania in its full majesty.

They took a brief rest, glad for the horses' spirits to refill. They drank from the small, shallow river that had the same source as Yvaq's water supply but branched out a few leagues northward. Dalen left to be sure they were not being observed.

The ride to Yvaq would come soon enough, in any case.

Sonja removed her boots to shake the stones out. The sand of the Bleak Road had been one thing, but this was Hyrkania, and it would be stones, no matter how cunningly you wore your clothes.

Aria looked at her sadly and then smiled unexpectedly. Sonja found herself smiling back, without conscious effort.

"Well, we made it. And we're not even dead yet," said Aria.

Sonja nodded. "Of that, I am not entirely certain. But it's a pleasant thought, Aria."

Aria stood to brush bits of tree needles off her mount. She was turned away from Sonja so she didn't have to meet her eyes. "He loves you, you know."

Sonja sat upright, unprepared. "What? The boy? No. No, he loves you; he only has eyes for you. You needn't doubt."

Aria continued brushing her horse absently. "He does love me. But I am a woman. You are a creature of legend."

Sonja was uncomfortable but lacked the agility to change the subject convincingly. "I'm not at all that. I never wanted to be anything but Sonja."

Aria turned to face her, still smiling. "I believe you. I believe *in* you, my lady."

It was too much for her on this day of terrible discovery, this second discussion of her value from bedmates she'd known for only a few days. Sonja stood and wiped the dust from her coverings. "I do not ask that of anyone. I do not want it."

Aria knelt by the water, cupping her hand for a drink, cold and clear. "You say you don't care about people, yet you are tortured by leaving your love. You say you don't care about your country, yet here you are."

Sonja was now annoyed. "Your man is safe from me, girl."

Aria's face was unreadable. "There is room in our hearts for one more, lady."

Dalen returned, leading his horse.

"It's time," he said.

The entire ride to the ruins of Yvaq, the smell of death loomed like a slaughterhouse left to bake in the sun.

She hadn't told them of the Hunter's Asp. Of the many, many dead souls she seemed to encounter when wearing it during slumber.

She hadn't mentioned the terrible giant thing, that demon that had spoken to her in image and prophecy. He had *found* her, he'd said. In the darkness.

And she was aware that she'd been cold, always cold, since putting the damn circlet on. Yet she was reluctant to take it off. Sentiment, she supposed.

A memory of how cheaply she had sold her loyalty and love.

Maybe it *was* a curse.

She looked at the Asp on the ride to the ruins, and its emerald eyes, eyes that matched her own, strangely, seemed to glow...How had she never noticed that before?

"SONJA," said a voice in her head, one she recognized with trepidation. It was the voice of the demon.

"TURN AROUND," it said. "THERE WILL BE NO FURTHER WARNING. DO NOT INTERFERE."

The voice came through like a befouled temple, seemingly lining the inside of her skull with acrid fungus. "What are you, demon? Why are you doing this?"

Dalen and Aria heard her talking but had long since become used to her speaking to Sunder, and deliberately left her to her privacy.

"I AM A SOUL WITH A GRIEVANCE, SONJA."

Sonja shuddered; she couldn't help it. But again, she had her special gift: She did not fear death.

"So it's sorcery. You're a wizard, then. I've killed a few, demon. Shall I tell you how they died?"

There was silence in her head for a moment.

"Badly," she said. "They died badly, is how. It could happen to you, trickster."

The voice came back, louder and deeper than before. "YOU THINK ME A WIZARD, GIRL? I AM NOT A WIZARD."

A burst of pain shot through her head, like a crossbow bolt, and she did the unthinkable. She fell from her horse.

As she lay breathless on the stony ground, she clutched at her head in pain. Dalen and Aria reacted with alarm, coming toward her to dismount.

"I AM THE DEATH OF YOUR HOME, SONJA OF HYRKANIA."

She passed out briefly. Both of the faithful, kindhearted soldiers were holding her up in a sitting position. Sunder looked at her almost apologetically.

"I'm fine. Don't fuss. It's dark. There was a stone in the road," she said.

Dalen was genuinely alarmed. "A stone? Sonja, you fell from your mount. Is anything broken?"

She stood, with some discomfort. "Quite possibly my ass, thank you for your concern."

She shook off their comforting arms and walked to Sunder, who seemed to bow slightly, as if to make her mount easier, which, to be honest, she found both welcome and patronizing.

She'd only been half-kidding; she had taken a jolt, and even sitting astride Sunder, she was noticeably tender. "Come on, lazybones," she said, and hitched her horse to a fast trot, just to prove that she could.

All three had been soldiers. In Sonja's life, she'd been a thief, a prisoner, a pit fighter, a pirate, a general, and more. She'd seen massacres; she'd seen the victims of torturous brutality that made her question the point of humanity.

But all agreed... They'd never experienced this before.

The entire city was razed. Even worse, somehow, the ashes and black scarring of the land were a perfect circle, meaning someone had tended the fire. It hadn't been left to its own course. They'd stayed to watch it burn, all neat and ordered.

There were bits of the framing of wooden houses left, some still burning, most simply smoking as the fuel that fed them became untenable. Even some of the stone and mud structures in the center of the village had burned hot enough to distort and melt partially. It must have been an impossible inferno.

They stood in the center of the aftermath, trying to comprehend what had happened here. Breathing was difficult, but all felt there should be some witness, some record that this had been a real city, with real inhabitants, just a day before.

Sonja found she couldn't speak and took a reluctant Sunder around the perimeter of the controlled burn. They met up again in the center of the black circle, still glowing red, yellow, and blue in spots.

"Whatever happened here... The people were not taken," she said. "There's not a single footprint of man or horse." Her throat caught; she knew that fire terrified horses. "No cart tracks in any direction."

Dalen looked in disbelief. "How is that possible? There would be... there would be bones if the town was burned, yes?"

Sonja's face went cold. "Yes. There would be bones. And signs of carrion."

Dalen shook his head. "Unless they buried the survivors right next to those who perished in the flames..."

No one responded; it wasn't needed. It was what they were *all* thinking. The victims were quite probably buried while they were still alive.

Aria knelt, touching a handful of cooling ash. "So what do we do? How do we fight a force that could do this?"

Sonja looked down at the pair. They wanted, needed her to be the hero she never wanted to be. But hero or not, she found she was quite incapable of letting this go unanswered.

"We are Hyrkanians," she said. "We hunt them. We find them. And we *trap* them."

Aria stood up, wiping her hands together to brush off the ash, ash that quite possibly was full of the burned remains of her own country-men. "My lady Sonja. If you please," she said, on the verge of tears, "what you told that Zamoran captain, Grapas, I think...what you told him about the curse. The Curse of the Hyrkanians..."

Aria's eyes looked up with hope and desperation.

She spoke gently, as if unwilling to share this moment with the dead. "Is it true?"

Sonja turned her mount away.

"Today it is."

As night fell and a blessed cooling of the ground came forward, Aria noticed it first.

"My lady. You're bleeding." And she pointed to Sonja's arm. To the Hunter's Asp, its eyes suddenly the color of rubies, instead of emeralds. Blood was dripping from below the circlet, in thin rivulets.

As if it had rough metal in its circumference. As if it had teeth. Instinctively, she reached to pull at it, repulsion rising in her gorge. But the harder she pulled, the more painful it became. When Dalen and Aria rushed to help her, she swatted at them, pushing them away.

"Don't *touch* it. It's connected somehow," Sonja said. "Gods damn it, it's *in* me! Am I to be punished for a harmless theft forever?"

They heard a noise behind them, a completely unholy sound, like broken bones and ligaments trying to function, and the lifting of burnt wooden walls that had collapsed completely.

They all turned and saw their first creature. It appeared to be female yet was nearly seven feet tall. One brilliant blue eye opened to look at them; the other had bubbled to mush running down its cheek.

It was nude and covered in ash. The odd, vine-like tattoos made of carefully burnt tissue snaked all over its body...Its hair was mostly burnt off at the scalp, bone clearly showing underneath. Its fingers and toes were elongated, more animal than human.

Its eye surveyed the area, as if the creature was remembering where it was. Then it muttered a grotesque screech without opening its mouth, ash bellowing out of its body as if it were a forgotten cooking pot over a raging campfire.

It came at them.

To their credit, they all three stood their ground. All three reached for their bows, Sonja with her double-curved Hyrkanian model, while the other two were forced to use the sturdy but less accurate bows they'd taken with them from Zamora.

Sonja hit the mark first, dead center in the creature's forehead. The shot was true and hard, and the point came fully out on the other side. The thing didn't even slow. Dalen and Aria, proficient archers themselves, scored hits in the heart and throat.

It slowed down not at all.

Its muffled screams were terrible; they made Sonja think of eternal torment. The two Zamoran steeds pleaded to be let free, to run anywhere, to be anywhere but in proximity to this thing.

Sunder was made of sterner stuff. Sonja drew her sword and urged Sunder toward the creature, yelling to the remaining pair of their trio, "Its eye. Take out its *eye.*"

Sunder's hooves thundered. Whatever this thing was, this terrible thing, he wanted very badly to crush it under his hooves. Foam flecked on his muzzle as he aimed straight for it.

Dalen made the target, shooting another arrow through the

thing's eye, and it let out another loud muffled screech. Sonja raced directly toward the creature, who did not retreat, even without its one terrible eye.

The creature spun, impossibly fast, and swatted its great arms outward, smashing into Sunder's front flank, barely missing the soft flesh of Sonja's leg. Its claws drew blood as the bravest horse Sonja had ever ridden was knocked completely off his feet. Sending her spilling for the second time today.

Sonja held her sword up and away from her body as she fell, Sunder lying stunned, attempting to rise, three claw scratches along his exposed side. She didn't want to accidentally slice herself or her mount in the tumble. Dalen and Aria had abandoned their bows, simply thrown them down in the mud and ash, and were coming straight toward the thing, pale and wet somehow in the moonlight.

The creature paused to scream, blind and raging, at the moon's soft light. It made the sound of rusted metal being scraped against a boulder.

Dalen, with his long legs, made it there first and sliced at the creature's torso, only to receive the same kind of brutal backhand that had knocked down a horse just moments before.

Sunder was rising, anxious to get back to the fight, standing sideways between Sonja and the creature. Aria hacked at one of its arms and succeeded in cutting nearly halfway through, but the creature ripped its arm away with her sword still in it, leaving her defenseless. The muffled screaming was unbearable.

The thing reached its clawed fingers toward Aria's eyes, intent on blinding the noisy things that had blinded it. It grabbed her hair and pulled her completely off the ground, the claws of its other hand pulling back to strike.

Sonja got her footing, squared her boots fully into the ash for leverage, and then *ran* full speed at Sunder. "Sunder, *hyakh!*" she shouted, lifting one leg up to nearly the top of the horse's spine. He froze, as commanded, as she used her momentum to carry herself up and over him, at last pushing off with her powerful legs, bounding from her horse's back into the air between him and the monster.

She screamed a scream she hadn't made since she was ten years old and slew the bear that was trying to eat her. She clutched her sword's hilt with both hands and raised her arms above her head.

When she was about to collide with the beast, she thrust her blade down from the crown of its exposed skull all the way, hilt-deep, through its brain, throat, and heart. Letting go of the blade, she let momentum carry her, tumbling through the soft ash and scorched earth.

The creature staggered, seemed to pause a moment, and then its knees twitched and buckled as it fell backward against the stone and ash, making a grotesque cracking sound as it hit, and the small bits of remaining fluid in its skull poured out in a gush.

The three took a moment to breathe, all too wary of the thing they'd just killed.

"It's a monster," said Aria hopelessly. "We're fighting monsters."

Sonja shook her head. "It's a demon, isn't it? It looks...looks like what our storyteller said of the twisted realms."

They approached slowly, Sonja moving closer to its face.

Its mouth was stitched shut in tiny, strong stitches.

"It's a Zamoran," Sonja said, astonished and disgusted. "A gladiator who refused to fight." She fought the urge to vomit.

Aria shuddered, then turned away. "It's a demon, or demon-made."

Sonja felt a burning pain in her arm, under the Asp. It felt like malice incarnate. Like it hated her.

The voice of the demon came to her, and it was clear Sonja could hear the words. "SHE'S WRONG, SONJA. WE ARE NOT MERE DEMONS. THAT WOULD BE A MERCY FOR YOUR KIND."

They heard sounds all around them, broken limbs trying to reattach. The people of Yvaq were returning.

From the ground where they'd been buried alive.

They were all around them, in every direction.

The demon's voice returned. "WE ARE MORE LIKE NECRO-MANCERS."

33

DEMAND FROM DECAY

As stated in the previous chapter, the art of warfare changed dramatically at the end of the Iron Age. Where previously, combat had been settled primarily by conscripted armies, and service was expected, even mandatory, throughout most lands, new strategic minds realized it was possible to attack an enemy on more than one type of battlefield.

There was the psychological. This meant primarily demoralizing or misinformation campaigns. Many a people were conquered after losing faith in their leadership, leading to desertion and migration from areas where armies were being culled out of the general population. After the slander was revealed, whether true or untrue, it was too late.

In this era rose the prominence of rudimentary espionage, everything from poisoned water sources to loyalists posing as locals in the enemy camp. The benefit here was that one man or small group might do as much damage as a battalion of trained skirmishers at a fraction of the cost.

But another method came into practice at this time, one that is the first tool in aggressive diplomacy to this day: that of economics.

Realistically, it became clear in this age that if you want to destroy a country, you do not need to fight them on their home field. You can starve them. Alienate them. Remove their allies. All through the judicious use of sanction and deprivation.

Simply put, a battle can wound a people. But destroying a country's trade route disables it for generations.

It is clear, historically, that once these strategists came to relevance and significance, it signaled the end of the solitary fighter forever.

Thedren Sysfan, *Economics in the East*

MAKKALET, TWO DAYS' RIDE FROM YVAQ

The king was a liar.

All kings were.

But most had a circle of faithful among whom the truth could be shared, examined, argued, and exploited. It was this circle that he had lied to, for reasons he steadfastly felt were worthwhile, even though it came at (likely) great personal cost.

Gahresh, king of the Wooden Throne, master of Makkalet, high lord of Hyrkania, commander of the King's Eye, and everlasting general of the Assembled Glorious Cavalry of the Steppes, had made his choice. He was the official descendant of Danska (though he had serious doubts about the truth of that claim, as well), and he had been placed in the position of leader during the worst time since the fall of Hyrkania, many centuries past.

He had sent his son, Arahka, on a hopeless mission, protected by a chosen handful of elite guards and his most trusted general,

Dahmarhk, veteran of many bloody campaigns and a thousand unpleasant duties. He had told his son that the mission was glorious and vital to the continuation of their line and land.

It was a lie.

He'd sent his son on an impossible mission, and in the wrong direction, with the aid of Dahmarhk, who was almost a father to the prince, and more than willing to take this last mission, regardless of what it meant to his honor and name.

There was no glory to be had in the task he had given the prince. The truth was simpler but could never be conveyed aloud to anyone save Dahmarhk and the king himself.

He had sent his son away because he knew in his heart that Makkalet would fall. These invaders had demolished Yvaq in the space of an afternoon, and that city no longer existed. Makkalet, being the capital, was fortified with great stone walls and guarded parapets. But there were no walls that could repel these invaders. Makkalet would fall, and everyone in it would die or worse.

He intended, however, to go out howling.

Gahresh had never been a great warrior. In his lifetime, it hadn't been necessary. But now, sitting on the throne commissioned by Korath the Wise, drinking excessive amounts of his private stock, surrounded by the carved wooden scenes of great victories and acts of valor, he felt that, at last, he would take his place among the great.

He would be dead. But he would be legend.

And his son would be alive.

There would be no happy ending to this story, he was certain. His son would not return in triumph, not against these monsters. The Wooden Throne, symbol of a new and better Hyrkania, would burn to cinder, and his own head would likely be displayed as a reminder of who really owned this land.

But his son would be alive.

A bit unsteadily, he called for one of the King's Eye to bring him his sword, and woe betide all if it was brought to him less than gleaming. After a time, his dressers fastened his cloak, and he went to inspect his troops. Sword at his side, helmet in his hand.

He went out to face the damned.

Sonja, Dalen, and Aria naturally and wordlessly flanked one another. Sunder cantered anxiously...He loved a fight; he wanted no part of whatever this was. The Zamoran steeds had been let to leave the area, but fear kept them from going too far—they seemed to need to remain in eyesight of their human protectors.

"Your bows, where are they?" Sonja asked, without turning her head, as the dead, fallen citizens of Yvaq, living beings just a day ago, began to crawl their way from the dirt and ash.

"Hideous" did not begin to describe them. Their skin was of bluish or greenish pallor, their eyes bulbous, as though they had died gasping and their faces still reflected that. Most were carrying grievous wounds; many had had limbs ripped off entirely, and others had had much of their flesh removed in clawlike relief.

The story of the attackers was told in the open wounds of their victims.

They began to walk toward the trio. "We dropped them, my lady, back at the epicenter of the black circle," said Aria, who fought to keep the quaver in her voice to a manageable level.

"All right. We move slowly. Don't break the triad; watch your partners' backs. You are the only shield they have," she said. Sonja was not afraid of death.

But this wasn't truly death, was it?

Dalen spoke as they moved in unison, cautiously. "They're not like the demon. They're smaller. Less...manipulated."

Aria responded, as they were almost at the bows, "That wasn't a demon. I know what it is; they spoke of it in whispers in the king's court."

Sonja, without turning her head from the creatures, shot back, "Well, perhaps you might be good enough to tell us before we die. I hate unanswered questions."

The sarcasm meant nothing to Aria, who was truly terrified. "It was a gaunt. They walk between life and death, forever starving, forever wanting. And they live in jealous hatred of the living every moment of their miserable existences."

"Upon reflection, keep any further information to yourself, please," Sonja said.

Aria didn't listen or couldn't help herself. "These are their dwyers, the recent dead, mindless on their own, under the thrall of the gaunt lords. I thought all this was nonsense."

Sonja raised her sword as threateningly as she could. The creatures made no attempt to stop or slow their progress. "And yet here we are."

Dalen broke ranks to put a hand on Sonja's shoulder. "We don't all have to die, Sonja. You have Sunder. Take Aria and go. I'll keep them… entertained." He raised his sword, and Sonja saw the steel in his face.

Aria cried out, "No. *No.* That isn't a strategy—that's death!"

Those of the creatures that still had working eyes stared silently at the three, their milky irises reflecting like silver in the moon's harsh light.

"Nevertheless," Dalen said.

He took his bow, already covered with ash, from the ground, and broke from the trio, running headlong toward the dwyers, and Sonja held Aria back as she screamed.

"We have doubled the men on the watchtowers, sire. None will approach the Stone Gate without being seen, I swear it," said Commander Sagja, standing in for General Dahmarhk in overseeing the city's defense. He was bright and a loyalist, and his courage could not be questioned.

But he lacked imagination, and Gahresh was certain he would not survive the invasion. He had the use of only one hand, for one thing.

"One soldier each in the towers, Commander, no more," replied the king.

The soldier's face fell. "But, sire, surely advance warning..."

"The attack will not come riding and carrying banners and playing the flute, soldier. I've told you, place your watchers on the ground *inside* the walls. At distances where at least one other sentry can see them. The first hint of a tremor, sound the alert. Is that clear?"

"Yes, sire."

"I want carts, with barrels of lamp oil, at every key crossroad in the city, and a lit torch for every sentry. The moment the ground opens up, dump the oil in the aperture and throw the lit torch down after. Is that clear?"

"Sire, what is it we're facing?" asked Sagja, utterly puzzled.

"I don't know for certain, valiant Sagja. But whatever pops out of those god-cursed sewers, lay at it with every blade and arrow in the city. Do not cease until whatever foul thing arises is in pieces at your feet. That is the command of the king."

Sagja straightened. Strategy was not his strength—he knew that. But defending his people, his king, even to the point of death? That he could do. "It shall be done, sire."

They felt a sudden vibration and heard a deep thunderous sound coming from the dirt below their feet, like a boulder falling from a great height onto a rocky surface far below. Braziers and trade goods fell, and the king himself nearly lost his footing.

Sagja drew his sword. "They're coming."

Reluctantly, Gahresh drew his, as well.

"They're here," he said.

Sonja was not prone to freezing in battle. But for a moonlit moment, she was uncertain what to do.

Dalen was firing his arrows at the undead Yvaq citizens. It did seem that an arrow to the brain took them down, unlike the hideous thing Aria had called a gaunt.

But there were too many. And Aria, struggling in Sonja's arms, would not be reasoned with. She'd follow Dalen to death—hells, she'd *leap* to follow him. Dalen's plan was sound, but she could save only one; Sunder could not fully gallop and maneuver with three adult riders.

"Let me go, gods-cursed fraud! Stealer of dreams! Let me go," Aria screamed, which seemed to attract more of the shambling corpses.

Sonja decided on a plan. She pushed Aria none-too-kindly toward Sunder, who was clearly receptive to any plan that involved leaving this foul-smelling area and the shadowy remnants that walked upon it.

"No. I won't *leave* him," she shouted.

"We're not leaving him, girl. We're just giving him some room."

Reluctantly, Aria climbed aboard, already drawing back her bow and firing twice before Sonja could get her leg over to the other side. "Sunder, *han-yash*," she shouted, and both women had to hold on as best they could as the roan ran directly toward Dalen, surrounded by the foul things.

Dalen had acquitted himself honorably, Sonja noted, as at least six of the bodies had returned to what she hoped was their final rest. His blade was coated in the blackish ichor that had replaced or curdled the lost souls' blood. Each stroke made a wrenching sound, like dropping a too-ripe melon.

"*Sword, left*," Sonja said simply, not turning to look at her passenger. She herself trusted Sunder to steer and placed her own sword in her right hand, to the opposing side of his great flanks.

They ran directly through the center of the mass of shuffling bodies, Sunder's hooves and momentum crashing many into broken dolls in the ashy mud, as Aria and Sonja messily decapitated each head that came into their vector. For a moment, they were a death engine.

One of the dwyers latched on to Dalen's sword arm with its teeth. He switched his blade to his other hand and re-killed the foul thing, but its bite was deep and venomous.

Sonja, finally at her target, chopped brutally enough that the head of the thing and most of one arm and shoulder slid away noisily.

Aria shouted, "We could make for one of the standing stone buildings, barricade the door somehow...?"

Sonja thrust her blade through another throat and twisted. "They come up through the ground, King's Eye. We'd only be offering them a more comfortable place to murder us in."

They were surrounded. They could dismount and resume their back-to-back defense, but that would leave Sunder's might unused. And he could not carry Dalen. Aria watched in sad assessment of their odds as the gap they'd just made with their mounted charge filled in with moving bodies silently.

Dalen slashed two bodies at once, but the blow was inaccurate, and both needed a second slash to the throat to put them down. Either he was fatigued already, or...or the bite was infectious.

Finally, Sonja spoke. "All right, dismount. Get off."

Aria began to protest but did as she was told.

Sonja turned to her comrades. The blackish blood of the dwyers had spattered her face, giving her a savage aspect. "All right. This is the plan. Sunder will run a straight line through the mass. We follow behind him as a phalanx, as quickly as we can. Whatever sorry excuse for a path he clears, you follow, do you understand?"

Both of the disgraced deserter guards nodded. Even in exile, they'd come back for king and country and would die for that cause. And no one would ever know.

Yet they did not hesitate.

Dalen spoke, smiling through the blood and ash. "This isn't going to work, is it?"

"No. Now shut up and get ready to run." Sonja held her sword in one hand and her dagger in the other. She slapped Sunder's rear flank hard with the flat of the sword. "Sunder, *gyash*."

The horse took off, and to their credit, for a moment, the trio kept up, as bodies were knocked sideways and flung into broken heaps, some of which still tried to move and crawl in their murderous lust.

It was not enough. A stray shambler had retained enough sense to carry a scythe and manage to graze Sunder's chest in passing. Panicked, riderless, the horse regressed to instinct and bolted haphazardly, leaving a path the runners could not follow.

They fought like lions.

It was not enough.

"An honor to die with you both," Aria said.

"Oh, do shut up with that," Sonja said. She grabbed her arm and kissed her tenderly on the mouth, her own mouth parting slightly. She couldn't explain it; it simply made sense at the time. Regrets were for sitting at home by the fire, and this was whatever was the furthest opposite pole from that.

Aria then grabbed Sonja's face in her hands and returned the kiss with even more fire. None of them said anything; they all merely smiled, that grin that comes when death is inevitable but you are glad you don't have to face it alone.

They turned their backs to one another, ready to face the onslaught for as long as they were able. The shamblers, numbering perhaps two hundred, converged on them. A thundering began on the edge of Sonja's hearing, the blood in her veins pulsing more vigorously for this, her final moments.

Sonja's last thought in that instant was to hope her horse was safe and headed as far from here as hooves could carry him.

The grim silence of looming death was shattered by the sound of thundering hooves.

It was a company of soldiers, Hyrkania's finest, racing down the slope toward the black circle, arrows flying expertly, cutting down entire swaths of the creatures. Carefully avoiding the trio in the center of it all.

As the company came closer, Sonja saw its banner, the horse's head banner of the prince, and indeed, recognizable by his finery, he was leading the charge, an older veteran at his side. The company shouldered their bows and drew their swords, a magnificent display.

The trio still had creatures to dispatch and did so joyfully. Aria let out a soldier's war whoop, loud and clear.

And then it was bladework for all until their sword arms were numb with exhaustion.

34

HEALING TOUCH

Our faces spoke of anguish,
and our bodies quaked in fear.
"Take the low road," spake the king,
"for you're not welcome here."

We pleaded for kith and kin
not to simply disappear.
"Leave our city," spake the king.
"You are not welcome here."

We climbed into the hole they'd dug,
forced down by blade and spear.
"We bury you now," spake the king.
"You are not welcome here."

Author unknown, verse found
during Gahlitzah archeological
expedition

To the surprise of many, Gahresh, king of Hyrkania, was turning out to be far more of Danska's lineage than any had thought.

The first of the eruptions, as the guards had begun calling the mounds of dirt, stone, and rock that bloomed up from below in the city's streets, had still managed to startle the citizens despite the warnings of the king. The mounds had a terrible odor and made an explosive din when erupting through the pavement stones of the city's roads. They never appeared inside houses or stalls; they avoided the rudimentary sewer system. Whatever other hellish thing they might be, they were not random.

The first to come through, in the largest market in the city, was a missed opportunity. The guard had not been prepared for the swiftness of the bulge in the road, and the fleeing craftspeople, fearing an earthquake, knocked over the cart with the barrel of oil and the torch along with it, setting a good portion of the area on fire and missing the target entirely. The sentry sounded the alarm, and soldiers arrived in numbers, swords and distinctive double-curved bows at the ready.

But nothing emerged from the eruption. The soldiers were terrified, to be truthful, but were eager to shed blood to prove their courage and valor.

But nothing came from the eruption.

Nothing except an unsettling moaning sound and the odor of the abattoir.

A second barrel was hastily brought from another sentry point, poured heedlessly down the gap in the top of the mound, and set to burn by torch. A man's screaming was heard, hideous and prolonged. Another smell was added to the terrifying scent wafting from below: that of burnt flesh.

The sentries took this as a good sign; they'd repelled the invaders before the attack had even truly begun. Gahresh was not so sure.

Commander Sagja approached with a salute. "I'll muster a party, sire. Stalwart fighters, all, to send into the breach below. With your permission, I'll lead the way myself."

The king shook his head. His commander was more brave than wise. "No, Sagja. You are not expendable. You are not allowed to die; that is an order. Do you understand?"

"But, sir, they're on the run... They didn't know we were expecting them."

"That world is not ours, Commander. We have no chance squirming after them in the tunnels only they have traveled."

The alarm sounded again, from the other side of the city. Soldiers broke ranks to go protect the sector, leaving their area unprotected. Citizens fell or were pushed out of the way.

The second mound appeared, and this time, the sentries responded flawlessly and with speed. Dozens of arrows were fired into the gap in the mound's center, followed by the barrel of oil, once again lit on fire.

And once again, there followed a cacophony of agonized wails, but blessedly, this one was much shorter. Three more times this pattern occurred, each time having a more unsettling effect.

The enemy was below them but unwilling to surface. Gahresh surveyed the last eruption, still churning smoke from the burning fuel spread below.

What was this tactic? Were the creatures simply so alien that they did not understand warfare, but only the massacre of unarmed citizens?

Whatever the motivation, it unsettled the soldiers and rattled the nerves of the city's population. Some citizens had taken to pounding their fists on the gates to be let out, fearing the collapse of the ground beneath them more than the orders of the soldiers. Others climbed onto the tallest roofs they could find, and more than one had fallen when a tremor came concurrently with the eruptions.

It became quiet for a moment. No one spoke. Everyone waited for the next eruption. And it came, but not like before.

Each mound, all at once, vomited up a series of bodies.

Even the king and the commander stepped back as a man's corpse, dressed as a soldier and charred through to the bone in places, landed at their feet, broken like a wooden fork smashed against stone.

His hands were bound, and his face, half burned away, showed he was alive when his own comrades poured the burning oil down the gap. He ended in agony, it was clear.

Sagja knelt, his face confused and angry. "I know this soldier. He's assigned to the—" Sagja stopped and looked up in every direction around the city. "Eastern watchtower."

The king followed his gaze. Every parapet, every watchtower within his line of sight, was empty of men.

Then began the screams of the widows and orphans.

It turned out to be a taxing business, killing a town that had already been killed.

When the bladework was done, the crown prince, Arahka, dismounted, and his advisor and protector, Dahmarhk, did not. They both approached the exhausted, blood-splashed trio.

The prince was handsome and had proven himself valiant. But Sonja had no love for monarchs and little ability or desire to hide that predisposition. Dalen and Aria immediately knelt deeply on one knee in the bloody mess around them. The prince surveyed the area and noted the mass of dead dwyers surrounding the three.

"Well, well. This is indeed a strange sight. A Hyrkanian woman traveling with two Zamoran soldiers? I imagine there's a tale to tell in this," said the prince, with a slight grin.

The pair knelt even more deeply. "Your Majesty...," they sputtered, but neither seemed capable of continuing the discussion.

Sonja bowed perfunctorily but with a genuine gratitude she hoped would make up for her lack of due worship of the throne. "You arrived just in time, lord. You have my thanks."

Arahka looked at her with a sideways glance, amused at her impertinence. He was about to speak, when his general, still mounted, interrupted sharply. "Raise your faces, soldiers. Let me see your eyes." Dahmarhk's voice was iron, with no sense of the civility the prince had shown.

Dalen and Aria raised their heads but still kept their eyes looking down, through habit and training. "I know these two. They are not Zamoran, unless they have tricked their way into that country's armed guard. The girl stole secrets of the king himself to sell to our enemies! They are deserters and traitors to the court."

The loyalists that they were, they did not utter a sound in their defense.

The mood of the gathering instantly changed. Grimly, Dahmarhk gestured to his captain, a trusted vet of many campaigns. "Captain, I order you, tie these traitors to the fastest horses we have, and ride them over the steppes until the flesh is gone from their treasonous bones."

The captain pulled his sword, without hesitation, and began to dismount. Dalen and Aria clasped hands tightly; they'd been preparing for this since the day they left the mountains.

Sonja found herself responding without thinking. She drew her bloody dagger, dripping with ichor, and stepping behind the prince, she put the blade to his throat. "I wouldn't, Captain."

This garnered the attention of every soldier in the company. They'd rescued traitors, apparently, and it put them in a cantankerous mood. Twenty bows had arrows pointed at Sonja in moments.

Dahmarhk was aghast; this was simply too much to bear. "From your voice and bow, I deem you a kinswoman. What kind of Hyrkanian-born would threaten the future king?"

The prince calmly added, "I have just been wondering that same question, my lady."

Sonja felt slightly embarrassed. "Look, it's not as if I *want* to kill you or anything."

"That is pleasant news, indeed, my lady," answered the prince. "What is it exactly that you *do* want?"

Admittedly, she hadn't quite prepared for this line of questioning. "All right. Good question. Yes. Well." She nodded toward her traveling partners, still abjectly bowing in the ash and blood. "Those two. I would very much request that you not murder them, if it's all right with you."

Dahmarhk fumed. "And what of their knowing treason, lady?"

"Their only crime"—gods preserve her from ever needing to utter such a poetical statement again—"is being in love." She felt like a bard. It was a revolting sensation.

The prince nodded. "I see."

"They may be deserters, but they came back, under penalty of your stormcrow general's bad disposition, to fight for you and for Hyrkania. Would their deaths not serve you better if they arrived while slaying monstrosities? A waste of good soldier flesh, I say, to simply string it out over leagues of stone when it could be on their bones, doing your good works."

The general scowled. "You're not seriously considering this, my prince? What happens to the next batch of deserters and cowards? Do we deny them their seconds at supper?"

The prince nodded sagely, as if considering. "A trade, then, my lady. Surely you would agree that their lives are worth bartering for?" A brave man, to negotiate with her blade at his neck.

Sonja listened but did not drop the dagger. "What trade, lord?"

The prince stood straight, tall enough that Sonja had to change her hold slightly. "The cost is this, Sonja the Red. Their lives, their history forgotten, for your vow of servitude to me."

She bit her lip in frustration. "You know who I am."

He smiled, as if there were not a blade at his throat. "I had thought you a legend. But in your pride and arrogance, I honestly fail to see how you could be anyone else."

*   *   *

She tried defiance, but she knew he'd outmaneuvered her. "I do not bow to monarchs or thrones."

"It is not my father, nor the chair he sits in, that you would swear your oath to. It would be to myself, and no other, and the oath would end with my death. Is it agreed?"

In her life, all her life, Sonja had valued freedom above all else. This oath, she knew she would regret it. She knew what she was giving up. "Agreed."

"Agreed, what, my lady?"

She lowered her dagger. "Agreed, Prince Arahka, son of Gahresh."

Sonja silently cursed herself. *Weakling*, she thought. *Sentimental child*, I am.

She handed the dagger to him, hilt first. She stepped in front of him, making as if to kneel, but he held the dagger's blade on her shoulder gently.

"That won't be necessary, Sonja. I think I prefer you standing." He spoke to Dahmarhk, in the voice of command. "They're all wounded. Take them to the healer; get them looked over."

He walked over to where Aria and Dalen still knelt, and pulled his sword. For a moment, Sonja felt she'd misjudged him and he was going to murder them for her effrontery. But he simply laid his blade upon their shoulders in turn. "Rise, former soldiers of the King's Eye. I say that your position and rank are to be restored, pending oversight by a captain of my choosing."

The pair kissed his hands, grateful tears flowing from their eyes, and for once, Sonja did not equate the tears with darkness. They both ran to her arms, and she briefly held them, allowing their joy to wash over her.

She had to let them go, of course. Such displays in front of the enlisted soldiery were quite looked down upon.

The prince smiled, a kindly smile that Sonja quite liked, as she found she quite liked the man bearing it.

"Welcome home, warriors," he said.

From a distance, they were being watched.

It had been four hours of anxious waiting in Makkalet, and to the king, Gahresh of Danska's line, the silence already felt funereal.

There had been no further eruptions, no voices in the night. No theories on how twenty sentries, trained guards all, had been plucked from towers and turrets and dragged underground without being seen or heard.

The silence was unnerving. Like having the enemy hiding in your home as you try to pass the hours until they strike. Gahresh had ordered each mound flattened and filled in with broken bits of glass, sharp stone, and pottery, and each flattened pile covered with over-turned carts and stones rolled from just inside the gates. It wasn't much, but it would make entry through those venues very painful and difficult indeed.

Commander Sagja approached, saluting with his right arm, the effect all the more powerful considering he had lost his right hand in battle years ago. Defending the crown, defending the city. A soldier's sacrifice.

Gahresh felt the weight of thousands of lives on his shoulders. It was dark, and he strongly felt that if the enemy were to attack, they'd attack under cover of darkness, where they held every significant advantage. Yet so far, nothing had presented itself, no message, no asking for surrender, no attack.

"My liege," began Sagja, speaking slowly, as though hoping to delay a conversation he knew to be inevitable.

"Yes, Commander," said Gahresh, who had been on post for

hours, alongside the men and women who guarded his life. He didn't know their names and felt that he should. Dahmarhk would know; he knew them all.

"It's...it's simply this, sir. I feel I could be more efficacious to you if I knew what these things *are*."

The king smiled. This was as close to disloyalty as the commander could get, it seemed. "Yes. I wish I had a better answer to that, my friend. No one alive knows what they truly are now...but once... once they were cast out of this city, in the cruelest way possible."

No further explanation seemed on offer. Sagja turned to practical matters. "You need rest, sire. Rest and food. Let me be your sword, my liege—it is my duty and honor."

The king had to admit that sounded appealing. He began the process of arguing with his soldier, with the plan of eventually giving in, when there came an explosion far louder than all the previous ones combined. Sagja reacted in horror as he realized where the sound had come from.

"The *stables!*" he shouted, turning back to his king, who waved him on.

"*Go. Go*, save what you can" was the king's breathless response.

The commander took off, shouting for his soldiers to follow.

The king shook his head. The citizens could forgive the loss of some soldiers. They would never forgive the breaking of the royal stables.

Nor would he forgive himself. He felt suddenly, impossibly tired.

He saw the flames of the stables in the distance, against the far wall of the city. And he heard the cry of the horses.

35

AN END TO
EVERYTHING

She walks in thunder and leaves in shadow.

Esperanza Mojile, *Sonnets of Sonja*

Dahmarhk was not pleased and let the prince know. "You have no idea what you've done, lord. This will invite deserters in every rank. It will become legend that you can betray the throne and return with threats and protestations of regret."

Arahka considered for a moment as the soldiers set up their camp for the night. "General. Will these future deserters return protected by Red Sonja? She is practically a goddess herself in the eyes of our people. Then let them come. The woman has the status of myth... and she fights for our cause. That will rouse every farmer and blacksmith in the land. And she vowed her loyalty to the crown—"

"To you, Arahka, not to the crown."

"Fine, yes, to me. But she had a point. Two soldiers mean nothing in this battle. If they die of torture, we gain nothing. If they die in combat, at least they'll take some of those creatures with them, I'll wager."

The general sighed. "I have always been at your side, Prince. I have done all I could to raise you to lead us. If my counsel is now unwanted, that is for you to say."

The prince's face did not register the meaning of Dahmarhk's words. "Mitra's fist, General, can you not imagine it? *Red Sonja* leading our people to war, riding that magnificent beast of hers? The people will follow her to the end of everything."

After recovering their mounts, they'd seen the healers, and various bandages and unguents were applied to their minor scrapes and wounds. Dalen had required a searing for his bite, but it appeared not to be fatally infectious.

The healers were baffled at the Hunter's Asp, and the agony Sonja experienced when removal was attempted led them to decide it was beyond their skill to continue.

They were given a simple tent, built for six, but Dahmarhk had insisted no soldiers mingle with them. His ire was evident; this was not how wars were won, he'd stated. For her friends' sake, Sonja had commiserated with him and apologized, then showed a hand gesture that was a beloved vulgarity in Khitan realms the moment his back was turned.

They took supper from the mess cart gratefully. It was a simple goat soup and bread, but for three hungry fighters raised on Hyrkanian food, it was nearly orgasmic. Sonja walked through the general camp, intending to thank the soldiers for their skill and courage in the earlier skirmish. Many times her life and skill had been used without note from those she'd fought for, and she'd carried that feeling for a good, long time.

The soldiers were aware of her fame and were not immune to it, but her simple, plainspoken words of thanks made them think of her as one of them, and soon they were laughing and offering her ale, telling her of their homes and families.

In many a soldier's heart that day, a weight was lifted. Sonja the Red had returned and would fight beside them. The fog of hopelessness lifted some in her wake.

A burly bear of a soldier named Gryosk opened his tent and shouted at her, "Ho, redhead, if you really want to show your gratitude, how about joining me in my bedroll this evening? I could show you my own greatsword."

She shook her head and said, "You wouldn't know what to do with it if you found it, large one," and the company laughed hysterically, none louder than Gryosk himself. It had been decided. She was one of them.

Aria watched from a distance, sitting next to Dalen on a fallen log near the stream they'd used to water their mounts. "I'd worked in the frost mountain post for a year before my fellow soldiers remembered my name, and if she asked them to follow her instead of the crown, I believe half of them would go."

Dalen kissed her on the lips, with more passion than he'd intended. "I knew your name. It's Marja, right? Bettina, maybe?"

She punched him as hard as she could in his good arm, and they both laughed. He mock-fainted from the pain, and they laughed and gazed into each other's eyes. They'd survived so much, traveled so far, to regain their rank, country, and reputation in one evening, under this remarkable moon—it was overwhelming, and Aria's eyes began to water.

Dalen touched his forehead to hers. "The moon is making you look even more beautiful than usual."

She sighed.

"Marja."

She pulled back to punch him again, then laughed as he took her fist and opened her fingers to kiss them. "It'll be dawn soon. We had best get some rest."

She kissed him again, her tongue darting into his mouth. "I have what I believe is a better idea."

After a short time, Sonja returned to their tent. She was carried a bit aloft in her demeanor, as always happened when she had somehow survived the unsurvivable. She opened the flap, smiling and laughing to herself, the cares of the past few days forgotten. Sonja did not think of yesterday, and tomorrow was not to be known.

As she stepped in, she saw her tentmates had combined their bedrolls and were both naked in the soft moonlight. They broke their kiss to look at her sternly. "Oh, Tarim! I had no idea... Pardon me, carry on, soldiers, fine work, and good fortune," she managed to babble. The tent flap caught on her sword sheath, and she nearly brought the tent down by simply turning to exit in too great a haste.

Aria broke the silence. "The soldiers love you already, Sonja."

Uncertain what to do, Sonja nodded but did not turn around. "They were very nice. Do you know, I think I'll go see if there's any more of that goat stew in the pot. You two go about your business—don't mind me."

Aria said, with more intensity this time, "Sonja. They are not the only ones."

The Devil turned, raised an eyebrow, and remained blessedly silent for once. Aria moved the top blanket, revealing their willing flesh. In Dalen's case, more than willing, perhaps. "Grab your bedroll, Sonja. We'll make room," the small woman said, her voice honey and smoke at once.

Sonja laid her bedroll down beside Dalen, and Aria shook her head. "No, sweet Sonja. Your place is as before, in between us." Dalen reached out his hand, and she slipped out of her garments and weaponry, into the warm spot between them. They reached across her naked body to touch each other's hands.

And then they set their hands free to explore.

Then their lips.

Then their all.

They did not get much sleep that night, and in the morning, each required additional servings at breakfast.

After breakfast, it was time to decide the plan. Her friends would likely have to carry on under the general's mark. She hated to leave them, still pleasantly remembering the taste of them on her tongue. But her guts churned a little bit at the realization that she had an obligation to foster, and it hit her like an arrow. She was bound to the prince's whim, and it chafed her like a leash around her spirit. It had been a necessary choice; she would make it again. She had feelings for the pair, and her heart tugged a little with the knowledge that she would likely never see them again.

After she checked on Sunder's feed, the general came up behind her, on foot, and without the niceties of a greeting said tersely, "The prince begs for an audience, She-Devil. At the officers' camp. Will you allow me to accompany you?"

She shrugged, and they walked together. Despite the heat of the morning, he was formally dressed in full leather armor, like an avatar of a different time. As they walked, it was Dahmarhk who broke the silence. "You must understand. I have been as family to the king for a very long time. The prince is many things, laudable things. But he has a kind heart. It is my job to have the hard heart in his place. For his sake and his father's."

"Families are what we make of them, General. You have my respect for your loyalty."

This seemed to quell his resentment a bit, and he added, with emotion in his voice, "Don't hurt him or allow him to be hurt. This is what I beg of you, Sonja the Red. Don't let him down. Please."

With that, he turned and walked away. Sonja headed to the campfire, past the prince's guard, who eyed her warily, entirely without the camaraderie and joviality of the rest of the company.

She sat on a cleverly built portable chair across from the prince, who was having his breakfast alone. She felt for him, suddenly. The weight of an entire people was in his hands.

He looked up at her and smiled. "You're leaving us, I take it."

Surprised, she nodded. "I'm sorry, my lord. I took a vow and I meant it. I'll return to you. But I came back to find someone, my lost brother. And I can't do it in a dark cemetery in the middle of nothing."

"Responsibility is a choice, always, Sonja. I myself am supposed to be chasing spirits in the empty Southlands. I hope you find your kin, as I would love to meet the littermate of Sonja the Red. Do you know their whereabouts?"

"The last he was seen was Makkalet, lord."

"Ah," said the prince. "Then you must speak to my father's council. Give them this dagger; tell them I ask of them to grant you every cooperation. Fair enough?" He handed her a dagger, which was, she supposed, like many a royal...too pretty to be genuinely lethal.

She thanked him and stood.

"I'll expect that back, Red Woman. Once you have found your man. We'll figure out some way to release you from your vow after the day is won, something painless and covered in glory—would that suit you?"

She agreed that it would.

And walked away thinking it was one of the few times she'd spoken with royalty and not wanted to wash afterward.

She retraced her way to the makeshift paddock and found Sunder happily eating the remainder of his breakfast, unchallenged by even the hardiest of the other warhorses. She looked longingly at the tent where her friends, the deserters, were doubtlessly packing their gear, anxious to fight for their land and the prince who had welcomed them back.

They'd be waiting for her. And she would be gone.

Sighing, she mounted her horse and rode toward the capital, feeling very much like a deserter herself.

36

THE HEART OF
A PEOPLE

That woman. That cursed, red-haired woman.

Anonymous brigand's final words

I t was impossible, but the horses were gone.

When Gahresh made it to the blazing stables, dry hay exacerbating the inferno, Sagja was already there, stunned into silence, standing as a man transfixed and lost at the same time.

Heedless of the danger, oblivious to the heat, the citizenry crowded around the fire, weeping and shouting their outrage. To Gahresh, it seemed clear . . . He had tried to burn them in their holes, and they had sent the fire back to him tenfold.

And they had taken the soul of the city. Simply to show that they could.

He cursed. He cursed and raised his sword. And he looked at the faces in the crowd, angry and wounded and fearful.

It was his time to raise the ghosts of his ancestors. It was time to be king. At long last.

One of the admittedly small lot of kingly graces bestowed upon him was a voice that carried over crowds. His ancestors had used it to command on the battlefield. He used it now, over the sound of the inferno.

"People. There is a darkness under our feet, a world we have never known. The beings that wish to steal the hearts out of our chests. They seek to make us beg and weep and bow," he said, and the people fell silent, under his spell, despite the terror they felt.

"I will not have it.

"For the sake of our fallen fathers. I will not have it. When they come up to the land above, I will fight them, until my very last breath. I swear to you, I will give them the nightmares they seek to give to us.

"We do not fight for ourselves; that is not our way. We fight for our children, our wives, our husbands. We fight for all. We give all for all."

Someone in the crowd shouted, "All for all." More joined in, a whispering chorus. "*All for all.*"

"I ask you," the king shouted. "Will you hide under your soft bed, waiting for death? Or will you join me, join our people, and *send these beasts back to the grave?*"

The crowd hollered and shouted. Many raised what poor weapons they had. He knew they'd heard him; they thought of one another, rather than just the loss of the horses.

Commander Sagja bowed and escorted the king back toward the House of the Wooden Throne. He was smiling, firmly taking the king's arm. "Well done, sire. Bloody well done. We need to get you out of there. They'll be hoisting you on their shoulders next, and there's a war to be fought."

The king nodded, although a small part of him felt being hoisted by the crowd would not be without its pleasurable side.

"Follow me, lord." Gahresh couldn't help but realize... he felt younger than he had in years. He'd meant it; he'd fight until he had nothing left to fight with. *Let that be my legacy*, he thought to himself.

The commander opened the lock to the great oaken doors of the throne room, and the smell of smoke was overwhelming... wafting from the stables across the square, he imagined.

When the door fully opened, Gahresh saw that the Wooden Throne, uniter of his people, symbol of his rule, was on fire and already blackened and charred over half its surface. He cried out. More even than the city, more than the horses, it had been his responsibility to protect and cherish. And it burned in front of him.

"The people will take this hard," he muttered to no one.

Before the dais was a mound, an eruption of dirt and stone, like the ones in the streets four hours earlier.

"It really was a rousing speech, sire," said Commander Sagja, a curved blade in his good hand. Sagja, who had cherished the throne more than any man or woman under the king's command, spoke in a voice that cracked, just a little.

It felt wrong. The king turned to his loyal soldier just as he heard a dagger being unsheathed.

Sagja stabbed the king in the liver, twisted, and ripped upward, hard enough to hit and crack two ribs in the dagger's path. The king's eyes widened; his mouth worked but no sound came out.

Using the blade, still inserted hilt-deep into the king's innards, he pushed the king helplessly to the gap at the top of the mound. Then just a little bit farther.

The king screamed as the unearthed sod beneath his feet disappeared, and he fell into the void.

Where mottled gray-blue hands with elongated fingers and yellow cracked nails ripped him to shreds as he kept screaming.

For a time.

37

LOVE AND HATE IN TIMES OF WAR

We weep for the warrior, the wizard, and the wife
We weep for the father at the end of his life
We weep for the sun and we weep for the moon
We weep for the babe who was taken too soon
We weep for our king, and know there is none greater;
I ask you my friend, who weeps for the traitor?

Author unknown (verse translated by Sofia Dulois)

After a span of time, in the room of the burning Wooden Throne, a ghastly, horrific figure rose out of the gap in the secret mound, right in the heart of the city of Makkalet, still spattered in the blood of the freshly slaughtered king.

Commander Sagja knelt. He bowed his head, appearing to show

respect, but truthfully, he couldn't bear to look at the face of the gaunt ruler.

The King of Spiders, the Lord of the Chasm, Emperor Tol of the Underground Kingdom, the Demon of the Asp.

At last, the creature stood astride the gap of the mound, fully eight feet tall and muscled like the taut limbs of a jungle cat. His skin was pale with a greenish tint in this light, his overlong arms and legs offset by the obvious power of his being.

His body was festooned with vine-like scars, and Commander Sagja realized that these would be their version of tattoos: body art that they could feel, in the darkness, where color meant nothing. Along the vines were painted spiders, white with red eyes.

The emperor looked down toward the soldier, his preternaturally long neck moving in a manner that would induce horrors in the night for a long time to come, in any unfortunate enough to witness it. Tol sniffed, once, twice, three times, then bared his filed, sharp teeth.

Sagja did not look up.

"The city is yours, Emperor."

Tol surveyed the room, his eyes adjusting to the light.

He carried with him in his massive, terrible hands the king's simple gold crown and tried to place it on his oversized head. When it wouldn't fit, he pulled it looser, until it was as misshapen as his own form, but it did at last stay on his cranium.

A final piece to prove legitimacy, then.

He stepped onto the dais.

And sat fully on the Wooden Throne as it burned around him.

He smiled. Emperor of dirt, and now king of fire.

Who could stand against him?

Sunder's hooves crashed and smacked against the ancient stone pavement of the Long Road, a single-cart runway that traversed the entire east-west distance of Hyrkania and had once been illegal for commoners to use at all, under pain of dragging.

Sonja rode with a ferocity that would have killed a normal horse. Breeze in her hair, thunder between her legs. She meant to find her brother, if he yet existed. And after having seen the black circle, she meant to kill every gaunt that entered her field of vision.

They thought they knew Sonja. They all thought they knew her.

She would show them that they knew nothing at all.

She would show them darkness. Darkness unending.

When the sun was at its highest, she looked for an oasis. The horse was in need of shade and water. She stopped reluctantly at a glade of some size, surprised at this section of the steppes. Vegetation spawned around a small but fertile pond and crawled up into the rocks of the lower cliffs, providing shade and a freshness to the air. Most welcome after a full day of breathing in the cooked remains of her countrymen's lives.

She dismounted, and Sunder went to drink. The grasses were not the soft manicured blades of wealthy castles and temples; they were desert greenery and pricked and cut if one wasn't altogether cautious. She had had visions of being followed, likely by Sylus the Blood Man, but detected no trailing rider within the limits of her vision and put the thought out of her mind.

She'd deal with him as need dictated, when necessary. If he even lived at this point.

She lay on her back. She thought sad thoughts; there was no other word to describe them. Her betrayal and run from Ysidra, her stealthy abandonment of Dalen and Aria.

Just as everything she had ever loved had left her, she had done the same to everyone who ever loved her back. For the first time in a very long while, her freedom felt like a weight to be carried on that dry and thirsty road.

A voice spoke to her, so low in volume that it sounded almost welcoming. "Sonja. Hear me."

She sat bolt upright, grabbing at her sword, but saw no one in the glade save Sunder, who looked at her briefly and went back to drinking from the pond.

She recognized the voice, and her skin crawled. And worse, it came from inside her own skull. No, not her skull… The voice came from the Asp, the cursed Asp. "Sonja. Do you hear my words?"

She stood up, ready to fight, craving it. "Get on with it, gaunt. I know what you are now."

The voice that replied was still grotesque, but there was a note of regret in it, somehow. "Do you? Shall I tell you how we became what we are, favorite daughter of Hyrkania?"

Sonja shrugged. "If you must. And why do you speak so much more clearly now?"

"I speak to you in a voice you understand. It is the Asp that translates for us."

She looked at her arm; the eyes of the circlet were glowing green. She tried once more to take it off, but it now felt almost as if it were attached at the bone, and would not budge even slightly.

"I don't care what tricks it does. I just want it gone," she spat.

"It is an adornment that is costly—for the wearer, I mean. Have you felt tremors of its power? Have you had that much awareness?"

Sonja thought. She wanted the answers, and so she was willing to provide a few herself. "I've been cold. Even under blankets, even in the hottest sun. And I've seen… things."

"Yes. You see the dead, Sonja. I am certain you have deduced this for yourself. The more recently killed, the closer they are, and the more coherent they remain. The long deceased, they are harder to see and understand."

Sonja said nothing.

"The cold, do you not understand this, Sonja? It is the cold of the grave, which you grow closer to every moment you wear the Asp. Every day you stink of it a little bit more."

"Where did this thing come from, demon? Why was I allowed to have it?"

"I am not a demon, Sonja. I am a living thing. You may call me Tol. As for the Asp, there are thirteen, actually. I have one. My allies have two more. And one was stolen by Turanian raiders centuries ago. The rest are buried and will likely never be found."

"And that's how you 'found' me."

"So said, it is so."

She sat down again, remembering the circle of black ash that had once been a town. "Why are you killing Hyrkanians? To what purpose, for what *reason* would you murder children and mothers like this?"

"I will tell you, Sonja. If you will listen. But I warn you. It will change you."

Makkalet was a city, then. A fine city, of its time.

But it was a brutal place. Lawless and unkind. Strangers were sent away into the desert, without allowance to our water supply. Then our rangers, the closest thing we had to governance, would follow their trail and rob the bodies.

There was a king. Danska. By the ramblings of history, a fearless warrior, protector of the weak.

In reality, he was a vain, cruel man. And greedy beyond understanding. He could have had a city of purest gold. It would only have tempted him to wish for more. He enjoyed public executions, particularly for those accused of "disloyalty."

Which could mean anyone who whispered anything Danska didn't favor. Often, he would complete the execution himself, chopping the victim's head off with one of his beloved ceremonial blades. Whether it was poor coordination or sheer malignant cruelty, he would often miss the first several strikes, until the victim was gashed and torn and begging for death.

The city had a Zamoran neighborhood at that time. We kept to ourselves and were quiet and peaceful. We knew the ragings of the king and his army, and had no voice in the city's running.

But we were of the Spider Kingdom, and we practiced our faith. Quietly, at night. We were foolish to believe it made us safe. We thought our families were considered part of the city, if not a significant part. We prospered, after a fashion. But we knew to be careful in ostentatious displays of our modest wealth. For jealous eyes are angry eyes, Daughter of the Steppes.

There was an illness. A real plague, unlike the fake one your Gahresh dreamed up. Even murderous Danska heard the grumblings of discontent and fear. It became truth that the populace became more afraid of the pox than of their king, poor aim with a sword or not. Bloated bodies filled the streets. People vomited everything they attempted to consume.

We of Zamora had conquered the disease long hence and still knew the recipe of inoculation. We gave of it, freely, in gratitude to our neighbors and friends.

Danska could not have another savior in his city. It could not be countenanced that anyone, Zamorans in particular, could have saved the people.

So he blamed us.

We caused the plague.

We murdered our neighbors.

And it was only Danska's quick thinking that saved the survivors.

We tried to fight, but it is impossible to fight a lie that people want to believe, Sonja.

They robbed us and beat us, tortured us to make us confess each other's guilt. My own wife called me the Father of Death. She died in my arms, unable to hear me forgive her.

We were marched, starving and in shock, to a grand cave with no second entrance. The king himself marched us inside, by barbed whip. He asked if anyone would speak for us, and no one did.

No one.

They sealed off the cave with stones and then cement. We were left in darkness, to starve to death. Most of us lost our faculties.

But some remembered the old ways. Some remembered the names of the Elder Gods, names which would test your sanity simply to hear. And we learned there are worse things than darkness and worse things than death.

We were given gifts. The ability to move earth, crawl like worms. Even the roots of the trees that give you shade belong to us. There is a city below, Sonja, and it contains wonders to witness.

We made a pact. It went beyond simple vengeance. It was a promise to remember, remember what was done to us.

And to repay that debt if it took the rest of eternity.

She stood again. He'd been right: It wasn't anything she wanted to hear, and she felt burdened with the knowledge. Talking through the Asp was painful, her head aching with each crawling word.

"So alive centuries beyond your time. You have been deeply wronged, Tol. I do not doubt. A debt is owed. But you murder innocents, and that I cannot countenance."

Tol's voice said, "It doesn't matter if you understand."

She shook her head. "No, it does. Why, then, did you try to warn me away? I'm Hyrkanian. I have Danska's blood, however thin, in my blood."

Tol's voice shrank a bit. "You intrigue me, Sonja. You care not for your homeland but risk all to defend it. You care deeply for people, yet you are always alone. You loved your family, yet you have spent all your life trying to forget them."

"It is my life to live, Tol," she said, bite creeping into her voice.

"For now," said the dark voice.

Images flew like ravens through her memory. The black circle of death and pain in Yvaq. The burned family on the Zamoran border.

"Tol. I am sorry for what happened to you. But I am coming for you. If I can, I will stop you."

Tol's voice boomed, the dark, cruel voice that was his own and not a version filtered through the Asp. "I DON'T THINK YOU WILL, DAUGHTER OF HYRKANIA."

And then she passed out for a time.

When she awoke, there was a sword pointed at her throat.

An ebony sword.

Ysidra stood over her, tall and determined.

"We need to talk."

38

THE ART OF
THE ENEMY

Heyo, they pull you from the fire
Heyo, they make you out a dwyer
Heyo, you die in your old age-o
Heyo, awaken in a cage-o

Heyo, a grave they place you in
Heyo, then they take you out again
Heyo, you'll be an endless sleeper
Heyo, they bury you still deeper

Heyo, they call you back for more
Heyo, the gaunts are at your door
The gaunts are at your door

Do you hear them as they roar?
The gaunts are at your door

Author unknown (collected from
the diary of Sir Thomas Blake, 1834)

Aria sniffed, holding back tears, as she packed her few possessions. Dalen, already packed, watched her with a pain in his
heart. It killed him to see her cry.

"She left us, not even a farewell," she said once again. "Did we
mean nothing to her, nothing at all?"

Dalen felt that for once, he understood the complexities of the day
more fully than Aria. But he lacked the words to take away her hurt
at being abandoned by the single person whom she admired most,
the person she had sculpted her life to resemble.

"Wipe your tears, my love. We leave with the company and must
break down the tent."

A soldier they didn't recognize coughed politely into his fist at the
flap of the camp tent, too big for two people, making Sonja's absence
even more acute. If he'd heard the discussion, he was too decent to
mention it. He was carrying something in his free hand, but it was
obscured by the canvas.

Aria and Dalen both turned to face him. "By order of General
Dahmarhk himself, I present you with these. The general requested
I tell you that he regrets his harsh words yesterday and that he is
proud to serve beside you as soldiers in the prince's company."

Aria audibly gasped as they were presented with the soldier's
package: two cleaned and neatly folded uniforms of the prince's
guard, with the head of a horse proudly displayed as his badge in
carved leather across the chest.

The soldier grinned kindly. "The general says welcome home, soldiers of the mark."

The general in question strode through the officers' camp, the fire long since cool in the hot midday sun. The prince was already mounting his horse. The plan was to trace the gaunts that had murdered and raised Yvaq and enslaved the corpses of its citizens. It could not be allowed to happen again. Hyrkania would not survive widespread knowledge of its enemy.

"My prince," the general said, bowing deeply before him.

"I do wish you wouldn't do that, General. It's decidedly uncomfortable," said the prince.

But the general was in no mood. "My prince, a courier has arrived, one of my best men from Makkalet."

He had the prince's full attention.

"The city is under siege, sire. It is a matter of perhaps a day or two before the entire city is"—he gestured to the black circle—"like this, lord."

The prince's face went pale. "Is there more, General?"

Dahmarhk nodded. "Your father, the king, is missing and can't be found, lord."

Orders to the contrary were swiftly forgotten.

The prince's company was returning home.

Ysidra. In the fog of slumber, Sonja forgot the events of the past week and recalled only the pleasant times they'd spent together. It was the way of her memory; it picked and chose at the strangest of times. It played favorites, and it left many details of note in shadow for as long as it could.

She attempted to sit up, to embrace the queen in exile as she had each morning for many days. But the point of the woman's sword bit her throat slightly, drawing blood. Sonja noted the solitary guard of the queen's Wolf Pack watching her sadly, his bow drawn and aimed at her heart.

And as had many memories in the past few days, everything that had passed between them came gushing back.

"Ysidra, I—"

Ysidra held up her free hand. "Stop, Devil. I will hear no entreaties or apologies. Leave me with that much dignity, I ask you."

Sonja swallowed this, a bitter taste in her mouth. "How did you find me?"

The queen considered the woman before her and sighed. "Captain Grapas of the Zamoran outreach patrol found us. Eventually I got the story from him. He says he has done as you requested and spoken with the mayor. Any refugees will be cared for as best they can."

Sonja nodded. One soldier in Zamora at least was a man of his word, and this made her quietly happy for some reason.

The queen continued, "He also said he would have done so, Curse of the Hyrkanians or not. Whatever that means."

"I'm not going to hurt you, Ysidra. May I be allowed to stand?"

The queen was lost for a response for a moment. "'Not going to hurt me?'" she almost shouted. "You crushed my heart. You took my tribe, my family, my position from me. I see you; you didn't even wait a fortnight before finding new bedmates and abandoning them as well!"

It was all true—she knew it. Sonja never thought of the past or the future. But others lived every day thinking of one of those or the other.

Ysidra's face broke its practiced sheen of disdain. "You were my home, Sonjita."

"You have good reason to hate me, Ysidra. And I am sorry. I don't even know why I took the cursed thing, contract or no. But I again must suggest you let me stand."

The queen sniffed. "Why would I do that, Devil?"

Sonja nodded her head toward the pond.

"Because Sunder thinks you're going to hurt me, and that will not end well for any of us."

The two exiled turned to look at the chestnut giant, who had stopped drinking and was looking right at them, muscles tensed, preparing to charge.

It was decided the queen would lower her sword.

Sonja stood and nodded to Raganus. She'd always liked his bone-deep loyalty and love of a simple life. The guardsman did not respond, and that stung a bit.

She surveyed her former lover, her betrothed. She was still beautiful, a contrast of colors, size, and attitude to Sonja herself, but she continued to look as though she carried the weight of the world inside of her, while Sonja at her happiest carried nothing of her past with her at all.

"When did you know, Sonja? When did you know you were going to take the Asp?"

This question somehow hurt more than the threats. She knew the truth would help no one, not herself, not Ysidra. But the time for lies was long past, regardless of the wounds that would result.

"Before I ever met you, Queen. I was hired by a notorious hoarder of stolen wealth. The Falcon, he is named. He coveted it. Now I know why. He knew taking it by force would be loud and costly. So he asked me."

Ysidra shook her head.

Sonja was all in; there was no point in stopping here. "I thought it would be an adventure, a lark."

The queen turned away for a moment. When she turned back, Sonja could see that something had simply given up in her eyes; something fiery had died. "I loved you, Sonja. Then I hated you. Now I simply pity you."

That landed hard, but there was nothing to say that would make it hurt less. "Did you know, Ysidra, what the Asp could do?"

Ysidra walked over and patted Sunder. She'd missed him very much, and the horse's tense stance diminished immediately. "I knew. Why do you think I chased you? There was a time, in my madness, I wanted you to kill me."

"So that you could—"

"So that I could haunt you forever, yes, through the Asp. And you will laugh at me, but even that seemed preferable to never seeing your face again."

There was silence between them, a gulf that could not be reached across. "I reconsidered, Ysidra. I want you to know that. That day you showed me the windmill. I decided I could not steal the thing, could not hurt you like that."

Ysidra nodded. "And yet it preyed on your mind."

"Yes. Every moment, like how you still see the sun after closing your eyes."

"It must've wanted you to take it very much."

Sonja joined her by the horse's flank, both touching the giant, gentle now, quieted by their touch. "I have no excuse. I was afraid of being tied to anything, even my queen of ribbons."

"I do see that, Sonjita. You think I don't, I know. But I see it. Have you tried taking off the Asp?"

"It will not allow it. It is part of me until death, I fear."

The queen nodded.

Ysidra hummed for a moment, the lullaby Sonja had forgotten the words to, which the queen sang to herself when she was lonely or sad.

"Well," she said, after a time, "I am now as you have been, Sonja. A vagrant, a pauper, loyal to no one and responsible for nothing. And whatever dream there was between us, that dream has faded away."

Sonja could only stare at her. She lacked the words to respond entirely.

"So let me help you save your country, as I find my royal appointment book utterly free of entries at the moment."

Sonja was silent.

"I didn't come here for revenge, Sonjita. I came to undo the evil the Asp has helped bring into this world. Are we riding together or not? Because I'm going to Makkalet to fight, regardless."

They were together, three fine riders on three fine steeds, though only Sonja's was Hyrkanian bred. The other two were bought at dear cost from a man Grapas had suggested.

Ysidra, freed of her burdens for the first time in her life, even smiled at the cool breeze in the air. Which made Sonja's heart melt a little.

"This doesn't mean I forgive you, Sonja," she shouted, her hair blowing wildly against her face in the wind.

Sonja agreed. "Understood. I am a terrible scourge of a person. But to be fair, they *do* call me the Devil."

"And a barely adequate lover, as well." Ysidra laughed like the song of birds outside a window.

"That is altogether too far, my queen."

"Well. Competent, certainly."

"I'll take it," shouted Sonja, remembering every bit of why she had fallen in love in the first place.

Yes, love. She'd fallen in love.

She'd ruined it, she knew. But it had been love, a word she had primarily used for ale and horses previously.

Sonja did not live in the past.

So she rode on, heedless of the frost that had not left her since she donned the Asp. There was a little warm glow, instead, and it felt like the hands of a healer.

Within five hours' ride, they began to see the smoke from the great city of Makkalet's smoldering fires.

39

WHERE YOU MUSTN'T FOLLOW

And then came the Woman in Red.

Author unknown (carved in rock at Cave Bantias)

The riders stopped well short of the Stone Gate of Makkalet, for fear of being spotted. The watchtowers and parapets had guards in them, but their gait and stature appeared to be wholly inhuman, and it seemed impossible to approach with stealth; one might as well simply go up to the gate and knock on it.

If Sonja were alone, she might attempt that, for the sheer bravado of it. But it would most certainly get all three of them killed on the spot.

They dismounted while they strategized. "Well, any ideas, my brilliant comrades?" Sonja asked.

Raganus chimed in, helpfully. "Yes, we turn around and go back to that tavern we passed an hour ago. Or we could wait for the creatures to die of old age, dance in, and declare it a victory."

Sonja and Ysidra were unsure how to process this version of the taciturn guard and thus smiled awkwardly.

"I'm sorry," he said. "I hate monsters."

On this there was general agreement. Ysidra spoke up. "I could sneak in, try to get help to open the gates."

Sonja sighed. "Respectfully, Queen, that is asking rather a lot of you and staking our lives upon it."

Ysidra raised an offended eyebrow. "I've twice snuck up on Sonja the Vigilant since this adventure began."

"I believe I liked it better when you people were moody and petulant," said Sonja. "No, I think there is another way. Come with me; stay low... These things don't see well in the day, but night is coming, and then those odds turn against us."

She looked at her two companions. She'd done them both so wrong and yet asked so much of them already. She vowed to herself that if it was within her power, she would trade her life for either of theirs and call it a good death under Tarim's eyes.

"Ysidra, you said in your spying that the prince's army was coming. You're absolutely certain?"

"Yes, but they weren't prepared. It'll be...what, two hours at least, perhaps more. And regardless, they're mounted, and the Stone Gate is closed and watched. They have nothing for a siege assault with them; they were hunting the moving dead."

"You're saying it's hopeless," Sonja said.

The queen said nothing.

"Good. I'm tired of all this triumph and glory and living happily to old age," Sonja said, and rode in an arc around the Western Wall of Makkalet.

The people of the walled city were fully in panic.

The newly admired king, unpopular in peace, somehow beloved

in war, had disappeared, and many said he had deserted. Many citizens and even some soldiers had made to climb the wall but had been ripped apart by the number of gaunts coming out of the shadows like the spiders they took their inspiration from. The screams came irregularly, but the terror in them was enough to reach into a person's guts and twist.

Some simply gathered in their homes, holding their loved ones, as if hoping to not be noticed, childlike and mistaken.

The rest fought. The death of the soldiers and their callous reintroduction to the surface world had lent fire to many a heart, and the theft and disappearance of the royal stallions was a furlong too far for many more. They fought with blades, slings, and bows, but many lacked proper weapons and chose spades, cleavers, and clubs. The few actual skirmishes that had occurred had ended in man and gaunt beaten and torn in the most unlovely ways.

The burnt soldiers who had been murdered in the depths were stacked, as respectfully as possible, on their backs in the town square. Hyrkanians buried their dead, and if any survived, these men would have their rest.

Although, after the events of the past weeks, perhaps that was a custom that needed reevaluation.

An hour before dawn, the first of the dead soldiers opened his eyes.

The rest followed.

One after another, they stood on burnt and ruined legs, still smelling of the fire that had killed them and the unholy presence that had brought them back.

They had been raised. They were dwyers now.

And they did as Tol commanded.

40

BLIND IN THE DARK

No direction but down, my lord
No future but in the ground
No direction but down, my lord
Is where I shall be found

Traditional Hyrkanian battle song

Sonja's green eyes, the eyes of an unmatched archer, examined the perimeter of the castle, looking for something in particular, until at last she found it.

A cave entrance, not unlike the one she'd taken and decorated with the bones of a bear.

"It's there. They must have some entrance, no matter how cunningly hidden, to bring in the dwyers and supplies they need for this. It's there—do you see?"

Raganus shook his head. "You're not proposin' we enter that

tunnel, through a kingdom of spiders, peopled with ghastly beasts in defiance of all-natural law, are you?"

Sonja did not turn around. "Yes, but you needn't make it sound so cheery."

Ysidra looked at her last loyal defender of all her people. "Raganus, I free you from all obligation to me, with my everlasting gratitude. Go home. Tell them I forced you to follow me and you renounce my treachery. Live a life of joy and forget this place."

He shook his head. "I don't think any of us will be doin' any of that, and I won't desert my queen. Festrel would never forgive me," said Raganus. "Besides, you'd both be lost w'out me."

Sonja smiled. "It's settled, then."

They headed for the cavern's small entrance, nearly invisible from the road. And Sonja once again smelled the scent of death by fire, which she had tried so hard, for so long, to forget.

The prince slowed his steed's gallop slightly so that he could talk to his general, the man he considered a second father, who had been more present in his daily life, guiding him, than had the king himself.

The feared veteran was getting old. They both knew it but never spoke of it. He'd long since earned whatever restful pensioner's dream he had in mind, and the prince aimed to make sure he took it. Fishing or farming, hunting or bed-hopping, he'd earned every right to whatever folly made his last days pleasant.

In truth, he loved the man, grim though he could be—brusque, even cruel at times.

"Thoughts on our approach to the Stone Gate, Dahmarhk?" he said when the older man moved forward to ride beside his prince.

"Nothing useful, sire," he said sourly. "Our people are unbeatable on horseback, and yet a wall and a gate leave us helpless. That will have to change, as I've told the king many a time, gods bless his crown."

The prince had never heard his father's trusted general without a strategy, and it was discomfiting indeed. "You'll think of something. But as we are less than two hours away, I pray you, think of something *soon*."

The general looked at the young man—boy, really—he thought of as his own son. "I tell you now, Prince. If that gate is not open, we might as well turn back entirely, for we are never entering our homes again."

They were watched from the rear of the company by Aria and Dalen, in their fine new uniforms, oblivious to the fact that their mission was doomed.

The three arrived at the cavern entrance. It was dark, of course. But it seemed a darkness none of them had ever previously experienced. It had a palpable feel; it lingered on the skin. They had only one torch between them—steadfast Raganus always thought of the worst possible outcome and prepared as best he could. They lit it from his tinderbox, and all blessed its flame, weak though it would be.

Only Sunder, of the horses, would willingly go into the tunnel. The Zamoran horses, who had never spent a day underground, simply refused to be led inside, showing the whites of their eyes and foaming at their mouths as their riders pulled back on the reins. In the end, they were simply let go, their saddle and gear taken away. They had better odds on their own, in any case.

Those remaining entered the tunnel, which felt for all the world like being digested, consumed, inside the intestines of a monster the size of the world.

It wounded Sagja on some deep level to see his city fall, to see his people so demoralized and fearful. In truth, he felt they had let him down. He'd expected better. He threw back his cloak and pulled up his sleeve on his good arm.

The Hunter's Asp wrapped quietly around it stared at him with blank, dull eyes.

The voice came before he felt the presence of the great creature behind him. Tol. Tol the Emperor, he'd insisted on being called, though it galled the soldier to do so. "THEY ARE COMING."

He did not turn around. As much as he felt contempt for the terrified scurrying of his city, he himself found no good reason to look at the creature's face.

"The prince? Of course he comes—was that not the point of it all?" asked the commander.

"NOT THE PRINCE. THE DEVIL."

He knew the creature meant Sonja, and he found the courage to be a bit disrespectful to the owner of the voice, for the first time in many, many years. "If this woman, this 'She-Devil,' actually ever existed, she's likely long since dead or a fishmonger's wife, somewhere."

Tol's voice was calm in response. Eerily so. "ARE YOU CERTAIN, COMMANDER?"

Sagja summoned what remained of his resolve. "Worry about the real dangers, Emperor—our plan is treacherous. We could all die tonight, and then your dreams of blood payment will come to nothing, and you will go back to the grave for real this time."

Tol smiled, a rictus so hideous that it stung to witness it. "YOU THINK I AM THE STRATEGIST, THE LEADER OF MY PEOPLE."

This puzzled the commander. "Are you not? Are you not the emperor? Because you certainly say it enough."

"THERE ARE WORSE THINGS THAN ME IN THE CITY OF GRAVES. SUDHI-YA GUIDES US ALL, HYRKANIAN."

And there it was, a reminder that even in alliance, the ancient pact of the gaunts was still in place.

And for all his treason this night, Commander Sagja of the King's Eye was still a pure-blooded Hyrkanian.

They walked in double file, Sonja in the lead, holding the torch, with Sunder beside, followed by Ysidra and Raganus. The air was cold and damp, and the silence was oppressive. It felt like every step and whisper was being heard and recorded halfway around the inside of the world.

They walked in broken, shuffling steps. It was slow, nauseating progress, and only Sonja, who had lived in a cave for two brutal years as a child, managed to keep her spirits somewhat out of the mire.

Every surface they touched, by accident or for balance, felt tainted, like spoiled meat. Sonja recognized the feeling, the chill they all carried in their spines.

The cave and the Asp were one. She didn't understand it; she just knew it to be true.

It was Sunder who smelled the gas first. He stamped his feet and attempted to turn back, but the passage was too thin. Soon they all recognized it, a natural gas leak, under the city.

Raganus whispered, "I heard a tale in a tavern, a leak like this in a copper mine below the southern border. When the miners didn't return from the cave, they was found dead as doorways, to a man."

Ysidra added, "Perhaps it's intentional. Someone comes by with a torch. The gas is ignited, just enough to burn them to cinders. The gaunts don't carry torches, do they?"

It was decided, at some great pain to all concerned, that to continue they'd have to douse the torch.

Tol stepped into the market square. For the first time, a gaunt, an alabaster giant, a spider king, was in full view of the citizenry, as dusk began to fall. Fire, smoke, and screaming were all around him, but he seemed oblivious to it all.

He was surrounded by the undead soldiers, vomited up from the mounds just hours before. Those that could held their swords at the ready.

"HYRKANIANS. HEED MY VOICE."

He raised his arms, as if in triumph. There were wails and great sobs coming from all directions.

"NONE OF YOU WILL SEE THE MORNING. MAKE WHAT PEACE YOU MAY. AND KNOW THIS, WHILE YOUR HEARTS STILL BEAT…"

He squinted his goat's eyes, glowing in the darkening air.

"WHEN YOU DIE, WE WILL BE WAITING FOR YOU STILL."

Commander Sagja stood in the shadows. He had to admit it was, as political speeches go, succinct and possessed of uncanny clarity.

They walked in total darkness, using Sunder's eyes as guide. When a bat flew toward them, Ysidra, the bravest woman Sonja had ever known, shrieked and grabbed her free hand in her own. Sonja squeezed and felt sincerely, *This might be my last pleasant memory.*

When they no longer smelled the pocket of gas, they attempted to light the torch again, but their eyes had not adjusted to this level of darkness, and they gave up trying.

Which meant following the tunnel by feel, tripping and cursing, lightly touching the walls with their fingers while at the same time shuddering at the sticky sensation of them.

There were crossroads in the tunnels, places where the walls would end as another wing of the passages cut through. They required a walk of faith, with no walls to guide them, until they got to the other side and found the tunnel they hoped continued to their destination. But direction felt lost here, and their internal compasses failed them all.

After a worrying downhill grade (no one wanted to go farther under the surface), the path began to level out, and they heard something hideous yet familiar. Grotesque but almost...almost something. It was singing, but from a cursed throat, like the music of death itself.

Sonja recognized the melody of the impossibly deep, guttural voice in the caverns ahead.

It was the lullaby of her mother.

41

THE VOICE OF MEMORY

"Mother, turn on the light. I cannot see in the dark."
    "That is the last kindness I may give to you, my daughter. It is better that you do not."

Zamoran campfire tale

For a moment, she heard her mother's voice, more clearly than she had since the day she lost her forever. Whether it was a cruelty of the Asp or simply the melody bringing back scattered islands of remembrance, she couldn't say.

"Sonjita, remember the day. Remember the faces."

She knew it meant something, but she could not say what.

Ahead of them, there was a dim light, and they heard an echo as they came closer to the singing, bouncing off the walls blindly like the bat they'd faced earlier in their journey downward.

They came to the cavern's central hall.

And there they met Sudhi-Ya, Mother of Gaunts.

42

MATERNAL URGES

There are demons in the dirt.

Traditional eastern European folk ballad

The central cavern was massive and surely would have collapsed upon itself if not for the clever engineering of its solid central pillars of rock, spindly in places, stout in others.

There were small, meager lanterns on the walls, placed irregularly, and dwyers scuttled about like cockroaches, performing duties it was impossible to discern. Sonja thought it likely that the gaunts could work and live in darkness but their resurrected servants could not, and she thought of the cruelty of placing light only where their duties lay, as if further restricting them to unending servitude with no hope of respite.

But far worse was the massive, unhallowed greenish-white monstrosity lying against the rear wall, being washed and scrubbed and fed, all at once, by the dwyers, loving in the care of the thing, feeding her a bloody red meal from a bowl made of bone.

She mewled as she ate, like an infant, and the mashing of her massive mouth was instantly nauseating to witness. She was mostly spider, but with extra, useless extremities, a pair each of human arms and legs, dangling motionlessly among the eight hairy spider legs that held her upright.

Twenty feet tall she was, at least, and bulbous at the largest segment of stomach. The hard surface of her flesh was pale, with a green mottled tint, like the gaunt Sonja had killed at the black circle. Her legs pinwheeled chaotically.

She had a misshapen, nearly translucent head, a thousand eyes wandering around aimlessly, never falling on anything for more than a moment. She ate from the bowl, its contents poured into her mouth lovingly by a dwyer, and the entire cavern smelled of illness and fungal growth. And in between her hideous gulping, she sang the song that was the only gift Sonja still possessed from her mother, in an impossibly deep, razor-throated voice.

Quiet child, so fair and deep
Mother will watch you in your sleep
Restless eyes and dreaming heart
Mother has loved you from the start
Quiet child, wrapped in fur
Sleep in silence, do not stir
Daughter, sister, mother, wife
We'll walk with you all your life

Sonja felt her stomach clench but forced herself to listen. *It was just a song,* she thought to herself. Thousands of mothers sang it every night to their young.

Worst of all, worse even than the lullaby, Sudhi-Ya, the White Spider, was in the act of giving birth.

To a fully grown, living gaunt, mewling and squealing as it worked its way out of her womb, covered in ivory albumen.

"Gods above," Ysidra whispered. "How does such a thing come to be?"

Sonja thought she knew the answer: through hate and murder. But she was unable to fully connect those thoughts.

Raganus stated it most plainly. "It gives birth to the monsters. We can't ever win if that thing lives to make more of them."

Sonja thought of the black circle of Yvaq, and her face became hard. She handed the doused torch to Raganus, turned, and embraced them both.

Ysidra's face showed alarm. "Sonja. What are you doing?"

The She-Devil took her dagger out and swiftly mounted Sunder. "Follow me as best you can. Arm yourself; prepare to run."

She put the dagger between her clenched teeth and drew her bow.

And then she charged Sudhi-Ya, Mother of Monsters.

43

EXILE UPON EXILE

"Am I not the clever one?" said the traitor to the king.
"I've lived to see you come undone and haven't lost a thing."
"It's true," the king said, as he bled, "but you'll not see my flinches.
"You see the brave man dies at peace; the traitor, by the inches."

Sir Fagin Rastar, *Comedy and Death*

Sagja was a born loyalist.

His father had been a captain of the city's guard, a defender of the gate and a trainer of men, and he'd instilled the idea of duty in his young son, more through example than wordy lessons. There was no question of his future . . . He'd been given a wooden sword at the age of three, and learned the love of it, the feel of the hilt, the impact of a target fairly pierced. It thrilled him his entire life through.

When other children of the guard took to play or to fish or to read, Sagja set himself increasingly complex imaginary challenges and judged his performance against imaginary villains and creatures, going through a great number of ever sturdier and more ornate wooden swords.

Until at last, at ten, he was given a proper sword, made for his hand. His father smiled; his mother fretted. But if he was to pick the greatest single moment of his life, it would be that moment when he took his first real blade from his father's hand.

Better still, no one admonished him. No one cautioned. No one treated him as an infant.

No one said *Be careful, Son* or *Never use this unless our lives are in danger.*

He didn't need to be told. The truth was, as eager as he was to defend his family, his home, and his king, he was slightly repulsed by the idea of getting blood on his fine blade. The thought of it was somewhat nauseating.

It would never shine in the sun again, not like that first day, not with blood on it.

He practiced twice as hard every day.

And when he was brought into the soldiery, a fledgling guardian of the gate, at a mere fourteen years old, even his mother cried prideful tears.

He did not cease his training. And soon other guardsmen joined his sessions, silently entering the square behind him and imitating his movements. He did not turn to acknowledge them. In truth, he knew few of them by name at all.

But they had observed, and they had chosen. This was a young man to be followed. Who was worth following.

His rise through the ranks was surprising to no military man but somewhat appalling to the political retinue of the court. He had the king's ear, though he never used it in self-interest.

Still, his preeminence as a respected figure was seen with jealous eyes, and an assassin was hired.

Sagja lived.

But his sword hand was ruined.

There was no bitterness. A sense of longing, of being untethered, yes. Yes. There was all of that and more, along with a sense of unconquerable fear that his days as a guard were done.

He blamed no one. It was just the way of it all.

Instead, his king did him the great honor of visiting his recovery bed. And on that day, he made Sagja a commander. Loyal, humble Sagja, who now outranked his father, who kept his eyes steady at his father's proud salute.

On the seventh day after the attempt on his life, Commander Sagja rose from his bed, quietly donned his casual clothes, and walked out of the hospice, unnoticed and against orders.

He walked to his training square quietly. Thinking briefly of what he had lost and then dismissing those thoughts into the morning air.

He knew the road was long and would be hard. And he would have to face it alone, commander or not.

When he arrived in the square, it was filled with soldiers of every rank, every duty in the city. To a one, they raised their hands in silent salute.

Sagja walked to the front of them and turned away as he always had.

He moved his sword from his right to his left hand.

And resumed his training.

It was hard. No, it was nearly impossible. His left hand felt like an intruder, a foreign thing. It lacked all the subtlety that had made his swordwork such a joy to witness.

There were times he almost despaired. But the soldiers behind him in the training square seemed to sense those times and redoubled their efforts, and he found himself unable to surrender.

One day, he asked a lieutenant to stay after to spar. The first parries were awkward and overly energetic. But something odd happened.

When the lieutenant thrust too hard, too close, Sagja reacted, and his hand, his left hand, made the counter. Made the counter by reflex.

He realized he could not force one hand to be the other. He had to allow that one hand to work to its own advantage.

And so he did.

His courage, his determination, became almost a legend, and when the father of a comely daughter, himself a nobleman, approached Sagja about a marriage, Sagja consented.

When he met the girl, Saria, he felt romantic love of a kind he could never have imagined.

His father approved.

Sagja woke each day with a happiness he never had thought possible, in the arms of his beloved wife.

There were two blessed children, twins, raised in sentimental adoration. When they were three, he gave both his son and his daughter a gift.

A wooden sword.

And the first lesson of duty.

There was a fire.

For the rest of his life, Sagja equated the smell of smoke to loss and grief. There was no question of another wife, no thought of siring another heir. He found he could not simply switch hands in this.

Both his hands felt empty and without meaning.

*   *   *

His father died that same year. A wasting disease that left him bab-
bling at unseeable creatures in the air. Far worse than seeing him fall
in battle was seeing his father lose a fight that did not truly exist.

Sagja felt weakness in his soul. His men looked up to him, the people
worshipped him, and the king relied upon him.

And he felt unworthy of it all. His grief made him doubt. And
without conviction, he was nothing.

In going through his father's few possessions, he came across
something he'd never seen before. He stared at it helplessly.

And it seemed to stare back at him.

44

NO PATH TO RETREAT

Neighbors are lovely things. On the other side of the wall, I mean.

Wai Fe, emperor of Khitai, Fourth Era

M any of the Hyrkanians resisted the invaders. They were not cowards and had nowhere left to run.

They cut dwyers by the dozen and even slew some of the lesser gaunts.

But it was clear they were losing. They had no leaders, and their efforts were unkempt and desperate.

And the Stone Gate remained closed.

And Tol, with his dwyer retinue of former Hyrkanian sentries, strode through the city on his terrible yellow-nailed feet, completely unhindered.

*   *   *

It hurt her eyes to even look at the thing. But to aim, she needed to see.

Sonja of the Hyrkanian Steppes came thundering directly at the giant creature, half spider and half human, firing arrows as her horse filled the stone cavern with the sound of approaching thunder.

The first two shots took out the creature's primary eyes, and she roared and howled, attempting to sit up, to crush and chew her enemy. But they were two eyes of a thousand, and she would not be slowed or blinded. The dwyer servants were without much in the way of wit, and it took a moment longer for them to see the danger.

Which was a moment too late.

Sonja fired two more arrows into the thing's throat, and that did seem to shut her up properly.

The beast was still alive, and in her fury, she threw her many spindly arms out against the wall behind her, strong enough to crack the stone, bringing part of the cavern's ceiling down.

Sonja would have been incapable of stopping at this point even if she'd wanted to do so. She shouted in Ancient Hyrkanian at Sunder, words to the effect of *"Run right over this filthy bitch, oh lord of all steeds."*

Sunder obliged, running right through the creature's legs and over the nearly crowned gaunt on its cursed day of birth and right up Sudhi-Ya's grotesque body. Sonja switched to her sword and dagger to hack and slash the mother's flesh and those of the dwyers trying to protect the massive creature.

When Sunder reached the mother's head, his hooves dashed into her flesh and cartilage, with the full weight of horse and rider both, and Sonja shoved her sword through her remaining brain with all the force left in her arm.

Raganus and Ysidra ran behind, slaughtering the wailing and weeping dwyers, praying to the gods that this time, they never found their way back.

Sonja hollered out—screamed out, really. Let them hear her. Let them *all* hear.

"The Red Woman returns, you insect-humping wretches!"

But Sudhi-Ya was not a creature much dependent on her brain, sadly.

The dwyers were many and had been given only one command.

"Protect the gaunt queen." They were violent and ferocious, but they were not capable of independent strategy without a gaunt overseer. For Ysidra and Raganus, killing them was repulsive, and they soon found themselves covered with the ichor of the brainless, slug-like creatures.

Sudhi-Ya, a gaping wound extending clean through to her brain, reared back and slapped at Sonja with her massive spider's limb, and Sonja was knocked six feet off Sunder, landing hard on the uneven stone floor.

For a moment, she felt the loathsome hair on the mother's murderous forelimb, before seeing a constellation of stars behind her own eyes, somehow.

As she was staggering to her feet, another blow, like a tree trunk in a hurricane, sent her tumbling again, and she felt two ribs crack painfully.

On the creature's third attempt to strike her, she mustered the strength to bring her sword down hard. It did not penetrate whatever carapace the mother had, but the effort caused the creature to utter a shriek that made Sonja's guts tense.

The creature moved with alarming quickness through a tunnel in the dark.

And Sonja again smelled the gas.

Sonja looked longingly at the bright lanterns on the cavern wall, then lovingly at her comrades, who were still fighting the mindless horde behind them.

She turned to run after Sudhi-Ya.

A moment later, Sunder followed. They would not be parted.

In the tunnel, in the dark, Sonja walked beside Sunder, trusting his eyes, holding his mane for both guidance and comfort, truth be told.

From the darkness beyond, they heard the singing, now distorted and animalistic. Sonja swore she heard the song in her heart before her ears.

Quiet child, sulfur and deed
Mother wi' eat you in your sleep
Tasteful eyes and savory heart
Mother has loved you from the start

They walked on. They passed two of the mother's living young, freshly birthed, as she moved in shadow, leaving a trail of milky fluid and a long, writhing, blessedly detached umbilical cord in the dirt behind her. Sonja had nearly stepped on the first in the darkness, causing a shiver even she could not suppress.

She killed both without regret. Sunder snorted in approval.

When they reached the hissing, drooling, bleeding mass of spider and flesh, all remaining eyes turned toward Sonja. The eyes pleaded with her. The creature's strength was bleeding out in milky liquid and dead offspring.

Her mandibles twitched. She was trying to say something, trying to beg for mercy, perhaps. Sonja was transfixed and appalled, wanting nothing more than to look away.

The mother's mouth opened.

"Myyyyyyy babiesssss."

Sonja ran her sword right into the creature's open skull and stabbed again and again until all possible signs of life were long gone.

And perhaps a bit longer.

The trio and their sole remaining mount made their way through the tunnels, now armed with lanterns ripped from the walls of the final resting place of Sudhi-Ya, thank all the gods there were. They favored any path that appeared to lead upward, and felt that they could not entirely go wrong using up and down as their guideposts.

Tol had told Sonja, via the Asp, that his people had been turned by spider magic into gaunts, but apparently one of them had become a queen. Nature does find ways to keep even its dirtiest secrets from falling away entirely.

She shuddered.

She heard his voice in her head as they switched tunnels again. "I know you are here, Sonja. Though I can't see you. You can yet live through this. Come to me. Kneel to me."

Sonja spoke slowly, at some effort. "I'm afraid I have a previous obligation, Tol."

"This is your last chance."

She smiled. "See you soon, Emperor of Shit."

And she cut the connection, leaving Tol to rage alone on the surface.

They came at last to another winding area, where the air no longer smelled so much of slaughter. Sonja cocked her head at the sounds... It was impossible. But here it was. The smell came moments later... her favorite smell in all the world.

"Horses!" she cried. "They've taken the *horses!*"

She ran ahead, oblivious to her friends, thinking only of seeing once again the royal stallions of King Gahresh. Revenge against Tol, even the search for her brother were momentarily forgotten in the moment of blind rage.

It was another large cavern, but shallower than Sudhi-Ya's cursed bedroom, as if built for this purpose. They came upon it, and even Raganus was stunned at the sight, the majesty of the king's collection, quite literally the finest horses on Earth, held in the filthy cavern by iron-thorned posts driven into the ground along its edge.

Sonja ran to be among them, to calm their fears. Tol would likely have taken them to dishearten the populace, which it would surely have done. Or perhaps he'd intended to feed them to the abomination she'd just slaughtered.

She touched each of the great house's horses in turn, Sunder watching with subtle jealousy. "We have to free them," she said. "I'll not have them end up in some ghoul's stewpot. I won't."

Ysidra was sympathetic but logical. "How do we get them out, Sonja? Carry them on our backs?"

It was Raganus who found the solution. "There's a ramp here; it needs pulling down. They planned this. It's quite cunning." He pulled on a chain, and a concealed ramp came down from the roof of the cavern, painted and rigged to look like a stable stall floor to those in the city above.

Raganus walked to the blessed surface, breathing deeply, Sonja and Ysidra to follow. None had ever been so delighted to breathe even the smoke-filled air of the capital city.

"Well. This won't do, I'm afraid," said a voice in the darkness. "It's not part of our plan, do you see?"

Commander Sagja stepped forward with military precision and posture. Even Sonja had heard of the man, a legendary soldier. He drew his sword in ceremonial style, the last thing many a dueling opponent had ever seen in their too-short lives.

"So, between your own people and those below, you chose the spiders. Is that right, Commander?"

The man did not lower his eyes. "There's no resisting them, Sonja. I've made an agreement, and they will let our people live."

Sonja sneered and pulled her own sword. "And I'd heard you were smart, soldier. Come on, then. Let's see what you can do."

Sagja's face was sad. He stepped forward, blade raised.

Sonja sighed and started to move toward him. Raganus reached out his arm to stop her. "Beg pardon, Red Lady."

He pulled out his own sword in a manner no one could call elegant. "Go see to the horses. Save your city. I've got this traitorous son of a bitch."

Ysidra kissed him on the cheek. It was his time, and she would not interfere with his decision. She followed Sonja back into the hidden stable. It was the last time she ever saw her guardsman alive.

There were a dozen gaunts in the market square, hideous creatures all, surrounded by willing dwyers, given the hideous duty of collecting people from their homes to be slaughtered. These were those who had attempted to stay hidden and were being rewarded for it in fear and blood.

It was an abattoir, a culling ground for people.

The gaunts, each one a giant, cavorted and capered, eager to taste the blood of historic vengeance. The tallest of them grabbed an elder woman by the hair, lifted her completely off the ground, nearly to the point of her scalp being torn off, and pushed the woman's head into the dirt, while she prayed to Mitra.

They all turned at the sound, even the dwyers, of a mountain tumbling down, coming directly at them.

Sonja came, laughing, her sword raised, on the back of Sunder, his hooves flying and sparking on the stone market square. But she wasn't alone. Behind her was the entire collection of the king's royal stallions, who seemed to forget for the moment that they were pampered show horses, and instead remembered what it was like to be at war. The sound was ruinous to all but a Hyrkanian, to whom it was the voice of angels.

Ysidra rode the first stallion, the king's own favorite, her sword held high.

They collided with the confused invaders, gaunt and dwyer alike, trampling them underfoot like eggshell kindling. Bones cracked and skulls exploded, and for the first time in a century, the gaunts knew fear.

Ysidra looked back, stunned to see that not a single citizen had been injured, and she didn't see how that was even possible. Sonja grinned and shrugged. "They're Hyrkanian, Queen," she said, as if that was all the explanation necessary.

Those in the square who had been doomed to die set upon the gaunts and their servants, pummeling them with stones and whatever weapons they could scrounge. It may have come late, but their willingness to fight had arrived.

Sonja and Ysidra fought side by side through the streets, using swords, since bows alone were not certain to kill the bigger gaunts. The streets ran with blackened blood.

But there were too many sons and daughters of Sudhi-Ya, and they were but two fighters in a city with no allies and no exits for escape.

As Raganus approached dueling distance, Sagja held up his sword in polite deference to tradition.

"I detect an accent from Turan, so I suggest we use the rules of your land. No stopping until one is dead, of course, but there's no reason to be savages, don't you find?"

Raganus smiled and rubbed his chin with his free hand. "Well, the thing about that is..." He rushed the legendary soldier, using his fist around the hilt of his sword to smash Sagja with all his might in the man's handsome face, exploding his nose, sending blood gushing like a geyser, and knocking the man through the window of the nearest hovel behind him.

He smiled. "I'm sort of not *allowed* in Turan no more, sir."

He climbed through the window, ready to make the traitor swallow his own sword if necessary. And if he died here, tonight, so damn well be it.

Wolf Pack forever, he thought to himself.

They turned a corner, next to a crossing of the streets where the buildings on all four corners were burning. On the far side of the crossing, in the center of the street, was Tol, surrounded by the dwyers he'd made of the watchtower soldiers.

And each wore full Makkalet armor.

The stallions would not go any farther, would not attack those they thought were their protectors, even with the stink of death upon them.

Tol shouted out to Sonja.

"YOU SHOULD HAVE LEFT, DEVIL."

Sonja's eyes narrowed. "I could say the same thing about you, dead thing."

She turned to Ysidra, urgently speaking into her ear. "Take the stallions. Get the Stone Gate open—do you hear? Nothing matters except the gate. If the prince can't get through, every living soul here dies and comes back as their servant. Do you understand?"

Ysidra looked at Tol, who was still surrounded by soldiers. "Sonja...you can't..."

Sonja reached over and kissed her, hard. It wasn't romantic, but it was love, of the best sort she could spare.

"*Go.* Go *now.*"

Ysidra thundered off, the stallions following the king's mount, as they had their entire lives. Sonja checked the grip on her sword and stretched her arms backward to make sure she wasn't too stiff, pulling hard enough to bring her shoulder blades together with an oddly satisfying crack.

"Well, Lord of the Latrine," she said, grinning at the giant in front of her, surrounded by his murderous servants. "Let's see what you can do when your enemy isn't some poor goat farmer in his home, sleeping."

And she charged again, for the final time that night.

45

THE STONE GATE

Oh, and screw your mother, by the way.

Reportedly stated by Red Sonja (may be apocryphal)

Miserably, and unaccountably, it began to rain. Summer storms were not uncommon in the region, but this seemed a bad omen for all involved. Dark clouds pregnant with a pounding rain.

It lessened the advantage of those on horseback on the cobblestone roads of the inner city—bad news for its defenders.

Ysidra rode through the dampening streets with the stallions pounding behind her, slowly but with purpose, purpose that made the gaunts step aside as best as they could. She struck down those that realized the peril a moment too late. Dwyers scuttled but lacked the cunning of their overlords, and many would have to be washed from the hooves and undercarriages of the king's finest at some point. One or two had been bitten in passing, seemingly in spite for having taken up space when the stallions came running.

Ysidra hoped the creatures were not infectious, but the horses were never going to be fully tamed during times of war.

Most of the gaunts were not using weapons, relying on their hardiness and ferocity, and the terror of the citizenry, to win the day.

It was a mistake on their part, Ysidra thought. And for a moment, she felt like a queen again, with a life of meaning, on a night of storms. She felt alive.

The people cheered, seeing a woman of regal bearing leading the full complement of the king's stallions through the streets of the city. Ysidra did not allow herself a smile, but she did nod in passing and was gratified when the cheers redoubled.

She headed for the Stone Gate as best she could, but like most cities of that age, the streets were random and unmarked. And even at the speed she was going, in the rain, a dead end could be disastrous and potentially fatal.

Ahead, a group of brave local soldiers were using swords against a circle of gaunts and losing; two uniformed corpses were already on the ground. She steered her mount to one side—there was no time to stop—and handily sliced the head from the stoutest gaunt as the rest of the stallions followed, their discipline remarkable. She would have to reconsider her disdain for show horses, entirely.

The gaunt's head rolled downhill, making a sound she found most satisfactory. It moved her. *To hell with the rain,* she thought, and spurred the king's horse on at speed.

We can win, she thought.

She raced to the set of stairs leading to the pegs in the city wall that would allow the Stone Gate to roll open. The horses could not follow her there; they'd crash right through the wooden riser to the city wall's upper surface. And at the top of the stairs, guarding it from just this situation, was a mammoth gaunt, nine feet tall.

And carrying a mace.

They'd decided to use weapons, apparently.

The prince lost his temper just outside the Stone Gate, in the pouring rain. "General Dahmarhk. Are you telling me there is *no* approach to this wall that can be made from this side? Our city is *on fire*."

The general merely stared at the massive gate as the people he'd spent a lifetime defending were inside, screaming and dying.

Aria was close enough to see the pain on the old man's face.

Raganus, in some poor citizen's abandoned house by means of a broken window, lifted the traitorous commander by his shirtfront, and it tore in the doing. If he'd been less kindhearted, he could have stabbed the dog while he was down, but in truth, that course would simply never have occurred to him.

He was momentarily surprised to see a flash of gold on the man's arm, an exact mate to the Hunter's Asp that had caused his people so much heartache and led to the death of his only real friend. His wonder cost him, as Sagja, bleeding down his face, stabbed the Wolf Pack rider through his guts, smiling.

"Die, Turanian pig," said the soldier. "Soon Hyrkania will make slaves of your kind again. Soon your people will *beg* for our mercy."

Rather than remove the commander's blade, Raganus chose instead to lift his enemy entirely off the floor by his arms, crushing them to the man's side. He thought for a moment about how he might beat this gifted swordsman with his own less elegant skills... and then he decided it might be better simply to bash the man's head against the wall until nothing remained but a stain.

And so that was what he did.

*   *   *

Ysidra made it to the bottom of the stairs to the top of the Stone Gate, dismounted, and looked directly at the king's own stallion, who regarded her with patient but somehow insulting regard.

"I don't...I don't speak Ancient Hyrkanian. I don't know if you really—that is, I don't know if Sonja, or the others of your city, if they and you can *actually*...uh...," she stammered.

The horse cocked his head and snorted.

Ysidra put her head on the horse's great muzzle and held his cheeks in her hands. "Thank you for carrying me here, bearer of kings. Get the rest of them somewhere safe, please. They do not know the way, and need your guidance."

Reluctantly, the king's horse pulled away.

The other stallions followed.

The Queen of the Outcasts drew her sword and began to climb.

Toward the monstrous gaunt at the top of the gate, his mace swinging slightly in the rain.

Sonja rode Sunder directly toward Tol, and he had had sense enough to move four of the dead soldiers in front of him, swords across their bodies, either by some command of his or by some dim light of repeated training left in their decaying minds. She noted the Asp he'd used to speak to her and to communicate with the dead on his arm, identical to her own.

She could not use the power of her own Asp, did not even fully understand what those abilities were. But she felt its angry power, nonetheless, like an iron on her flesh.

She looked in Tol's dead, lidless eyes and recognized his loathing for her. Or perhaps it was hate for all Hyrkanians. Didn't matter. She knew he believed he would drag her from the horse and cut her open in the street. She had a different plan.

As the giant horse ran at the emperor of gaunts, Sonja stood on Sunder's back, using her sword for balance, one foot on each end of Sunder's spine. It was not a tenable position for long.

"Mitra bite your *ass*, gaunt," she hissed.

The horse collided with the armored former soldiers. The sheer combined weight of the shared mass of their resurrected bodies caused the rest of the phalanx to fall back on their already unsteady, damaged feet, and Sonja leapt at Tol, blade first.

Tol turned at the last minute, and the blade missed his throat, to dig deep into his chest, where his heart should be, or whatever desiccated husk filled that empty space. He grabbed her arm, the arm carrying her own Asp, and hurled her hard into a market stall. One whiff and she knew it sold fish. She landed in pain and more than a bit of ignominy.

Worse still, her sword was still stuck in the creature's chest as he walked toward her.

No one would call Raganus an imaginative man. He liked a simple world of duty and labor and did not dream of grander things, as a rule.

So when he reached down to pick up the traitor's Asp, as it had, upon the man's death, fallen from his arm, it might have been the single most speculative moment of his entire life. He was not given to fancy.

But Raganus was a keen observer. And he had spent ten years watching every movement of his queen's person.

He knew the cost of wearing the Asp, and he did not shirk paying it.

He placed the thing on his arm—it seemed to grow slightly to fit. And he saw a different world.

With the man he'd just killed standing before him.

*   *   *

Ysidra realized the gaunt had the better strategic position, waiting for her at the top of the stairs, while she was still on the final flight to the top of the Stone Gate. There was no way to open the gate but from the top of it, and that hideous creature was between her and the mechanism she needed. For a moment, she wondered what Sonja would do.

And it came to her.

"Hello, forgotten corpse," she said. "Rejected again by the recently dead? Not to be cruel, but have you considered washing?"

The thing raged at her, all gangly limbs, on the narrow stairs. He clumsily swung his spiked mace, missing her head by inches. She ducked under his reach as he passed, being just more than half his size at best, and dragged her sword across his ankles as his own weight did the rest. His arms pinwheeled helplessly, and he began to fall forward, but she was already past as his weight took him crashing through the wooden railing and over the side to the rocky ground far below, headfirst. She made it to the top safely as his body made a popping sound and then he moved no more.

There were four large stone pegs that were inserted through the top of the wall and into the top of the wooden door of the Stone Gate. All four had to be lifted from their locking position before the door could be opened outward. One person could do it, even a not particularly large person. If their will was strong enough.

She took out the first peg by its iron chain. Three more to go.

Below, she saw Sonja fighting the emperor, and her heart fluttered uncomfortably.

She pulled out the second peg. This one was harder and required her to brace her legs and pull up with both arms. But she freed it and moved to the third.

It was then that she saw four dwyers climbing the stairs toward her.

*   *   *

Dalen pulled at the general's sleeve, pointing up at the woman on the Stone Gate's upper wall.

"General. Look. She's trying to open the gates!"

The prince looked, to see the four creatures coming for the woman on the gate. They'd be upon her in moments.

Perhaps there might be at least part of a city left in the morning, after all.

Dahmarhk turned to Dalen and asked, "How's your bowcraft, guardsman?"

Dalen smiled and pulled the first arrow from his modest quiver. "Adequate to the task, I believe, General."

Ysidra blessed the guardsmen as the dwyers fell, one after another, making perfect little splashes in the puddles atop the gate as they died.

Raganus looked at the image of the commander in the spirit realm. He knew what the Asp could do, better than Sonja, better than anyone but a bearer themselves. But he'd never worn it, and it was difficult to believe what he saw in front of him, the image and soul of the very recently dead.

He tried speaking to the specter, who seemed in a state of confusion and disorientation. Perhaps that was the cost of dying with your brains bashed in. "You. Soldier. Why did you betray your people?"

The specter shook his head. "No. Made agreement. Keep my people alive. The Spider. The horror beneath us. Where am I where is my body *where am I?*"

It was useless. He tried a different tactic. "Commander. Can you make a grip? Can you hold something, on my orders?"

The specter willed himself through great effort and put out a hand, in a grip, as if to hold a sword or club. But more interestingly... so did the very nonspectral corpse on the floor with half its head missing.

"I want you to carry something for me, dead fellow."

Sonja didn't have her sword, as it was still clumsily hanging out of the gaunt emperor's chest, seemingly stuck in bone. She had only the small, gem-encrusted dagger the prince had given her.

As Tol approached, she swung the short blade in a vicious horizontal arc, but she'd underestimated the gaunt's speed, and she nearly wrenched her arm when the dagger's blade met no resistance.

He backhanded her with a cracking sound that shook her senses. And she slammed into the clay wall of the nearest house so hard, she heard shelving fall on the other side. She stood shakily, her impacted left side barely functioning at all.

Tol moved toward her, taking her blade out of his own chest, then raising it high above his head.

Ysidra, arms aching, pulled the third of four restraining pegs loose, her hands bloodied by the massive chain, slick with the cursed rain.

And in the rain, she didn't hear the footsteps approaching her from behind.

For a moment, Sonja felt adrift, a rare sensation for her, particularly in battle. The gaunt, stronger than she was and nearly as fast, held a sword, her own sword, and she had no counter save the tiny, ceremonial dagger. She'd have traded all its jewels for even the trash sword she'd been given in the Zamoran arena, corrosion and all.

Worse, she couldn't feel her left side at all and could summon movement only at some cost, in pain and concentration.

Tol walked toward her, the blade reflecting the moonlight through the clouds, casting sparkles on the wall behind her, and his own Hunter's Asp, a mere glint in the darkness. "We were mistreated, Sonja the Red. Buried alive and left to rot. We've earned this city's blood."

Sonja leaned her weakened left hand against the wall for what little support that gave her trembling legs. She'd at least die fighting. "This isn't the way, Tol. I didn't intend to be your enemy. But here we are. Do what you must."

Tol's face showed a look of disgust. "You disappoint me. You're not a god; you're not a hero. You're just…"

Sonja raised an eyebrow. "Yes? What am I just, spider thing?"

Tol looked at her with contempt. "Just a woman. You are simply a woman, and nothing more. Nothing grand, nothing miraculous… just a woman."

Sonja threw back her head and laughed.

"It's true, great Tol. But you forgot what else I am."

Tol's chin went up, so he could look down on her more clearly. "And what is that, Sonja?"

Sonja's laughter stopped, her green eyes flashing. "I am *Hyrkanian*, Emperor of Rubbish. *Sunder. Sarat!*"

Tol barely had time to hear the hooves cracking the cobblestones like a hammer hits an anvil.

46

FOR THE LOVE
OF OTHERS

It is often said of Sonja that she never truly loved anyone or anything, but I do not think that's true. Certainly she loved her horses, she loved carnal pleasures, and she loved food and drink in abundance. As for people, I believe she loved as best as she was capable. And that is the tragedy of it all.

Lady McAubrey, *The Life of the Red Woman*

Whether Tol felt pain as mortals did, no one truly could say. But as the great warhorse slammed him into a pinwheel motion that completely separated him from the ground, his face contorted with what looked like agony.

Or perhaps it was surprise or vexation.

In the end, it made no difference.

As Tol regained his balance slowly, he stood to his full height and realized he'd dropped her injurious blade. He'd heard it clatter a good few yards away.

Tol arranged himself as proudly as possible. "Will you let me reach your sword, Sonja the Red?"

Sonja grinned. "You know, I just don't see how that would work out for me, Tol."

"I understand."

Instead, he ran at her, hands extended like claws.

The first swipe, Sonja dodged. She thrust at him with her dagger, but again, he was fast, and she had only half her body working. She screamed in pain when he used his other hand to shove her injured side back into the wall, causing blinding flashes behind her eyes.

He took that moment to grab her hair, pulling with all his formidable strength. Sonja tried to stop her fall but could not, and she landed hard on the rain-slicked stones.

Tol opened his mouth wide, showing an appalling number of sharp white teeth. "What a feast you'll be, Red Woman."

Sonja struggled, his hands still in her hair. "Call the cursed horse again, and I'll kill him, Sonja. I'll make of him food for the Queen Under the City. I'll grind him while he's still alive."

She could smell his fetid, gravestone breath.

It did what will alone could not seem to manage. It repulsed her.

She took the dagger and stuck it through his open mouth into the hard palate above.

She yanked it out, blackish ichor pouring down from the wound, then she summoned her anger and stuck it hard in his belly, just above the groin, tearing upward, until she fractured the lowest set of ribs, loudly and wetly. The dagger stuck inside the thing's flesh, which he did not seem to notice.

He pulled her up by the hair, her toes barely touching the stone below, either unaware or uninterested in his guts spilling out of his open wound.

"SUDHI-YA IS GOING TO LOVE YOU, DEVIL."

Sonja was in pain, finding it impossible to get purchase. Her dagger was stuck in the filthy creature who was holding her just long enough to taunt her before snapping her neck.

With effort, she choked out, "What, do you mean that great huge diseased bug in the caverns below? The one that makes a lullaby sound like syphilis?"

Tol's eyes went wide, and his mouth gaped open most unattractively. She loved the look in his goat-goblin eyes.

"Because I cut that sallow bitch in half, and my horse crapped on the remains."

Tol screeched in outrage and fury, perhaps even in grief. Sonja abandoned her footing, her weight now painfully dangling by her hair entirely, as Tol opened his mouth to bite her, most likely in the face, almost certainly to death.

She put her feet against his thighs to steady herself, pulled the prince's dagger from his gut, and reaching through the pain, jammed it into his eye and twisted. A second shove placed its hilt deep into his brain.

He dropped her, screaming, cursing words no one in Zamora or Hyrkania could possibly remember.

As he bent forward, Sonja retrieved the sword, jammed it into his jaw from underneath, and stepped back to regain her breath.

It took him a long time to die.

So she cut off his head and limbs to speed the process a bit.

She was nothing if not considerate.

Ysidra shouted in joy in the warm eastern rain. Standing between the third and fourth peg, leaving only the fourth and final peg still in the door.

But her elation and relief would not allow her to let the moment go unnoted. *"There's the Curse of the Hyrkanians, after all, impotent scarecrows,"* she shouted to the city below, so that even the witless dwyers paused in their sacking and murder.

Sonja looked up, her smile fading at what she saw on the wall above the Stone Gate. *"Ysidra!"*

The queen had not been watchful, as an arm came around her throat, and she felt the first of five punctures in her body, quick as a snake, deep as death.

She felt the first three but was already dying as the last two hit.

Sylus stood over her, cackling. He bent over her, hoping to watch her Hidden come forward, as he'd waited for since meeting her that first wounding night. "Show me, show me, Queen of Nothing. You came all this way, only to fail. Show me that *pain*, you *useless vixen*."

"I won't, sneak," said Ysidra painfully. "Don't you know who I am?"

Sylus smiled, a mean little smile.

"Oh, you mean the exalted Queen of Nothing? Is that what you are?"

"No, fool of an assassin," she said. "I'm Sonja the Red's Blood Man."

If Sylus had known more about Ysidra's people, about their skill with beads and secret compartments in their clothing, he might have been more cautious.

Instead, she showed him *her* "hidden."

He screamed as the beaded knife stabbed through his eye.

Sonja slashed at the soldier dwyers in front of her, bereft of real purpose without an overseer but still programmed to kill. Tears filled her eyes, but she still had some flame in her, some warm lovely place where she thought the queen could still be saved. Where good hearts were rewarded, and cruelty was condemned.

But running for the stairs as fast as she could, she realized that no such place existed.

A gaunt general was rallying the troops through terror and rage. Even with Tol and Sudhi-Ya dead, the outcome for Hyrkania was in doubt. He aimed to at least spill enough blood that they would never again forget this night. "May they drown in it," he prayed to the eight-legged god with a thousand eyes.

"Kill all. Burn everything. Leave nothing for the dawn to break upon!"

It sent the dwyers into a frenzy, for they had been programmed for this. A memorable gesture, just in case things did not go as Tol had hoped. His general gave the order designed to chill the blood of the remaining citizens.

The dwyers began gathering all the children they could find in the market square.

The commander's corpse held the torch firmly, if awkwardly, and did as he was ordered by the new holder of the Asp. He had no choice in the matter.

He was being directed past the winding tunnel, through the great chasm, and past that, to the tunnel on the other side, below the city, in the dark.

If he'd still had the power of scent, he might have smelled something in the air.

Ysidra was crawling toward the fourth peg, leaving a trail of blood on the stones as rain fell upon both her and the Blood Man.

Whatever faculties Sylus had once had, whatever artifice allowed him to pretend to be as normal men, were now utterly gone. He thought only of hate, hate for the women who had seen through him, had thwarted him, had *defied* him.

And like many who fetishize anything, whether gold or knowledge or war, eventually that was all that kept him going.

He could have killed her. But he would have been cheated out of seeing a queen's *true self,* and that he could not abide. He clapped one hand over his ruined eye, but the anticipation was too great; he would not succumb to pain or blood loss.

He had to see. He had to see what was inside of the queen, what was truly hers. If it was his last such feeding... so be it.

He watched with his good eye, watched her crawl to the fourth peg. His fingers twitched uncontrollably at his side.

She tried to pull it up with fading strength.

"Help. Me," she said. "They'll all... all die if we don't."

He looked out over the wall to the streets below. Hundreds, thousands of terrified people, dying in rapid succession.

He almost wept with joy.

Sonja ran up the stairs, taking them two and three at a time, nearly slipping more than once as rain slicked the path.

She could've killed the Blood Man that night in the shithole tavern in Radolan. She'd seen something, something in him that was wrong.

She should have killed him. But she hadn't. She hadn't.

Mitra forgive her, she hadn't.

Sylus knelt down by Ysidra, sprawled as she was, dying.

"You know, I don't normally go past five strikes, but you are taking an ungodly amount of time to die," he said.

He pulled out the dagger, the queen's own dagger.

"Remember this, Your Majesty?"

*   *   *

The prince shouted at Dalen, the better between the two of them as an archer. "Do you have it?"

"I do, lord," Dalen said, wiping the rain from his eyes before pointing the arrow at the kneeling man on the Stone Gate.

"Do you *have* it, soldier?"

In answer, Dalen sent an arrow flying.

The children of the city were put in a circle in the center of the market square. They looked out to see only pitiless eyes. Boy or girl, some tried to fight, to run, even those just above the age of toddler.

Gahresh would have been proud, if he had lived.

"*Kill them,*" said the gaunt flatly.

Sylus fell beside Ysidra, whose breathing was irregular and weak. He had an arrow in his arm, and he was certain that a *man* had shot it, which ruined his entire theory on *women* being the carriers of evil in a sinful world.

Lying flat on the surface of the gate, he knew the archers below could not see him.

He pulled it out of his left arm. And stabbed it into Ysidra's back.

Commander Sagja had not been a dwyer long. There remained a small bit of his own mind underneath the ancient spells of the Asp. He knew what he was being asked to do. Unfortunately, he was compelled to go on and could not stop it.

He briefly screamed in his own mind as he walked, torch in hand, into the alcove of the trail where the gas had been leaking, and as he shoved it through the hole with all his remaining strength, he was incinerated into nothingness. And the vein opened wide, allowing limitless gas to escape from far deeper in the earth than even Tol had ever journeyed.

The explosion rocked the entire city, as if Mitra had slapped the city walls. The Wooden Throne Hall burst outward and up like an active volcano, and stones the size of houses flew upward, landing in the roads or on dwyers too dim to run.

Fire shot up out of the gap and ceased to stop, burning off the excess gas forty, fifty feet in the air.

As the dwyers regained enough sense to move toward the children, a figure appeared before them, blocking their path.

"Hold, dead things. I'm Aria of the prince's guard. But you may call me Aria the Redeemed."

She fired six perfect shots into the shambling creatures' skulls. The children bashed them with fallen stones, just in case.

Sylus saw Sonja coming through his blurred vision, and enough reason returned to him that he knew this was the end. He raged inside. He was the evolved man; he was the favored of the gods. He saw what was inside people, truly inside them.

For his last such read, he was finally correct.

Because he looked in her eyes, her emerald eyes, and saw only rage.

He was screaming that it wasn't fair as she threw him from the Stone Gate's wall and into the massive fire below.

Ysidra was reaching for the final peg and had pulled it nearly halfway out. Sobbing, Sonja put her own hands over the queen's and pulled the final peg out. The pulleys were released of their counter-weights, and the doors swung wide open.

She heard the clattering of hooves as rider after rider flowed into the city center, sending the dwyers to a resting place, this time to a place from which they would not return.

47

RECKONING

Pain is for the living; death is for us all.

Author unknown, "Lament of the Gravedigger"

Sonja knew there was fighting left to be done as she knelt in the rain. But she lacked the strength to leave Ysidra on her journey across the last river.

She laid the queen's head in her lap as her eyes fluttered open. Her mouth trembled, then formed the words Sonja knew would come. "The city—the gates—"

"You lifted them, love. The doors are swung wide. Because of you." She took Ysidra's hand and kissed it softly.

They listened to the rain for a moment; the sounds of battle seemed very far away. "Ysidra, there are healers below. Perhaps—"

The queen smiled weakly. "I would not make it down the stairs, Sonjita."

Sonja put her fists against her temples. She wanted to scream. At great effort, the queen said, with clarity, as if they were the most important words ever spoken, "Sonja. Do not return the Asp to my people. Promise me."

"I promise."

The queen's face smoothed, and she closed her eyes, a bit of grace Sonja would be unable to muster for some time to come. "Kiss me. Kiss me for the love we had, and the love we foolishly threw away."

Sonja wiped away tears.

Tears meant death, she'd always said.

That was wrong, she thought. *It was the other way around.*

Ysidra's eyes opened, looking in her direction, but also looking beyond. "Hurry, Sonjita. Hurry. I'm already gone."

Sonja kissed her soft lips, and when she pulled away, it was as Tol had said of her. *You care deeply for people, yet you are always alone.*

She wiped her eyes once more and said softly, "May you again find home, Queen Ysidra, Rider of the Windmills."

It was Dalen and Aria who put a cloak over the queen's body, and another around Sonja's shoulders. They led her away, Aria openly weeping.

"Sonja, I am so...I am so sorry," she said.

Dalen looked at her with such empathy it made her feel worse for him than for herself, momentarily.

Sadly, that feeling would not last.

She thought very highly of them both, cared for them, even.

But could only imagine that they would live happier, longer lives without her. The great truth of Red Sonja, in her own hidden heart, was that leaving the people she loved was the best gift she could give them, she was certain.

Sonja walked like a broken woman to the first stair. Every cut and bruise she'd collected on this journey spoke its name aloud as she stumbled. But at some point, she looked out at the battle still taking place, and she straightened her shoulders, shrugging off the well-intentioned support of her two young friends.

No. Acquaintances.

Strangers.

She walked down the rest of the stairs alone. She drew her sword as she walked. Toward combat, toward death.

Not for her.

For every undead bastard foolish enough to get in her way.

At the bottom of the stairs she saw Raganus, shirt removed, bloody bandage around his guts. She saw he had an Asp of his own, but didn't ask how. It simply didn't seem important in the moment. He looked at her with a hope that broke her heart again.

She shook her head softly, touched his shoulder as she passed. For a big man, he wept with surprising grace and tenderness.

She took out the prince's gem-filled dagger and threw it over her shoulder. It was useless, and it was past time she stopped caring about the value of *things*. She pulled out the queen's dagger, a plain, unadorned thing, with a simple wolf carving on the hilt.

That went in her free hand.

And the Sonja who walked the length of the city and back again, dealing death to every unholy creature she saw, was terrifying even to the hardened soldiers of the prince's own guard, the same men she'd broken bread with, laughed with.

They had said they believed Red Sonja was a legend.

That night, she proved them completely accurate, and they spoke of her in whispers for many years to come.

After a time, random dwyers started turning on their gaunt owners. That would be Raganus's doing—she knew it; she felt it. She even fancied she heard him weeping in grief, though he was nowhere within sight.

After the streets had been cleared, Sonja went door to door, chasing out each gaunt or unturned dwyer and killing them word-lessly. By dawn, the people of the city were almost as afraid of the silent redhead covered in blood as they were of the creatures that had tried to conquer them and nearly succeeded.

But legends die hard, harder than the people who become them, and time would tell this story differently, and some young girl or boy somewhere would hear the story and think, *I wish I could be like Sonja.*

They couldn't know. How could they know?

Aria and Dalen were sent to ask her to stop, after she had gone through every home twice. Her arms trembled with fatigue, her weapons were slick with ichor, and her eyes were expressionless and fixed on nothing.

"Sonja, rest. Please," said Dalen.

And at last, she allowed herself to be taken before the prince, cov-ered in blood and gore, shot through with grief, the very image of the aftermath of war.

She was brought to one of the finer homes inside the city walls, a temporary camp, as the actual throne room and residence had been destroyed. The prince sat. In a chair. A normal, meaningless chair on a simple riser. But he stood when she entered.

A fatigued Dahmarhk sat beside him. Whatever happened, this would be the old man's last campaign.

Aria and Dalen, her escorts, made to leave, but Sonja bade them to stay.

She looked up at the prince, who was wounded in several spots, but nothing life threatening. She thought the kingship looked good on him. She stepped forward and handed him a twisted circle of gold, bent at irregular angles. He looked at her inquisitively.

"It's the king's crown, sire. Tol took it for his own. Uh. I'm afraid it got bent a bit."

"I see," said the prince.

"It was like that when I found it."

"Of course. Thank you, Sonja."

He looked down at her kindly.

"I am sorry for your loss, honored lady."

"Everyone here will have had loss this night, sire."

"It is true." His throat clenched. His father had been found, recognizable only by his signet ring, still attached to his broken, swollen finger.

"I am told the city would be lost without you and your friends. Is there anything I may offer you in return? Anything you ask."

She thought a moment. "My friends fought for you. Their tribe are exiled from Turan. They deserve better. They earned better."

The prince smiled. "This I can do. And it shall be done. Tell the stout one he is home, and to bring his tribe. I will see to it myself. They will wander no more."

She thought of Ysidra, and how this was all she'd ever wanted, and the feeling was deep and bittersweet. She fought back tears.

Her eyes then narrowed with memory. "Swear you'll treat them better than the Zamorans, so long ago. Swear."

"I swear. Anything else, my lady?"

She struggled for a moment. "Sire, I want to be released of my vow to you. I am not meant for such oaths, and I carry them unwell."

"This does make me sad, Sonja. But I give you back your freedom. And my vow to you that you will always have a home here."

She didn't really have any more words at the moment and bowed politely. "I'm going to leave, sire. I thank you for your kind gifts."

His face fell. "Surely you can stay and rest awhile, Sonja? Even one night?"

She began to turn, but he took her arm gently. He embraced her, clutching her to him.

"Please stay," he whispered. She began to protest. He said again, "Please stay . . . Tomato Head."

She closed her eyes.

Sometimes the things you lose, you find when you are not quite ready.

She agreed to stay a night and was given the best room in the house. Aria and Dalen volunteered to guard her door—insisted on it, really—and refused to leave their post for any reason.

Her room was luxurious, with food and wine kindly provided, of an elegance far beyond even that of the star gladiators' quarters in Zamora. She picked at some of it, but it tasted of nothing. Perhaps it was the Asp's doing.

She was preparing for bed in silken sheets when there was a knock at the door. She'd been expecting it.

"You recognized me," the man said.

Sonja nodded. The general let out an exhausted sigh.

"When did it happen?" he asked.

Sonja sat up, on the edge of her bed. Her sword and dagger were within reach. She debated with herself about reaching out for them. "When you fought tonight, with the fires behind you, General. You've aged. You had no beard then. It was your voice over the flames and smoke that I remembered first."

"I won't apologize, Sonja. The king had no heir and couldn't produce one with a dozen mistresses. We needed a son. A year old or less."

"Of low birth," she said. "So no one would question him."

"Yes."

"From a village with no one alive to bear witness."

Dahmarhk strode forward angrily. "That was not my doing. They weren't supposed to kill anyone. Did you see me hurt anyone? No? Because I committed no violence that day; I swear it on the prince's head."

Sonja squinted. She'd set her memory free with each fire she'd encountered, but it had come back a wounded bird with many missing feathers. "I don't remember you stopping them, either."

He sat in the chair at the desk she would never use. "No. I suppose I did not. We, too, were starving, Sonja. We became raiders to survive. It...I can't explain the cruelty. Perhaps it made the task easier accomplished when we didn't think of the villagers as human. It has haunted me, I swear."

"Good," Sonja said, staring into his eyes for signs of a lie.

He waited in silence. "Are you not going to kill me?"

"I haven't decided, General."

He stood and straightened his clothes, imperceptibly wrinkled. "Then if you'll excuse me...I'm an old man, and I need to pass water. Should you decide you have a blood message for me, I'm three rooms down, next to my prin—my king."

Sonja waved him away. At the door, he hesitated. "I do thank you for your service, Red Lady. You saved our city, and I am grateful."

"General Dahmarhk," she said as he was about to turn the handle of the room's grand door. "Someone was colluding with Tol. It would not be possible for him to know the city's workings without coming to the surface. He would not know the workings of the Stone Gate. Someone was collaborating with Commander Sagja, coordinating from without to within."

The general frowned. "What you say must be true. I will find the traitor, and he—or she—will be punished to the limits of their endurance. Do you find this acceptable?"

She simply watched as he left.

But she did find it acceptable.

"To the limits of their endurance," at the very least.

Arms aching, heart clouded, she fell back on the bed and slept before she remembered to remove her boots.

48

A ROAD IS A SERPENT WITH MANY HEADS

And she found herself, at last, able to rest.

Gaven Arune, *Sonja at Dusk*

She overslept breakfast, and when lunch came, she slept through that, too. Her loving guards had been told to let her rest under the authority of the new king, and it was a duty they were proud to serve.

When she finally did get up, she found fresh new clothes made and laid out for her. Nothing fancy, not silk and brocade, but comfortable clothes for the rider with no fixed destination. She thought them quite fetching, really, and put them on. Her other clothes were soaked with blood, in any case, so she forgave the presumption. There was a coin purse, as well, filled with coins bearing the previous king's face, and that made her breath hitch for a moment.

When she opened the door and saw two faces quite dear to her, she smiled—she couldn't help it. "And what did you do this time, to be burdened with such a crap detail?"

Dalen smiled. "We volunteered."

Aria added, "And actually, we've been promoted."

She grabbed them both to her, breathing in their warmth, love, and joy. She would need it in the coming days, she was certain.

"Take care of each other, as it's obviously clear no one else would have you."

Aria wiped joyful tears from her eyes. "Sonja, we—"

Sonja put a finger to her lips. "We'll meet again. I promise. Be happy. Be well. Both of you."

And she walked away before they could say anything that might change her mind.

She passed the second set of guards, who looked at her with a bit more awe than she would have liked. Did they not realize she had failed the one who mattered the most?

She was escorted to the prince's table, a beautiful, flower-bedecked wooden table very unlike the burnt, scarred table she'd had growing up. Would anyone ever love this table as much as she had loved that pauper's relic? She doubted it. But it was pretty enough, and evening birds were singing, glowing colors in the candlelight.

The prince looked pleased to see her and stood to kiss her on the cheek, holding her hands to steady her tired arms.

"Is there anything you'd like, Sonja?"

She thought about it and said simply, "Meat."

"Yes, but what *kind* of... Never mind, meat it is."

This she liked. Why people were always trying to complicate meals, she did not understand.

She looked at him squarely, something he clearly had not had happen in some time. "You have something you want to tell me."

"You see quite a lot, honored guest. What I have to say is this, my lady. Regardless of what you know, or what you think you know"—he reached out to hold her hand, kindly—"I am not your brother."

She pulled her hand back away. "Of course you are. You're Shia, our youngest. I couldn't...I couldn't find your bones. You were taken by Dahmarhk!"

"No, Sonja. For your sake, I wish that were true. I was born to a nameless prostitute the king fancied he had fallen in love with. He bore no legitimate children, so I was taken and a story made to fit." He looked in her eyes, knowing this would sting to hear.

"It's a lie. I don't know why, but you're lying to me."

"Do not call your king a liar, Sonja. I beg of you."

She shook her head; she wanted nothing more than to leave and never return. She had successfully forgotten the worst night of her life, and fate had forced her to live and relive it all over again, for nothing. For nothing.

"Sonja, listen to my words very carefully, please. Then you may do as you wish, and I will not try to stop you. Agreed?"

Reluctantly, she nodded.

"We are a country that has fallen, lady. We are trying to get up, and it is a slow, hard process. My father was a good man. And he is gone, and the people know someone took him in the night, inside our Stone Gate and walls. They know he was taken despite his guards, his army, and his people. He was plucked like a chocolate from a candy plate."

She stayed quiet. *Let the man speak*, she thought. It changed nothing.

"The people are afraid. They do not feel safe; they do not feel protected. Almost worse, our enemies will feel energized and emboldened. We can't even protect our king in his own home. How long before an army comes—bearing a Khitan flag, or Zamoran—telling us they are our new masters?"

He reached out to hold both of her hands.

"Sonja. If I am the orphan son of a dead blacksmith, with no papers, no lineage...then it stands that I cannot *also* be the son of a king who died trying to save his people. Do you understand?"

She looked away and thought of places she would rather be, and wondered how quickly she could get to any of them.

He looked her in the eye. "If I am your brother, Sonjita, beloved, then I cannot be the king who will protect all these foolish, wonderful horse lovers we've both grown so fond of. It breaks my heart to say this—do you know why?"

"Why?" she managed to say past dry lips.

He held her hands tighter. "Because no brother on Earth could be more proud to have a sister like you."

It was too much. She looked at the birds and listened to their song.

"Do you understand? Do you believe me, Tomato Head? For our people, do you believe?"

She did something she had dreamed of doing, one last time, since she was ten years old. She brushed his blond locks away from his forehead and kissed him there and smelled his skin as if he were a toddler. A toddler and not the king.

She drew herself straight and said as she turned, "Don't call me that."

She walked away from the table; she'd lost her appetite completely.

"Only my brothers call me that."

And then she was gone.

She'd packed her few possessions. The horsekeepers had considered it an honor to watch over her personal steed and had quite spoiled him. Sonja stifled a laugh when they brought him to her, his mane braided in bright colored beads in elaborate fashion. He looked mildly embarrassed, but she swooned over him. No sense being cruel to the stablekeeps.

Raganus came up to her, his horse's reins in his hands. "I'll follow you until the veil if allowed, lady."

"It would be my honor, Raganus the Wise."

He scowled as if she'd made sport of him, but she meant it.

"You mastered the Asp in hours. I thought it a useless trinket for days."

They set out, and a comfortable silence settled in. Neither felt much like talking.

About a half day's ride from Vilayet Sea, whose name, again, seemed a bit grand to Sonja, who still felt it was more of a great lake, they splurged on a pub for the night. Neither felt like hunting or cooking; it seemed a bit of a drudgery when both had hearts so heavy. At their table, they had Sonja's favorite (meat) and Raganus's favorite (everything) and washed it down with a good, dirty ale that smelled like it had been kept in someone's laundry drawer. On this particular journey, it could not have made them merrier if it had been the finest Kothian beer.

She looked at the Asp, the eyes dead in color, for which she was very grateful. "Do you think, Wise Wolf, that you might be able to get this gaudy thing off my arm?"

He looked at her, then the Asp. "I could try. Shall I?"

She pulled her arm away, a bit too quickly. "No! I mean, no, thank you. Not tonight. Perhaps tomorrow."

He looked at her with understanding and went back to his ale. A woman across the tavern was looking at him with obvious interest, and Sonja pointed it out to him, wished him well, and went to her room.

She could not explain what she intended to do, but she was afraid he might guess, in any case.

She called to the Asp. She made no incantation; she knew no spell nor demons' names. She simply spoke to it and told it of her need.

And Ysidra stood before her. Beautiful, brilliant Ysidra, who had been the first to show her windmills.

"My love," she said, and Sonja's eyes burned a little.

Sonja wanted so much to hold her. Ysidra looked at her with kind, understanding eyes. More than that, she wanted just to speak to her, to be able to talk to her forever. To dance with ghosts at last.

With the Asp, it could be.

"Your people have a home, Queen. You earned them a place to belong, at long last."

Ysidra closed her eyes and smiled. It made her more beautiful, somehow.

"And Raganus is a hero. If your people are wise, they will make him king."

"Sonja."

"The city is safe. That was your doing."

"Sonja."

Sonja felt a weight in her chest.

"Sonja," Ysidra, the recently departed, said. "You have to let me go."

Sonja bowed forward; it suddenly felt very difficult to sit without falling over. "I can't. I can't. You say this because you know I can't."

The queen looked down at her with one final sweet smile. "I say this because I know you can."

At Sonja's pleading and Ysidra's kind mercy, they spent an hour sharing memories, laughing, and crying.

Then, when Ysidra went back to sleep, Sonja spent an hour with the Asp, working and learning and searching for something very specific. When she found it, she went back to work and left orders.

Upon awakening, she found the Asp off her arm, with no marks left behind, lying innocently on the floor.

It had seen her.

And found her wanting, somehow. She could not disagree.

The next morning, Sonja found the tiny village's blacksmith, a burly man who did fine trade overcharging travelers for fixing cart wheels or the shoes of overworked horses. He tried to intimidate her, and when that didn't work, he tried to overcharge her. She told him to shut his bloody lip or she'd throw him in the trough, and did it herself.

The Asp was glorious, but it was gold, and gold was soft. Sonja fired up the forge, warmed the Asp until the shape became indistinct and the emerald eyes fell out. The blacksmith begged her not to; he seemed to take destroying a work of good jewel-making as a personal insult.

This time, she only had to scowl to get him to stop.

She took his hammer to the anvil, as her father had taught her long ago, and she pounded first the emeralds, to a fine green powder. The gold she pounded into foil, then pounded into tiny bits of foil by the thousand.

She flipped a coin at the blacksmith, one with a large portrait of Gahresh the Bold.

At the edge of the sea (*great lake*, she thought), Raganus hugged her as if she were his sister, with a suddenness and ferocity that felt like it might have bruised a rib or two.

She didn't complain. But kissed his cheek and touched her forehead to his. And then her last human travel partner was gone.

She overpaid for a ticket and, on second thought, made it two tickets, as well as a steerage slot for Sunder (who had no love at all for boats), for passage across to the other side, the Western Steppes, gateway to Zamora. And halfway through, she scattered the remains of her Hunter's Asp over as large a body of water as she could, and threw the box she'd kept the dust in over the side as well.

The shore was barren save for the small dock and toll shed. There was no one to meet her, and she felt there may never be anyone waiting for her for a long time to come.

She mounted her horse, and she looked to the east, toward Hyrkania, too far for even her eyes to see. She wrapped her new fine fur cloak around her; the days were already getting colder, would only get colder in the days to come.

As she rode, she debated. East? She'd just left there. West? Too soon, and there might be some animosity over the guards she'd killed.

North? Too cold.

South it would be, then.

And briefly, she thought of her last hour with the Asp, before she destroyed it. Tol had been able to "find her in the dark," he'd said. And he'd said there were four active Asps that remained unburied and in use.

So she faced the dark. Tol was dead; the king had his Asp and no desire to use it. Sagja was dead; Raganus had his Asp and seemed too honest to be tempted to abuse it.

And Sonja had hers—at least, she'd had it. Now it was at the bottom of the sea in thousands of glittering specks.

That left one unaccounted for. So she searched in the dark, until she found a small glow, which she followed as best she could, until it became a shimmer.

Then it took human form.

An older man. A general.

Dahmarhk.

Suddenly, the traitorous actions of a loyal-to-the-crown officer like Commander Sagja made all the sense in the world. He was following orders, the orders of his supreme military commander, whom he worshipped as almost near to the gods.

The gaunt emperor and his monstrous mother were unstoppable. He'd been told... by his *general*. The king could not protect the people. A treaty had to be brokered with the demons. They were saving their country, he'd told Sagja.

But there mustn't be questions, so a coup was out. Coups meant loyalty was divided, sometimes for generations. No. To make the people agree, they would have to be conquered. Humiliated. Terrified.

She saw it all. And she was certain the prince was completely unaware of the entire plot.

Well. Reasonably certain.

Perhaps it was better not to know.

She'd shown mercy to the general for his other offense. It was so long ago, and he *had* saved a child, perhaps. Perhaps.

But working with the gaunts, and a tumorous growth like Tol... against his own people, children, even...?

Her mercy had been entirely misplaced.

So in that hour, she had talked to the Asp. And she asked about how to make dwyers.

And as it turned out, there were *hundreds* of bodies of recently dead Hyrkanians inside the city walls of Makkalet, just from the siege alone.

Hyrkanians bury their dead.

But these hadn't been buried *yet*.

She felt ill using the Asp; it held no temptation for her any longer.

But this one time...?

Yes. This one time.

49

THE COLDEST OF COMFORTS

The siege and the triumph of the Hyrkanians did have one positive out-come, in an increase in stability for the entire region. Certainly, it was noted that the country had a just, strong king and council for the first time in a century. But also, it can't be denied that a country that would detonate and explode their capital city was not one that could be easily discounted.

Tasir Ra Manye, *Rise and Fall and Rise Again*

Dahmarhk awoke as he always did, in the arms of two women well paid to pretend to love him. He knew the truth—that they despised him. It didn't matter to him; perhaps he even enjoyed that a bit.

He'd never admit it. But perhaps. A bit.

He'd had his sheets imported from Turan. He loathed getting out of them, so soft was their touch and so cunning their design. He found himself famished and irritable. He'd planned for so long.

When he opened his eyes, he flung himself backward against the headboard in terror. He tried to yell, but nothing came out of his mouth but a long gasp. The two women spent no time at all trying to shield him. If he'd longed for loyalty in this life, perhaps he should have spent his days in kinder pursuits.

They ran, but they raised no alarm.

No one was coming to save him.

At the foot of his bed, his elegant, beautiful bed, he saw the ghastly pale face of a soldier he'd known who had fallen to the gaunts. Then another, then another.

He ran for the door, still in his underclothes. The recent dead, standing angry and tall, numbering in the hundreds, facing him with black accusatory eyes in the hallway all the way to his chamber door.

"Don't make your commands too complicated," the Asp had informed Sonja helpfully. And she'd followed its advice.

"Kill the traitor who let the monsters in," she'd said, with a mental portrait of the general in his military finery.

And so they did.

And it took longer than expected.

They were admirably thorough.

Chores done, Sonja patted Sunder and headed south. She rode pleasantly for a day and decided she'd make a camp for herself at the edge of the woods, near a small but picturesque freshwater creek.

She pulled off the bedrolls and gear, leaving one blanket on

Sunder's broad back. She gathered his feed and said, "We're on a new road, my friend. Can you feel it?"

He made a disgruntled snort.

"No, no, no. It'll be warmer down south, and I have a Falcon's nest to scorch. You'll love it."

He made the noise again.

"I am *not* a liar. Mind your manners."

And then she lay down and slept the sleep of a contented bear in its cave over a fish-filled lake.

ACKNOWLEDGMENTS

I have a small legion of people without whom I would not have been able to consider this book, let alone finish.

To start, my beloved husband, who believed in me when I did not. And to my son, who kept encouraging me in his quiet way.

To my mother, who insisted I write Red Sonja in the first place, as she was a fan of the movie, and my sister, who has never failed to tell me she was proud of me.

I want to thank Nick Barrucci, who convinced me I should write Sonja for his company, Dynamite Entertainment, and Sonja's guardian and protector, Luke Lieberman, who has always made me feel like part of the She-Devil family.

Thank you to the many fantastic artists who made my previous Red Sonja stories come alive, especially Walter Geovani and Jenny Frison.

Thank you so much to my support team, agent Ari Lubet, literary agent Yfat Reiss Gendell, and legal advisor Mahdi Salehi. I wouldn't trade them for a vat of gold.

Much love to the many creators whose work I've adored who supported and encouraged and advised me when I started writing professionally, including Mark Waid, Tom Peyer, Bill Morrison, Terry Delegeane, Larry Ganem, Dan DiDio, Colleen Doran, Bill

ACKNOWLEDGMENTS

ɔienkiewicz, Geoff Johns, Scott Snyder, Tom Taylor, Joe Quesada, Tom Brevoort, and so many more.

A She-Devil salute to the many creative geniuses who gave birth to Sonja or dressed her up just right over the years, most especially including Robert E. Howard, Roy Thomas, Barry Windsor-Smith, and the legendary Frank Thorne.

I am incredibly grateful to all the people at Orbit, who went miles beyond the call of duty to make this book happen. Warriors, the lot of them.

Thank you to a line of rescued greyhounds who have been my constant companions my whole career.

And finally, thank you forever to those of you who bought my stuff for saving me from a lifetime without telling stories, the thing I love to do most in the world.

Gail Simone
4/14/2024